The Shipkiller
is a breathtaking tale of an incredible hunt . . .
of one man's rage pitted against a colossus that
is unscathed even by the watery battering rams
of a hurricane. The *Leviathan* is stopped by nothing—not by the primeval forces of nature . . .
not by her most brutal winds, not by her wildest
seas. But Peter Hardin—alone in a small sailboat,
and himself eventually hunted by armies, navies,
and anti-terrorist forces—will not stop until he
has made this monster feel the enormity of its
crime. *THE SHIPKILLER* is an epic adventure,
relentless in its high drama and suspense, vivid,
explosive, and utterly unforgettable.

"GREAT TENSION TO THE LAST PAGE!"
—San Francisco Chronicle

"The pace grips from start to finish . . . [it]
spills over with intense drama, color, romance,
authentic backgrounds, and a thrilling booklong
chase."

—San Diego Union

THE SHIPKILLER

Justin Scott

FAWCETT CREST • NEW YORK

THE SHIPKILLER

THIS BOOK CONTAINS THE COMPLETE TEXT OF
THE ORIGINAL HARDCOVER EDITION.

Published by Fawcett Crest Books, a unit of CBS
Publications, the Consumer Publishing Division of CBS, Inc.,
by arrangement with The Dial Press.

ISBN: 0–449–24036–3

Alternate Selection of the Book-of-the-Month Club
Selection of the Playboy Book Club
Selection of the Nautical Book Club

Printed in the United States of America

10   9   8   7   6   5   4   3   2   1

For Gloria Hove,
My love, my beauty, my friend.

BOOK ONE

1

Gray squalls and yellow sunlight checkered the ocean horizons. *Siren*, a forty-foot ketch, rose and fell in following seas, lifting her stern to the swells, plummeting into deep valleys, a speck of wood and fiberglass three miles above the floor of the Atlantic Ocean.

Lingering atop a wave, she gave Peter and Carolyn Hardin a glimpse of a ship in the distance, a dark smudge crossing their wake in a patch of sun many miles behind. *Siren* slid into a trough. Walls of water rose on either side, slate gray. Vivid smears of robin's-egg blue spread beneath the surface like flat animals swimming.

Carolyn touched her husband's face with her lips. Hardin drew her close. When he looked back from another crest, the ship had vanished behind a hazy rain squall and *Siren* was alone once more, a single sail on an empty sea.

He glanced at the compass. North-northeast. Nine days out of Fayal, the Azores, two more days to Falmouth, England, if the weather didn't get worse. He looked at the sails. It was an action as automatic and regular as that of a good driver checking his rearview mirror in heavy traffic. The genoa jib had begun to luff. Hardin cranked its sheet. The winch ratchet clicked several notches and the fluttering stopped.

The two-masted boat was on a broad reach, sailing almost directly before the wind, her mainsail, mizzen, and jib run far out, bellied taut and full. The wind, like the slow, warm current, flowed from the southwest, fresh and steady.

Siren was twenty years old, overbuilt by skeptical designers when fiberglass was a new, untested material, and her broad and gracious hull needed such a breeze to make her lively. Hardin had crewed her when she was new and he was a young man. Three years ago he had bought her for his fortieth birthday.

He sat windward of the helm, his eyes sweeping the water, alert for a dangerous wave, his browned hand resting comfortably on the chrome wheel's elkskin wrapping. His broad face was weathered and faint squint lines arrowed toward the riant depths of his gray-blue eyes. A sturdily built man of medium height, he had a craftsman's quick, pliant fingers and a squarish body hardened by years of compensating for the ceaseless motion of small boats.

They had battled rain squalls all day on this, the third leg of their slow and easy crossing from New York. Then, quite suddenly, the squalls had withdrawn to the horizons, the clouds overhead had fanned apart like a spreading lens aperture, and the sun shone brightly. It made the sea sparkle and dried the decks.

They opened the forward hatches to let the warm air take the damp from the cabin and they shed their vinyl parkas and pants, and rubber sea boots—the foul-weather gear that they had donned against the cold, driven wet of the squalls. The wind slackened some more and they took off their wool sweaters.

Finally, with a hopeful look at the sun, Carolyn began unbuttoning her shirt. Hardin watched, thinking how beautiful she looked with her short black hair puffed by the breeze, her cheeks radiant, and her full, dark eyes sparkling. He cheered enthusiastically when her shirt fell to the deck.

They had been married ten years and their partnership had survived marked differences in ages, tastes, interests, and the ricochets of the fragmenting unions of their friends, to whom, over the years, they had come to represent a promise that pleasure did not have to be fleeting to exist.

Carolyn blew him a kiss, stepped out of her faded jeans and tossed him her panties. It was the beginning of May and her skin was still winter white. She lay on her stomach

10

on the bridge deck, which traversed the front of the cockpit, and braced her toes against the coaming. When the boat pitched, her leg muscles rippled with grace and power.

Hardin eyed the horizons speculatively. Overhead the sky was clear, but astern, holes of blue sky changed shape as dark cumulus clouds moved beneath gray stratus like interlocking iron plates. More squalls might be forming, but they were distant, ten or twelve miles off, and moving slowly.

He took off his own shirt and knelt beside Carolyn. The sun baked into his back. He kissed her ankle, her calf, the backs of her knees. She combed his thick brown hair with her tiny fingers. When she found a place that made him shudder, she asked, "Self-steering?"

Hardin looked again at the gentling sea.

"Self-steering," he agreed. "Don't go 'way."

Carolyn welcomed him back with a slow and intimate kiss.

They were deeply enfolded when *Siren* heeled before a sudden sharp and chilly gust, and cloud shadow enveloped the boat. Carolyn snuggled closer, goosebumps speckling her skin.

"What's happening, Captain?"

Hardin lifted his head and looked at the sea. Cloud banks and rain squalls had spilled into the sunshine. He could see clearly for many miles ahead, but the horizon was creeping closer on either side. Above, the sun boiled white behind the clouds like the mouth of a blast furnace.

"We better . . ."

"Now?" Carolyn asked wistfully. "Shouldn't we finish one thing before we start another?"

" 'Fraid it doesn't work that way."

She levered up on her elbow and looked over the side. Astern, a squall was mustering a long line of rapidly gaining low black clouds.

Carolyn greeted them with an exasperated gesture.

"You couldn't wait?"

Laughing and trading one-liners, they scrambled to

11

shorten sail. Carolyn took the helm while Hardin went forward with the storm jib and sheets. He hanked the small sail onto the forestay below the genoa, attached the halyard shackle, and led the sheets through a set of fair-leads and back to the cockpit.

Carolyn steered slightly upwind to spill air from the genoa so he could lower it. The headsail began to flap and a second cold gust made it crackle like pine branches in a fire. She coordinated the movement of the boat with his progress and the sail fell on deck.

He unhanked it and quickly stuffed it down the forward hatch; there was no time to bag it. Then he hoisted the storm jib hand over hand, took a wrap around the halyard winch, and cranked the sail up taut.

Carolyn let *Siren* fall off the wind and the storm jib filled. Then she eased the mainsheet and the mainsail spilled its wind. Hardin lowered the big unwieldy sail and Carolyn came forward to help gather and furl it to the boom with elastic cord.

She sagged against him, laughing.

"My legs can't take this. My knees are like peanut butter."

The squall closed swiftly, preceded by angry gusts that flicked the tops off the crests, flattening them. Spin-drift skidded over the water, trailing long lines like torpedo tracks. Quickly, they returned to the cockpit, reefed the mizzen sail, and put *Siren* back on her broad reach.

Hardin went below to secure the forward hatch. The cabin was neatly kept, warm with earth colors, and stocked for their long cruise. Checking that everything that should be was tied down, he hurried back to the cockpit and shrugged into his foul-weather parka. When he reached for the helm, so Carolyn could don hers, their hands worked briefly in tandem.

"Got it."

Carolyn put on her sweater and parka. Her legs were still bare, but the squall had arrived. She tossed the rest of their clothes down the companionway, shut the main hatch, and sat beside Hardin, bracing her feet on the op-

12

posite cockpit seat. He gave her the jib sheet and kissed her mouth.

A fierce gust hit the sails and frothy seas rammed the hull on the stern quarter, pushing *Siren's* beam to the wind. She heeled sharply. Hardin played the wheel, working to bring her stern to the mounting seas.

The squall brought darkness as if it had yanked a black canvas across the sun. The temperature dove twenty degrees; icy rain lashed the decks; jagged lightning fragmented the dark and painted the wild sea stark white. Waves scattered, collided, combined, and leaped high.

Carolyn played out the jib to spill the wind, and because Hardin was busy with the wheel took charge of the mizzen sail as well. *Siren* stood taller, filled, and tore before the squall like a frightened mare.

It was over in minutes. The sky lightened, the wind dropped, the temperature rose, and the seas calmed. Rain fell straight and hard, then stopped abruptly.

"Whew," said Carolyn. "Next time we reef the mizzen. She was running too fast."

"She can take it," said Hardin. He grinned and stroked Carolyn's bare knees. "Besides, the excitement was good for us. Things were getting a little dull around here."

"You've got a short memory. How'd you like to spend the night in the dinghy?" She leveled an imperious finger at the little white boat on the cabin behind the mainmast.

"Alone?"

"Alone. And here comes another one, so make up your mind."

A second dark line was overtaking them, a mile back. Hardin's senses were drawn to it. He stared at the approaching squall, trying to see through its fluffy gray leading edge into its dark core. He saw no unusual menace, no freak wave, no sign of extraordinary wind.

"What's the matter?" asked Carolyn, sensing his uneasiness.

"I don't know," Hardin replied slowly. "I just have a funny feeling."

He took binoculars from their locker and scanned the cloud line. "Looks more like rain than wind, doesn't it?"

He gave her the glasses. Carolyn agreed. It didn't have the hard darkness of a real squall, nor were advance gusts announcing its coming.

Hardin looked around. The first squall had veered east. There was sun ahead and it looked as if the weather would clear by night as the climbing barometer suggested. He glanced astern again, still debating whether to take in the mizzen sail. There was an adage: The time to reduce sail is when you first think about it.

"Let's reef the mizzen."

"Aye, Captain."

They reefed the mizzen sail.

Siren slackened her pace, stripped her storm jib and abbreviated mizzen, and the rain line gained at a faster rate.

Hardin scanned it again, hunting what bothered him. He saw nothing. When he lowered the glasses, he found Carolyn regarding him with a frank open gaze. She traced his lips with her finger.

"I love you."

"I love you."

"Hold me, please."

Hardin slipped behind her, took the wheel, and let Carolyn lean back in his arms. With one hand on the helm and the other around her shoulder, he sighted the sea over the top of her silky black hair. She unzipped his parka and rested her head on his chest. *Siren* moved peacefully, her bow still pointing the distant sunlight, her stern to the clouds.

Carolyn shivered.

"Peter, I'm frightened."

"What is it?"

"I don't know."

She looked out at the sea, then behind them. Her body went rigid in his arms.

"Oh, my God!"

14

Hardin turned and stared.

A black steel wall filled the horizon.

"Jibe!"

He whirled the wheel hard left as fast as he could, held it with his leg, and yanked in the jib sheet hand over hand. The racing winch ratchet buzzed angrily. *Siren* lurched downwind. Carolyn leaped to the mizzen boom, released the reef, and hoisted the sail to the top of the mast.

Sails flapping, *Siren* nosed around until the wind was dead astern and the black wall was bearing down on their port side. It was less than an eighth of a mile away—six hundred feet—and closing fast.

"Run it out!" yelled Hardin, spinning the wheel back to center and letting the mizzen sheet race hotly through his hand. When the sail was out at right angles to the boat, he threw a quick turn around the winch barrel and cleated the sheet. The jib blew back and forth with sharp snapping sounds, searching the wind.

Hardin hit the auxiliary's starter switch, praying it would start. It was an old engine and he hadn't run it since the Azores. The jib sheet tangled around a halyard cleat on the main mast. The pinioned sail flapped uselessly. Carolyn secured the starboard sheet and darted forward to free it. *Siren* plunged into a deep trough. Carolyn's feet slipped out from under her and she fell hard, skidding toward the edge. Hardin cried out. He was helpless, too far away to save her.

Her legs slid under the safety lines into the water. She grabbed a stanchion with one hand, clawing desperately with the other. The water pulled her farther off the deck. *Siren* lumbered to the port side and Carolyn used the lift to pull herself back on deck. She scrambled to her feet, leaped to the mast, and untangled the jib. Hardin steered left and the sail snapped full, the jibe completed.

Carolyn ran along the port deck and dove down the companionway. Hardin saw her face was white as the sails. Only she knew exactly how close she had come to falling overboard in front of the monster ship bearing down on them.

They were sailing across its path. Hardin stabbed again at the auxiliary engine's starter switch, his eyes on the enormous black hull. He had never seen a ship so huge. Already they should have been beyond it, but it was so wide that it seemed to be coming sideways. Less than four hundred feet of water separated them.

The diesel starter ground. Carolyn raced up from the cabin with their life jackets. She held Hardin's for him, while he steered with his leg and frantically pushed the starter, and secured it before she put her own on. All the while her eyes were glued to the black hull.

The diesel coughed alive. Hardin eased the gear lever forward and *Siren* put on two more knots. The ship was so close that he could see weld lines in the metal. It was taller than the tops of *Siren*'s masts, wider than a block of five-story brownstones.

And moving very fast. A giant bow wave crested over twenty feet. He saw no one watching over the side, no bridge, no lines, no lights, no name. Nothing but a blank wall, its flat lines broken only by an anchor that was bigger than *Siren*.

Hardin thought they would make it past the edge of the bow wave. Now he could see along the side of the ship, a sheer cliff that vanished in the distant mists. In its lee the sea seemed calmer, protected from the wind like the still waters of a lagoon. The wind was directly astern, the sails over the port side. *Siren* was still sailing at right angles to the ship. Hardin wanted to broaden the angle and head farther away, but he would have to jibe again to do that and he hadn't the time. He gunned the engine. *Siren* shuddered forward, but he had to cut the power the next moment as the cold diesel threatened to stall.

The mizzen sail fluttered. Then the jib.

Siren slowed, wallowing clumsily.

Carolyn's eyes snapped to the sails. "The wind?"

Hardin knew the full horror of what had happened.

16

The monster had stolen it, casting a wind shadow like a tremendous bluff. The sails drooped and hung limply.

He jammed the diesel wide open. It was too cold for sudden acceleration and it coughed and died. For a long moment the slack flutter of the sails was the only sound. The ship was a hundred feet away. Whatever powered it made no noise. Only the loudening hiss of the cresting bow wave announced its coming.

Hardin and Carolyn found each other's hands and backed toward the bow. They huddled there, clutching the forestay, watching in disbelief as the silent wall blacked out the sky.

The wave heeled the sailboat onto its side, where it lay like an animal baring its throat to plead defeat. Hands locked, Hardin and Carolyn tried to leap away as the black ship trampled *Siren* into the sea.

2

Siren died with a loud crack of splintering fiberglass.

Hardin leaped. The water was violently cold. He broke surface and pulled Carolyn to him. Something smashed his side. Pain coursed through his knee. Carolyn's hand was wrenched from his. He heard her scream once before the water buried him again.

The life jacket yanked him back to the surface. A tremendous blow struck him high in the back of his head. Everything seemed dark, though he knew his eyes were open. He was somersaulted over and over. His arms and legs seemed useless, but the life jacket kept him afloat as the metal hull brushed past.

Part of his mind exclaimed at its smoothness. Not a seam or a rivet protruded from the polished surface of the sheer wall. His head kept going underwater and he realized that the propellers were pulling him down.

Frantically he kicked off from the passing hull, but each time he started to swim away it drew him back to the long, straight vortex of rushing water between the ship and ocean. Again and again he tried to swim away, but each time he was drawn back until, surrendering to exhaustion, pain, and fear, he struggled only to protect his body from the metal.

It slid past for so long that he began to think he would be trapped forever between a moving wall and the sea. Each time he kicked, its forward motion spun him partway around and slammed his back into the hull. Had it not been for the bulky life jacket, he would have been battered to pulp. As it was, his knees and elbows were smashed horribly.

Suddenly it was gone and he was hurled into froth and foam that filled his nose and mouth and stung his eyes. He sank beneath the surface, the life jacket useless in the aerated water that the ship's propellers flung behind it. The froth entered his lungs; he coughed and retched as the heavy salt water pierced the membranes of his mouth and throat.

The froth congealed into liquid. The sea subsided. The life jacket brought him to the surface. He was alone on a piece of water as flat as a pond. A huge square stern was vanishing into the cloud. Above it was an enormous white bridge, topped by a pair of straight black funnels belching gray smoke. The air reeked with exhaust, but under that smell was the strong odor of crude oil.

Lettered across the black stern in stark white was the name of the ship: LEVIATHAN.

Beneath its name, its home port: MONROVIA, LIBERIA.

"Carolyn!" Hardin yelled.

He threshed around looking in every direction, but saw nothing. As for the ship that had run him down, it was gone, vanished in the cloud. Slowly the sea came back. Waves entered its wake, tentatively at first, as if fearing

18

its return, then with vigor, more and more boldly, until Hardin was bobbing from low troughs to high crests, screaming Carolyn's name, and trying to raise himself out of the water to see farther.

The cold was fierce, anesthetizing the pain in his elbows and knees, numbing his mind and body. Mists swirled closer, narrowing his view. He was slipping into shock when his hand hit something solid. He flinched with terror. Sharks.

Kicking and splashing, he heard his own voice yell like an animal's. He felt the terror take his body back from the realm of shock. Instincts assumed command. He reached for the knife that hung from his life jacket and tucked his aching knees until he was bobbing like a ball.

It hit him again, and again terror wrenched his stomach. It was on the surface. His hand closed on something. He brought it to his eyes. A splintered piece of wood. Teak. Part of the cockpit coaming.

Other objects bumped against him. Wood, Styrofoam. *"Carolyn!"*

A shape rose suddenly out of the fog. White and bulbous. He swam toward it, knowing nothing more than that it floated. The life jacket confined his strokes, so he extended his arms like a prow and kicked with his feet, his knees paining. The object glided away on a wave. Hardin forged after it, lunged, touched it. His fingers slipped on the slimy surface. He recoiled from the impression of living flesh.

Then he recognized *Siren's* dinghy. Or half of it, sheared in the middle as if cut with a knife, and floating upside down, kept buoyant by its Styrofoam packing. He gripped the broken end.

If he could turn it over and get in, he could search for Carolyn from its greater height. He stretched his arms and gripped each gunnel. Ignoring a new shooting pain in his right elbow, he kicked to maintain leverage and pulled down on one side of the shattered boat and pushed up on the other. It tipped partway before escaping from his hold.

Hardin swam after it, reached over its bottom, and tried to hold its stubby keel. Again, as it tipped toward him, he couldn't maintain his grip. He worked around to the broken end and tugged with all his strength on one side. Slowly, he got it to dip underwater. Then the buoyant Styrofoam refused to sink farther. He brought his feet up, jammed them against the inside of the gunnel and threw his entire weight on the broken dinghy. It flopped upright.

Hardin tumbled backward and broke surface, retching and coughing, the salt stinging his throat and eyes. He spotted the dinghy and swam after it. Its stern floated high while the open end was underwater. Reaching the open end, Hardin turned around and tried to sit on the bottom. The dinghy threatened to flip back over. He reached farther back, grabbed the interior braces and hauled his buttocks into the bottom of the boat. The stern rose higher. Letting the waves assist him, Hardin inched farther and farther into the shattered hull until, at last, he was propped in the stern, half seated, waist deep in water, his feet dangling over the break. He drew them in, still afraid of sharks.

"*Carolyn!*"

The dinghy lurched. It was like a shallow bowl. It would support his weight until he tried to move. Then it tipped dangerously and threatened to fling him back into the ocean. He experimented cautiously, moving his body until he had propped his shoulders against the transom so he could see over the sides.

The fog and rain clung close to the surface, offering less than fifty feet of visibility. He saw the debris of his boat, pieces of the teak decks, a cupboard, some shredded sailcloth. Had it been ground up by the ship's propellers?

Siren's fiberglass hull would have sunk quickly. He shivered. It was probably still sinking, with a mile or two yet to fall before it touched the cold, muddy floor, the enormous water pressure crushing the light bulbs. The cabin lights and reading lamps first, then the smaller, tougher globes in the running lights.

"*Carolyn!*" He caught a glimpse of the front half of the

dinghy. He strained to see more clearly. Had she gone to it the way he had gone to his half? A current swirled it around, revealing the gaping emptiness of the shattered hull. It drifted from his sight.

He called her again and again and cupped his ears for response. Nothing. He raised his head as high as he could and scanned the shrinking circle of his vision. It was getting dark. Had she lost her life jacket? Was she sucked beneath the ship? Was she a hundred feet away, unconscious? He called her name for hours.

3

The Ultra Large Crude Carrier LEVIATHAN was the biggest moving object on the face of the earth. It carried one million tons of Arabian oil, and it drove through the ocean like a renegade peninsula.

The seas that *Siren* toiled up and down were nothing to the gigantic ship. Its blunt bow smashed them like a battering ram, and its square stern laid the North Atlantic as flat as a sheltered bay.

LEVIATHAN was one thousand eight hundred feet long —over a third of a mile—so long that in squalls its bow was invisible from its bridge. It was so wide that the distant smudge glimpsed earlier on the horizon, which Peter and Carolyn Hardin had reckoned was the side of a passing ship, had been in fact LEVIATHAN's bow pointed straight at them.

Two days later—during which time LEVIATHAN had off-loaded at Le Havre and begun its return voyage to the Persian Gulf—two elderly and relatively small hundred-thousand-ton oil tankers brushed hulls in the crowded English Channel. There was no explosion and damage was slight. The empty ship, outbound in the proper traffic separation lane, proceeded into the Atlantic, effecting repairs as she went. The inbound ship, fully laden and conned by an aging master who preferred to ignore traffic schemes, suffered a number of crushed hull plates and leaked some cargo. The spill was less than two hundred tons.

The floating oil blew onto the coast of Cornwall, where it caught several thousand migrating gulls resting on the beaches. Fisherman, farmers, shopkeepers, and painters descended the rocky cliffs and collected the victims, which were poisoning themselves by preening the crude oil from their feathers. The people set up a field station to remove the oil and keep the birds warm until they had dried.

Dr. Ajaratu Akanke, a young African woman, joined the rescue late in the afternoon when her hospital shift had ended. By then the beach was littered with dead birds and the cries of the living were growing faint. She had done this before, and when she saw that most of the birds left were dead, she walked beyond the main slick, which had covered the pebbles with several inches of sticky tar, and searched where no one had had time yet to look.

She was tall and very dark, with high cheekbones and a narrow nose and delicate lips that spoke of an Arab or Portuguese slaver generations back in her family. A plain gold cross hung from her neck on a slender chain.

She found a cormorant wedged between two rocks where the tide had left it. Its eyes blinked dully through the thick crude that coated its head and body. The diving bird had apparently surfaced in the slick. There was no doubt it would die, so she snapped its neck with her long, graceful fingers.

She put the corpse in a plastic carry bag, so the oil wouldn't kill a scavenger, and looked for more birds. About a mile from the main body of searchers, she rounded a high rock flecked with oil and stopped short. A man, half naked, in a yellow life jacket, was lying on the pebble shelf, his legs white, the skin shriveled from

22

long immersion. She knelt beside him, expecting more death.

Hardin awakened clearheaded. He knew he was alive. He knew he was in a hospital. He guessed from her manner that the striking black woman standing next to his bed was a doctor.

She was counting his pulse from his left wrist. Her cool fingers had broken his sleep. She said, "Good afternoon," in a cultured, upper-class British accent.

"Where is my wife?"

"I'm sorry. You were found alone."

Grief ripped through him. "What day is it?"

"Thursday."

It had happened Sunday. "Did they find her body?"

"No."

"Maybe . . . Where are we, England?" he asked, prompted by her accent and his memory of *Siren*'s position rather than his surroundings. It was a bright, airy room; his was the only bed. There were windows on two sides and sheer white curtains blew tropically in a light, warm breeze.

"Fowey, Cornwall," said the woman. "On the Channel coast. I found you on the beach."

Hardin sat up and tried to swing his feet off the bed. His right knee wouldn't move. "Maybe she's farther down the coast. Did anyone else find someone?"

"No, I'm sorry."

"Maybe a boat," he said, ransacking his mind for hope. "Maybe the French."

The woman placed coffee-black hands on his shoulders and firmly pushed him to the pillow. She said, "The authorities are all aware that a man was found at the edge of the sea. Where you've come from no one knows, but they trade information. Had a woman been found, alive or dead, they would know."

Hardin tried to resist and found he was too weak. The outburst left him trembling. He sagged back on the bed, his eyes half closed, a dark, empty space expanding in his

23

heart. It was more than he could bear and he took refuge in inconsequentials.

"I'm a doctor," he said. "I've suffered a mild concussion."

She eyed him cautiously. "You've been unconscious for a full day here. How long were you in the water? What happened?"

"In that case," amended Hardin, concealing a stab of fear, "I've suffered a severe concussion. I was last conscious Sunday night. . . . Skull fracture?"

"No."

"Projectile vomiting?"

"Not yet."

"Respiration?"

"Normal."

"Is that why you didn't tube me?" Throat and nose tubes were ordinarily inserted into unconscious patients to prevent respiratory blockage.

"I, or a nurse, was with you at all times. I would have employed tubes if you had remained unconscious much longer."

"I've been sleeping off the exposure," said Hardin.

"Perhaps." She wiped his forehead with a cool cloth. "What is your name?"

"Peter Hardin."

"I am Dr. Akanke, Dr. Hardin. I want you to sleep."

"Please."

"Yes?"

"Seven degrees, forty minutes west. Forty-nine, ten north. My nearest last position. Tell them to look for her somewhere around there, please."

She made him repeat the numbers. He thanked her, then followed her with his eyes as she glided from the room. His gaze shifted from the door to one of the windows. The breeze pushed the curtain aside. He saw the sea, green and sparkling, far below.

He awakened in the dark, his scalp prickling. He tensed, waiting for the movement to repeat. It was coming again. He sensed it, couldn't see it, but he knew it was moving. It was black. It was coming straight at him. He sprang off the bed. One of the windows was wide open. It reached the floor. He ran through it. The black followed, flanking him. He ran and was suddenly in the water where he couldn't move fast enough. The black advanced, pushing a white wave before it.

Hardin yelled.

He heard a soft sound and felt safe. Dr. Akanke's face was close to his. Her voice was liquid smooth.

"A nightmare, Dr. Hardin. You're all right now."

The harbor master kept calling him Lieutenant, because Hardin had mentioned in the course of the lengthy interrogation that he had served as a lieutenant aboard a United States Navy hospital ship. He was an old man, and despite his pleasant manner was clearly incredulous.

When Hardin realized that he was about to repeat all his questions for the third time, he said, "You don't believe me."

The harbor master shuffled his notes. "I hardly said that, but it is rather incredible, now that you mention it."

"I'm lying?"

"Your memory . . . your injuries . . . Dr. Akanke says you have a concussion. . . . I'm not—"

"I saw the name on the stern."

"You could not have survived," he said flatly.

"I did survive," said Hardin. "A ship named LEVIATHAN out of Monrovia sank my boat and killed my wife."

"Lieutenant, LEVIATHAN is the biggest ship in the world."

"You've said that three times," Hardin yelled. "What the hell am I supposed to do about that?"

The harbor master made clucking sounds and backed from the room. "Perhaps when you feel better."

Hardin swung his feet off the bed and half rose. Shooting pains locked his knee. He fell back, his face contorted. The old man looked alarmed. "Lieutenant?"

25

"Was LEVIATHAN in the area in which I was found?" Hardin asked quietly.

"It off-loaded at Le Havre on Monday night. Still, I feel . . ."

"Get the hell out of here," Hardin said savagely.

The local police inspector was a youngish, intelligent-looking man with a sympathetic smile and cool eyes. He began with a grim assurance.

"I'm sorry, but there's been no sign of your wife. We've double-checked the Channel ports and are in communication with the French and Irish."

"She could have been picked up by a boat without a radio."

"Unlikely." The inspector leaned forward. "Now, Dr. Hardin, we have to verify who you are. Whom do you know in England?"

Hardin mentioned a few London doctors.

"We would like to fingerprint you."

"Who the *hell* do you think I am?" The pain in his knee was making him irritable, but he agreed with Dr. Akanke that his head trauma precluded the use of pain medication.

"This harbor is a port of entry," the inspector replied blandly. "We are often unwilling hosts to Irish gunrunners, drug smugglers, and all sorts of illegal aliens—Paks, Indians, what have you."

"Which do you think I am?" Hardin asked angrily, focusing his hurt for Carolyn. "A Pakistani or an IRA terrorist swimming ashore with a howitzer in my teeth?"

"That's quite enough for one day, thank you, Inspector," said Dr. Akanke. She had been waiting at the door. Now she swept into the room, flanked by two nurses who guided the policeman out. As soon as he had gone, she put a thermometer in Hardin's mouth and said, "You're in no condition for shouting."

It was a day since he had awakened in the hospital. The harbor master and the police officer had stirred a deep anger that had begun to smolder inside him.

"I want to call New York."

"I suggest sleep. We've already contacted your embassy."

"I'll sleep after I call my attorney, Doctor. Would you please arrange it?"

She bridled at his tone.

"Please," said Hardin. "I'm very upset. There's somebody I have to talk to."

"Very well."

Twenty minutes later an attendant arrived with a telephone on a long extension cord. The overseas operator verified each end of the line and told them to go ahead.

"Pete," said Bill Kline. "What the hell is going on? They said something—"

"We got run down by a ship."

"You okay?"

"Carolyn's missing."

"Oh Jesus Christ! How long?"

"Five days."

"Oh," Kline moaned. "Oh, no. . . ." The line hissed quietly for a while. "Is there any chance?"

Hardin took a deep breath. He couldn't lie anymore. The water was too cold. He himself had survived by a miracle. Another wasn't likely. "Not much of a chance . . . none."

Hardin closed his eyes and listened to his friend sob. Kline had worshiped Carolyn. He had contributed to the ruin of his second marriage by comparing her to his own wife.

"What happened?" he asked.

"We got hit by an oil tanker. LEVIATHAN."

"LEVIATHAN? Jesus Christ, didn't you see it?"

"It came out of a cloud bank wide open. We didn't have a chance."

"Weren't they using radar?"

"I don't know what happened, Bill. Our radar reflector was up."

"What did they say?" Kline persisted.

Hardin said, "It didn't work that way, Bill. They didn't stop. I was in the water for four days."

"What? They just ran right over you and kept going?"

"Right. Now listen, I want you to bring charges against them."

"Well . . ."

"I want to get whoever's responsible. Can you be here tomorrow?"

"I can't, Pete. I got a client subpoenaed to Washington. I gotta go with her. Besides, you need a local guy. I'll line up my corresponding English solicitor. Top guy. Where are you?"

Hardin told him.

"Hospital? You okay?"

"I'm okay."

"And it happened in British waters?"

"No," said Hardin. "High seas."

"Oh . . . Well. My guy'll be there tomorrow for sure. I'll contact State, and I'll have American Express transfer funds. You need anything else?"

"Clothes."

"Sure. I'll go over to your place right now." At the mention of their apartment, Hardin thought of Carolyn's clothes and how her closets held her fragrance. Kline's voice broke. "Is there any chance?"

"I'm still hoping," said Hardin. "But . . ."

After a while, Kline said, "I'll take care of things here."

Hardin hung up, sick with grief. He had made her death real by telling Kline. Now the lawyer would carry the news to her family. As he lay back with his hand on the telephone, a frightening wave of nausea swept through him. He waited for the violent vomiting that would indicate he had sustained damage to the medulla oblongata, the brain stem. Instead, he slept.

The next day Columbia Presbyterian, Carolyn's hospital, called for confirmation. She had taken a leave from her staff position, and their Atlantic crossing had been the start of what was supposed to be a long, lazy four months before she reported back to work.

Then a young woman from the American Embassy arrived on the London train with a temporary passport, a British visa, and official solicitude. She seemed awed by him, as if she were meeting a character in a television drama, until he said that he wanted embassy help in pressing charges against the owners of LEVIATHAN. She patted the blanket and said, ritualistically, "First you have to get better."

She was followed by a couple of London reporters who telephoned repeatedly after failing to insist their way past Dr. Akanke in person. Hardin was tiring and, thinking the press might help, mentioned a few details before Dr. Akanke interrupted him with the news that Carolyn's father had come.

Ira Jacobs was a trim, short man in his sixties, expensively dressed, but ill at ease with his Protestant son-in-law who seemed to achieve so much with baffling ease. Carolyn had inherited his dark eyes and small hands, and seeing him amplified Hardin's pain.

Jacobs looked on the edge of collapse. Grief had deepened his jowl lines, blackened the pockets under his eyes. Carolyn's mother, he reported, was under sedation and couldn't travel. He stood stiffly by the bed, refusing a chair, and said he wanted to know what had happened.

Hardin described their last moments together.

Jacobs sobbed. Tears dripped from his cheeks. He raised his eyes accusingly. "Why didn't you watch out?"

"We were watching. It came out of a cloud bank."

"Why did you sail in clouds?"

"We didn't choose to."

"It was stupid. You took my daughter."

"Ira," Hardin pleaded.

"What a crazy thing, sailing the ocean. She was a brilliant physician. She was so beautiful. She had everything to live for. You didn't even leave me her body."

Hardin forced himself to meet her father's anguished

gaze. He reached for his hand. Jacobs jerked it back. "Why did you drag her along?"

"We loved each other, Ira. We sailed together. It was part of our lives. Our marriage."

Jacobs wrung his hands. "She didn't even leave children."

"That was the choice we made. We were happy."

"All you did was play. She was a serious person before you got her." He started out the door, then whirled back, his face contorted. "I always hoped that marriage wouldn't last. God, I was right! She would still be alive if it hadn't."

The black wall came for him that night, oozing like tar, and he knew if it caught him it would smother him, fill his nose and throat and trickle down his windpipe into his lungs. He knew he was dreaming. But when Dr. Akanke shook him awake, he clung to her, shaking with terror.

The solicitor's name was Geoffrey Norton. He was younger than Hardin, pleasantly dressed in a sport jacket, blue shirt, and bright tie, and he said he would do everything he could to serve him. He asked Hardin, apologetically, to tell him exactly what had happened to him, and listened intently.

When he had finished, Hardin said, "It was damn close to murder, pure and simple. I want the captain and crew of that ship brought to justice."

"Why?" asked Norton. He made it sound like a point of information, not a challenge.

In waking moments, Hardin had thought of that. He said, "I want to put other captains and crews on notice that they've got to do whatever's necessary to look out for small boats. This isn't the first rundown of a private boat, but this time they hit the wrong man."

A smile wandered across Norton's mouth. "That simplifies matters, doesn't it?"

"If that doesn't work for you," Hardin said briskly, "I'll get another lawyer."

"I have no difficulty with your motive," said Norton. "The law is largely an orderly process of redress."

"All right, what do we do now?"

"I've already discussed this with an Admiralty solicitor —a specialist in maritime law. He explained the procedures one would follow, and he helped me isolate LEVIATHAN's owners."

"What do you mean isolate?"

"When you collided, LEVIATHAN was under short-term charter to CPF–French Petroleum. The ship is registered in Liberia, owned by a Luxembourg consortium consisting of British, American, Arab, and Swiss investors, and managed by a Liberian shipping company called ULCC Ltd. Ultra Large Crude Carriers Limited. They are a fairly new company, pioneering in bigger and better ships. They have an office in London."

"I don't care who owns it."

"We will state our claim to ULCC Ltd.," Norton replied.

"Why don't we go right to court? Press charges?"

"It's not done that way. LEVIATHAN's management company will check our claim against the log and any report by the ship's master."

"The captain isn't going to report it if he didn't stop."

"Probably not," Norton agreed. "But according to my sources, the company will conduct a scrupulous investigation."

"Fine. What if no one saw it happen?"

"Could another boat or ship have witnessed the collision?"

"We were alone."

"I'm in touch with the RAF unit that searched for your wife after you were found. Thus far, we've no reports of wreckage."

"It's been six days," said Hardin. "Besides, *Siren* was fiberglass. She would have sunk like a stone."

"Yes, of course. If ULCC Ltd. denies liability, we will have to refer the matter to the Admiralty solicitors. They would inform LEVIATHAN's company of our intention to pursue the matter. They in turn would refer it to their legal department and notify Lloyd's, their insurer. We would attempt to negotiate a settlement. If that failed, we could petition to sue in the Admiralty. As you can imagine, it would begin to become expensive."

"Wait a minute," said Hardin. "I don't want to sue. I want the captain punished."

Norton laid his note pad on the table beside Hardin's bed. He crossed his legs and folded his hands. "Unfortunately, as the incident occurred in international waters, the government has no authority to prosecute."

"Then what can I do?"

"You can sue the ship's owners."

"They weren't running the ship."

"You'll never bring the captain to an English court."

"I want those who were directly responsible for my wife's death."

Norton looked out the window. Hardin watched his blue eyes flick from side to side as if he were reading old briefs imprinted on his brain. He turned back to him with a smile.

"We could sue the ship."

"What do you mean?"

"Proceed *in rem*. Arrest it."

"What do you mean, arrest it?"

"It's an old custom. But quite valid. An Admiralty marshal would nail a writ to her mast, arresting her to be held for trial."

"Stop the ship?"

"Actually, he'd use cellotape. It's difficult getting a nail through a metal mast."

"Stop the ship?" Hardin repeated, intrigued by the idea of such direct and physical action.

"Until the owners posted bail. Then, of course—"

"Oh." He was disappointed. "They'd put up money and go."

"However," said Norton, "this is all rather speculative at present. We would have to persuade the Admiralty

32

court of the merits of our case." He went on uneasily. "The burden of proof will be on you."

"My wife is dead," said Hardin. "My boat sunk. They found me on the beach."

"That is not proof."

"Are you saying that I don't have a case unless LEVIA-THAN's crew admits they ran me down?"

"I'm sorry."

After Norton left, Hardin realized what had happened. The lawyer had come as a favor to Bill Kline even though he knew that he couldn't help him, and had courteously walked him through the facts until he saw the truth.

When the black came again, it was too real to be a dream. He escaped, thankful for whatever instinct it was that enabled him to differentiate between nightmare and reality.

A police patrol found him limping barefoot on a dark road and returned him to the hospital.

"Good morning," said Dr. Akanke.

She shone a light in his eyes and took his pulse. "You're looking much improved."

Hardin nodded. His body felt like one he remembered. "Do you know you've slept twice around the clock?"

Hardin shrugged.

"We were beginning to consider taxidermy."

Hardin looked from the window to her face. She had not cracked a smile. Even her brown eyes were fathomless. She inserted an electronic thermometer between his lips. It looked like an ordinary glass-and-mercury thermometer, but it was made of aluminum, and instead of calibrations on the side, it had a tiny LED readout the size of a thumbnail.

Hardin turned his head so she couldn't see him click his teeth on the metal probe.

Her eyes widened when she removed it from his mouth. "What's the matter?" Hardin asked.

"You have a temperature of one hundred and eight degrees."

"I feel kind of warm."

She pressed her hand to his forehead and her shoulders drooped with relief. "You're all right. It must be broken."

"Try it again," said Hardin.

She reset the probe and put it in his mouth. Hardin handed it back in a moment.

"Ninety-nine. Much better. There's still a little fever." She regarded the thermometer dubiously. "Odd. It's never broken before."

Hardin took it back, placed it in his mouth, and clicked his teeth.

"Now it says a hundred and seven." She laughed, tentatively. "You made it do that."

"It's mine."

"I beg your pardon?"

"I designed it."

"You did? They're very dear. You must be frightfully rich."

"This is an early model; pediatricians complained about bad readings. I found out it was susceptible to chewing. Some of them had a soldering defect. The new ones will give you point-oh-one accuracy on a hungry tiger."

"Interesting," said Dr. Akanke. "I suspected you had jaw injuries."

"Jaw? My jaw's fine."

"Apparently so. You just smiled."

Hardin looked away.

"It's not wrong to forget your grief, Dr. Hardin."

"Thank you," he said, dismissing her.

She replied, firmly, "I want you to get up today."

"I'll think about it."

"I want you up and I want you to come with me."

"Where?"

"My rounds."

"I don't practice anymore; I make instruments."

"I'm recently graduated, Dr. Hardin. I'd like some advice. There's a woman in the village."

"I don't know if I feel up to it."

"Sit in the garden this morning. We'll see how you feel in the afternoon."

Hardin stayed two days in the garden, ignoring the magnificent view of the Cornish coast, gazing vacantly at the sea beyond. The hospital was atop a hill that overlooked the Fowey harbor, a slender deep-water anchorage, well protected because its mouth, a slash in the high coast cliffs, offered a meager entrance for the Channel's wind and waves.

The town of Fowey, a mix of white and pastel houses, clung to the steep shore on the west side of the harbor. A quarter mile across the water on the east slope was the tiny village of Polruan. Behind the hospital, farms spread north from the sea, draping the land in green and plowed-brown checks.

Gradually, prodded by Dr. Akanke, Hardin lowered his bleak gaze from the sea and focused on the life around him. He noticed a small ferry crisscrossed the harbor every five minutes between Fowey and Polruan. It was little more than a motorized rowboat. People boarded from sloping stone quays.

Dozens of sailing hulls rode moorings in the blue water. Ketches, old yawls, and gleaming new sloops shifted like clock hands with the turning tide, pointing north, then south, then north again. Now and then a small freighter entered the harbor and steamed a half mile inland to a gray pier to load, Dr. Akanke explained, clay from Cornish mines for Dutch potters.

He consented to ride along on her rounds. They drove north down the hills to a car ferry that crossed the River Fowey several miles up from the harbor, then took a narrow hedge-lined road to an isolated farmhouse. Hardin waited in the Rover 2000 with the windows rolled down, breathing the earthy spring odors. They stopped at several more houses, and each time when Hardin declined to go in with her, she did not push it.

The farmyards were pretty, the houses well kept, but

35

the tall hedgerows lining the narrow roads made him feel claustrophobic. They topped a rise and the sea was suddenly beneath them, glaring in the noon sun like shattered mirrors. She pulled off the road at the edge of the cliffs and got out of the car. Hardin followed and they walked a trodden earth path that meandered toward the rim of the cliff.

"Sheep?" he asked.

"Tourists." She picked up a cigarette wrapper.

He squinted at the water polishing the black rocks far below and thought of Carolyn in the cold sand at the bottom of the ocean, or drifting in her life jacket, long dead, prey to the birds. He wrenched his mind from that.

"What's wrong?" asked Dr. Akanke.

"I was thinking of my wife."

"I'm sure she felt nothing. It's a miracle that you survived."

Why me? he wondered. And what had she felt? What pain and fear? They walked silently while he grappled with his imagination.

Dr. Akanke intervened. "Isn't this beautiful country?"

"Where are you from?" he asked.

"Nigeria."

In that single word, her voice wasn't British. The name rolled like proud music from her tongue.

"You speak like an Englishwoman."

"I've been at school here since I was a teenager."

"Do you ever consider going back to Nigeria?"

"I leave for Lagos within the month." Shielding her eyes with her dark, graceful hands, she looked out at the sea. "Your wife was a doctor."

"How did you know?"

"Her father told me."

Returning from his first long solitary walk, Hardin came in the front door of the hospital. A middle-aged Englishwoman in a plain dress jumped to her feet with an expression of relief. Then her face fell.

"Yes?" asked Hardin, drawn to her grief-stricken appearance. A wet, gurgling cough sounded behind a closed door.

She shook her head, biting her lips. "I thought you were my son. He's coming from Plymouth." Her voice broke and she sat in the armchair behind her.

Hardin knelt beside her. "Can I help?"

The coughing started again. The woman cocked her head and listened intently as the spasm went on and on, rising to a ripping, rasping noise that hurt to hear. When it finally stopped, her tensed body sagged with relief.

"My husband. Throat cancer. So fast," she said wonderingly. "He was healthy two days ago and the doctor says he'll die by night. . . . The boy is coming from Plymouth."

Hardin nodded. Dr. Akanke had mentioned the case yesterday.

"I didn't want to call at first because he has examinations, but it will be over soon." She looked exhausted, her round face pasty white. The coughing resumed. "It must hurt him so. I want him to die."

"I know," said Hardin, taking her hand.

"It's not wrong."

"No."

And suddenly he was crying, sobbing his anguish against this stranger's breast. Her son, a handsome university student, found them there. He thanked Hardin for comforting his mother.

4

The balmy May weather Hardin had enjoyed in Cornwall gave way to chilly spring rain in London, and after a day of fruitless shuttling between the British Admiralty and the American Embassy, cold fury blasted the last remnants of depression from his mind.

Fed up with the runaround, he telephoned Bill Kline in New York. Kline, unable to convince Hardin of the futility of legal recourse, called friends in Washington; and the next day whoever weighed power at the embassy decided that Peter Hardin deserved the personal attention of an assistant chargé d'affaires named John Cave, a bored young man who wore a Links Club necktie and occupied a handsome office with a view of the garden.

"I'm sure you're aware that I intend to bring charges against the captain of the ship that ran me down. I've learned that he is named Cedric Ogilvy and I believe that he is a British subject. I want a decent introduction at the British Admiralty to somebody who can authorize an investigation."

"LEVIATHAN is of Liberian registry," Cave responded. "A flag of convenience."

"I don't give a damn who owns it. I want the captain."

"How is John?"

"I just met the man," answered Hardin, his patience fading. His knee had been throbbing all morning and he felt feverish in the overheated office of the Admiralty civil servant Cave had sent him to. He loosened his tie and his wilted collar.

"Well, Dr. Hardin, I've discussed all this with some of our lower-echelon people—those you met yesterday—and I think I'm aware of all the facts. Unfortunately, sir, there is nothing we can do for you. If you weren't the only witness and this were a clear-cut case of malfeasance, we might seize the ship, but neither supposition is true, to our knowledge. And a mere hearing would be worthless because we have no power of subpoena over a Liberian ship."

"But the captain is British," Hardin said doggedly. His hair fell on his brow. He pushed it back. It had grown uncomfortably long and he felt disheveled and out of place in these orderly buildings. A simple memory clutched his heart—Carolyn always cut his hair. He hadn't gone to a barber in ten years.

"Commanding a foreign-flag vessel owned by God knows who," replied the civil servant. "I'm sorry, sir. I can imagine what it's like for you."

He flinched from Hardin's empty eyes.

Hardin left the Admiralty and walked the Embankment in the rain, perspiring from fever despite the damp cold. His knee hurt and kept threatening to lock. He cut through the Temple Gardens, decided outside the solicitor's door not to stop at Norton's office, and walked some more, growing desperate, not knowing what to do next.

He felt alone and out of place in the lunch-hour bustle of Fleet Street. The narrow sidewalks were crowded, the pubs and wine bars jammed. Hungry, he ducked into a pub and ordered a hot meat pie, but fled the cheerful warmth before the barmaid brought it, unable to bear his thoughts of Carolyn and the trips they had taken to London.

He walked into the old City, threaded a maze of narrow streets and tall gray buildings, found Lloyd's of London, and questioned a doorman in a red frock coat who sent him across Lime Street to the company's Hull and Cargo sections. On the second floor Hardin found a blue-carpeted office with big windows and rows of modern wooden desks heaped with papers, folders, bulging envelopes, and telephones, and manned by youngish men in bright shirts, loosened ties, and rolled sleeves.

His coat dripping, his hair soaked and pasted down, he stood uncertainly beside a table of instant coffee fixings under a color pinup. After a while, someone noticed him and asked if he needed help.

Hardin tried to order his reeling brain. He wasn't entirely sure what he was doing here, but he knew no other place to go. He brushed his hair from his eyes and said, "I'd like to talk to somebody about an accident at sea."

"Cargo or hull?"

"Hull, I guess."

"This is Cargo. I'll take you there, it's right around the corner."

He was led to a glassed-off area at the back of the Hull office.

"My name is Hardin. My boat was run down by LEVIATHAN."

There were two men in the office, both in white shirts. Their suit jackets hung over the backs of their chairs. One stared, the other rose with a careful smile.

"I've heard your story, Dr. Hardin, but I'm not quite sure what you're doing here."

"Lloyd's insured LEVIATHAN," Hardin replied. "If I sue, you'll be involved."

"Not directly, I'm afraid. It's not like automobile insurance. The shipper is responsible for his own defense, if defense is called for. We merely advise."

"Listen," said Hardin, "I don't want to sue. I just want to bring charges against the captain."

"That's out of our ken." He looked over at Hardin and smiled again. "Could I offer some advice, Doctor?"

Hardin brushed at his hair. "What?"

"Your position is hopeless. You can't prove that LEVIATHAN collided with your yacht. It's as simple as that."

Hardin saw a familiar expression on the man's face. How often had he assembled his own features into a mask of wary sympathy when a patient complained of sickness for which there was no reason?

He returned to the Admiralty with no plan in mind, found it closing, and was standing bare-headed in the rain when an ancient black Rolls pulled up to the curb and a loud voice hailed him from a lowered rear window.

"Dr. Hardin!"

The door opened and a wrinkled hand motioned him in. Recognizing an old man he had glimpsed in one of the offices at the Admiralty, Hardin climbed into the car and pulled the door shut. Silently, it entered the traffic, piloted by a white-haired chauffeur and heading toward Trafalgar Square.

The wrinkled hand pushed a button and a glass partition

slid up. "I'm Captain Desmond," said the man in the backseat. "Royal Navy, Retired."

"We spoke yesterday?" asked Hardin, wondering what secrets the old captain could have from his aged chauffeur.

"We were in the same room. I overheard. You've had an incredible experience, sir, and I speak as a man who's been shipwrecked four times: the first on a windjammer in the Chilean nitrate trade, and three times by German torpedo."

The car proceeded magisterially through the London traffic, passing by sidewalks jammed with civil servants marching home beneath a rippling canopy of black umbrellas.

Hardin's anger, close to the surface, erupted. He was tired of the ghoulish interest his experience attracted. He said, "I'd appreciate the miracle of my survival a bit more if my wife had shared in it. I'll get out at the next light, thank you."

"My wife drowned when a ferry hit a German mine," said Desmond. "It was a year after the war had ended. You've reminded me of my fury at the absurdity of it."

"A million-ton tanker steaming full speed through visibility shorter than the space it needs to stop in is more than absurd. It's criminal."

"I hadn't your luxury of someone to blame," replied Desmond. "My anger died long before my pain." He gazed at the city, his lips working. "Such speed is common practice. They depend on their radar. Did you have a reflector?"

"Of course," Hardin snapped.

"Some yachtsmen don't," Desmond said mildly. "Too much windage."

"I wasn't racing. I had a big one on the mizzen. I don't see how they could have missed it."

"Could it have been carried away in the squall preceding the collision?"

"No. I know my boat."

Desmond said, "I would hypothesize that in the con-

41

ditions you've described they set their radar to maximum range, which reduces short-range resolution. Or perhaps it wasn't functioning at all, though that information would be in its log."

"Which I can't get to without an investigation."

"I don't think a reputable shipper would cover up such information."

Hardin snorted a disgusted dissent.

"No," said Desmond. "The tankers are not known for mechanical reliability. Breakdowns are so common that they're routinely entered. It would be very difficult to conceal the fact that a repair crew had done work."

"Nothing electronic is infallible," said Hardin. "Somehow, either through breakdown, oversight, negligence, or something inexplicable, they didn't see me. And godammit, they should have lookouts."

He fell silent, staring out the window as they rode down The Mall past Buckingham Palace, toward the wild horses on Wellington Arch. The Rolls swung through a set of pillars marked In and Out in front of a stone building next to Hyde Park.

"Would you have time to join me for a drink?" asked Desmond, as the car stopped smoothly.

Hardin shivered. His clothes were soaked inside with perspiration and outside from the rain. A doorman was approaching the car with a big umbrella, and though he felt conspicuously unkempt, the amber glow of the building's windows was warm and inviting.

He accepted, and followed Desmond through spacious, dark halls to a small room where they took armchairs in front of a coal fire.

"Whiskey and soda," said Desmond to a young Italian waiter.

"Scotch, straight," said Hardin.

"You look tired," said Desmond.

"Yeah." He massaged his knee in the warmth of the fire.

Desmond was very small. His trim body couldn't have weighed more than a hundred pounds. The top of his

42

head, which was ringed with a band of snowy hair, seemed nearly separated from the bottom by the deep squint lines that radiated from his eyes.

"Can you help me?" asked Hardin.

Desmond shook his head. "Do you realize that whatever the intentions of the corporation which owns LEVIATHAN, and the intentions of the oil company that chartered it, and the intentions of the captain and crew, none of them really believe they did run your boat down?" He raised his hand to stop Hardin from interrupting. "Wait. LEVIATHAN is so enormous that it could put a fifty-ton trawler under the sea and it wouldn't feel a tremor. It wouldn't surprise me if she's done it already. They've been disappearing regularly off Africa since the supertankers began to round the Cape."

"Well, *I* didn't disappear," said Hardin. "I *know* LEVIATHAN ran me down. I know it killed my wife. I know it sank my boat. And I'm going to do something about it. I'm sick of hearing about how it's too big to stop, and too big to see small boats, and too big to know when it runs them down."

The drinks came. Desmond raised his glass with a wintry smile and sipped; Hardin drained his quickly.

"We're all responsible for what we do," he said. "That's the way it works. If they can build them that big and surmount the technological difficulties in building them that big, they can surmount the technological difficulties in sailing them, including looking out for small boats."

"Have the other half," said Desmond, nodding to the waiter, who returned quickly with a second scotch. "I agree with you, Dr. Hardin. However, it's questionable how much they've ever surmounted such difficulties. There are limitations, really. Physical limitations. LEVIATHAN is the latest generation of ULCC. She's Japanese built; they fitted her with proper engines, twin screws, and twin rudders for better handling, but even so, she can't be stopped in less than four miles. A million tons, sir. Can you imagine the inertia?"

"I've seen it in action," said Hardin. "What it comes down to is it's too damned big for the ocean."

"A million tons of oil is an awesome economic tool," said Desmond. "She makes her own market. Simply by choosing in which port to off-load."

The drinks drove a soft wedge between Hardin and his anger. It permitted him to accept the comfort of the deep chair and the warm fire. He nodded politely while the old captain rambled on about his life at sea and the great changes that had swept merchant shipping in recent times.

"Age is the worst threat the ULCCs present. All ships, like all men, are doomed. Rust and vibration will have their way. Plates wear thinner each year, corroded by the sea without and the oil within. Welds part, seams open, machinery weakens, and metal fatigues.

"LEVIATHAN was launched only last summer. In less than a decade, she'll have begun to deteriorate. By all that's right, then they should send her to the breaker's yard. But little is right with the sea these days, and prudence often runs a poor second to profit. What if there's an oil shortage that year, or the scrap-metal market is soft? What if LEVIATHAN is worth more afloat that year than as scrap? What if her owners sell her to a shipper willing to take a chance?"

Desmond looked into the fire. "She'll die an awful death. She'll break down someday and go aground. Or split in two. Or sink. And I pray to God that she'll be empty, for if she's laden, she'll wreak incalculable destruction on some shore of Europe or Africa. She'll make what the *Amoco Cadiz* did to Brittany look like a minor spill. A million tons of crude oil. That coast will still be a desert long after it's forgotten what destroyed it."

"If they keep on running it the way they are," said Hardin, "it'll crack up before it gets old."

"Not likely," replied Desmond. "Certainly not with Ogilvy in command. He takes his responsibility very seriously. And he understands—"

"You know him?" Hardin interrupted.

"Cedric? Vaguely. He was my gunnery officer for a month or two on the old *Agincourt* just before the second war. I had a command in the Gulf. Oversized gunboat.

"He was barely more than a boy, fifteen years my junior, I'd imagine. Now of course, he's the most envied ship's master in the world. Snagging that berth was quite a plum. Funny about Cedric and the tankers. He hates the Arabs; and now he's in the Gulf every two months like clockwork. It must gall the hell out of him that they're patrolling the waters we used to."

"It galls the hell out of me that he's on the bridge of that monster after what he did to me."

"You've used the right word," Desmond agreed. "It is a monster and Ogilvy is not entirely in control. No man could be."

"Someone is always responsible," said Hardin. "And it's the captain at sea, Master before God! At this very moment LEVIATHAN is following his route and the crew is following his orders. If he posts lookouts, there are lookouts. If he doesn't, there aren't."

"In point of fact," Desmond said, chuckling, "Cedric Ogilvy is most likely nursing a pint in Hampstead right now and wishing his wife would let him smoke in the house."

"They relieved him?" asked Hardin.

"Oh no, no, no. They rotate captains. He's on two trips and off one. He'll be home for six or seven more weeks—I say, Dr. Hardin, stay for another. It's an awful night."

But Hardin was already hurrying to the door.

Ogilvy's house was in a section of large detached houses built in a terrace row at the turn of the century. A tall woman with white hair and a long plain face answered the door. Captain Ogilvy was still in the City on business. She expected him home in an hour.

Hardin declined her invitation to wait and walked to a pub he had seen around the corner on the main road.

The Lancers' Arms was a free house, a simple mix of

country woodwork, hunters' kit—dusty horns, guns, knives, and whips—hanging from the low ceilings, and plastic fittings on the beer taps.

He ordered a pint of bitter, found it watery, and switched to scotch. He had eaten nothing since breakfast at his hotel, and the whiskey on top of those he had had with Desmond had more effect than he intended. He was on his second or third, he didn't know which, teetering between giddiness and oblivion, when Captain Cedric Ogilvy walked in.

He was blandly handsome, a ruddy-faced, white-haired man of sixty, tall and erect, though Hardin saw a slight shuffling of his feet which signaled the early stages of hardening arteries. Two regulars at the bar greeted him, showing pleasure at the captain's acknowledgment. Ogilvy took a seat by the fireplace.

The barman poked the wood fire and went back to the bar in response to a patron's demand that he be permitted to buy the "captain" a pint. Ogilvy invited his neighbors to join him at the fire.

Hardin remained alone at the bar drinking and listening and wondering where exactly Ogilvy had been at the moment LEVIATHAN had run him down. The bridge? Chart room? His cabin? The deck? Had his hard eyes glanced at the radarscope, missed a dim blip, ignored an odd flicker? Had he labeled a pinprick of light a glitch? Had, in fact, he even been on watch?

It was easy enough to dislike the man. He talked in a loud voice, stopping only long enough to allow a contribution to his monologue. He seemed opinionated and thoroughly imbued with a careless assurance that, Hardin guessed, came from years of talking to subordinates.

One of his friends bought a second round. During the exchange Ogilvy's big, thick fingers drummed restlessly on his knee. Someone asked him about LEVIATHAN's performance. He lowered his pint, untouched.

"She's a titan. Quite simply, the greatest ship in the world." He started to raise his glass, then stopped again. "My only regret is that England didn't build her, but it

46

took the Greeks and Japanese to show us that our out-moded marine traditions were holding us back. There's a new technology of the sea, gentlemen, and in a word, it is big.

"Build them big. Automate them so you don't have a hundred men running around the engine room. Staff them with a few good officers—mine are British, you know. Took them with me when I left the P and O. Big ships are fast and comfortable and they get the job done. And that is what the sea has always been about, gentlemen. Getting the job done."

"Regardless of whom you kill?" Hardin asked loudly.

All eyes turned to the bar where he toyed with his empty glass. He held it out for the barman to fill.

"I beg your pardon, young man?" asked Ogilvy.

Hardin, noticing that the barman was not pouring more whiskey into his glass, rapped it sharply on the wooden bar. The insistent drumming sound told him he was getting drunk. He put the glass down and answered Ogilvy.

"You killed my wife and sank my boat with your *big* ship, sir."

The other people in the bar exchanged startled glances, but Ogilvy stood up, clearly understanding, and replied, "You must be the fellow who's been slandering me at the Admiralty."

"You deny it?" yelled Hardin. His voice rang loud in his own ears.

"Absolutely," said Ogilvy, stepping out of the circle of chairs and approaching Hardin at the bar. He had small, bright-blue eyes, and up close, Hardin realized, this was a much tougher man than his bland face implied. *"I deny it!"*

"You had no lookout," said Hardin, pushing the hair from his brow. "You don't know what happened."

Doubt flickered in Ogilvy's eyes, then disappeared like a candle flame in sunlight. "LEVIATHAN ran no one down," he said firmly.

"You ran right over me, you son of a bitch. I saw your name all over the stern."

Ogilvy turned to the gaping men at the fire. "This young man is obviously in need of medical help. He's been bandying about wild accusations at the Admiralty, ignored, rightfully. He seems to be searching for a villain on whom he can blame his wife's death. I suspect he knows he was responsible for whatever accident he suffered and feels guilty."

Hardin hit him.

Ogilvy cried out and stumbled backward, clutching his face. His friends sprang to his aid, shouting in dismay. Confused, as if he were unable to figure out a movie he had entered late, Hardin watched them cluster about the captain.

Ogilvy's face was wracked with pain; and the body staggering backward belonged to an old man. Blood poured through his cupped hands. It spattered his white shirt and enraged his friends. They helped him into a chair while the barman, a stocky two-hundred-pounder, came for Hardin, his fists raised expertly.

He threw two quick, stinging jabs and a right cross that took Hardin high on the cheek and slammed him against the bar. Bobbing and weaving, he threw two more jabs, one of which opened Hardin's lip, and went for the body.

Hardin sidestepped. The body punch hit the bar. The barman, angered, charged wildly. Hardin laid him flat with a barstool. Then he sat down at a corner table with his back to the wall and his head in his hands and waited for the police.

He was charged with public drunkenness and assault and battery, and put in a cell with several drunks who kept threatening to beat up a frightened Jamaican boy accused of housebreaking. He gave the hospital in Fowey as his address in England. The black wall came for him at dawn, pushing the comber before it. Carolyn tumbled on its crest, her arms and legs pinwheeling. He ran to help her and grabbed her hand, but the wave tore her away. He awakened to the sound of his shouting and the Jamaican shaking him and pleading, "Sair, sair, you've a dream, sair."

The police took him to magistrate's court in the morning. Acutely aware of the disadvantage at which his dirty, disheveled appearance put him, Hardin intended to ask for a lawyer and a postponement and, if denied, would request help from the American Embassy.

Before he could, an assured young man took charge of the unfamiliar court proceedings, and it took Hardin a while to realize he was not a prosecutor but his defense attorney. After the charges were read, a police constable described the scene he had found at the Lancers' Arms. The magistrate's face wrinkled with distaste at the mention of Ogilvy's age. The situation became marginally clearer for Hardin when Dr. Akanke swept into the courtroom in a tailored blue suit and white turban, cast him a worried smile, and took the box to testify that she had treated Hardin for physical and mental trauma.

The magistrate questioned her rather sharply. When he cast doubt on her qualifications, the well-dressed young man asked to speak with him privately. He was joined by several others, including two black men. The group conferred at the magistrate's bench, the magistrate turning several times to his clerk for advice.

"Bring the prisoner forward," he snapped at the bailiff. Hardin was hustled to the bench. The magistrate looked perplexed.

"Your presence in my court, Dr. Hardin, has attracted an especially qualified solicitor, a gentleman from the Foreign Office, and two Nigerian envoys, not to mention the American ambassador's assistant chargé d'affaires lurking in my anteroom. Were these worthy personages here to attest to the character of a hooligan who struck a gentleman twenty years his senior, and assaulted a barman who came to the old man's defense, I would ignore them and remand these serious charges to a higher court.

"However, as they've journeyed to Hampstead to support the testimony of your doctor who contends you're not entirely responsible for your actions, I am persuaded to

49

release you in her care. But I place you under the strictest probation. If you ever go near Captain Ogilvy again, I will send you to prison. Is that clear?"

Dr. Akanke drove Hardin to his hotel for his clothes, then headed toward Cornwall on the M3. He hunched against the far door of the Rover, thinking how when he had called Kline for help at the embassy, Kline had said, Come home.

Come home to what? The streets they explored when it was too cold to sail? Their favorite restaurants? The subscription seats at Lincoln Center? Or would he find a place they'd never been and stare with filling eyes, knowing she'd have liked it too.

He thought of Ogilvy and LEVIATHAN.

When they passed Shaftesbury, he sat straight, and said, "Thank you. Where'd you get the big guns?"

Dr. Akanke drove with both hands on the wooden wheel of the powerful car and her eyes stayed on the road as she answered.

"Racialism has become a serious problem in England, particularly in the cities. I was afraid the court would disregard my testimony because of my color, so I asked my embassy for support."

"And they wheeled out two diplomats and a senior man from the British Foreign Office? That's some embassy."

She threw him a quick smile. "It wouldn't do to have me insulted. Many people believe that my father will be the next chief of staff of the Nigerian Army. Others assume I will marry the son of an important politician."

"Why did you come for me?" asked Hardin.

"You're my patient. You've obviously not recovered."

"I have now."

She frowned dubiously. "Are you suggesting that assaulting that man was some sort of catharsis?"

Hardin smiled to put her at ease. "No," he said. "It was a mistake."

"I'm glad you see that."

50

He saw it clearly. He had attacked the wrong enemy. No man, no captain bore such responsibility that hurting him would slake Hardin's fury.

While Ogilvy worked his Hampstead garden, while Dr. Akanke drove him through the ordered beauty of Dorset, the monster was out there—host to another captain who imagined he was in command—steaming back around Africa like the relentless arm of a deadly pendulum.

5

She had never met a medical man like him. He told her he hadn't studied surgery, but he acted with the boldness and abrupt decisiveness of a top surgeon, and in that he reminded her of her father. But her father was a Yoruban Nigerian soldier, and this man was a white American widower, and something told her it was just as well that she was going home in a month.

She was twenty-seven years old, just surfacing from the drudgery of medical training, and she found herself noticing the oddest things: his rare smiles broadened his wide mouth but didn't show his teeth; the resonant sound of his voice; how he brushed his hair from his forehead when he bent over a page.

His powers of concentration were enormous. She stood over him, her shadow on his book for several minutes, and he didn't notice. He was lying on the grass in the hospital garden surrounded by books and magazines. Since they had returned from London he had spent most of his time reading about shipping and maritime affairs. Therapy, he had called it, when she had asked. Once a day they talked for an hour. He refused to speak with the staff psychiatrist, but he answered her questions openly and candidly and thanked her several times for helping him put things in perspective.

He said he felt much better and she believed him. His anger seemed gone, vanished as if it had never existed. He no longer snapped at people, nor did he stare into space with the rage smoldering in his eyes the way he had.

She made a shadow bird on his page and flapped its wings. He looked up. "Hi."

Ajaratu said, "Would you like to come to my office?"

"Here's fine. You could use the fresh air."

She thought he had started to say "sun" and caught himself. She knelt beside him, conscious of how light his skin was even though it was tanned.

"How's the therapy coming?" she asked.

"Fine." He reached to straighten the stack of magazines, but they fell, fanning out like a bridge hand. Ajaratu riffled through the copies of *Safety at Sea* and *Fairplay* and reached for a glossy color magazine that had a picture of a soldier on the cover.

He took it from her and stacked it with the others. "No dreams last night."

"Wonderful."

"At least none I can remember."

"How's your knee?"

"Stiff."

"Is it still locking?"

"It wants to," said Hardin. "I'm getting so I can anticipate it and move accordingly."

"Perhaps you won't need surgery."

A nurse came into the garden and said there was an overseas call for Dr. Hardin. He apologized. He received one or two a day. "Excuse me. I'll be right back."

He returned quickly. "Lawyer. Sorry."

"Important?" She wanted to see where his interest lay.

He looked at the sea. "The insurance came through on the boat."

"Did your wife carry life insurance?"

Like lightning, the anger flashed back in his eyes. Ajaratu waited. She had asked deliberately to gauge his reaction. "Yes," he said quietly. "Any more charming questions?"

52

"I'm sorry, Peter. That was thoughtless. You were going to tell me about your business."

"Not much to tell," said Hardin. "I took in a partner to run it day to day and my lawyer watches him. I own the patents. It works."

"Then what do you do? Do you invent new instruments?"

"Or go sailing." He grew reflective for a moment. "It's funny, but it's hard for me to connect with the person I was when I built the temperature probe. It seems so long ago, even though it's only a few years. In retrospect it happened so fast—I thought of it; I designed it in a morning; spent some time ironing out the bugs. Bill Kline did the wheeling and dealing. We had a mad scramble setting up a factory and then all of a sudden the money was rolling in. Sometimes I still can't believe it happened." He laughed. "I doubt I could do it again."

Ajaratu smiled. Before she had realized how quickly Hardin would recover, she had telephoned Kline to learn details of his life that might help her care for him. The lawyer's version of the invention was less casual. "Twenty hours a day seven days a week for a year and a half. That's how long it took him to put that thing in production. Incredible determination. Once he knew he had the right idea, you couldn't stop him."

"That must have been difficult for his wife."

"Carolyn?" The lawyer paused. "Yes, it was hard. But she was back in med school then, busy as hell, and they worked it out, just like they worked everything out. She was an incredible woman . . . How's he doing?"

She had told him not to worry. Now, of course, he would know from talking to him that Hardin was quite well.

She said to Hardin, "The director suggests you should be released."

He grinned at her. "I guess I have been using this place as a hotel. I'll get a room in the village."

"Don't rush," she said. "We've got some extra beds." She crossed her arms around her tucked-up knees and gazed down at the long, narrow harbor. "What do you intend to do?"

Hardin nodded at the bright hulls riding their moorings. "I'm going to buy a boat."

The wealthy Londoners who owned the sailboats left them in the care of a scrawny old Cornishman with a sly face. His name, Culling, was emblazoned on the sheds and barns in his boatyard at the north end of the harbor on the Fowey side. He listened without comment while Hardin explained what sort of a voyage and boat he had in mind, then led him into a shabby wooden rowboat, yanked a cord on a Seagull outboard, and steered toward the middle of the harbor where his moored charges pointed the tide like sheep facing the dog.

A fresh wind raised a chop on the water and snapped the yachts' halyards musically against their aluminum masts. Hardin was impressed. These were deepwater cruising and racing boats. They droned past a spectacular white hull, a Sparkman and Stephens Nautor Swan built in Finland. Hardin gazed longingly at her powerful lines. It would be hard to imagine a finer single-handed cruising boat. They were rare in the States, but he had once seen one in Boston.

Culling slowed the little engine and said, "There she is. A gentleman's cruising boat."

Hardin whistled. There she was. A graceful, fast Hinckley Bermuda yawl. Another American design, Tripp, but much older, with a long overhang and pretty as a picture.

"How did she get over here?" Hardin asked as the yardman veered alongside and backwatered expertly by spinning the Seagull on its mount.

Culling shrugged. "She's going very cheap. Needs some cleaning up, but a bargain."

Hardin climbed aboard and looked around. She hadn't been cared for with much enthusiasm lately. Her chrome was pitted and the first winch he touched was frozen. Not that that necessarily mattered. The Hinckley was a

54

solid, Maine-built boat and he was looking for more than a bright paint job.

"I'll need some time to look her over," said Hardin.

"Enjoy yourself." Culling lay back in the rowboat and covered his eyes with his cotton hat and appeared for all intents and purposes to fall asleep.

The companionway hatch slid open with great difficulty. He had to brace himself to shove it back enough to skip down into the cabin. She was dirty below and smelled damp. A rumpled blanket was mildewing on a forward bunk. He started at the bow and worked backward, checking out the lockers, sail bins, bilges, and cupboards, hunting her strengths and weaknesses, assessing what damage her previous owner had done her.

He found half-empty liquor bottles, cocktail mixes, paper napkins, plastic cups and plates, and few spare parts and tools. Shackles, blocks, rope, twine, and tape were all in short supply. Whoever had sailed the yawl from the States had not been the last person aboard.

He pulled the mainsail out of its bag. The cloth had deteriorated along the entire length of its foot. Dacron's sole weakness was its chemical instability in sunlight, and the sail was ruined because it had not been covered when it was furled to the boom.

He shone his penlight into the depths of a locker and discovered that the bulkhead between the main and forward cabins had separated slightly from the hull, but when he pulled up the floorboards in the stern, he found little water in the bilges, and the stuffing box around the engine box seemed tight.

He went back up on deck, thinking that a good fiberglass boat, as the Hinckley was, could survive the sort of careless owner who had had this one much longer than could a boat built of wood or steel. Wood rotted and steel rusted, but fiberglass just waited for better times.

The standing rigging, the wire stays and shrouds supporting the mast, looked all right, though some corroded fittings would have to be replaced. The running rigging, the halyards and sheets, was worn. At the bow, Hardin leaned against the forestay and gazed the length of the yawl. The stay felt very tight.

Culling lifted his hat from his face and called from the rowboat, "Like her?"

"Maybe."

Hardin walked the deck, testing the safety-line stanchions, finding several loose. The mainmast's backstays and shrouds were as taut as the forestay. He stepped into the cockpit and checked again the tight sliding hatch cover. Not only were the tracks clean, but someone had chiseled them wider in an unsuccessful attempt to make the cover slide more easily. He reached down and fingered the top step of the companionway. It was loose. Recalling the crack between the cabin bulkhead and the hull, he leaned over the side of the boat and eyed its length. He stood abruptly and stepped across the yawl and into Culling's rowboat.

The yardman grinned. "Yes?"

"She's a banana."

"Banana?"

Hardin slapped the hull. "She's bulging amidships. Some damned fool's been tuning the stays too tightly. The tension's distorted the hull."

"You know your boats, sir."

"I know a crook, too," Hardin shot back.

Culling seemed undisturbed by the accusation. He wrapped his starting cord around the outboard's flywheel. "There's another I'll show you."

"I don't think so," said Hardin. He sat in the bow of the boat, facing back.

Culling yanked the cord and the motor buzzed like a jar of mosquitoes. "Won't take a minute. It's on the way to the quay."

Hardin nodded glumly. The old thief had a lock on every decent boat in the harbor. He watched the panorama of the towns and hills swing in a circle of soft peninsular colors. Of all the beautiful places he and Carolyn had

56

visited, none had such pale, clear, revealing light as Cornwall.

The view stopped swinging and when Culling slowed the little engine, Hardin turned around and saw the Nautor Swan, twenty yards ahead. Even moored it looked like a prowling shark.

"That?"

"That," said Culling.

The Swan had the short, sharp lines of a bayonet, powerful rather than pretty, with its bow not especially raked and its squarish stern chopped at a distinct forward angle. A sliver of cabin wedged barely a foot above the deck at its highest point.

Hardin turned from the straight lines of the hull to Culling's sly face. "What are you up to? She's got to cost more than I have."

Culling's gamin features softened. "Her owner is bankrupt and his creditors want their brass. She's worth fifty-five thousand pounds, but they'll take forty-five."

"You're kidding," said Hardin. Eighty-five or so thousand dollars was more than he intended to spend, but a bargain price for a used yacht that must have run a hundred and twenty thousand new.

"She's a treasure," said Culling, "and as I've the job of selling her, I'll decide who deserves her."

Hardin smiled thinly at the maimed Bermuda yawl. "I passed the test?"

"Thought you would. Mind your footing now." Culling brought the rowboat gently alongside, and this time joined Hardin as he stepped aboard.

She was beamier than her sharp profile suggested, and Hardin paused for a heady moment at the aluminum helm to drink in her wide teak decks and lavish fittings and imagine what a joy it would be to work her. This was an ocean yacht capable of driving as hard and far as a man could push.

Her sleek cabin grew from her molded fiberglass hull, rooted as integrally as a knife's cutting edge to its blade.

Where wood might offer comfort or beauty she was wood; the decks, sheet cleats, and handrail had weathered gray.

The cockpit was small and shallow. Hardin lifted the teak seat covers and found stowage lockers, including one with a life raft, sealed tight from the bilges. Double two-inch scuppers would drain her quickly if she shipped a sea.

She had jiffy reefing and stainless-steel Lewmar sheet and halyard winches, and her stays, shrouds, and safety lines all gleamed corrosion free in the bright sunlight. On a panel above the hatch, visible from the cockpit, were the black dials of Brookes and Gatehouse racing instruments for wind velocity, wind direction, speed, and the farthometer readout for water depth.

"Three years old," said Culling, stroking the safety lines with a loving touch. "Thirty-eight feet overall. Twenty-nine on the waterline. Fin keel. Six-foot, four-inch draft. Eight tons displacement. Seven thousand pounds ballast. She's been to the Canaries, Rio de Janeiro, Fort Lauderdale, and home by the Azores."

"You've maintained her?" asked Hardin.

"Aye. Not that she needed a lot. The owner treated her like a lady. Go below. See what you see." He slid the smoked Lucite hatch cover open as smoothly as if it were on roller bearings.

Hardin studied it with a wary eye until he determined that it was three quarters of an inch thick and seated in deep tracks so that a wave couldn't rip it off. Although he worked with the latest technology and most modern materials, he was, at age forty-three, old enough to have started sailing when boats were still made of wood and carried canvas sails sheeted with manila line, and he had a conservative mistrust of amenities like plastic hatches.

He descended the companionway into the main cabin. She was a miniature teak temple inside, light and airy, with the rounded lines and edges that showed that the Finnish carpenters had known they were building a boat instead of a house trailer. He took a long, appreciative look at the craftsmanship, then put the beauty from his mind and turned to the essentials.

Her lockers looked good. They were clean and orderly and packed with the tools and repair materials found on a well-maintained boat. The sails had been protected from the sun and stowed properly. He worked his way through the sail bins, checking the enormous inventory.

The owner had been slightly sail happy and had spent lavishly. If he took this boat, Hardin would have to leave some behind to make room for supplies. The rope lockers were similarly equipped, the bilges dry, and the diesel auxiliary, shielded by a heavily soundproofed box, clean, its hoses recently replaced.

"Twenty horsepower," said Culling. "Two and a half to one reduction. Twenty-five-gallon fuel tank. You've got a three-hundred-mile range at six knots."

"Clockwise screw?" asked Hardin.

"Sixteen inch propeller." Culling nodded. "The folding kind."

"Generator?"

"Alternator off the main engine."

To drive the equipment he planned to install, Hardin would need a fair-sized generator. He gave the switchboard and circuit breakers a quick look. Like everything else on the Swan, they were orderly and clean.

"Okay," he said. "Let's haul her. I want to see the bottom."

Culling nodded invitingly at the narrow cut in the cliffs. "Care to sail her first?"

Hardin shook his head. "First I want to make sure she isn't wearing a reef."

Culling smiled. "I'll slip the mooring. You run her in." He detached the double lines that held her to her mooring and nodded complacently when the diesel muttered eagerly at Hardin's first touch on the starter button. Hardin wondered for the hundredth time if they might have escaped LEVIATHAN if he had replaced *Siren*'s balky engine before their Atlantic crossing.

The Swan steered responsively; he regretted not having the time to take her for a sail first. But he had to know by evening if this was the boat, because he needed other things equally important to his plan.

From the water, Culling's boatyard appeared as a circle of well-kept boat sheds ringed by enormous tumbling-down boathouses. Rusting tracks emerged from the water and disappeared into the dark of the boathouses like the bones of beached sea monsters. Hardin asked the purpose of the ruins and Culling replied that early in the war he had maintained a repair station for MTBs—the motor torpedo boats that fought the Germans in the English Channel.

Hardin pointed the Swan toward a smaller, functioning railway and followed the yardman's shouted commands until her hull was wedged firmly on the underwater trolley. A winch engine chugged lazily, a cable lifted from the water and hauled her up. Culling propped a ladder against the hull.

Hardin climbed down, stepped under the sharp bow, and began tapping the fiberglass with the wooden handle of an awl. He tapped sharply every few inches, methodically testing the entire surface, his ear cocked for the telltale soft or hollow sound that would reveal delamination of the glass layers or a faulty repair.

He spent two hours working the awl over the hull. Twice, when he got a sound he did not like, he turned the tool around and jabbed the point into the fiberglass. The first time he discovered a tiny delamination, which had probably been there since she was built. While it showed no sign of getting worse, Culling nevertheless circled it with chalk.

The second seemed more serious. The awl sunk sickeningly deep into a soft spot in the middle of a two-inch dent. It looked as if the boat had hit something small and hard while moving fast. Hardin tapped all around the area, assessing the damage. When he was positive it wasn't structural, he let Culling circle it.

After he was done with the outside of the hull, Hardin said, "Please fix those spots and paint the bottom."

"You haven't sailed her yet."

"I'll pay whether I buy her or not. Would it be all right if I stay after dark?"

"I'll run power into her."

"Thank you." Hardin eyed the yardman thoughtfully. "Mr. Culling? You know who I am, what happened to my boat?"

Culling nodded, his bright eyes curious. "Yes. I heard. Sorry about your missus."

"I'm building some electronic equipment to stop this sort of thing from happening again. A big-ship warning device."

"How you going to do that?"

"I've got a couple of ideas. A long-range, low-power radar, for one. And a passive sonar listening device. Something to give early warning. The thing is, I'll be testing the gear on my cruise. I wonder if I could install it here before I leave. I'll need some work space."

"That depends on how much," said Culling. "Summer's coming. . . ." He hunched his thin shoulders apologetically.

"I just need a corner out of the way. Could I put up a bench in one of those old barns?"

"That's all? Of course." He seemed relieved that he could do the favor.

"I'd like to keep the project quiet until I've sailed," said Hardin. "I want to perfect it before I talk about it."

Culling smiled with crooked teeth. "There are no secrets in the village. But they don't travel far."

Hardin climbed into the boat and started tapping all over again from the inside. Then he tested the electrical system, the diesel engine, pumps, fresh- and saltwater plumbing, winches, and the rudder, making a list of parts that should be repaired and replaced.

It was late at night when he was done. Culling, who had provided a meal and an endless supply of hot tea, pointed his flashlight at the Swan's stern. Her gold-leafed name was peeling.

"Shall I fix that while she's up?"

"Change it," said Hardin. "No port. Just the name. Black paint."

"What name?"

"Carolyn."

6

The shattered hull of an abandoned MTB filled an enormous boat shed far from the main entrance of Culling's yard. Her bow, riddled by machine-gun fire, cleaved fiercely toward the harbor as if she were straining for a grave denied her. Her stern was lost in darkness.

Hardin built a workbench in the shadows of the dead fighting boat—three thick boards on four round legs sawn from an old boom—hung fluorescents to supplement the daylight that streamed in the shed's open front, and laid out his tools on nearby beams.

The first thing he made was a long, narrow plywood box, a mold with tapered sides and rounded inside corners, which he coated with paraffin and lined with four layers of fiberglass cloth bound together by epoxy resin. He repeated the procedure on a separate flat piece of plywood to which he had screwed two chrome angle irons.

The laminated fiberglass had to cure. He used the time to shop for electronic equipment in Plymouth and Bristol. Then he extracted the fiberglass box he had formed in the wooden mold and, using a fine blade, sawed out its narrow back, epoxied the flat piece with the angle irons to the top of the box, and refastened the cutout with hinges and a rubber seal.

He had created a long, slender nacelle, two feet wide

and six feet long. It had rounded corners and a stream-lined front, connectors on top, and a small watertight door in back.

He carried it to the edge of the harbor, filled it with rocks, and submerged it to see if it leaked. Culling wandered over to see what he was doing. He helped Hardin pull the nacelle out of the water, rolled a cigarette on licorice paper, and watched without comment as the doctor opened the door and pulled out the rocks. Finally, after he tipped it up and the last of the rocks tumbled out as dry as they had gone in, Culling lighted up and asked, "Coffin?"

Hardin ignored him. He admired the old yardman's skills, but he deliberately maintained a distance because Culling always seemed to be watching.

"Can you haul my boat?" he asked.

"Now?"

"Now." He had waited until after four o'clock when Culling's men went home. They were alone.

"Aye. The way's clear."

"I'll need her up for a couple of hours."

"Aye."

"I can put her back in myself."

"I'll stay about."

Hardin rowed out to the Swan and ran it up to the rails. When the boat was out of the water, he drilled four holes into her keelson and fastened the nacelle to the bottom of the hull, between the fin keel and the propeller shaft, with long chrome screws. Culling watched with interest.

"Begging your pardon, Doctor, but what the deuce are you doing?"

Hardin finished tightening the quick-release wing-nuts, stepped out from under the boat, and straightened up. It was time to give Culling something.

"It's a sonar nacelle."

"Sonar? That's big enough to smuggle a corpse."

Hardin laughed. "It's got to be big. It's really a big ear. It will be lined with foil inside. What do you think?"

"Don't know."

"I'm not inventing anything new," Hardin continued. "I'm just trying to make it cheap and simple enough so an offshore sailor will use it."

"What about your radar?"

"That's next. Same principle. It's got to be cheap and simple, and since it's on a sailboat, it can't use too much power."

"Is that what all that gear is in the shed?"

"Some's radar," said Hardin. "Some's sonar."

A black box was a black box and the lying came easily. As a doctor and an engineer he was accustomed to working in an exclusive world, privy to secrets of biology and physics that were as mysterious to most people as the Latin language had been to a medieval serf.

Culling eyed the nacelle which hung behind the keel like the cabin of a blimp. He tested the chrome angle irons. "Don't know much about radar and sonar," he commented. "But I tell you one thing. A box this size'll have enough buoyancy to tear it right off your boat if you don't ballast it."

Hardin opened the watertight door. "I'll let her fill for the test. I'll give it a lead bottom if it works. Do you think it'll drag?"

Culling looked at it from several angles. "Hard to say, Doctor. She's such a finely shaped hull, you can't tell what a little change'll do to her." He squatted down and measured the bulk of it with his hands, handling the nacelle the way a good cook would heft a fresh chicken. "I'd like it a bit smaller."

Hardin squatted beside him and eyed it dubiously. "Dammit, I think you might be right."

Culling scuttled out from under the boat like a slow crab and carefully straightened his gnarled frame. Kneading the muscles of his lower back with bony fists, he said, "You'll find out soon enough when you take her to sea."

It was the first time he had been in deep water in the month since the rundown, and the sight of a giant oil tanker as he sailed through the slit in the cliffs into the English Channel scared the hell out of him. It stood as sharp in the sun as a toy on a gameboard, empty, riding high, its hull dark red and black, its superstructure gleaming white, gigantic, dwarfing the ships around it, yet barely a quarter the size of LEVIATHAN.

The Swan nudged him away from his fear. She sliced authoritatively through the Channel's sharp chop, a stiff sailer with little inclination to heel sharply or roll. He had started the engine, just in case she needed help clearing the narrow inlet, but she'd sailed well to windward, and he'd gotten her out on a single starboard tack.

Now, running before the southwest wind under mainsail and genoa, he steered her east along the English coast and nervously eyed the procession in the outbound shipping channel. He had never seen so many big ships at once.

Tankers and bulk carriers—grain and ore ships—predominated, riding tall and black in the sparkling, sunlighted water. Freighters were smaller, the old ones sprouting vast deck cranes, the more modern stacked high with rectangular containers.

The ships became so monotonous in their black and gray anonymity that a fruit carrier with ebullient green stripes on its flared bow was a startling sight. White, it was a beautiful ship with fast-looking lines and the Star of David proud on the funnel. Hardin was reminded of a trip he and Carolyn had taken to Israel.

The day waned. Hardin scanned the coast, checked the distinguishing features against his chart, and readied a pair of anchors. The ships filed into the setting sun in neat and orderly procession, the color of the clouds, decks burning red, then flaring out to ash. The Channel waters turned a rich blue-gray, not the slate of the North Atlantic, but lusher, as if they drew color from the fertile soil of England and France.

It was almost dark when he entered Portland Harbor. He found anchorage near the mouth, lowered his sails, and sank exhausted into his bunk.

He awakened at dawn, his hands and muscles stiff from handling the sails, his palms sore. Ravenous, he ate apples, cheese, and cereal, brewed coffee, and ghosted out of the harbor on a light morning breeze. By nine the wind had freshened. He pushed the Swan and made Chichester, late that night. Her performance under a variety of conditions—sailing to windward, on a reach, and before the wind—seemed largely unaffected by the nacelle riding behind her keel.

The next morning he awakened late and was preparing to raise sail when the Chichester Harbor Patrol bore down on his anchored boat in a fast motor launch. A customs officer asked permission to come aboard. Hardin presented the Swan's registration and his passport. A second man waited in the launch with a dog.

"In from Fowey?" asked the officer politely.

"I stopped at Portland."

"And you're heading?"

"Rotterdam. I'm cruising the Rhine."

"We won't be long. You can come with us or go about your business."

Hardin said, "I'll do what I'm doing."

The officer called the dog. It was a half-breed shepherd. The launch pilot slipped its lead and it bounded under the life lines and into the cabin.

Hardin faced the light breeze and decided upon a genoa jib. He went down the forward hatch, got the sail, and squeezed past the officer, who was going through one of the lockers. The dog whined with excitement. Hardin scratched his ears.

"What do you do?"

"Chester's a sniffer," said the man.

"Dope?"

"Explosives."

Hardin nodded his understanding. He had expected this. The IRA still posed a constant terrorist threat. These so-called customs men were probably Special Branch.

"Do you search every boat that comes in here?"

"We spot-check. And we recognize strangers."

He made Hastings that night and started early the next day on a run across the Channel which brought him to Calais in eighteen hours, exhausted by the nerve-wracking job of keeping out of the big ships' way as he crossed the east- and westbound traffic lanes. It was blowing hard the next morning, and the North Sea was fierce as soon as he cleared the harbor. He beat all day against a heavy chop and only got as far as Ostend on the West Flanders coast.

The next day was worse, a full gale from the east, but Hardin tacked out of the harbor past small-craft warnings and beat east along the unfamiliar shore. He hadn't the time to wait. A mist settled in and he overshot the entrance to the inland water route across Holland to Rotterdam. Fearing the breakers that muttered ominously to starboard, he forged on, and that afternoon, as the fog rose, reached the Hook of Holland.

He dropped his sails and powered into the Nieuwe Waterweg past Europoort—an enormous complex of silver storage tanks and VLCC berths that sprawled over a low, flat, smog-wreathed plain, bounded by blue-gray forests of slender smokestacks that fed a yellow sky. Ten miles from the sea he turned into the Nieuwe Maas, and followed the diked channel that twisted through the basins of Rotterdam Harbor.

Each basin was ringed by deepwater berths, railroads, and warehouses. The sky, bluer here than above the chemical fumes of Europoort, was seen through silvery thickets of piping, forests of cranes, and clouds of black cables.

The harbor was a fountain of movement, a switching station where goods were delivered, stacked, stored, and sorted. Gigantic yellow railroad gantries plucked containers off gray, green, and black freighters from Europe, Asia, and the Americas. Floating pneumatic grain elevators surrounded bulk carriers and drank their dry cargo. Pontoon cranes transferred bales and pallets from anchored ocean vessels to coastal steamers, and bluff-bowed river barges off-loaded sacks and boxes from the Continent.

Hardin's sailboat, an angry white sliver frosted dull by

67

the North Sea's salt spray, sliced between the ships and painted boats like a shark that shunned the beauties of a coral reef for the scent of distant prey. He stood in the cockpit, the harbor chart at his knees, heedless of the color, indifferent to all but obstacles.

A tug cut across his bows and nosed against a freighter. He threw his engine into reverse and waited while a docking pilot in an immaculate uniform climbed a ladder to the freighter. Before the tug backwatered out of his way, he spotted a torn cargo net floating beside him. It looked useful. He hauled it aboard with a boat hook and spread the knotted manila over the coach roof to dry.

He motored past Rotterdam, into the Noord and then the Merwede River, then the Waal. The broad, diked rivers offered long, clear views down upon an orderly green land as flat as the sea. As the sun set behind a distant evenly spaced single row of feathery trees, he turned off the river into a small canal, moored alongside the earthen bank, ate some cheese and fruit, and fell asleep to the land sounds of cars and trucks on a nearby road.

He woke to the incongruous combination of the boat rocking and the earthy smells of a rural June morning. A glance out the fore hatch showed the cause of the motion. A barge had passed, its bluff bow raising a gentle wake. He washed, drank coffee, cooked eggs, and consulted his charts.

The diesel muttered awake and moved the Swan smoothly from the bank, back into the Waal, toward the River Rhine and the German border. Hardin lounged at the wheel, steering the straight easy course, enjoying the beauty of the flat land and the warmth of the sun.

She would have loved this. They had stopped in Amsterdam on a quick trip years ago, but hadn't had the time to see the Dutch countryside. He thought of her sitting next to him. His throat tightened with an awful feeling. What had she looked like?

What in the name of God had she looked like? He dashed into the cabin and started to search his wallet for her picture before he remembered that everything he had was new, bought after LEVIATHAN had killed her.

At nightfall he tied up outside Wesel and the next day drove a rented BMW to Frankfurt. He bought an old Army field jacket, checked into the Schlosshotel Kronberg—a secluded castle-hotel in a northwestern suburb—and slept.

He awakened in the evening, drove twenty miles southeast to Aschaffenburg, parked his car on the outskirts of the garrison town, and walked to the raucous section of bars and nightclubs that serviced the nearby encampment of the United States Seventh Army's Second Regiment.

German hookers eyed him speculatively from dark, narrow alleys lighted by blinking neon. He bought drinks for people in bars where lonely soldiers sipped three-dollar beer while they waited for something to change, and he learned that the Second was a three-in-one-out. One week a month, the infantrymen arrived in Aschaffenburg with three weeks' pay in their pockets and three weeks' field maneuvers to forget. That explained, said a bespectacled ordnance corporal, the enormous MP presence. The corporal asked if Hardin wanted to buy some hash.

The MPs stopped him on the crowded sidewalk. He had tried to steer clear of the patrols, but they were on him suddenly, each man a head taller than he, their short billies looped menacingly to their wrists. A sergeant with a brusque military drawl demanded his papers.

He'd made a mistake choosing a field jacket that fit as snugly as if it had been tailored for him. He'd meant to blend in with the soldiers to put them at ease. Instead he looked neither soldier nor tourist, but something in between that interested the MPs.

He hesitated, and that made them curious. Two who had been scanning the street over his head now watched him instead, the glimmerings of excitement lighting their eyes. What had they found?

He had no choice. Quickly, he handed over his passport wallet. If the sergeant wrote his name in his notebook, he would leave Aschaffenburg immediately. The sergeant grunted his surprise.

"What are *you* doing here, Doc?" he asked with the automatic respect Americans give physicians.

"Traveling around Germany."

"This ain't Germany. This is a piss hole."

"I got homesick," Hardin smiled. "I wanted to hear States talk."

The sergeant grinned. "Yeah, I know what you mean." He handed back the wallet. "Watch your ass. It's a tough town."

"Any place you recommend against?"

The sergeant snorted. "Off-limits joints. And a few others. You can tell looking at 'em. And stay out of the Florida Bar if you don't want something social that itches where it hurts." He tossed a mock salute and herded his men back into the street.

Hardin continued walking, searching, dodging the MPs. He saw nothing that surprised him, nothing he hadn't seen years before on shore leave in the Philippines or Japan. Here the teenagers peddling drugs and eyeing the streets with bitter envy were fair and blond, like their sisters in the bars, but excepting the color of the camp followers, Aschaffenburg was like every town outside every American military base in the world, and if the girls' arms were plumper than in the Orient, the needle tracks looked the same.

Around midnight he found the Florida Bar—aptly described by a group of soldiers who passed it as "a real creepo joint"—on a dimly lighted street beside a burned-out building with boarded windows and old off-limits signs. It stank of spilled beer, hamburger grease, and cigarettes. Liquor prices festooned its filthy mirrors. In addition to a long bar, it had small round tables and a swing door in the back with a diamond window that showed a lurid red light in another room.

Most of the Florida's customers were drinking beer and shots. They looked like lifers, twenty-year men, their faces hollow with the empty shadows of trouble and ignorance, their eyes dull with drink and stupidity, their brains roiled with murky fears of what would happen when their hitches were up.

Hardin knew them well. As a navy doctor he had bandaged their contusions, stitched their stab wounds, and picked broken glass out of their bodies every night his ship gave shore leave. And even before then he had known them from his intern nights in the emergency rooms of New York hospitals.

He took a spot at the bar near the door and ordered beer. The enormous bartender smacked a bottle onto the dirty Formica and demanded nine marks. Hardin paid with a hundred-mark note. Offered no glass, he drank from the bottle, his change stacked conspicuously beside him.

He drew attention immediately. The younger customers began shuffling past, muttering offers to sell drugs. Hardin ignored them. Some of the more persistent laid their wares on the bar. Hardin was surprised by the amount of heroin offered. The bartender approached, glowering menacingly, and they hurried away. Hardin ordered another beer.

A weasely-looking corporal, a forty-year-old lifer with gray skin and trembling hands, sidled up to him. Manufacturing a labored smile of rotted, broken teeth, he mumbled, "Hey, Buddy."

Hardin nodded.

The soldier eased tentatively onto the next stool. His faded sleeve bore darker marks where lost chevrons had once adorned his uniform. "How you doing?"

"Great," said Hardin. "How you doing?"

"Name's Ronnie." He pawed some crumpled bills and loose change from his pocket and counted it hazily on the bar. "Buy you a beer?"

Hardin pushed his own money at the bartender. "On me, Ronnie."

The corporal took it hungrily, downing half before he stopped, apparently remembering his original intention. "What are you doing in Germany?" he asked.

"Business."

Ronnie nodded and drank some more. Hardin watched him closely, waiting, fascinated by the man's pretense to nonchalance while his face worked like a small wary animal sniffing the wind. Suddenly, he blurted, "I got a forty-five automatic."

"Got or can get?" Hardin asked quietly.

Ronnie's eyes lighted. "I got it stashed right outside. Fifty bucks."

"Anything bigger?"

"Sure." He wet his lips. "I can get a M sixteen. Seventy-five bucks."

Hardin shook his head. Wrong man.

"Sixty."

"No, thanks, Ronnie. Not interested."

"Come on. Forty," he pleaded. "I'll get it in the morning."

"Haul ass."

The corporal slunk back to his table. Hardin ordered another beer, satisfied that he had the right bar.

A fat, pretty woman in her thirties looked him over and asked in English thickly accented with German if he wanted some fun.

"Later." He pushed more marks at the bartender. "A drink for the lady."

She smiled her surprise and asked for schnapps.

"What's your name?"

"Katrin."

Hardin nodded at the door with the red diamond. "Got a friend back there, Katrin?"

She hesitated only a second. If the free-spending American civilian preferred *zwei*, he would be served. *"Ja."*

"Ask her if she would like a drink."

Katrin returned with a wide-eyed Hilda, who also drank schnapps. Sitting between the two women, nodding occasionally at their attempts to make conversation, Hardin watched and waited.

Men passed in and out of the back room. Once, when three boisterous master sergeants greeted them by name, the women left Hardin with apologies and led the three into the back room. The group emerged in ten minutes. The sergeants plowed out the front door and the women rejoined Hardin at the bar, where each accepted another schnapps and worked unselfconsciously at repairing her lipstick.

After an hour, during which Hardin was offered more drugs, and a hand grenade by a drunken file clerk, the place started to empty out and he concluded it was a wasted night. He was reaching for the rest of his money when a big, rawboned Spec. 3 with a hawk nose that sat like a meat hook on his bloated face lurched up to the bar and demanded beer in a thick southern drawl.

He wrapped an immense hand around the bottle and grabbed the rump of the nearest woman. She squealed; the soldier gave Hardin a challenging smirk and watched for his reaction through slitted eyes. Though he was only in his late twenties, alcohol had already pasted his features into a puffy ball and his head was balding as if his hair was fleeing the debauch.

Hardin put his money back on the bar. He had seen the man's quartermaster's insignia. Supply. Pointing at the bartender for another beer, he tipped the stack of bills along the Formica. The soldier eyed the money with puzzlement, then, as if murkily realizing that his challenge had been met with another of a different sort, he slapped a rubberbanded roll of deutsche marks on the bar and ordered another beer, his arm still around the German woman, his fingers digging.

He chugged the second beer, dropped the bottle on the floor, and asked, "How much?"

Hilda's eyes flickered toward the roll on the bar. "Eighty marks."

"In a pig's eye. Fifty."

73

"Seventy."

"How 'bout you?" he asked Katrin, but Hilda seized his arm and steered him toward the back room, saying she would take fifty.

He was back in ten minutes, alone.

Katrin cast a nervous eye at the diamond window and moved closer to Hardin.

"Beer!" yelled the southerner. "Mock shnell! Fuckin' makes me thirsty."

The bartender brought the beer. He too glanced at the diamond window. The private reached in his pocket. His jaw dropped.

"Friggin' kraut cunt stole mah roll!"

He reached clumsily for Katrin, who was already backing away. She screamed. Moving faster, bellowing rage, he slapped her, drawing blood from her mouth, brushed past Hardin, and lurched toward the back room. A pair of waiters tried to intercept him, but he grabbed a beer bottle from a table, broke it on the back of a chair, and slashed the air with its jagged edges.

A blackjack appeared magically in one of the waiters' hands. He waited coolly for his chance, then stepped inside an awkward swing and smashed the private's face.

The soldier staggered, dropped the bottle, and clutched his nose. The second waiter drove a flurry of hard punches to his stomach and groin until he sagged to the floor. They kicked him a few times, and when he was no longer twitching hefted his limp body between them and lugged him out the door.

Hardin followed, a full bottle of beer in his hand. The waiters dropped the soldier in front of the burned-out club and returned to their own bar.

Hardin cast a wary eye for the MPs. The street was empty, the racket of the earlier evening stilled, the teenagers gone. He knelt beside the unconscious soldier. There was a military identification card in his pocket. Roscoe Hendersen. Specialist Third. Supply Corps. Second Regiment, Seventh Army. He heard measured footsteps. An MP patrol. He stood quickly and pressed into the

74

shadows, hoping they wouldn't turn down this narrow street, because if they found Hendersen, they would take him away. They passed on the main street.

Hardin waited until he couldn't hear them anymore, then poured his beer onto the soldier's face. He revived, moaning. His head lolled on the cobblestones. He blocked the flow of beer with his hands, sputtering, and when Hardin stopped pouring, his meaty fingers moved gingerly to his nose. Hardin knelt beside him.

"Don't touch it."

"Shit. Hurts like a sumbitch." He pawed at his swelling cheeks. Suddenly he struggled to stand. Hardin helped him until he had him on his feet, swaying against the building.

"Who the fuck are you?" he asked, pulling away. "Oh, yeah, you was in there. Big fuckin' help you were."

"Not my fight."

"Yeah. Shit." He shrugged Hardin off and lurched toward the Florida.

"Where you going?" asked Hardin.

"Gotta get mah money."

"She's gone."

"I'll get it outa the rest of them bastards."

"They'll kill you."

"I need it."

"Hold it," said Hardin. "Just stop. Right there. How much did she get?"

"Three hundred bucks. And some kraut change." His rough, slurred voice took on a worried note. He said, quietly, "I owe these guys some money. They want it tomorrow."

Hardin shook his head in amazement. It looked like the "new army" was drawing on some of the same basic material that had fueled the old. Where did they come from? The Supply Corps was the road to riches for anyone with half a brain and the larcenous instincts of a four-year-old in a candy shop. How did this fool get in debt to loan sharks?

"How long you been in, soldier?"

"Six years," Hendersen mumbled.

Hardin nodded; somebody had to move boxes.

Hendersen tried to brush past him. Hardin hooked a foot behind his ankle and shoved the bigger man's chest with his open palm. Hendersen sat down hard and bellowed his anger. Hardin stood just outside his reach.

"You're too shit-faced and busted up to go back in."

"I need mah money," Hendersen said doggedly. He licked at the blood trickling down his upper lip.

"How much do you owe them?" asked Hardin.

"I told you. Three hundred bucks. These guys don't fuck around. They'll kill me if I don't pay 'em."

That was the last thing the loan sharks would do. Instead, they would make Hendersen their man in Supply. Until the sergeants found out. Then *they* would kill him.

Hendersen started to stand again.

"Stay there," said Hardin. "I want to talk to you."

Hendersen dropped back. He cupped his hands around his nose and watched Hardin over his fingers. "What about?"

"Maybe I can replace some of that money."

Slowly, Hendersen lowered his hands. "Yeah? How?"

"I'm looking for some ordnance. It's worth a couple of hundred bucks."

"What kind of ordnance?"

"Something I can carry. What can you get?"

"Maybe a mortar."

"No."

Hendersen stared. "How big you want? You think I can just carry any old thing off the base?"

"I know you can."

"What do you want?"

"A Dragon."

"You're kidding."

"Four hundred dollars for an M forty-seven Dragon."

"Four hundred bucks? Jesus Christ!"

For a second, Hardin thought he hadn't offered enough, but Hendersen's next question assured him he had.

"What the hell do you want a Dragon for?"

"Four hundred bucks. Delivered outside the base tomorrow."

Hendersen struggled to his feet, pulling his way up the side of the building. He looked down at Hardin with a crafty expression. His swollen face was yellow in the glow of the single streetlamp. "You really need it, don't you?"

"Right."

"*Five* hundred dollars."

"Good-bye, Roscoe." Hardin turned away and walked briskly toward the main street. The private lumbered after him.

"Okay, okay. Wait. Just wanted to . . . you know."

Hardin stopped. "Can you get it?"

"Sure I can get it. We been pulling a whole shipload of the fuckers in from the field. Gotta ship 'em to NATO depot for dismantlin'."

Hardin had read that the Dragon was being phased out. He said, "I want it operable."

"It'll work."

"I'll warn you right now, Roscoe. I'm going to tear it down and make sure before I pay you."

"It'll work. Guaranteed."

"I'll give you fifty bucks for the service manual."

Hendersen grinned. "You got it."

"Where do we meet?"

The private suggested several places which Hardin rejected. Finally, he described a remote spot that sounded safe. Then he said, "You gonna give me a down payment?"

"No."

"What if you don't show up?"

"Sell it to the Red Army."

"Shit. I don't know anybody in the—"

"I'll show up, Roscoe. You better go get your nose fixed."

Hardin went back to the Florida Bar, had a beer with Ronnie, and bought his forty-five.

It was quiet, but for the calls of birds. Hardin lay in the rafters of a tumbled-down barn and watched an army Jeep trail dust up the narrow dirt road, the driver readily identifiable by the white bandage that wrapped his face between his mouth and eyes.

Hardin lowered himself to the earth floor, slipped out the back of the barn, and watched the front door through a jagged crack in the stone wall. The Jeep skidded to a stop.

"You in there?" called Hendersen.

Hardin waited.

The big private appeared in the doorway. When he saw the BMW parked inside, he dropped to one knee and fumbled a gun from his pants. Hardin edged around the side of the barn until he could see the Jeep. A long canvas bag lay in the back. He lobbed a rock at the Jeep. It clattered off the hood. Hendersen flung himself to the ground and leveled his gun at the noise.

"Drop it," said Hardin.

Hendersen stiffened. Slowly, he looked over his shoulder, gazed into the cavernous barrel of the army-issue forty-five automatic that Hardin was holding in a two-hand grip, and dropped his gun.

"Back away from it."

Hendersen slithered aside. Hardin left his cover at the corner of the barn, picked up Hendersen's weapon, and tossed it into the high grass

"Wha'd you bring a gun for?" asked Hendersen.

"For yours. Get up. Open the bag."

"You going to pay me?"

"If you brought what I wanted."

Hendersen watched the forty-five as he opened the duffel bag, pulled out some pillows, and slipped the bag from a wooden crate about four feet long and a foot square.

"Open it," said Hardin. "On the hood."

Hendersen grunted with effort as he lifted the crate out of the Jeep and walked it to the hood. He pried off the lid with a long screwdriver. Hardin stepped closer. The Dragon lay in excelsior and reeked of oil.

"Go sit under that tree."

"You ripping me off?" Hendersen asked miserably.

"No." He waved the gun. "The tree."

He waited until the private had sat down with his back to the bark. Then he slipped his gun in his belt. Roscoe reached inside his jacket and pulled out something shiny. Hardin froze, kicking himself for not frisking the soldier for another gun.

"Okay if I have a snort?" asked Roscoe, raising a flask.

Hardin exhaled. "Yeah. Enjoy yourself."

He took out his screwdrivers and pliers and, consulting the NATO service manual, opened the Dragon. Then he probed its secrets with the electronic test equipment he had purchased in Wesel. When he was sure that the electrical guidance system was functional, he put the weapon back together. Then he banged the lid shut on the crate, worked the canvas bag around it, and loaded it into the trunk of the BMW. It was brutally heavy. He backed the car out of the barn, left the engine running, and walked over to the tree, gun in hand. Hendersen watched anxiously, wetting his lips, his eyes shifting from Hardin's to the automatic.

Hardin tossed the money at his feet. The private looked surprised.

Hardin drove straight to the pier at Wesel, loaded the heavy bag onto the Swan, returned the rented car, and by nightfall was motoring smoothly down the Rhine. He stopped at dawn in a quiet cove at the side of the river, tossed the forty-five overboard, stowed the Dragon, and slept for several hours. Then he continued down the river, bypassed Rotterdam on the inland canal route to the North Sea, spent the night in a Dutch fishing village, and the next morning raised his sails and pointed west.

He made Calais that night, entering the French harbor in the dark, slept, and left at dawn. Driving hard, he sliced a long diagonal across the Dover Strait and reached Eastbourne by nightfall. Southwesterlies prevented him from getting farther than Chichester the next day. He beat

79

out of Chichester in the morning against a stiff west wind and spent a tough afternoon rounding the Isle of Wight.

He was pleased with the Swan. She would do what he wanted and kept on making tough situations easier, sailing very close to the wind and negotiating the rough chop around the island so smoothly that she could have been on rails. She might do even better without the nacelle disrupting her passage.

As he neared St. Catherine's light, a squat, white cylinder in a forest of radio masts on the southernmost point of the Isle of Wight, a fast, steel-hull motor yacht flanked by a pair of lean cutters thundered into view from the direction of the Solent and passed close behind. Their triple wake raced after the Swan. She lifted her stern, rolled angrily once, and continued on the wind, which bore, briefly, the reek of diesel fuel.

7

Miles Donner contemplated the drift of sunlight that the rippling waters of Le Havre reflected on the ceiling of *Orion*'s lavish salon. Though deep in discussion with the twelve men and women aboard the motor yacht, he automatically weighed the technical aspects of photographing the ephemeral effect.

Donner looked soft. He had sensitive features, full lips, warm eyes, bushy brows, and the easy demeanor of a pleasant, middle-aged English gentleman who did awfully well at something professional—a physician on the Surrey cocktail circuit, or a writer of ladies' fiction sold in America, or, as he was in fact, a commercial photographer, a master of natural light who specialized in travel promotion. It earned him a good living and it was a perfect cover. With his British passport, he could hop a plane anytime to take pictures anywhere.

The meeting was conducted in Hebrew. It was a chance to exchange information and be with your own, away from cover. The yacht was registered to a Swedish steel company. Whenever it served the Mossad, it was accompanied by a pair of armed launches capable of matching her thirty knots.

LaFaur, head of the large French station, had the floor. He was high-strung and vain, and often acted as if he were in charge of European operations, which he was not. That power rested at home. He was describing a Paris field agent's recent nervous breakdown. The man had suddenly disappeared.

"I immediately instructed my office to follow the usual search procedures. We quickly learned that neither the Palestinians nor the Russians had done him harm. The same was true of our 'friends.' And yet he had vanished. We went so far as to canvas the jails and hospitals in case he had met with a genuine accident.

"Nothing." He looked around the table. Donner returned his gaze. La Faur looked away. "Do you know where we found him?" he asked pompously.

Grandig of the German station cast Donner the faintest trace of a smile and raised his hand.

"You found him at Orly Airport."

LaFaur's face fell. "How did you know that?" he snapped. "That information was not released for general consumption."

Grandig smiled easily. He had the bluff, round appearance of a Munich tavern owner, a brilliant methodical mind, a low calm voice, and a quiet sense of humor.

"Where," he asked, "does a Mossad agent go when he is in trouble?"

"But—"

"It was a guess, LaFaur," he said soothingly. "Something similar happened to us last month in Bonn." He took the floor, the humor gone from his voice.

"We've suffered some terribly demoralizing fiascos re-

81

cently. They increase the pressure on our field people. Our man actually lived in the airport for four days before we found him."

"It only took us two days to find ours," said LaFaur.

"Perhaps we should strike a medal," said Grandig.

LaFaur looked indignantly at Donner. Donner smiled and shrugged.

Grandig continued. "Our man put his clothing in a locker and shaved and bathed in the men's room. He wanted to be close to the aircraft, because a Mossad agent's only friend is the pilot of an El Al airplane."

The others nodded. Several stared at the polished table. All had worked the field and all knew the isolation. Donner sympathized with them. Unlike his younger Sabra colleagues, who were raised in Israel and had to be taught the lore of their assigned countries, he was a British subject and England was his natural home. He had been born and raised there, but for a few boyhood years in Palestine. He had read history at Cambridge and had lived in London for the last thirty years.

He had been a Zionist when Partition had come in '48, and he had tried to return to Israel for the defense, but his superiors had persuaded him he could do more good in England. At their orders, he had drifted away from his Zionist friends, slowly, the way a man loses interest in a movement, and gradually created the details of an English life. It began to resemble his own life as the years passed, a confusion that kept him in limbo as a man with one home and another homeland, and a man who sometimes felt himself getting old waiting for the end of an endless war.

"Reputation is our strongest weapon," Grandig continued. "And the fiascos have blunted it. Killing that waiter in Norway . . . agents arrested . . . our Brussels station head's desk exploding in his face. We're too small to say 'Wait till next time' the way the big powers can. For us, each time is our only time."

"Enough," smiled Donner. "Tell them the good news."

"What good news?" LaFaur asked suspiciously.

"As you know," Donner said, "the NATO forces are continuing to phase out the Dragon M forty-seven anti-tank rocket."

"That is not good news," said the woman who ran the Rome station. "In six months those rockets will be landing on our security patrols."

"Wait until Grandig tells you what happened."

"Miles helped," said Grandig.

The woman from Rome was very beautiful and notoriously short tempered. She wore charcoal-dust eyeliner, the *kajal* preferred by Arab women, and the vivid border around her dark eyes set them off like flames. "If this is a contest of coyness," she snapped, "I'll decree Grandig the winner. Would you please get on with it? We have a lot to do today."

"This is a good operation," said Grandig. "Good cooperation between my unit, and the Dutch unit, and our people in North Africa. We discovered a Palestinian plot to smuggle the weapons. They are buying them from an American master sergeant and paying the 'Sohn' of Kohler und Sohn, Landwirtschaftliches Mechanismusaufnehmen, to hide them in his father's tractor shipments.

"The tractors are placed in sealed crates and stored in bonded warehouses in Rotterdam, where they are not required to be inspected by Dutch customs since it's trans-shipment. Two days ago, they shipped them out on a Russian freighter to Tunis, where the weaponry will be sorted out of the farm machinery and sent east through Arab territory."

"How will we stop them?" asked LaFaur.

Grandig grinned at Donner. "Miles arranged for a small crate from an English company to be placed aboard the ship at the last moment. I imagine it contained something fulminous."

There were smiles around the table.

"Wonderful," said the new Brussels man.

"Until next time," said Grandig. "There are too many of those weapons around. Right now the Americans have a curious mystery on their hands concerning the Dragon. Or, more precisely, one Dragon."

"One weapon," said LaFaur, "is a German problem." He lighted a cigarette from the butt he was smoking, and it passed through Donner's mind that LaFaur might be in trouble himself. He had gotten rather jumpy since the last Station Head party.

"Any weapon is an Israeli problem until proven otherwise," Donner said firmly.

"Go ahead," said the woman from Rome.

"A Dragon was stolen, clumsily, from the Seventh Regiment encampment at Aschaffenburg. The Americans were fairly casual about it. They might have disciplined the soldier responsible and left it at that, but the German police, as you can imagine, were not. Not with the latest inheritors of the Baadar-Meinhof gang flailing about."

"Our interest," interrupted LaFaur, "is less obvious."

Grandig ignored him. "They maintain informers in NATO ordnance sections, as do we, for just such occasions, and when they found out about the theft, they demanded that the American Army assist in a full investigation to unearth the recipient of the weapon.

"It was rather like artillery where one elevates the barrel to shoot high in the air. The police sent their requests to the top of the Bundeswehr. The results cascaded explosively upon the American base commander.

"Several soldiers were charged with dereliction of duty and it was suggested to the prime miscreant that he cooperate. He told a preposterous story, which no one believed. As the man was an alcoholic, the Germans employed the single expedient of denying him drink. His story remained the same.

"He claims that he sold the weapon—for four hundred dollars, mind you—to an American civilian."

"You mean an *Arab*-American civilian," said LaFaur.

"No. The soldier was positive and his description tends to uphold his story. The man was American. Not German. Not *Arab*-American. Just plain American, if there is such a thing."

"A criminal," said Donner.

"That's what I thought," said Grandig. "But, as the uproar waxed, the American investigators questioned the Military Police who patrol the recreational area where the man made contact. One MP patrol recalled having stopped an American civilian and checking his papers. Only the patrol sergeant actually saw the American passport. Unfortunately, he neglected to record the information."

"He remembered nothing?" asked LaFaur.

"He's unconscious," said Grandig. "A stool was broken over his head in a barroom brawl. We are trying to determine if the incidents were related, but all we know so far is that the only person who saw our man's name is lying unconscious in the base hospital."

"Will he recover?"

"Probably. Policemen are issued hard heads. In the meantime, we have one interesting piece of information that suggests the man might not be a criminal. The other military police said that their sergeant addressed the man as 'Doctor.' Or 'Doc.' "

"A physician?" asked the woman from Rome.

"The Americans think so. They tend to reserve the title for medical practitioners."

Donner's eye returned to the ripples on the ceiling. The Dragon M 47 antitank missile system was a TOW—tube launched, optically tracked, and wire guided. And a TOW was a potent weapon. In battle, one man could stop a tank. At an airport, he could destroy a jet liner at a half-mile range.

The American might be an ordinary criminal. Or he might be a free lance representing IRA provisionals, or the German Red Army, or Italian Red Brigade, or Palestinians. Donner would make the investigation his first order of business when he got back to London.

Sunlight glanced off the harbor master's binoculars as Hardin sailed beneath his cliff-top observatory and entered Fowey harbor. Weaving among the anchored yachts and fishing boats, he steered for Culling's yard, dropped his

85

sails—first the jib, then the main—and drifted to his mooring. By the time he had snared the slimy rope and fastened the double bight, a harbor-patrol boat—an outboard launch—was buzzing alongside. The officer greeted him by name.

"Good trip, Dr. Hardin?"

"Fine, thank you."

"Where did you go?"

Hardin led him below to his chart table and showed him his course plots.

"What did you do in Rotterdam?"

"I sailed right on through to the Rhine."

"Unfortunately our EEC dispensations don't apply to our American guests. Did you make any purchases? Alcohol, tobacco, diamonds?"

Hardin grinned at the man. "I don't drink much when I sail, I never smoke, and I don't have a girl friend."

The customs officer smiled back. "Do you mind if I have a look around?"

"Not at all."

He began poking through the Swan and Hardin went back on deck. Culling waved from the dock, a hundred yards away. He was still there, ten minutes later, when the customs man ferried Hardin in, and as the launch skimmed away, he asked, "How did it work?"

"You were right," said Hardin. "It's too big. I felt a tug on the rudder." He stepped around him and walked to the shed where he had his shop.

Culling called after him, "Dr. Akanke is looking for you."

Hardin kept walking. The trip to Germany had taken longer than he had estimated and he still had to assemble the radar components, build a reflector, run the waveguide, install the new generator, and provision the boat. He had been sailing since dawn, but he sat at his workbench on an upturned box and plugged in his soldering gun. After the days of distance scanning, seeking buoys and landmarks, it took a while for his eyes to adjust to the close work. It had been an exhausting trip.

He spent several hours soldering new connections for the radar transmitter, the cathode-ray tube display, and the remote controls. Then, after running a battery of electrical tests, he set aside the delicate electronic components, and shaped and bolted several lengths of aluminum tubing into a rectangular frame.

Next, he took up hammer and crosscut saw and built a rough wooden trough four feet long and a foot wide and bellied a foot deep in the center. Viewed from the side, it had the shape of a uniformly rounded banana. He pressed half-inch chicken wire into the hollow and bent it to the curve of the trough. Then he lifted out the chicken wire, gingerly placed the airy crescent on the workbench, curved face down, and braced it from behind with the aluminum frame.

He soldered a metal T in the middle, and when he was done he leaned on the workbench, too exhausted to move, staring at the antenna. After a while he looked at his watch. The hands blurred before his eyes. Three in the morning. He'd been at it ten hours straight. He was reaching for the light switch when he heard footsteps approaching the open end of the boat shed. It was a dark night and only the Channel lights shone in the harbor. A shadow moved across the reds and greens.

"Still at it," said Culling.

"Just finished."

Culling moved into the garish light of the fluorescents.

"I was just leaving," said Hardin, wondering what he was doing at the yard at this hour. "I've got to borrow a dinghy and get some sleep."

"What's this?" asked Culling.

"Radar antenna."

"Made out of chicken wire?"

"It works."

Culling nodded. "I like that. You've a way of making things simple."

"Things that work *are* simple." He reached for the light switch. "I have to get to sleep."

"What's in the box?"

"What box?" asked Hardin, his voice loud in the quiet barn.

"The nacelle thing under your boat."

"Water. I told you, I left it open for ballasting."

Culling shook his head. "You went for something and you got it."

"What are you talking about?"

Culling walked slowly around the circle of light, pausing to nod and gaze at Hardin's tools and equipment. He fingered the dipole antenna in the middle of the crescent-shaped reflector. Hardin watched, his mind in turmoil.

Suddenly, Culling looked him straight in the face.

"You're not an Irish gunrunner. You're not a drug smuggler. What contraband could you have gone for?"

Hardin broke the long silence. "Don't you think," he asked quietly, "that if I had gone for contraband it would be dangerous to ask?"

Culling chuckled his quiet, knowing laugh. "I do not think you're the type of man who would harm me."

"Can we leave it at that?" asked Hardin.

"I keep asking myself, what is he up to?" said Culling. He nodded at the workbench. "What is he doing in my yard?"

"I'm building a long-range radar."

"And sonar?"

"Yes. And I'm leaving very soon."

Culling stared at him a long time. Then he walked around the bench to the bow of the old MTB. He caressed the curve that loomed above their heads.

"A brave lady," he said, speaking half to himself, half to Hardin. "She took a direct hit off Cherbourg in the autumn of forty. Almost blew her out of the water. Smashed her starboard engine. But she brought her boys home, what was left of them. When we pulled her in here, we found her back was broken. She couldn't have gone another mile."

As he described the wooden boats dueling the German coastal squadrons, the old man's memories built images in

Hardin's mind. He saw at dusk the small gray MTBs slipping out the slit in the cliffs and heard their engines thunder south. And he saw the boatyard at dawn, when Culling's men lined the quay, waiting for the damage, and behind them the ambulances, and then the group commanders, counting the survivors in the misty morning light.

Culling stroked the blistered wood. "We stripped her parts, then they moved the MTB base up the coast and that was the war for this yard . . . Here, I'll show you something."

He walked Hardin into the darkness beside the boat and ducked under the hull amidships. Hardin crouched beside him.

"Got your little torch?" asked Culling.

Hardin flicked on his penlight.

"Over there," said Culling. "That's it."

The beam settled on a wide steel scoop that protruded from the bottom of the boat.

"Water intakes for cooling the engines," Culling explained. "There's another one there and two more on the starboard side."

"What about them?"

"Every night they had a kill, there were some boats they always had to tow home because these intakes were blocked and there was no water to cool the Rolls-Royces. Do you know why?"

"No."

"We had exile crews on the MTBs. Free French. Poles. Dutch. Some hated the Germans more than I could imagine. And when some of those young boys sank a German E boat, they put the helm over and ran back through the survivors. Back and forth through the swimming men. Their flesh blocked the intakes and the engines overheated and stalled. I know. We had to clear them."

"Why are you telling me this?"

"They wasted the chances we gave them," said Culling. "It was more important to sink German boats than kill

German sailors. They disabled their own boats when they should have continued the attack."

Hardin stood slowly and rubbed his bad knee. "I'm not sure what to say to you."

"You're safe in this harbor," said Culling. "Stay as long as you need."

"An out-of-pattern operator."

"An apparent free lance."

"Out of nowhere."

Miles Donner's informal inquiries at MI 6, at the Deuxième Bureau, and at the CIA produced nothing about the theft of the Dragon that the Mossad hadn't already learned. The MP was still unconscious and the Germans were checking on every American doctor who'd entered their country in the past six months.

Donner didn't put much stock in the doctor theory, and even if the apparent free lance was one, he wouldn't have entered through Immigration. But the thought of an unknown roaming Europe with an antitank weapon made him very nervous, particularly since the other agencies' informants had turned up no hints of big IRA Provisional or Red Army operations in the offing. That made Israel a very likely target.

He cashed in a number of one-time favors and repeated his unofficial questions at higher levels. The answers were the same. Nothing new had broken. One thing. It wasn't new, but a tough, elderly MI 6 agent—a man who had done the impossible and infiltrated the Jewish Irgun terrorists before Partition—raised a question that had been bothering Donner.

"Why didn't he kill the soldier who sold him the weapon?"

Donner walked the streets of London trying to picture the man. He wanted him to be something simple, like a bank robber or a highwayman looking to stop an armored bullion truck, but that was wishful thinking. A criminal, even a clumsy amateur, would have murdered matter-of-factly to cover his tracks. An idealist? He shook his head. That sort would kill faster than a professional.

Not that he himself wasn't an idealist, he thought quickly, but you didn't kill a man who might be useful again. And if a man posed a threat, you shouldn't be dealing with him in the first place. He shook his head again. Guessing why the man hadn't killed was getting him nowhere. He needed facts.

He availed himself of sources at Fleet Street, but the newspaper reporters could add nothing. Stymied, he entered their morgues and systematically pored through the recent past, looking for upcoming public events that might provoke a terrorist attack. He began to feel the unusual sensation of panic.

8

"I say, Mr. Culling? Is that Dr. Hardin up there? Or is it a clever monkey?"

Ajaratu Akanke sounded angry.

Hardin looked down from his perch in a bosun's chair atop the Swan's mast. The boat lay fifty feet beneath him in the shape of a woman's eye. Ajaratu stood beside Culling on the quay, blocking the hot June sun with her hand. Her lab coat hung open, and with her head thrown back her wheat-colored cotton blouse stretched tightly over her soft-looking breasts and the lean muscles of her flat belly. A blue turban covered her hair and a stethoscope dangled from her pocket.

"It must be a monkey," she said. "Dr. Hardin would have told his physician that he was back from his sail days ago."

"I'm really sorry," Hardin called.

Culling rallied to his defense. "He's a busy one, miss. All day on the boat and half the night in the shed."

"How are you, Peter?"

"Fine."

"What are you *doing* up there?"

"Running waveguide."

"Really? What sort of waves do you intend to guide?"

"Radar."

"*In*side the mast?"

"It's hollow."

"Curious."

She bent her head and listened to Culling. Hardin continued lowering the flexible square tube into the mast. His tools were in a canvas sack slung over his neck.

"How are we doing down there?" he called.

Culling hopped onto the boat and disappeared below. Moments later Hardin felt him tug the lower end of the waveguide. He fed more into the mast and Culling pulled it out of the hole he had cut in the aluminum near the Swan's ceiling and ran it back to the chart table where Hardin was installing the radar.

Culling appeared in the cockpit. "That's enough."

Hardin fastened his end to the reflector mounting that he had already bolted to the mast.

"Peter?"

"What?" He shone his penlight into the mast. He would fasten the waveguide at the bottom, but it looked as if it might flap loosely in the middle. It had to be secured halfway down, but the mast was less than a foot in diameter and there was no way he could reach halfway down it with a tool.

"Can you hear me, Peter?"

"Yes, what is it?" He wiped perspiration from his eyes.

"I said, how's your head?"

"Busy."

"I'd like to examine you."

If he drilled a pair of small holes halfway down the mast he might be able to hook a loop of wire around the guide and draw it tight. Have to be careful not to puncture the guide, though. He should have drilled the holes first.

92

He was rushing, getting ahead of himself, making small mistakes.

"I said that I'd like to examine you."

Hardin's lips compressed with frustration. He should have thought about fastening the guide before he ran it down the mast. He was falling behind. The radar wasn't finished and he still had to install the new generator to augment the boat's alternator, then provision the boat— storm sails—he'd meant to take the main to the sailmaker this morning to sew a third line of reef slabs—clothes, charts . . . The list seemed endless.

"Peter?"

"I'm very busy."

"I gather that," called Ajaratu. "Perhaps I could conduct my examination over dinner."

"Tonight?" His mind whirled. He had to get started on the generator. "I have to work kind of late. . . ."

Her voice turned professional. "Then I'll expect you in my infirmary at nine tomorrow morning, Dr. Hardin."

She spun on her heel and stalked back to the white Rover. Her light wraparound skirt flowered open as she thrust angrily into the driver's seat. The car shook when she slammed the door. Hardin tried to untangle himself from the bosun's chair, his mind unexpectedly lingering over a fleeting glimpse of her long, slim thighs flickering like black fire.

"Culling! Stop her!"

Culling scampered after the Rover which was backing and filling, turning toward the drive, bracketed between spurts of flung gravel. Hardin cupped his hands over the top of the mast, pulled himself up, and kicked his feet free of the canvas seat. Then, taking his T-shirt which hung from his back shorts pocket, he wrapped the cloth tightly around the aft stay, clamped his hands around the cloth, and slid down the dizzy angle from the top of the mast to the stern.

He landed lightly, favoring the bad knee, jumped to the quay, and ran past Culling after the Rover. Ajaratu watched him come. Her full brown eyes were as clear and deep and cool as forest springs.

"You *are* a monkey."

"I apologize," Hardin panted. "I get too far into my own head sometimes. I would like very much to have dinner with you."

"If you're not too busy."

"Eight o'clock?"

"I'll pick you up here," she said. "We'll eat at a casual place. You can bring your tools."

The car shot around the old boat and disappeared in a cloud of dust.

Culling chuckled. "Quite a lady, the Duchess."

"The Duchess?"

"Aye. We named her that when she got here. It's in the back, you know."

"What's in the back?" asked Hardin. Culling, he had learned since they had been working together the last few days, held a complex opinion on everything that caught his notice.

"Aristocracy. Their backs don't been like ordinary folk. She's got that back."

Hardin considered Ajaratu's erect bearing. "So she does."

"Paint her white and she could be the Duchess of Cornwall."

Hardin looked at him sharply, but there was no malice in his tiny blue eyes.

That afternoon, while he was drilling the holes in the mast to secure the waveguide, Hardin punctured the tubing. He had to rip it all out, shop thirty miles away for more, and then hoist himself back up the mast to install the new. He was in a foul temper when Ajaratu picked him up for dinner.

She was sitting in the backseat of the Rover. A grinning hospital orderly ushered Hardin in beside her and chauffeured them past Fowey toward the cliffs. Ajaratu explained that as this might be her last dinner out in England, she intended to enjoy it without worry about passing a Breathalyser test. At her request, Hardin opened the champagne which lay between them in a bedpan full of ice.

At the cliff tops, they took the bottle and walked from the car and watched silently as the sun dropped into the sea. Hardin felt the strains of preparation slowly slide from his body. A gentle melancholy took their place. Champagne and the shanghaied—but amply compensated —driver were Carolyn things to do. He refilled their glasses.

They ate dinner at a restaurant in Fowey. It was a tourist place with pine-paneled walls and a panoramic view of the harbor and the dim cottage lights of Polruan on the opposite shore. As it was early June and a week night, the room was nearly empty. When they had eaten, the proprietress bought them brandy and told Ajaratu how sorry the village was that she was leaving.

"All packed?" asked Hardin when they were alone again.

"I shipped the last crates to Lagos this morning. All I've left are my suitcases."

"Excited?"

"No, I'm a bit confused."

"About what?"

She sipped her brandy, swirled it luxuriously in her mouth, eyed its color in the light of the candle. "All sorts of things. This and that . . ."

"Like what?"

She met his eyes. Then she looked away and her voice lightened artificially. "Funny things. Wondering what it will be like not to be special-looking anymore. For most of my time in England I've been the one black flower in a field of lilies. I'm noticed. It won't be quite like that at home."

Hardin grinned. "You'll be noticed. You're a very beautiful lady."

"Thank you." Her cheeks darkened.

She was wearing a pale-blue dress that bared her arms

and the fine lines of her neck. He tried to think of a term to describe the color of her silky skin. He hadn't thought of it before, but it was neither black, nor brown, nor any shade he could describe with a single word. A blend, he decided, a deep rich hue somewhere between dark coffee beans and shimmering crème de cacao.

"Who's this lucky politician?"

"Did I tell you about him?"

"Mentioned it."

"Actually, he's the *son* of an important politician. I'm not sure he'll amount to much. He's well intentioned, but's it's hard to be a man with such a man for a father."

"Oh, yes."

"Spoken like the son of such a man?" asked Ajaratu.

"In ways."

"You never tell me about him."

Hardin smiled; the brandy was giving him a beautiful buzz.

"I've been chasing after him since I was twelve. That's how old he was when he ran away to sea. He was born in eighteen eighty-seven and you could still do that in those days."

"He was much older than you."

"Oh, yes. Almost fifty when I was born. He fought his way up to second mate on a square-rigger in the South Pacific when he was sixteen. And I mean fought, because in those days any rank under chief officer had to be defended with your fists. The chief knew how to navigate, so hitting him was a serious offense. Anyway, my father got his master's ticket. *Then* he went back to New York and became a doctor. All on his own with no help from anybody."

Hardin looked out the window. A brightly lighted coastal freighter was slipping into the harbor, curiously out of place against the dark hills and the few remaining lights in Polruan. The freighter passed from sight, heading up to the clay docks, and Hardin found Ajaratu's face reflected in the glass, watching him.

"And he had a comfortable life by the time you came along," she said softly.

"That's right."

"A quiet life."

"Yes." She was pumping him. He felt threatened, and added brusquely, "A number of living-room therapists have told me that's why I joined the navy and why I sail, and why I quit practicing medicine. They've concluded that I can't take my own life seriously when I compare it to his. They're full of crap."

"I didn't say a word."

"I joined the navy because I like the sea. Which is one of the reasons I sail. I quit practicing for various reasons, among them the simple fact that electronics fascinated me. Why else would I go back to school when I was thirty-six years old? Carolyn had gone back then, too, studying gynecology, so it meant we had some lean student years."

A smile lighted his face. "And as far as taking life seriously is concerned, when we first met, Carolyn said I was the most serious thirty-three-year-old since Alexander the Great. . . . She got me to lighten up."

He sipped his brandy reflectively. After a while, he looked back at Ajaratu. "You know something? The trouble with having an older father is that most of his life has happened already. When you get back to Lagos you'll see your father doing what he does, general-ing . . . being important. I missed that with my father. All I ever knew were stories about things that happened before I was born. They seemed very important and unsurpassable."

"What if none of them were true?"

"Oh they were true, all right. He was too comfortable with himself—and with me—to be a man who had to make up a life. . . . I just wish I had seen him in the midst of triumph. He'd already won. I wasn't born in time to see him swagger down a gangway with a new promotion, or step out of a storm in streaming oilskins. I think I'm getting a little drunk and romantic."

"I saw mine step in dripping blood. Before the civil

war. A mob attacked my mother because she was Ibo. He killed two men with a ceremonial sword, but now he sits at a big desk like any other busy executive." She bit a knuckle. "Strange, I never told anyone about that. My mother and I left Nigeria soon after."

"Will you marry when you get home?" Hardin asked.

Her eyes flashed and her English grew imperiously precise. "I'm not all that sure I'll be married at all."

"The Lovely Lagos Spinster? I don't believe it."

She laughed. "Perhaps I'll knot my hair in a bun and devote my life to lepers in the jungle."

"Where *will* you practice?"

She made a face. "My father has arranged a position in a clinic. I told him I wanted to work with the poor, but if I know him, there'll be a policeman outside my office screening my patients. It wouldn't do to have his daughter mingle with the wrong types." She drained her glass and laughed.

Hardin signaled the waiter for refills. He said, "Rich people get sick, too."

Ajaratu leaned forward, her face suddenly intense. "I want to do something I can hold in my life."

"What?"

Her hair, drawn back and skewered by an elaborate ivory pin, reflected the glow of some nearby candles.

"Something special. Something important I can look back on. I don't know. I'll probably wind up going back to university. I'd like to study—you'll laugh—I think I want to study psychiatry."

Hardin laughed. "No kidding. I knew I was a guinea pig."

The waiter brought the brandy.

"Would you take a degree at Ibadan?"

She looked surprised. "Now how would *you* know about Ibadan?"

"It's the top research hospital in Africa. I wondered why you didn't study there instead of London."

"The civil war. My father sent us to England as soon as

98

the fighting began. I was in my teens then, and by the time it was over I was already in university."

"Where's your mother?"

"She died. The climate here. I was raised by a retired British colonel who had been my father's CO before independence. He had sons and no daughter. They sent me to a convent school."

"No wonder you're confused about going back to Nigeria."

"I've been back since for vacations."

"What's it like?"

"A frontier. Just like your wild west was once. Very optimistic. People are busy making money and building, and they are full of enthusiasm. I'm really excited about going home."

"No longer confused," said Hardin. "I'm glad we settled that."

"Did we?"

"Something the matter?"

She shook her head. "Tell me about your sail. Where are you going?"

"Monrovia first. Near you. A thousand miles or so."

"Then?"

"Brazil." The lie came easily. He'd used it often this week.

"You are testing a radar, Mr. Culling said."

"Right. Kind of business and pleasure together."

"But hasn't radar been invented already? I don't understand what you intend to do."

"I'm working on a simple warning device which will sit on top of the mast out of the way of the sails and give more than twenty- or thirty-mile range of ordinary small-boat radar."

"The jib is the forward sail?"

"Yes. If I can make it work, I'll try to rig it so it can be stowed below and run up the mast with a halyard—excuse me." He produced a pen and sketched a design on a paper napkin. He'd become so involved with the lie that he had

99

just come up with a nice idea for rigging the thing. Pocketing the napkin, he returned to the conversation with another apology.

"When do you leave?" Ajaratu asked.

"As soon as I can. I don't want to get caught in the hurricane season."

"How long will it take to sail to Monrovia?"

"Three weeks or so. She's a very fast boat."

"Alone."

"I'm alone." The pain was always close. He felt it disturb the pleasure of the brandy like ripples in wind-riled water. What, he asked himself again, could he have done better?

"Does it get boring?"

"No."

"What happens when you sleep?"

"The boat sails. A steering gear, directed by the wind, controls the rudder. It'll hold an approximate course."

"But what if you're near land or in shipping lanes?"

Hardin's eyes narrowed fractionally. He said, "Then you don't sleep. In fact, as far as sleep is concerned, you could do me a favor. I need some stay-awake drugs and some antibiotics. I can't prescribe in England. Could you . . ."

"Certainly. Though you still ought to be careful with drugs until you've fully recovered from your concussion."

"I'm fine." He sipped the brandy. "See, I can even drink again."

"I've never sailed on a yacht," said Ajaratu.

"I'll be shaking her down with the radar antenna day after tomorrow," said Hardin. "Come with me."

"Wouldn't I be in the way?"

"You'd be a help if you let me put you to work." He smiled. "Come along."

Donner found it almost by accident in the London *Times*. He checked the dates in other newspapers. The *Mirror* had blown a short interview up to a shrill half page. He telephoned Grandig in Germany from a pay phone. Grandig called him back in fifteen minutes from another pay phone.

"I've been thinking about the Dragon," said Donner.

"Nothing new has occurred," said Grandig. His English had none of the charm of his Hebrew.

"I have a suggestion," said Donner. "Check all the local hotels and restaurants and car rental agencies for a man with a lot of money."

"Thank you," said Grandig, "but we're doing that already."

"I have a name."

"What?"

"Don't share it with your friends."

"Why not?"

"It might be for us."

Donner went home and typed a triple-spaced report to a man named Zwi Weintraub who was getting old and had trouble reading. When he had read history at Cambridge, Donner had been fascinated by General George Washington, who had had a fine sense of the relationship between power and information.

A superb horseman, young Washington had used his skill and extraordinary stamina to ride regularly between the frontier and Williamsburg to report to a few powerful men on the state of the war with the French. The fresh information had furthered their positions in the Virginia House of Burgesses and had put them in Washington's debt. Years later he had had their support for his own ambitions.

Washington's habit had served Miles Donner well in his own career. Since Partition he had always apprised Weintraub of his plans, often consulting him before he spoke with his direct superiors. Weintraub had risen in the ranks of government and gave Donner greater access to power and information than would ordinarily fall to a Mossad agent.

101

He drove to Heathrow Airport, where he handed the sealed report to an El Al copilot who would deliver it personally.

The sun had settled behind the hills when the Swan nosed to its mooring off Culling's yard in Fowey harbor. Ajaratu caught the pickup buoy and hauled the dripping pendant onto the bow deck. She ran the thick line through the chock Hardin indicated, and forced the eye over the foredeck mooring cleat. Then she turned to Hardin for approval, but he was already lowering the jib, so she helped him stuff the sail into its bag.

Her face burned from the sun. Her hair was caked with salt. Her hands were raw and every muscle ached from handling the lines and cranking winches. Loath to let the day go, she said, "I had a wonderful time. Could I take you to dinner as a thank-you?"

"I'm sorry," said Hardin. "I'm too tired and I've got to get up early."

"Next time . . ." Her voice trailed off. His radar had worked perfectly. He was ready to leave. She made herself smile. "I guess there won't be a next time."

He tossed the jib down the fore hatch. Then he stood up straight and met her eye. Her heart leaped. His face was so full of pain, yet it still held a memory of laughter. But even though he never laughed, and rarely smiled, she knew he had enjoyed her being with him.

"What is it?" he asked.

She took a deep breath. She had planned to ask at dinner or in the morning, but now, on the boat, with an evening sea breeze cooling her face and the first stars lighting the black east, she knew was the time.

"May I come with you?"

It was wrong. The moment she said it she knew it was wrong. He didn't understand.

"Where?" he asked.

"To Monrovia. I'd fly home from there. I could help you. I'll pay for my food and I'll stand watches and help get ready and I'll stay out of your way and only talk when

102

you want to talk. I could sleep in the back cabin. And I'd cook." Her voice trailed off. How could she have been so foolish to fall in love with a white American from New York just when she was going home to Nigeria? And *was* she falling in love?—that was the most disconcerting question.

He eyed her calculatingly.

She was strong and athletic and she had picked up the mechanics of the boat more quickly than most. Taking her with him could be an opportunity to arrive at his destination in better shape than if he sailed there alone. The single-handed trip to Rotterdam had been exhausting. Sharing watches meant better sleep, greater efficiency handling the sails, and therefore more speed, as well as a safer passage through the shipping lanes.

On the other hand, he'd lose several days dropping her at Monrovia. But if time was a problem, he could take her to Dakar, seven hundred miles closer, and at either port he could replenish food and water—and fuel, if he'd had to use it, something he might not be able to do later on.

What if she found out?

But she wouldn't. Because the next leg of his plan was nothing more than a cruise to West Africa, just as he told all who asked. Could he teach her enough so he could sleep while she was at the helm? It boiled down to that. He would take her if she could serve him. And he would find that out very soon.

He said, "There are five thousand moving parts in your car, and less than fifty on this sailboat. The difference is you don't have to be on intimate terms with each of its parts to drive a car."

Donner flew to Amsterdam; Grandig came by train. They met at Pechcadou, a quiet restaurant at the foot of the Brouwers Kanaal. The menu was French. The decor was thirties Art Deco, and the view from the tall dining-room windows was a long perspective up the floodlit eighteenth-century canal.

Between the black and mirrored bar and the dining room were glass tanks where the patrons were invited to choose their fish. Donner and Grandig sat first at the small private bar. Trading greetings, they looked like a pair of European diamond merchants or art dealers celebrating a lucrative agreement with an expensive evening out in a foreign city.

"Why Amsterdam?" asked Grandig.

"Private."

"From whom?"

"Everyone but you and me," said Donner. "Did you keep it quiet?" Next to Weintraub, he trusted no one more than Grandig.

"So far," said Grandig. "Hardin stayed two nights at the Schlosshotel in Kronberg. It's near enough Aschaffenburg, where the weapon was stolen. He drove a car he had rented in Wesel. How he got to Wesel is a mystery, thus far. We've found no record of his entering the country, unless it was a long time ago."

"A boat," said Donner. "He probably went up the Rhine."

"Of course. Easily done. . . . Who is he?"

"I can't tell you. It's between me and Weintraub."

"Unofficial?"

"Yes."

Grandig spun the remains of his drink around the bottom of his glass. "It is not good for us to have too many wheels spinning inside of wheels."

Donner smiled. "Consider it initiative."

"Do you know that they're investigating you?"

Donner concealed the shock with a smile. The jolt set his heart pounding. "Thank you for telling me."

"I trust you," said Grandig.

"Why are they investigating me?"

"You've been accused of not staying under discipline and of independence in the extreme. I don't know the issue, but I'm sure you can recall something."

Donner nodded.

Grandig said, "Probably something similar to this Hardin incident."

"I've been playing this game for thirty years, Grandig. I'm better at it than most of the new ones."

"That doesn't mean they'll like you for it."

Grandig picked up a menu and read for several minutes. Then he asked, "What do I do about the Dragon investigation?"

"I'd like you to do nothing, if you can without endangering yourself. We know that Hardin doesn't pose a threat to our interests. Let the Germans run in circles. They'll get bored."

"They might not."

"Why?"

"The American MP is recovering."

"Does he know the name?"

"He doesn't even know his own at the moment."

"Can you do anything to keep matters that way?"

"It's a little late for that," said Grandig. "Now that he's conscious, it wouldn't look natural."

They ordered dinner at the bar. Then the waiter led them toward the dining room, stopping at the fish tanks to let Donner choose his trout. Donner inspected the dozen fish swimming in the clear water.

"That one."

The waiter dipped his net. The fish scattered to the corners of the tank, but he had already trapped the fat trout Donner had chosen.

"Well done."

The young man lifted the net from the water. The trout struggled frantically, slapping the water with its tail, standing almost perpendicular in the clinging mesh.

"Hold him," chuckled Grandig.

With powerful thrusts of its glistening body, the fish thrashed out of the net and fell back into the water. The waiter scooped after it instantly.

"No," said Grandig. "Let him go. Take another. He deserves his life a little longer."

105

"Which, sir?" asked the young man, withdrawing his net.

"He's mine," said Donner with a gentle smile.

"The same fish, sir?"

Donner watched the trout circle the tank with agitated flicks of its tail. "The same," he answered. "Get him."

Culling's relief on hearing that Hardin was taking the African doctor was short-lived. He had sent many yachts to sea, and as they loaded the Swan he saw that Hardin was still provisioning for a long voyage rather than a cruise along the northwest coast of Africa. The three cabins were filled to capacity.

The fore cabin held the sails, sixteen hundred feet of nylon and Dacron line in half-inch to inch thicknesses, and two spare forty-pound high-tensile plow anchors. The anchors were stowed at the aft ends of the sail bins, one on each side to distribute their weight evenly. A third anchor, a 22 S Danforth "lunch hook," occupied a cockpit-seat locker beside the storm jib and sheets.

The head, and the hanging lockers that separated the fore and main cabins, were crammed with clothing, foul-weather gear, blankets, linens, towels, saltwater soaps, and medical supplies. Clearly, Hardin was a man who planned for comfort aboard, which was all right with Culling. He had noticed that the casual ones often took ill or just wore down until they couldn't cope.

The main cabin had a drop-leaf table and berths above and out-board of the settees on either side. Hardin's sleeping bag occupied one of those berths, neatly rolled and ready to be used on whichever was the leeward side. The storage spaces were filled with cans, bottles, and glasses, but the cabin itself was not cluttered—another aspect that Culling admired. You had to be comfortable in such a small, confined space. He wondered where Hardin had cached the contents of the fiberglass nacelle he'd removed from the hull.

Tonging a third fifty-pound ice block out of the cockpit, the old man struggled down the companionway into the after portion of the main cabin, which was separated from the forward portion by cutaway partial bulkheads. The galley was starboard of the companionway, the nav station to the port side of the steps. Whether Hardin was navigating or cooking, he would have quick access to the cockpit,

Culling put the ice in the cooler. The glassy blocks would charge it for three days on the relatively cool mid-June Atlantic. There was fresh food for the first week out—eggs, milk, cheese, bread in plastic, vegetables, cooked meat, oranges, lemons, apples, and juices—and dry and canned provisions for the time to follow—brown rice, dried potatoes, pasta, cereal, soups, canned meats and vegetables, condensed milk, jams, honey, raw sugar, peanut butter, cocoa, coffee, and tea.

Culling snooped through the lockers and drawers, hunting empty spaces. One drawer was almost entirely filled with brown bottles of vitamins. He slipped in a stone crock of Stilton cheese and shut it before anyone noticed. Then he buried a bottle of Cockburn's in the rice sack. By the time they turned to rice, they'd be glad of a good port.

Culling stepped around the companionway and had a final look through the nav station. A powerful shortwave radio, a local-channel VHF radio-telephone, and a loran navigator—the new longer-range C type—occupied the bulkhead above the chart table. In the drawers and slots beneath the table were charts and the supplementary *Africa Pilots and Defense Mapping Agency's Sailing Directions,* a sextant, a chronometer, and the Nautical Almanac. A spare sextant, a second chronometer, binoculars, flare guns, signal lights, and flags were stowed in a locker aft of the nav station. Spread on the teak chart table were the English Channel charts Hardin would use tonight.

The stern cabin contained tools, bottom paint, fiberglassing supplies, lengths of oak and teak, an extra propane gas bottle for the galley stove, two five-gallon plastic freshwater cans to augment the fifty gallons in the boat's two tanks, and spare diesel fuel, as well as extra food—

enough canned goods for Hardin to stay a long time at sea after he dropped Dr. Akanke at Monrovia.

She was putting her things in the stern cabin. It was private from the main cabin where Hardin was bunking, and Culling was sure that unless the port took hold one night, the arrangement would stay that way. From what he could see, she was little more to him than a willing deckhand.

Hardin was often reminded during the last hectic preparations of doing the very same things—stripping purchases of their excess cardboard and plastic packaging, stowing and restowing to distribute weight evenly, cataloging their locations—just two months ago when he and Carolyn had loaded the old *Siren* and pointed the ketch toward Europe.

As dusk gathered, and the hills of Fowey and Polruan lighted gently, he eyed the way the wind snapped the square black telltales that fluttered from the shrouds. He used to use strips of Carolyn's stockings, but he had discovered by accident on the way back from Rotterdam that black showed up better against the night sky.

The wind would be stiff on the Channel.

"Number three jib," he said to Ajaratu.

She ducked into the cabin and appeared in a moment on the foredeck with the sail. Hardin hanked it on slowly, repeating the process aloud so she would learn. He felt very calm. His preparations were complete, and in an odd way her presence seemed to postpone the pressure he knew would come after he had left her and the battle had begun.

Suddenly, when the jib was attached, they were ready.

Nothing was left on the quay. The decks were clear. The job was finished. As if in encouragement, the tide ended its slack and pulled *Carolyn* from the dock, tightening the mooring lines, tugging toward the mouth of the harbor. It was almost dark.

Ajaratu stepped onto the quay and embraced Culling. He patted her shoulder, but when Hardin took his hand to thank him, he seemed embarrassed. Facing the hills from which the breeze was blowing, he said, "You've got the wind and tide, Doctor. Not much more a man can ask."

Hardin hoisted the mainsail, letting Ajaratu winch it the last few feet.

"I'll sail her off," he said.

He loosened the bowline, wrapped it once around the cleat, and handed the tail to Ajaratu. Culling manned the stern line. Hardin took the helm.

"Cast off, Ajaratu."

She tossed the line to the quay.

Hardin sheeted the main. It bellied, pulling the boat from the dock.

He nodded to Culling.

The old man loosed the stern line and the Swan was free.

9

"You missed him," said Culling, warily eyeing the three men who had crowded into his little office at the front of his main shed.

"When did he sail?" asked the older one in the middle.

Culling scratched his head. "Oh, some time in the afternoon, I recollect."

"What time?"

"Four o'clock or thereabout. Are you gentlemen friends of his?"

"He sailed against the tide?" asked the man in the middle.

Several hours after they left Fowey, the Swan's bow began to rise and fall.

"What's that?" asked Ajaratu. On their first sail they had gone east.

"The Atlantic," said Hardin.

"Already?"

It was very dark and he sensed more than saw her next to him. He said, "It's telling us it's out there."

"Am I going to be seasick?"

"I hope not."

"That's not encouraging."

"You ought to get some sleep."

She fell silent.

He heard the mutter of a boat engine in the dark. It seemed to come from behind and he craned his neck to make sure that the shielded stern light was on. It was. A cloud covered the star he was steering by. For several minutes he used the direction of the waves and the wind as his guide, waiting for the star to reappear. When it didn't, he flicked on the dim red binnacle light and checked his compass heading.

Neither his red and green bow lights, nor his white stern light, were visible from the cockpit. They were shielded to show only twenty points off the bows and twelve from the stern. The sound astern grew closer and louder, then changed pitch; the boat had spotted his stern light and was veering to pass him at a safe distance.

His star returned. Just starboard of the mast, exactly where it should have been. He began looking for a replacement. Steering by a star was much easier than trying to follow a compass needle, but you had to trade it for a new one every fifteen or twenty minutes; otherwise, as it moved across the sky, you'd follow it to places you didn't want to go. He explained what he was doing to Ajaratu, and let her find a new star.

The wind was stiffening, still north from the land, blowing away the sound of the overtaking boat. But despite the Channel chop which ran across the fledgling Atlantic rollers, the Swan was riding comfortably. They were sailing between the outbound shipping lane and the coast, hugging the channel to avoid the charted rocks. The lights of giant ships studded the blackness to port. The coast was mostly dark.

110

A silent explosion of white fire obliterated the black sky and water.

"What is it?" cried Ajaratu.

A powerful engine thundered alongside. Icy spray drenched the cockpit.

Hardin shut his eyes and tried to shake the blindness from his head.

"Douse that light!" he bellowed.

A crisp English voice echoed through a loud-hailer.

"Yacht *Carolyn*. Yacht *Carolyn*. Heave to for boarding."

"Shut it off!" yelled Hardin. "I can't see a goddamned thing."

The light turned away, illuminating the sea in front of the Swan. Hardin squinted at the silhouette of a fast cutter in the reflected-back glare. The loud-hailer cracked again.

"Coast Guard! Heave to!"

Now, as the cutter closed, Hardin could see several uniformed sailors preparing to secure to the Swan. One of them carried a light machine gun.

"What the hell do you want?" Hardin yelled angrily, his eyes still aching from the light.

"Coast Guard weapons search," cracked the loud-hailer.

Hardin could see that it was held by an officer in a dark pea jacket. Weapons search? Could he talk them out of it? For a wild moment he wondered if he could come about and knock them off the cutter with the flying boom, but then what? The Swan could sail forever without fuel, but it could never outrun a power boat. He'd have to talk them out of it. Certainly, stocked the way she was, the Swan looked innocent enough.

"Okay," he said to Ajaratu. "I'll head upwind. Get ready to pull in the jib. . . . Now!"

He winched in the main. The Swan straightened up and began to pitch. The cutter loomed alongside, three feet higher out of the water, but expertly steered. The boats touched gently and the sailors scrambled aboard, cleated a pair of lines fore and aft while the officer and the sailor

111

with the gun watched. As soon as the boats were made secure, the launch engine quickened slightly and they ran in tandem with just enough speed to point their bows to the waves.

The officer handed his loud-hailer to one of his men and scrambled into the Swan's cockpit. He was middle-aged, with a full, sensitive face.

"There are safer ways to stop a boat than blinding its crew with a spotlight," snapped Hardin.

"Awfully sorry," replied the officer, his eyes flickering toward Ajaratu. "Weapons search."

"You're out of your territory," said Hardin.

"Actually, we're still in the limit. We don't ordinarily bother yachtsmen, but we've a report of an IRA cell smuggling French explosives into southern Ireland. Won't take a minute. If you would just take me below, sir, and show me your papers, we'll get it over straightaway."

"Your hull is pounding mine," said Hardin.

The officer signaled and a muscular young man whose arms bulged through his dark sweater slipped aboard.

"Bosun Rice will man your helm while we go below. Are you all right up here, Miss?" he asked courteously.

"Yes," said Ajaratu. "Do you want my passport?"

"We'll get it below with the gentleman's, thank you. Cast off, Rice."

The sailors jumped back onto the cutter with their lines. Rice took the shiny wheel with an appreciative grin and headed the Swan away from the wind, allowing the backed headsail to fill. Rice glanced at the binnacle.

"Two forty?" he asked Hardin.

"Good enough," said Hardin. That Rice was a competent seamen was apparent in his stance. Hardin led the officer down into the main cabin and opened one of the drawers under the chart table for their passports and the Swan's registry.

The officer reached up and slid the hatch shut. He nodded at the settee.

"Sit over there, Dr. Hardin."

112

Hardin straightened up with surprise. "How do you know—"

The man produced a small black gun and repeated, "Sit!"

"What? Who the hell are you?"

"Where is the Dragon?"

"What?"

"Sit down, Dr. Hardin."

Hardin sank to the settee, his mind whirling. The officer nodded toward the hatch.

"I don't believe that lovely woman up there is absolutely important to your plan. I will throw her overboard if you don't cooperate immediately. I'll drown her the way your wife was drowned."

Hardin rose trembling from the settee. The gun receded into the protection of the man's waist.

"What do you want?" Hardin whispered.

"Where is the Dragon?"

"I don't know what you're talking about."

"The soldier who sold it to you was arrested. Where is it?"

Hardin sat heavily. "You're standing on it. It's under the sole."

"Show me." He stepped back to the chart table and watched carefully while Hardin disassembled the drop-leaf table and pulled up the floorboards. Hardin showed him the wooden box. "Inside," he said. "Sealed. Watertight."

"Does it work?"

"Yes, it works."

"Can you use it?"

"It's a simple weapon."

"And your target is enormous."

"Who are you?"

"Does the woman know?"

"No."

"Why did you take her?"

"To conserve my strength."

"Good."

"Who are you?"

"I want to help you."

Hardin didn't believe him, but he said, "If you want to help, you can get off my boat and leave me alone."

"Without my help, your venture is too chancy."

"I'll worry about that."

"How do you intend to locate your target?"

"What target?"

The man smiled thinly. "I don't think you fully understand the sheer indefensibility of your position, Dr. Hardin. That launch is armed. Those men are mine."

Hardin glanced out the porthole. The launch was barely visible, a lean shape between the dark water and the black sky, its engine muttering idly, barely ticking over to pace the sloop which was plowing through the Channel under full sail.

"Why?" asked Hardin.

"We can shoot you. We can sink you. We can drown you. And your companion. No one will ever know. . . . How do you intend to locate your target?"

"Screw off."

"Or I can turn you over to the authorities."

Hardin felt his face betray him.

The man smiled. "Oh, that you believe? You can believe it all, sir, but we'll use that as a wedge." His smile vanished. "How do you intend to locate your target?"

"Radar."

"What range?"

"Fifty miles."

"*Fifty* miles? That's rather optimistic for radar."

"I built it."

"Fifty miles. Three hours' warning if your target travels at sixteen knots. Provided you close within fifty miles to begin with." His eyes slitted almost shut and he stroked the underside of his chin with his thumb. "That's not good enough. I can't allow such hit-or-miss conditions."

"*You* can't allow?" Hardin exploded. "What the hell are you talking about?"

"I want you to succeed."

114

"Then let me go."

"I *insist* that you succeed."

"I'll keep it in mind."

The man smiled. "You'll do more than keep it in mind, sir. You'll do exactly as I tell you."

"No," said Hardin. "It just doesn't work that way."

"We've already discussed my options."

"What do you want from me?"

"I want what you want. And I can help. I can track your target. I can alert you to any changes in its departure, or route, or destination. I will know its whereabouts every moment and I will give you ample warning to attack."

"What do you really want?"

"It doesn't matter what *I* really want, Dr. Hardin. I'm giving you LEVIATHAN on a silver platter."

The man pocketed his gun and worked his way down the tilting cabin sole to the radio above the chart table. "Come here, Dr. Hardin." He turned on the radio and manipulated the dial.

Hardin joined him. The man sat at the teak table, located a pencil and scratch paper, and wrote GMHN. "It's a good radio," he said. "I'm giving you a false call sign. GMHN. Gold-Mike-Hotel-November. I'll make the arrangements to document it. Reverse it for my call sign. When do you intend to attack?"

"Three or four weeks."

"I'll call next week and the week after. Then every night. Eight o'clock Greenwich Mean Time. Twenty hundred hours. We'll arrange a code because we'll be on an open line through the Portishead Overseas Station."

"What if I don't answer?"

"Once I get off this boat, Dr. Hardin, I obviously can't force you to do a thing. But I find it difficult to believe that you would ignore information on LEVIATHAN's exact position. Am I wrong?"

"You're right," Hardin conceded. And then, even though he knew he would not get an answer, he said, "But I want your name and who you're working for."

A staccato drilling sound interrupted the static hiss of the open radio channel.

"Bloody hell!" snapped the man. He turned it off.

"What was that?" asked Hardin.

"The Russian Woodpecker. They're testing a new over-the-horizon radar to track the United States Cruise missiles, and it's balling up shortwave all over England. If it disrupts our broadcasts, I'll try again in five minutes. They never last very long."

"Who are you?" Hardin repeated.

"Rather than concoct a lie, let me say that my name is Miles and that I am associated with a democratic state in need of a new weapon."

"What does that have to do with me?" asked Hardin.

"You're the prototype."

"Prototype for what?"

"The weapon."

BOOK TWO

10

The wind tested the steel cables that spiderwebbed between the ship's towering mass and the spindly-looking refinery pier. The wind was light, a gentle July evening breeze, and the cables were thick, but LEVIATHAN's hull, a wall one hundred feet high and eighteen hundred feet long—over four acres of windage—tempted it like a giant sail.

The strain on the cables was enormous. Double bow and stern lines, breast lines, spring lines, and midships cables, twelve in all, shared the load. They chafed against the ship's chocks and tugged relentlessly at its shock-absorbing mooring winches. Heavily greased wherever they touched metal, they stretched tautly between the mooring winches and the chocks, dividing the vast deck like low fences, a series of obstacles too low to crouch under and too high to step across without an effort.

The wind was from the southwest and as LEVIATHAN was pointing north, up Southampton Water toward the city where the rivers Test and Itchen meet, the greatest strain was on the stern cables, over which a group of Pakistani stewards were manhandling crates of fresh meat and vegetables. The wind speed increased from three to five knots for several seconds. On the bridge, the Doppler radar's LED screen showed that the ship's stern had moved three inches farther from the pier.

There was something indecent, thought the Southampton harbor pilot, about a ship in ballast. Empty, LEVIATHAN rode high in the water. The upper fifty feet of its hull was clean matte black but underneath that was another fifty feet painted red, the underwater part concealed

119

when the ship was laden. It was scarred where the mechanical scrapers had stripped off moss and shell life, but what was worse was the great bulbous protuberance which jutted from the bow, a fat, unseemly growth ordinarily draped by the sea. The pilot felt as if he were privy to a secret of nature, an impossible sight like the underbelly of an iceberg.

One of his colleagues had piloted the monster in the night before and he had been outspokenly angry; it was sheer arrogance to float a ship that big, much less bring it into Southampton Water. LEVIATHAN dwarfed the refinery, demanding attention, tearing the eye from the twisted miles of silvery pipeline, the squat storage tanks, and the tall, spiny catalytic crackers that covered the gentle hills like weed and shells scattered by the tide.

Bad enough lumbering through the open sea in the grip of its momentum, but insanity in harbor, mocking the very term haven, because no place the monster docked could ever be safe until it had gone. The winds, the tides, and the currents exerted their force according to resistance. They bowed to grace, but never bulk.

The ship had all the latest electronic guidance equipment, some designed especially for it, and the captain knew his position within a foot and his speed to inches per second. The pilot would use the aids, but not rely on them. He was a master mariner—at sea for twenty years before he'd retired to bring ships into his harbor—and he knew that with the colossal impetus LEVIATHAN generated, the instruments could tell him only what was already happening. It had been dead calm last night and still they'd needed six of Southhampton's strongest tugs to hold her.

But *now* there was wind. He watched it all day, fearing the night's work. It had begun stirring from the west in the afternoon, rippling the summer grass in his pony fields, miles from the sea. The Met forecast indicated it would remain west and might blow harder after dark. If it ever gripped LEVIATHAN, if the ship embraced it, nothing but grounding would stop her.

Throughout the day he had nurtured a terrifying image

of the giant drifting out of control, smashing into another ship, its thin skin rupturing, the residual oil and fumes in its tanks igniting like a thermal bomb, obliterating the harbor. Now, as the refinery's marine terminal manager drove him toward the ship on the narrow pier roadway, he repeated to himself an earlier promise. If the wind rose above ten knots, he would refuse to take it out.

"Swinging west," said the terminal manager, as if he could read his thoughts.

"Yes," said the second pilot, a younger man in the backseat of the speeding Mini. He was a backup man in case the first pilot was incapacitated in the middle of the job.

The pilot wondered about the luck of the draw. Of the fifty members of the Southampton and Isle of Wight Pilots Service, the refinery had selected six to pilot the crude carriers. The refinery wanted the best—their installation was as expensive as it was delicate and a mishap could put them out of business for months—and he was one of the six best. But why had he won the toss for LEVIATHAN? The man who had brought her in last night didn't want her again. He knew that the others had hoped to lose. He had been intrigued, as had his friend in the backseat. And they had won. It was as if the ship had selected them. Tonight, he wished it hadn't.

"Dropping," said the terminal manager. Like the pilots, he too had been a master mariner—a ship captain—and his assessment of the weather was more than a polite remark.

"I think you're right," said the pilot.

"I devoutly hope so," said the terminal manager. He looked as uneasy as the pilot felt. The bloody thing ought not to be here and all three men knew it.

Barely a tenth full, yet still holding one hundred thousand tons of Abu Dhabi crude, LEVIATHAN had had a draft just shallow enough to permit her into Southampton Water during the three-hour stand of high water which was created by a second tidal flood around the east side of the Isle of Wight. Ordinarily the giant ship would never dis-

121

charge at the Southampton refinery, but it had off-loaded half a million tons at Bantry Bay, Ireland, and four hundred thousand at Le Havre, and her managers had offered the remainder of her cargo for a pittance rather than waste time waiting for the French and Irish facilities she had glutted to take more.

London had overridden the objections of the terminal manager who had denied the ship entry on the grounds of safety. He leaned on the horn button; a camera crew scattered out of their way. The pilot smiled at the manager's grim expression. Corporations, he had noticed, could act as stupidly and illogically as people. Despite their flowcharts, memoranda, private language, dedication to profit, and facade of precision, they often did what they did merely because they wanted to. That was really why LEVIATHAN was here. So someone could take pictures and say "Look what we did."

The car sped alongside the ship and pulled up at the silver gangway that angled up the hull a quarter mile from the bow. The manager cast a worried eye at the cargo transfer arms, six elbows of pipe and hose that looked like the legs of a giant praying mantis.

"Be gentle." He smiled.

The pilot nodded politely, already half out of the car, his mind narrowing, shutting out nonessentials to concentrate on the job. The second pilot followed silently; they knew each other's habits.

The pilot straightened his navy-blue jacket and donned his white peaked hat. Then he started up the long slanting gangway. He climbed quickly at first, looking up, but the higher he went the more the slender stair bounced and he had to slow his pace to break the rhythm his feet had started. He looked down just before he reached the deck. Already he was higher than on most ships' bridges.

The wind gusted stronger on deck. This was his first real view of LEVIATHAN, and even in the fading light he was struck incredulous by its size. Twelve acres of green deck spread before him like a vast plain, broken here and there

122

by pipes and valves and divided lengthwise by a central catwalk connecting fire stations, and crosswise by taut mooring cables. Halfway to the bow, a Bell Ranger helicopter sat on the port pad.

Aft, the accommodations tower rose ten stories above the main deck, a gleaming white structure half as wide as the ship and crowned by triple spires—two slim black funnels and a tapering mast between them festooned with radar dishes and telemetric aerials. Slender bridge wings cantilevered over the sides of the ship from the top deck. They and the twin funnels, which spewed thin gray smoke as the engineers built steam, and the mast were incongruous touches of grace on the massive ship.

Followed by the second pilot, he walked toward the tower on a pathway marked with rough gray sand paint. The path humped here and there to cross lateral piping. It passed dark-green piping, yellow valves, white fire stations with red nozzle heads, and hissing black winches from which dragon tails of steam rose lazily until they were dispersed by the wind.

The pilot had to climb over several mooring cables, taking care not to smear grease on his uniform slacks. He already had oil on his hands from the gangway; that was standard on crude carriers. They entered the tower through a watertight door, stepping over a traditionally high sill, although it was hard to imagine seawater on this deck. An English seaman threw them a polite half salute and showed them to the lift, and there all semblance to an ordinary merchant ship ceased.

"Bloody great office block," remarked the second pilot as the spacious car silently ascended ten levels to the bridge deck. The pilot nodded. The ship sat in the water as solidly as a building on bedrock. The lift opened onto a broad carpeted hallway, a wide corridor like a foyer with lighted oil paintings on the wood-grained Formica walls, and potted palms on the floor. The pilots headed for a door marked Chart Room/Bridge.

It opened into an enormous, dimly lighted, windowless

123

room. Banks of computers occupied most of the space and yet, the pilot noticed, there was as much room around the oak chart table as you'd find around a lord's billiards table. Two young officers were attending the computers, reading the printout sheets which were spilling from them in steady streams. A cadet was pulling the Southampton Water and Approaches chart from the wide, flat drawers beneath the table.

The pilot passed through a heavy black curtain that separated the chart room from the bridge and stopped still. The view was breathtaking. One hundred feet above deck and two hundred feet above the water, big square windows swept the width of the bridge. It was like standing atop a twenty-story building. The city of Southampton was visible in the distance.

A number of low engine-control, communications, lighting, and electronics consoles squatted in front of the windows. Between the row of consoles and the bridge's rear bulkhead, a broad space ran uninterrupted from wing to wing. One hundred fifty feet separated the doors at either end of it. They were open to the evening breeze.

Amidships was the helm—a small yoke, smaller than the Mini's steering wheel—and ahead of the helm, hung from the low tile ceiling, were the magnified gyrocompass, the Doppler radar which showed position relative to the pier, the rate-of-turn gyro, and the knots and revs indicators. The pilot gazed at them for a moment. These were his.

At sea, satellite navigation, computer tracking of other ships, and anticollision radar were primarily in charge of the ship's position and well-being, but here, in his channel, the pilot worked with the most basic questions: Would the ship clear a buoy by fifty yards? How quickly was it turning? Was it going fast enough to turn? Was it going too fast to stop? When the bow left the pier, how would the stern follow?

But LEVIATHAN was too big. Its mass created uncontrollable momentum. Already in its short life it had overrun a sea berth in the Gulf, killing two men and holing its thin-skinned bow, and on another voyage it had ripped three cargo arms from the piers at Le Havre.

"You're late, Pilot!"

The voice carried across the bridge like a bugle. Cedric Ogilvy, the legendary P and O captain who'd left his old line for LEVIATHAN, did not look up from the instrument console he was studying. The pilot walked over to him.

Ogilvy was in full uniform, a rarity these days in the merchant service, and his sleeve carried four broad gold stripes. The pilot's sleeve bore faint stitch marks where his own four stripes had resided. It was the custom of the Pilot Service to remove your stripes so as not to embarrass a captain whose rank might be technically below yours. A courtesy. So few wore uniforms that it hardly mattered. Merchant masters manned their bridges in a variety of costumes that ranged from sweaters to nylon windcheaters. The pilot's favorite was an Italian captain who brought an old VLCC into the refinery once or twice a year dressed like a magazine model, in soft leather shoes, cashmere pullover, and a cotton shirt out of the best shop in Rome.

"Good evening, Captain Ogilvy," said the pilot, extending his hand. "I'm—"

"Late," said Ogilvy, nodding at the satellite navigation readout and not accepting his hand. The pilot looked at the screen.

SAT FIX	QLT:03	
GMT	20.03.00	
LAT	N-50	50.158
LON	W-001	19.524

It showed the satellites whose signals the computer was using to determine the fix, the time, and LEVIATHAN's latitude and longitude. Ogilvy tapped the second line with a long, thick, well-manicured finger. Greenwich Mean Time twenty-oh-three. Three minutes past eight. Three minutes late in reporting to the captain—the three minutes the pilot had paused to drink in the bridge.

He held his tongue. That sort of nonsense had gone out

of the merchant service years ago. Pompous old goat acting like he was still Royal Navy. And yet . . . it was common knowledge that Ogilvy was the only captain who had stayed with LEVIATHAN after his first voyage. The ship devoured captains. Last night's pilot said that the chap who had brought it in from the Persian Gulf looked to be on the edge of a breakdown. Neither time LEVIATHAN had gone out of control had Ogilvy been in command. Let his luck hold one more night, the pilot thought grimly.

He remarked on the wind, which he noticed was stirring the clothes of a seaman who was opening the bow thruster control panels on the starboard wing. Ogilvy met his eye for the first time. There was a hard edge beneath his blandly handsome face that had not been apparent at first. And something else, further down. Something strange, like fear, but it couldn't be fear.

Ogilvy stared at him for an uncomfortably long time before he spoke. He said, "You are two hundred feet above Southampton Water, Pilot. Of course it's windy. The matter of interest, however, is the force of the wind at deck level." He pointed at a dial. "The anemometer reads four knots. Barely force two. What?"

"Yes, Captain."

Ogilvy tapped the satellite screen's time line again. "We sail with the tide in forty-five minutes," he said, dismissing the pilot. Then he raised his voice.

"Number One!"

The chief officer, a slim dark, quiet-looking man, came running. "Sir?"

The pilot drifted away, trying to repress a smile. Number One? That was old Royal Navy with flags flying. The second pilot caught his smile and muttered, "Flogging on Sunday?"

They walked out onto the port wing overlooking the pier. Far below on the main deck the Pakistani galley crew were still carrying crates and cardboard cartons into the tower. The sun was setting behind the hills, and the wind was shifting due west, frighteningly strong. The lights of the refinery began to glitter in the deepening dusk.

126

He looked astern. Far across the marshes beneath Calshot Castle and the open Solent was the Isle of Wight, a dark-blue line on the southern horizon. It would be four hard hours before LEVIATHAN rounded the island and the pilot boat took him off, but he reckoned he would have matters in hand once he was stern to the wind in the Solent. First, however, he had to guide the long and ponderous ship through two sharp turns—right from the Calshot Reach into the narrow Thorn Channel, then a hard left, a full one hundred twenty-five degrees.

Three tugs were stationed dead in the water on standby as they had been all day in case LEVIATHAN tried to drift across the estuary and take the refinery pier with it. Three more were coming down from Southampton. He could see their lights a couple of miles away. The wind suddenly gusted sharply.

He heard cries of alarm and, looking down, saw the men on deck scattering like ants.

"Look!" shouted the second pilot.

He caught a glint of movement on the stern-most mooring cable. Midway between the side of the ship and the mooring winch, the cable had started to shred. The strands peeled away from each other, blossoming open like a steel flower.

The cable parted with a loud bang.

One end flipped high in the air, buzzing angrily, and disappeared over the side. The other end, that attached to the winch, slashed across the deck like a saber. It caught one of the fleeing galley stewards in the back of his legs and flung him twenty feet. He crashed to the deck, his white pants red with blood. A chilling scream pierced the hissing of LEVIATHAN's funnels and the hollow rumble of the tugs in the river. Ogilvy ran from the wheelhouse, looked down at the deck, and instantly shouted orders into the lapel mike of his VHF two-way radio. Seamen boiled out of the accommodations tower and ran to the nearest mooring winches. Urged on by a wiry bosun, a second deck gang began running a new stern line, humping a cable past the fallen man. At the same time, the tugs in the river nosed against the ship and pushed toward the pier. Only when the new cable was secured did the seamen gather around the fallen steward.

Ogilvy's radio crackled urgently. The pilot heard the word "hospital." The captain's lips tightened; he glanced at the setting sun and the darkening sky. Then his gaze fell on the Bell Ranger on the helipad.

"Send him in that damned helicopter," he snapped. "Number Two, get down there and see to it."

The second officer looked quite young, almost a boy, and he was staring, transfixed by the twitching form on the deck below.

"Now, mister!" snapped Ogilvy. "Hop to it."

The pilot's stomach was knotted with pain. Twenty years at sea and he'd never gotten used to its sudden violence. He stared at the hills and suddenly thought of his ponies, wild beasts he had captured in the New Forest and trained to be happy in his fields.

Ogilvy directed the removal of the injured man from his place on the bridge, issuing orders into his radio while they carried him forward to the helicopter. A man with a curiously red face trotted out after them and clambered aboard. The whippy blades began revolving. After a quick warm-up, the helicopter lifted off the ship with a thrashing roar and banked up the channel toward Southampton.

A heavyset man in a rumpled windbreaker hurried onto the bridge wing. He glanced at the Ranger vanishing into the dark, and looked down at the lighted deck where seamen were gathering loose apples and hosing away the blood.

"What happened?" he asked the white-haired Ogilvy, who looked ten years his senior.

To the harbor pilot's surprise, the captain answered him civilly.

"A stern line parted. Sliced the legs off one of my stewards."

The man nodded and gazed for a moment at the activity below. Then he turned to the pilot.

"James Bruce," he said, extending his hand. "Company staff captain."

"Checking up on me," said Ogilvy, with a faint smile.

"Troubleshooting." Bruce smiled back. He explained to the pilot, "We run constant inspections on our ships."

"Someone should have inspected that mooring winch," snapped Ogilvy, displaying emotion for the first time since the accident. "I can't very well be expected to turn her inside out the first day I'm aboard."

"You're quite right, Cedric," said Bruce. "I'll check your predecessor's maintenance charts before I get off."

Ogilvy flushed darkly. "What is the point of a captain taking leave if his ship is a shambles when he returns?"

"Cedric," Bruce pleaded, "even *you* need a rest."

"A lot of good that's done me. I'll be sorting this mess out as far as Capetown."

"It won't happen again," said Bruce. He glanced up the channel where the helicopter's lights had blended with those of the city. "You'll be wanting that helicopter."

"He can jolly well catch up!" snapped Ogilvy. "Number Three! Radio that man not to approach until we've passed Nab Light. Under no circumstances is he to attempt to land without my permission. Pilot! The tugs are ready. Stand by to single up."

Four tugboats pushed LEVIATHAN toward the dock. Another stood by with a line to the stern, and a sixth waited with a line to the tanker's bow. Their powerful engines jetted diesel exhaust high into the air. White water frothed behind their low sterns. Slowly, the docking cables slackened.

When all twelve cables were drooping equally, Ogilvy spoke into his radio lapel mike. The pilot raised his binoculars. Far below, on the main deck at the stern, Ogilvy's chief officer was relaying commands to LEVIATHAN's deck gang and the dockers on the pier. His second officer was doing the same at the bow, while his third, whose watch it was, hovered at the captain's elbow.

One by one the dockers dropped the extra cables, and

one by one LEVIATHAN's deck gangs reeled them onto the deck. Ogilvy paced the wing, his eyes in constant motion, and every time he passed near him, the pilot could hear through his radio the breathing of the men who were laboring at the steam winches. They loosed the cables until only three held the ship to the pier—a single line each at the bow, at the stern, and amidships. Singled up.

The pilot waited to be called, but Ogilvy seemed to have every intention of undocking and turning LEVIATHAN himself. He was welcome to it.

Thank God they dredged the mud shoals off Hamble Spit a year ago; it had greatly widened the channel opposite the refinery. Still, the giant ship barely had room to turn, and it wouldn't take much more than a minor miscalculation to block one of England's principal ports by sticking the monster's bow in the mud and straddling the channel like Hadrian's wall.

Ogilvy radioed orders to the tugs, to his officers, and to the dockers. Still ignoring the pilot, he faced LEVIATHAN's bow and spoke again.

A docker flung his arms high.

With a loud clank, the bow mooring cable dropped free of the pier and fell into the water, leaving a white trail like a jellyfish. Ogilvy spoke again: The midships line clanked loose. The tugboat at the bow was joined by a second. Together, they began pulling toward the middle of the channel.

Ogilvy reached into a small cabinet on the wing and engaged the bow thruster. Unseen and unheard, a two-thousand-horsepower diesel engine turned a propeller inside a tunnel that traversed the front of the ship. It pulled water in the starboard side and spewed it to port, pushing with the straining tugboats.

The bridge lights were extinguished. The thickening night moved closer to the ship. The pier and the refinery took on lighted shapes. A cool wind swept the bridge wing. Ogilvy ordered the stern cable cast off.

The last tie splashed into the water. Two Southampton tugs tightened up astern and pulled toward the channel.

The rest picked up lines on the outboard side and joined the effort to draw the ship from the pier. Water streamed from the taut hemp and the air trembled with the beat of their engines, but LEVIATHAN stood firm.

Ogilvy went into the bridge house and the pilot followed. The third officer took up a position by the engine consoles. A seaman waited at the helm. Small red ceiling lights illuminated the instruments and controls. The second pilot was already at the communications console, a VHF radiotelephone in his hand, conversing with the tugs and the harbor traffic.

"Right full rudder," said Ogilvy.

"Right full rudder," repeated the helmsman, turning the miniature yoke.

"Port, slow ahead," said Ogilvy. "Starboard, slow astern."

The third officer repeated Ogilvy's command and moved the plastic-knobbed levers which automatically controlled the engines, one forward, the other back. The engines engaged soundlessly with a barely perceptible tremor.

Then, by slow degrees, the world started to turn past the bridge windows. The distant lights of Southampton moved majestically across LEVIATHAN's bow. The pier angled away from the port side of the ship and the rows of red and green lights that marked the channel to the sea lined up in single file facing the starboard side. The pilot shivered; it was like watching the start of an avalanche.

Minutes passed. LEVIATHAN felt motionless, but the lights turned faster. The stern tugs dropped off, retrieved their hawsers, and scurried between the ship and the pier to help push the bow. Now the lighted outskirts of Southampton slid along the hull toward the stern, while the refinery—glittering like a space installation—swung to the other side.

"Stop engines!"

"Stop engines." The third officer moved both levers to Stop and recorded the changes in the Engine Movement Book. The harbor lights continued to shift as the ship kept on turning on its momentum. Several minutes later, as it lined up with the channel and was completing its turn, Ogilvy ordered the bow tugs away. LEVIATHAN's deck gang loosed their slack lines and heaved them over the side.

At precisely the instant it was facing the first channel marker—a quick-flashing white light a mile away—the ship stopped turning.

"Pilot!"

"Thank you, Captain," he said admiringly. It had been a masterful undocking. He turned to the second pilot. "Tell the tugs we've finished with them."

"Not yet!" snapped Ogilvy. "I'll tell them. I'll ruddy well tell them when I'm ready to. Is that understood?"

"I beg your pardon, Captain," the pilot said, startled by the outburst. Ogilvy's face set angrily in the dim red glow of the bridge lights.

The pilot stared down the channel, lining the marker against the window frame. In a moment the ship would drift. Out of the corner of his eye he saw James Bruce watching with a concerned expression on his fleshy face.

"Will you order ahead full, Captain, or shall I?"

Ogilvy turned to his third officer. "Tell the tugs we're done."

"Aye, sir." The third spoke into the VHF phone.

The pilot waited, his eyes flickering from the marker, to the compass, to the rate-of-turn gyro, to the zero-reading knots indicator.

"Thank you, Number Three. Port . . . starboard . . . ahead full."

"Ahead full, sir."

"She's yours, Pilot."

Ogilvy spun on his heel and disappeared into the chart room. A moment later the bridge deck shuddered as the twin propellers bit deep.

The gray interlude between day and night was over. It was quite suddenly dark, and the sky, the land, and the water merged at indistinct places. The flashing lights of the channel buoys, dim in the dusk, were now sharp pricks of red, green, and white. They were the only visual features that the pilot could trust, because the vague silhouettes of the hills and riverlands offered depthless perspective.

He stood close to the third officer. "Please give me six knots."

"Aye, sir."

"Helmsman. Steer one four two."

"Steer one four two," repeated the helmsman.

Slowly the shuddering eased and the great ship began to move down Southampton Water toward the Calshot Reach. The second pilot picked up a telephone at the communications console. As he swept the VHF channels, he reported to the pilot.

"The harbor patrol is ahead of us."

"Thank you."

"We've a ten-thousand-ton freighter, inbound, heading for Thorn Channel."

"Ask him to wait for us, please." The channel was less than a thousand feet wide beyond the turn.

The first channel buoy was coming up. The second pilot said, "*Seatrain* is behind us, just now leaving the Test."

"Thank you. Could you give me a bearing on the Reach light?"

The second pilot hurried out on the wing. You had to move quickly on a bridge this big. He sighted the grouped flashing white lights through a pair of vanes that rotated around a fixed compass card, then did a quick mental calculation from relative to compass bearing as he walked a hundred feet back to the helm.

"One four zero."

"Thank you," said the pilot. A moment later, he called to the helmsman, "One four zero."

Slowly, too slowly, the lights ahead moved right. The pilot watched the magnified fine-line compass overhead. The card ticked the degrees past the needle and settled, finally, on 140. He looked ahead. The grouped flashers were there, coming up fast. He raised his glasses and searched for the quick-flashing ten-second red Castle Point buoy he would use to begin his turn into Thorn Channel.

It was where it should be, twelve points off the starboard bow.

These were familiar waters—he guided ships up and down them day and night. But LEVIATHAN's great height altered his perspective and that took some getting used to. The grouped white flashers suddenly disappeared. He gripped his glasses, searching frantically before he realized that the distant bow had blocked his view. He hurried out on the port wing and leaned over the side and found the white flashers.

Quickly he walked off the wing, hurried through the bridge house, past the helmsman and the third officer, and out to the far edge of the starboard wing. Three hundred feet. It didn't seem possible a ship could be so wide. When the pilot on that ten-thousand-tonner saw LEVIATHAN coming out of Thorn Channel, he'd be glad of the port regulations that required him to wait.

The pilot leaned out over the water and eyed the Castle Point light to see how close the ship was to the edge of the Calshot Spit shoal. The stacks hissed above him. A gust of wind burst off the flats and tore at his hat. He jammed it on tighter and hurried back to the bridge house. He was afraid that the ship was moving too slowly.

Captain Ogilvy had come back on the bridge and was standing at the engine control console.

"When will we have six knots?" asked the pilot.

Ogilvy telephoned the engine room. So much for automation, thought the pilot. It was one thing to throw a lever demanding speed and quite another to get it. The instruments were not the machines.

He glanced at the deck-level anemometer. The wind was gusting to seven knots. Ogilvy cradled the telephone. "You'll have more turns immediately."

"Thank you, Captain."

He moved to the windows.

"What's that?" he asked his second, who was already studying a pair of white lights off the starboard bow. One was higher than the other and a dim red hung in the blackness between them. He picked them up on the radar.

134

A medium-sized blip, moving slowly east into LEVIATHAN's path.

"He's crossing into the North Channel," the second pilot said incredulously, grabbing the radiotelephone. Moments after he made contact with the harbor patrol boat, a single bright white light raced ahead of LEVIATHAN and hovered by the moving lights until they circled back in the direction from which they had come. The second pilot listened to the telephone and chuckled. "Coaster. He told the harbor patrol he thought he probably had time to make it."

But the pilot was already hurrying toward the wing. The white flashers were dropping behind. Overhead, he heard one of the radar dishes squeaking as it turned. He returned to the bridge.

"Helmsman. Steer ten degrees right standard rudder."

"Ten degrees right."

The great bow swung to starboard until the compass read 150. Eyeing the Castle Point quick-flashing red, the Calshot Spit white flasher and the distant quick-flashing North Thorn on the opposite side of the channel, the pilot ordered the rudder angle increased as the curve steepened.

"Steady up on two two zero."

"Steady on two two zero."

The white lights started to drift to the right. The pilot's eyes shot to the rate-of-turn gyro.

"Is she yawing?" he asked the helmsman.

"I've got her, sir. Steadying up on two two zero."

The pilot glanced at him. He was young and rugged-looking, with the intelligent expression and confident bearing of the sort of seaman who either breezed through his ratings test and became an officer, or, if thwarted, left the merchant service for better opportunities ashore.

The channel lights returned to their proper positions, and one of the open VHF local traffic channels came to life.

"LEVIATHAN. This is *Seatrain* right behind you."

The second pilot picked up the phone. "Hello, *Seatrain*."

The pilot walked to the wing and looked back at her lights. He had piloted several of the sleek container ships. They were big and fast. Four and a half days to New York. Faster than QE2. She'd be chafing to run.

He returned to the helm. The *Seatrain* pilot's voice sounded as clear as if he were on LEVIATHAN's bridge. "My minimum speed is six knots. When may I overtake?"

The second pilot looked at the first. He shook his head.

The second pilot spoke with a grin. "We suggest a lower minimum."

"That'll mean stopping," cried the voice.

The pilot took the phone—one eye on the next marker, a five-second white. "Sorry. No room."

"Thought so. Just wanted to give it a try."

"Cheero."

The pilot and his second exchanged smiles as they rang off.

They were almost through Thorn Channel. The Solent lay ahead, a broad, open wind chute. LEVIATHAN was doing six knots—barely steerage because her bottom was only a few feet above the dredged channel. The pilot glanced at the knots indicator. The needle, quivering at the six-knot mark, had begun to fall toward five and half. He beckoned for the third officer.

"I need more turns."

"Yes, sir." The young man telephoned the engine room.

The pilot eyed the light on the West Bramble buoy. Just before he was abeam the quick-flashing white, he started a slow turn to port. LEVIATHAN lumbered east into the Solent. He would have liked more steerage, but the stiffening west wind helped push her bow through the broad turn. He finished the turn at Prince Consort Shoal.

"Steady up on one zero eight."

"Steady up on one zero eight."

A pair of white lights, one almost atop the other, appeared dead ahead, looming larger than the others that dotted the black water.

"That's the freighter," said the second pilot. "I've got him on the phone."

"Thank you." He gave the helmsman a course ch᙮
to give the freighter more room. It was a small, aft-conn᙮
semicontainer with silvery boxes stacked between massive
deck cranes. He said hello to its pilot on the radiotelephone as it squeezed between LEVIATHAN and an anchored
Hovercraft tender.

The pilot exhaled. It looked like the worst was over.

An hour passed quickly, during which he located his
buoys, visually and on the radar, took his bearings, and instructed the helmsman. The channel lights pricked the
distance, moved in front of LEVIATHAN's gigantic bow,
grew larger, and slid past. All the while the wind grew
stronger. Six knots. Eight. Ten. Gusts to fifteen.

He put his face to the radarscope. Ahead, the channel
was clear. The distinctive electronic signatures of the
buoys filed up the screen—an almost straight path for six
miles. Then a forty-five-degree turn into the narrow Nab
Channel, which was reserved for deep-draft vessels. Once
through the Nab, LEVIATHAN would be in the English
Channel and he would be riding home on the pilot boat.

He straightened up and glanced around the dark bridge.
Ogilvy emerged from the shadows, spoke briefly to the
helmsman, and hurried onto the starboard wing. The pilot
listened to the peculiar shuffle of his left foot dragging
slightly on the polished linoleum deck.

"Tea, sir?"

A steward appeared at his elbow with a tray.

"Thank you."

The pilot bent over the radar for a final look. A cluster
of sailing yachts occupied the lower quadrant of the
screen, glowing like grains of white sand. They were
astern of LEVIATHAN, pointing Cowes and refuge for the
night.

The second mixed in milk and sugar and handed him a
steaming mug. He sipped gratefully and tried to squirm
the tension from his back. Good tea.

Abruptly, he put down the cup and stared ahead. The

137

quick-flashing red that marked the channel past Warner Shoal had moved left.

"She's yawning, sir!" cried the helmsman.

The third officer rushed to the helm, but the pilot looked at the knots indicator. The needle had dropped below five. He went to the helm, his heart pounding. The relief man was much older than the helmsman he had replaced. He licked his lips as he fiddled the yoke. The third officer put down a telephone.

"There's trouble in the engine room, sir."

"For how long?" the pilot asked quietly.

The third officer's youth was suddenly apparent and it occurred to the pilot that all of Ogilvy's officers were very young.

"Thirty minutes."

"You'd better get the Old Man."

"He's waiting for you on the starboard wing."

The pilot spoke to his second, who was hovering by his shoulder. "Put him on one two zero when you're abeam the Warner Shoal."

"One two zero."

"And call Eastern Docks and tell them we may need tugs."

The bow began to swing to starboard as the pilot headed toward the wing. He forced himself to walk normally. This was no place to run, not in front of a wet-behind-the-ears third officer and a jittery helmsman who was doing his damndest to compensate for the drift, trying to walk her back into the center of the channel. Everything happened so slowly, because of the ship's size, that it was impossible to gauge the success of the maneuver. He stepped out of the bridge house.

Ogilvy's officers were grouped around him, shadowy forms in the wing's darkness, while the captain spoke by telephone to the engine room. At his waist, beside the bow thruster controls, a dimly lighted remote-instrument panel showed the ship's course, propeller revolutions, and speed.

Ogilvy cradled the phone and turned to the pilot. In the dim reflected red light, he could see a tic in the cap-

138

tain's left cheek, a tiny movement like a fish breaking the water's surface.

"Pilot," he said stiffly, "I'm losing steam pressure. Water in my fuel bunkers has fouled my Number Two boiler's burner nozzles. My engineers need thirty minutes to clear them. LEVIATHAN will maintain four knots maximum."

"Will she obey the helm at four knots?"

"My helmsman can handle her."

"Can she turn into the Nab?"

"Not at four knots."

"Not even with the bow thruster?"

"I said no."

The pilot waited for more, but Ogilvy said nothing, which put him in a classic harbor pilot's dilemma. He was not familiar with LEVIATHAN's performance, nor did he know the man. Was Ogilvy's glacial calm a matter of heroic self-control or paralyzing fear? Was he warning about a difficult situation or was he predicting a catastrophe?

The pilot focused on the facts he knew. The Warner Shoal light was abeam. That meant LEVIATHAN was an hour from Nab Channel traveling at four knots. He asked, "When will you have steam?"

"One hour."

Fact or wish, the pilot couldn't know. He wondered if he should have kept the tugs all the way to Nab Light. Too late. He asked, "Can we twist her around by reversing the starboard screw?"

Ogilvy stared at the water.

"Pilot, my screws barely have purchase. They are partway out of the water and will remain so until I'm free of this inadequate channel and take on ballast. Therefore, twisting her around, as you so quaintly put it, may not be possible in this wind."

The pilot ignored the sarcasm. The captain had ample reason to be anxious. "Then we must stop before the turn into the Nab."

"It's too late to stop."

"I beg your pardon, Captain."

"It's too late to stop."

"We've *four miles*, Captain."

"Under the best of conditions I might stop her by putting both propellers full astern and trying to slalom from side to side. But with one boiler off the line, my propellers out of the water, the wind astern, and no space to maneuver, I do not enjoy the best of conditions. I haven't the power to half LEVIATHAN's momentum, and even if I had, I couldn't set anchors before the wind put me on the shoals."

"Are you telling me, Captain, that everything depends on restoring full power?"

"I'm telling you that LEVIATHAN's engineers will sort her out in one hour and until then you will experience some difficulty maneuvering."

"And what do you suggest if they can't?"

"I suggest you return to my helmsman. He needs your instructions more than I."

The pilot spun on his heel and walked as fast as he could to the bridge house, praying that Ogilvy's confidence was justified and glad that he was willing to stand aside. Apparently he recognized his limitations. A tanker captain spent most of his time on the open sea and only two days a month conning his ship through heavy traffic. He was not prepared for a close-quarters pinch in unfamiliar waters. That's what pilots were for.

A sudden blast of wind tore through the open bridge house. It was hitting the starboard hull now that the ship was angling toward the southeast. The helmsman was off his stool, anxiously playing his yoke.

"She's yawing across the channel, sir. I can't hold her."

"Are there any tugs nearby?" asked the pilot.

"The closest is ten miles," answered the second pilot.

Too far. He was alone. And three miles ahead, visible to the naked eye and bright on the radarscope, were the flashing red and grouped flashing whites that marked the curving entrance to the Nab. Three miles. Forty-five minutes. A mile beyond were three closely spaced orange

140

flashers that marked the channel itself past the turn LEVIA-
THAN couldn't make at four knots.

They drifted from side to side through the blackness
while the helmsman struggled to control the slow-moving
ship. The pilot helped as much as he could, conversing
directly with him instead of through the third officer.

"You can steer back across the channel, Helmsman.
You've a bit of room here. . . . Good . . . Good . . .
Steady up on one two zero now. . . . Good . . . Good
. . . Steady. Hold her!"

LEVIATHAN closed on a flashing white that marked one
of the many wrecks that lined the channel. The pilot took
a bearing on it. When it was time to turn, he stood beside
the helmsman, where the man could feel his presence in
the dark as they watched the compass.

"Steer one one zero."

"Steer one one zero."

At first the compass inched slowly toward the new heading: 119, 118, 117. It stopped at 117. The rate-of-turn
gyro slipped toward zero.

"Carry on," said the pilot.

"Yes, sir."

The helmsman turned the yoke further, but the compass stayed at 117.

"She's not responding, sir."

"Hard aport."

"Hard aport."

The helmsman put the yoke over as far as it would go.
His hands seemed absurdly large on the tiny implement.
Tinged red by the overhead instrument lights, their heavy
knuckles had the thick-skinned swollen look of an old
charwoman's. LEVIATHAN continued to plow forward,
pointing the southern edge of the channel.

The pilot looked anxiously from the rock-steady compass card to the blackness straight ahead. The knots indicator hovered at four. He felt an unusual anger rising in
his throat. What were they doing in the engine room?
Why did Ogilvy remain on the bridge wing?

141

He opened his mouth to order a crash stop. Both screws full astern wouldn't stop LEVIATHAN in time, but it might lessen the impact. There were rocks on the shoals as well as sand and mud, and they would tear her to shreds. The tanker would spill tons of residual oil into the Solent. She might explode or drift loose and block the port for weeks.

Then the compass card trembled past the needle and the ship resumed turning: 116, 115, 114. The distant bow moved like a giant shadow past the lights ahead, accelerating now, even as the helmsman eased the yoke back to arrest the turn. The pilot watched the compass. 112, 111.

"Steady," he cautioned the helmsman.

110, 109.

"Steady. You're past the mark."

"Aye, sir."

But still the compass turned. 108, 107.

"Bring her back," said the pilot, growing alarmed. "Steady up on one one zero." *Would she never stop?*

"I've got her, sir."

The compass slid toward 110.

"One one zero, sir."

"Steady as she goes."

He stepped closer to the helmsman. "Our next heading will be one five four. Can you do it?" he asked, aware that the third officer was listening anxiously.

The helmsman glanced at the knots indicator, still quivering at four. "I don't know, sir."

"Do you want stern power on the starboard?"

"That and the bow thruster might help, sir."

The pilot walked out to the wing to find Ogilvy. Unless relieved by the captain, he was fully in charge of the ship while piloting Southampton and Isle of Wight waters, but he wanted Ogilvy's help to determine what the enormous ship would do.

The wind was shivering the wisps of white hair that hung below the captain's hat.

"What is it, Pilot?" Ogilvy asked, his eyes on the water ahead.

142

"We must execute a forty-four-degree turn to enter the Nab. I suggest reverse power on the starboard screw."

"Do you now?" Ogilvy asked silkily. He turned and walked into the wheelhouse. The third officer hurried to him. "What's your speed?" Ogilvy asked the pilot.

"Four knots."

"Four and one half knots," said the third. "It just went up."

"Which is it, Pilot? Four knots or four and one half?" Ogilvy took up a position at the window just to the right of the one through which the helmsman peered. The pilot stepped back and looked up at the overhead knots indicator. He went to Ogilvy.

"Four and one half knots, Captain."

Ogilvy clasped his hands behind him and stared at the glass.

The pilot left him and watched the knots indicator. The needle wavered between four and one half and five knots. The rate-of-turn gyro showed that the ship was holding steadily to its course.

The pilot went onto the port wing. The hissing from the huge funnels seemed a mockery. He eyed the quick-flashing oranges for several minutes. When the ship passed between the buoys that marked the channel mouth, he returned to the helm.

The knots indicator still read only five knots. The second pilot looked up from the radar.

"Five cables."

Half a sea mile to the turn.

"We're coming into the Nab, Captain."

"Carry on."

The second pilot went out to the wing. He hurried back moments later. "First marker broad on the starboard bow."

"Ten degrees right standard rudder," said the pilot.

The third officer repeated his order.

"Ten degrees right standard rudder," answered the helmsman.

"Sir?" asked the pilot, approaching Ogilvy at the glass. "Shall we reverse the port engine?"

"No need," said Ogilvy, gazing at the orange flashers. "LEVIATHAN will turn quite nicely at six knots."

The pilot stepped back and looked up at the knots indicator. The needle quivered at six knots. The captain couldn't have seen it. He'd felt it. The legend was true. Cedric Ogilvy deserved LEVIATHAN.

"Is there anything else, Pilot?"

"No, Captain. Thank you."

"Number Three! See that the pilot gets off safely." Ogilvy walked onto the port wing with neither a glance nor a word to anyone else on the bridge. The last the pilot saw of him was the white of his hat and hair, ghostly on the edge of the wing.

Stung, he stalked onto the starboard wing, took a bearing, for something to do, and returned to the bridge house, where he talked the helmsman through the channel and pointed LEVIATHAN at the Nab Tower.

Yellow light flashed from the chart room as James Bruce stepped out of the shadows and disappeared through the blackout curtain. He had been on the bridge all along, the pilot realized, watching. Moments later the first officer left silently. It was almost midnight. The bridge was deserted but for the pilots, the third officer, and the helmsman. Ten minutes passed. The second officer entered from the chart room and spoke with the third, preparing to take his watch.

"Where's the Old Man?" the pilot heard him ask quietly.

"Port wing."

"Bloody hell, how long is he going to stay out there?"

The tension was leaving the bridge and the young third said with a grin, "To Cherbourg, at least."

"God help us."

"Call the boat," said the pilot. "Starboard side."

He gave the helmsman his last bearing. The black of

144

the bow swung toward the blazing white sea buoy, covered it, and let it peep out on the port side. In the distance, the green lights of the pilot boat bounced through the darkness, closing at a broad angle.

"We'll go off the starboard side, Number Three." He smiled in the dark. Now he was doing it, and he'd never been in the navy.

"Yes, sir." The third officer spoke into a phone, then threw some switches on the deck-lighting console. White light painted half a ship where there had been darkness, marking a path between the tower and a ladder midway to the bow.

"Off you go," said the pilot to his second.

A few minutes later, the man appeared on the main deck, an insignificant-looking miniature figure who walked the gray pathways and joined several sailors at the head of the ladder. The pilot went onto the starboard wing to watch. The lights of the pilot boat closed with the black line of LEVIATHAN.

Spotlights pierced the dark, lighting the water far beneath the ladder, showing a fiercely swirling sea. The launch, a narrow thirty-five-footer, cut through the froth and ran alongside, keeping pace with the moving ship. The wind whipped the sound of its twin diesel engines to the bridge wing. They sped up and slowed as the launch captain drew closer, than slowed to a hollow rumble as he made contact with the oil tanker's hull. Angled against its dull red bottom plates, the launch held her nose to LEVIATHAN. A man appeared on deck, looking up, and the second pilot waved down at him and stepped through an opening in LEVIATHAN's rail. The pilot went back to the bridge house.

"Thank you," said the third officer.

"Safe journey," said the pilot. He nodded to the helmsman, the younger one again, who gave him a relieved grin. Then he walked through the chart room, past the clicking banks of computers, past the second officer, who was examining his first English Channel chart while a cadet replaced the Solent chart, to the elevator. He rode to the main deck, where a waiting sailor accompanied him outside.

It was less windy on deck and warmer. Suddenly lights illuminated the forward end of the ship. He heard a whine overhead, saw lights in the sky, and seconds later the Bell Ranger lowered out of the dark. Several sailors ducked under the whirling blades and fastened the helicopter's skids to the pad.

The pilot remembered the injured man and Ogilvy's orders that the helicopter was not to land without his permission. He hadn't been on the bridge when the call came, nor had he heard Ogilvy's response. It was a reminder that his job was over and the ship was done with him, lingering a moment to let him off, then truly on its own, a place on the sea, beholden to no one.

A steam winch finished raising the pilot hoist as the pilot reached it. He stepped onto a platform and glanced down. The pilot boat was a speck in the frothy water a hundred feet below. The ladder locked into place. The pilot turned around and stepped back onto the wooden rungs. That was the hardest part, turning your back to the precipice. He climbed down three rungs, one from the bottom of the ladder, gripped the side ropes, and called, "Ready!"

Steam hissed. The ladder jerked suddenly, dropped, then slid down the side of the ship, gliding smoothly as small wheels rolled along the steel plates. The pilot held tight and glanced down. The deckhand was standing on the bow of the launch. He looked up. Far above, the sailor manipulating the ladder mechanism watched him descend.

Had it been a lucky bluff? Was it Ogilvy's good luck that the ship had gained sufficient speed to maneuver? It had come so close to losing control. He thought of the look deep in Ogilvy's eyes. He dealt with captains every day. He met good men and stupid men, and arrogance, and fear. Ogilvy had taken pains to put him down. The pilot decided that LEVIATHAN's captain *was* afraid. It said something for his common sense.

The ladder jerked to a halt. The pilot stepped onto the bow of the launch and the deckhand steadied his arm. He edged along the cabin, gripping varnished rope handrails, and lowered himself to the stern deck. The big diesels roared and the boat veered away. The pilot looked back. LEVIATHAN erased the stars, stretching between the horizons like a black cloud.

There were other pilots in the cabin. They exchanged quiet greetings. He sat next to his friend, drained. The launch ran a ways, pitching and rolling in heavy seas, then slowed and picked up the pilot from the *Seatrain* container ship. The new arrival spotted LEVIATHAN's pilot.

"I was running up your arse all night."

"We could have used the push."

"Blooming great pig," muttered the second pilot.

"Bad?" asked the man from *Seatrain*.

The pilot nodded. "Bad enough."

It was over. He dozed on the way to Portsmouth.

When they tied up at the brightly lighted dock in the naval harbor, each pilot dropped two 10p coins on the dashboard. The launch pilot, a master mariner himself, ritualistically protested the tip.

"A pint for the lad," said the pilot, nodding at the deckhand who was guiding them onto the dock.

In the taxi to the Southampton docks where they had their cars, the pilot looked at his watch. 0200. It was an hour's drive to his home in the New Forest. His wife would be long sleeping, but the ponies would come to the gate.

James Bruce wandered the deserted corridors of LEVIATHAN's lower bridge deck, brooding about Cedric Ogilvy, wondering if this would be Ogilvy's last voyage and wondering, too, about the absurdity of judging a man who was conning a ship he knew he couldn't handle himself. It was late. He saw no one in the library or the wardroom. The hospital was empty, the theater dark. The officers' dining salon's table was set for breakfast and the knives and forks tinkled faintly against each other as the empty ship's engines built to speed. There was, of course, absolutely no motion from the sea. No sea, no roller, no swell budged the ship, though when he had last been on deck, a stiff west wind was raising a nasty chop on the Channel.

The middle bridge deck, where the officers and petty officers slept, was equally deserted. He rang the elevator to take him to the captain's bridge deck, where his own luxurious guest suite was located. The company expected him to report on Ogilvy in two days. Was he too old? Had he lost his grip? Should he be replaced? That last was a bit of poor joke because they didn't exactly have a jostling queue of qualified men waiting at the quay for the berth.

Certainly Ogilvy wasn't the only ship captain in the world with a mean disposition and petty nature. Had he guessed he had sufficient maneuvering power or had he been lucky? Had he deliberately set up the pilot and his own third officer to embarrass them? Perhaps, thought Bruce, he could entice the chief engineer to reveal exactly what had transpired when Ogilvy had called for more power. Not likely. The men were of equal rank and unless a real grudge was held, and Bruce didn't know about one, the chief engineer would be circumspect in his reply. Nevertheless, he would try in the morning.

One thing was beyond dispute. Lucky or not, Ogilvy was winner hands down when it came to handling LEVIA-THAN. Bruce had boarded at Le Havre and had seen with his own eyes how the relief captain barely had control crossing the heavily trafficked Channel. Ogilvy made it look easy. Or was it a sham?

The elevator door opened, revealing an oiler in a dirty boiler suit. He ducked his head and reached for the control buttons.

"Which deck, sir?"

"Go where you're going," said Bruce, stepping in. "I'm not in a hurry."

The door closed. The oiler played nervously with his blackened fingernails as the elevator descended toward the engine room, then cleared his throat as if he thought he was expected to speak.

"Just takin' a breath of air, sir."

"Oh?" Bruce said politely.

"I go on deck whens I get a chance," replied the oiler. He sounded Glaswegian Irish, thought Bruce. The lift descended slowly. Bruce fancied himself a casual man who understood the ordinary seaman, unlike a lofty disciplinarian like Cedric Ogilvy, but he felt trapped in the lift, unable to think of anything to say to the oiler, yet feeling the obligation.

"Well, I imagine it gets rather hot down there."

"Oh, aye . . . but not so bad in the control room, sir. We pop in there for a wee cooldown."

"Yes, I imagine you do."

The elevator stopped and opened onto the roar of the engines, a deafening, deep, and thunderous din that obliterated the senses. It came as an afterthought that the thick and humid air was hotter than noonday in the tropics. While the body flinched from the noise and heat and the mind reeled at the enormity of the place, the eye fixed on the air-conditioned, soundproofed control room in the midst of the machinery. Refuge.

It contained the electronic monitors for the twin high-pressure boilers and the paired 35,000-horsepower steam-turbines, secondary, smaller boilers, freshwater evaporators, and a three-million-watt electric-power plant. Gray paint thickly coated the walls of steel and the mazes of pipe, the spindly catwalks and the studded decks.

Wisps of steam danced where certain pipes joined. Bruce shook his head angrily—dozens of steam leaks. LEVIATHAN needed a full day's repairs. Cedric would take care of it. He would shut her down on open water and plug them up.

"Sir?"

The oiler was hesitating in the doorway.

"What is it?" Bruce yelled over the roar.

"Can I talk to you?"

"Of course." He pushed a button and the door closed, blocking much of the noise. "What's the matter?"

"Nothing the matter, sir, really. Just . . . I go on deck

149

when I can. There's a point aft where you can see over the side."

Bruce nodded. There were wide notches in the gunnels for the stern cables. "Yes?"

"Not this last time but the time before. When we was coming up the Frog Coast?"

"Captain Ogilvy's last trip?"

"Aye. I was out gettin' air and gettin' wet." He grinned and his dark solemn face turned youthful. "Soaked to the skin I was. It squalled. I do that sometimes at the end of my watch. Warm up later in the shower."

"Yes," said Bruce. The seamen enjoyed extraordinary comforts on the big tankers. Private cabins with their own baths. A laundry service: clean boiler suits on each watch.

"I was watching the wake, sir. It's like a string we never let go. Tied to the hull, if you know my meaning, sir."

Bruce nodded. He had once seen a sailor throw himself into that string, mesmerized by the endless flow. The oiler rambled on. Bruce listened, his expression thoughtful, his mind elsewhere. So many sailors were like this man. Quiet loners who juggled unspoken words for days on end, then suddenly spouted fanciful thoughts—poetic, or naive—and just as suddenly fell silent again. He waited for the man to run down. Abruptly, he snapped alert.

"What?"

"Like I say, sir. It's my feeling we hit something."

"*Hit* something? When?"

"It all come bobbin' up in the wake." His blackened fingers played in the air. "Like knots on the string."

"What?"

"Pieces. Floating things. White things. Just a handful. Couldn't see too much. It was soft. Mist. And the deck is lofty."

"When?"

"Off the French coast, sir, as I was saying. The trip before last."

"What do you think the ship hit?" asked Bruce, trying to conceal his concern.

150

"I don't know, sir. Maybe that doctor's boat."

"Why didn't you tell the investigators?" Bruce asked sternly.

"They didn't ask the engine crew, sir."

Bruce ground his teeth. Every now and then the ancient engineroom–deck rivalry still reared its head. In times past, when the deck crew bunked forward and the engine crew aft, ships were often divided into two camps, each bristling with self-importance and convinced that the other, if not closely watched, would allow the ship to founder. Bruce himself had been a cadet in the old Clan Line *Mutlah* on a voyage beset with such hostility. The ore ship broke up at night, and at dawn the bow and stern floated separately and not a man on either waved.

The investigators who had examined Hardin's charges had failed to consider that an oiler might have been on deck. And an oiler not asked was insulted, so he had said nothing. Probably best this way. Let it be. "Well," he said, pushing the door button and admitting the engine roar, "Thank you for telling me. I'm sure it was nothing."

"Do you think we hit the doctor's boat?"

"No. And I wouldn't bandy that about. You'd upset people."

"Yes, sir. Um, sir?"

"Yes?" Bruce asked briskly.

"Why is that helicopter on board with a gun?"

"What gun?"

"A big machine gun, sir. Mounted. Some of the lads saw it when they tied her down."

"As far as I know," said Bruce, "we're delivering it to a sheik in Qatar." He forced a grin and patted the oiler's arm. "You know the Arabs. If we've got a toy, they want it."

"That's for sure, sir. Good night, sir."

Bruce ascended to the captain's bridge deck, cursing the Company, himself, the helicopter pilot, and Ogilvy for predicting what had just happened.

"There are no secrets at sea," Ogilvy had snapped that afternoon in his cabin. "You'll panic my crew. This is not a warship and these are not fighting men."

Bruce had paced about Ogilvy's cabin, pleading and cajoling, while the captain sat ramrod straight at his desk. He explained again the information that British intelligence had delivered to the Company's offices in London. Dr. Peter Hardin, the man who claimed that his yacht had been run down by LEVIATHAN, was suspected of stealing a man-carried antitank rocket and was last seen three weeks before sailing from England. The conclusions were obvious.

"He is mad," said Bruce. "And armed with a deadly weapon. We must protect the ship."

"I am quite capable of protecting my ship from a lunatic on a sailboat," Ogilvy replied. He stood abruptly, a head taller than Bruce and dressed in full uniform—navy pants and jacket, white shirt, dark tie, and gold on his sleeve—and he made Bruce feel uncomfortably short and round and a little shabby.

Bruce hooked his thumbs in the pockets of his windbreaker. There was nothing left to argue.

"Cedric," he said, unable to meet his eye. "The Company insists. You must take the helicopter."

"And if I don't?"

"I'm sorry. It's not just my decision."

Ogilvy had flushed darkly. His lips had tightened at first, but then his jaw moved up and down behind the flesh in an old man's expression of bitter defeat.

"If it's Hobson's choice, I'll take my ship." He raised one finger, which curled back into his fist as he spoke. "But remember, that helicopter pilot is under my command, no less than the lowest cook's boy in the galley."

As LEVIATHAN rounded the corner of France in bright sunlight the next afternoon, the Bell Ranger rose from its deck, buffeted by the passage winds of the ship's sixteen knots and a ten-knot crosswind blowing off the Atlantic. Angling its bubble nose toward the airflow, it headed

152

east for the port city of Brest. Aboard were its pilot and the company staff captain, James Bruce.

From the air it was possible to compare the enormous size of LEVIATHAN to the lesser ships that were steaming through the juncture between the English Channel and the Atlantic Ocean. Skirted with white froth like an island that chopped ocean waves into surf, the ship was almost double the length and breadth of the largest crude carrier in sight, and three times as long as the freighters. And even as ships they had flown over disappeared behind, LEVIATHAN remained visible. The pilot could still see it aft of him like a distant mountain range, when he spotted the yellow coast of France and zeroed in on a Brest navigational radio beacon.

He aimed for a landing in a white circle on the end of a pier in the harbor, working his hands and feet on the pitch sticks and tail rotor pedals to lower the helicopter levelly while it tried its damndest to fly up, down, forward, back, and sideways all at the same time. But despite the enormous concentration he conjured for the approach, memory tortured him. He had crashed in flames on a Texas dock pad just like this one, which was why his red face didn't move much and why one of his nostrils was noticeably larger than the other, and why two fingers of his gloved hand were curled as rigidly as the barbs on a wire fence.

A slight, swarthy man huddled just beyond the rotor wash, clinging to a cheap suitcase with one hand and defending his turban with the other. The new steward to replace the poor son of a bitch he had ferried into the Southampton hospital the night before.

There was a black limo waiting for the Englishman who had hired him. He felt his eyes on his face, but when he turned, once the craft was solidly on the ground, Bruce looked away.

"Here you are, my man," the pilot shouted above the whine of the engine. "You did say Brest."

Bruce gestured to quiet the engine. He let it wind down until they could speak without yelling. Out of the corner

153

of his eye he noticed the steward hesitating, wondering if he should come to the craft or wait to be called.

"Now listen to me," said Bruce. "They've seen the gun, but I've passed the word that you're delivering the helicopter to a shiek in Qatar. Try to support that story as long as you can."

"What the hell for?" said the pilot. "They're going to get kinda suspicious when they see me taking off every time a sail goes by."

"You won't see that many sails," said Bruce. "It's a much bigger ocean than you think, but the point is you mustn't rile Captain Ogilvy. In fact, try to stay out of his sight."

"Don't worry," the pilot replied with a distorted grin. "I don't much like him either."

"He doesn't want you aboard, but we insisted."

"I don't give a damn what he wants," said the pilot. "You hired me, you're the boss."

"No," snapped Bruce, appalled. "*He* is the boss. He is master of LEVIATHAN. That means that his word is law. Absolute law."

"Got it."

"Don't forget."

"The captain's the boss. I'll keep out of his way."

"There's one other thing. . . . We know that Hardin has a rocket and a forty-five-caliber automatic. We don't know what else he has."

The pilot had flown in Cambodia. "I been shot at before." He grinned again. His cheeks cruelly parodied the reflex. "But never by a guy in a sailboat."

"I wouldn't give him the opportunity," said James Bruce. "I would kill him first."

11

A week before LEVIATHAN sailed from Southampton, there had been a night when Hardin steered close to the West African coast—so close he imagined he could smell the Sahara Desert. The sea swelled gently. The sky was overcast, the night pitch-black. He looked for a light in the sea-lanes on the western horizon.

Ajaratu was sleeping on the port cockpit seat, unaware of the slight course change that had brought them near the land. It was quiet, and warm enough to wear shorts. Once when she moved in her sleep, her fingers brushed his bare leg. Hardin edged away, closer to the shush and bubble of the stern wake, and continued watching the darkness to the west.

LEVIATHAN was out there, close at hand, deeply laden and bound for Europe. But tonight it was only a mark on his chart where his course would pass its course.

"Land!"

Eleven hundred miles farther south, seven days later, the Swan was heeling before a strong northeast breeze off the coast of Sierra Leone. Ajaratu bounded onto the boom, clutched the sharply tilting mast, and waved exuberantly at an almost indistinguishable blue line between the white-caps and the darkening eastern sky.

"Sherbro?"

Hardin pointed the bow toward the island. The sails spilled the wind and the Swan righted. Ajaratu jumped off the boom. The compass card swung seventeen degrees. Hardin noted the bearing to the island, put the boat back on course, gave Ajaratu the wheel, and went below to the nav station.

155

On the chart, he penciled a line to Sherbro at the same angle as the bearing to the landfall. It put them three miles south of a dead-reckoned position he had plotted hourly since his noon sun shot by calculating the distance the Swan had traveled through the water, her course, her leeway, and the thrust of the Guinea Current. Fifty miles in eight hours. Three and a half thousand in three and a half weeks. The Swan was fast and they'd had good wind.

They had reached from England on stiff westerlies past the Bay of Biscay, and when the French waters were astern, they picked up an east wind—a powerful *levanter* —that drove them by Spain and North Africa almost to Grand Canary Island. Then, stranded between the dying *levanter* and the top of the northeast trade winds belt, they had ghosted south in baffling airs. It was several frustrating days before they caught the trades, but then the Swan responded with blazing twenty-four-hour runs that were making up the lost time.

He checked his navigation with the loran, and the electronic instrument gave a position satisfyingly close to the one he had plotted.

"Sherbro," he reported when he came back to the cockpit.

"Couldn't we just stop a moment? Just for vegetables. I want a carrot so badly I could eat the rudder."

"We'll be in Monrovia the day after tomorrow."

Her grin faded. "Yes. I keep forgetting. This feels as if it could go on forever."

"Sorry." He stared at the water. He had told her that he had to reach Rio before the hurricane season. It had a likely ring, even though, as far as he knew, Rio de Janeiro didn't have a hurricane season, but he was becoming practiced at concealment, and the small lies came more and more easily. He had taught her a lot about sailing the boat, but she was still a stranger to this world and she believed everything he said, even that his radio calls from Miles were weather reports.

The lying bothered him. He was reverting to the closed person he had been before he had loved Carolyn. After

156

many years with her he had come to believe that there were no hidden meanings, no secret messages, when Carolyn spoke.

"Peter."

"What?"

"Let her go."

"Take the wheel." He hurried below, climbed into his bunk in the main salon, and stared at the teak ceiling. She came after him almost immediately. He stared past her, across the cabin, out the port windows. As the boat was heeling, he saw only the deepening sky.

"Who's minding the store?" he asked.

"Walter." She'd named the self-steering gear after the politician's son she was supposed to marry, claiming that they shared similar attributes of tiresome dependability.

"Walter can't see ships and we're in the shipping lanes."

She fingered her gold cross. "Come with me. It's going to be a lovely evening. Come on, we'll have a drink before dinner."

Hardin gazed at her. She was always there. Several times he had stumbled into depression and each time she had coaxed him out of it. He said, "Don't you ever get tired of inspiring me?"

She grinned and her teeth gleamed like pearls. "I'm certainly not going to spend my first vacation in ten years with a grump."

Hardin's face turned cold.

"I'm sorry," she said. "I don't mean to make light, but you've seemed quite happy these past few days. I thought it would be all right."

He swung his feet off the bunk. "Forget it. Let's have that drink."

"I'll have my usual." She smiled happily and sauntered out of the cabin and up the companionway. Hardin paused to watch her go. She had beautiful legs and she was wearing a bikini. He smiled, recalling the tentative way she had worked up to the garment. At first she had worn shorts and a halter, then a two-piece that conformed prettily to her

157

long figure. Only after a week had she unwrapped a pale-blue bikini, still in the store's tissue paper.

Hardin had gradually stopped kidding himself and admitted that he enjoyed looking at her. She was simply too beautiful and interesting a companion to deny an attraction. But he felt too close to Carolyn, and too torn up inside, and too empty to want anything more from Ajaratu than her company and her strength, so he ignored the attraction exactly as he would have if Carolyn had still been alive.

He mixed two vodka and tonics, a weak one for her, and carved up the last two limes to extract decent wedges from the molding fruit. Ajaratu raised her glass. "To land. May it fall where it ought."

Hardin smiled with her and drank.

The sun was dipping toward the horizon. The sky was turning violet and the water dark blue. Wispy high cirrus clouds purpled in the west and stars lighted on the eastern horizon.

"It is heaven," Ajaratu said softly.

The boat was running under mainsail and genoa, pushed by a light wind from the northeast. The trades carried this evening a faint smell of land, a sweet hint of the African shore. The sun sank lower.

"What is that?" she asked.

"I'm not sure."

Hardin had been eyeing the strange shape for several minutes. It was as tall as it was wide, a blue smudge crossing her bow, miles ahead. He fixed it in his binoculars and whistled. Handing her the glasses, he altered course slightly west so as to pass closer to it.

"What is it?" she asked, peering through the glasses, adjusting the focus.

"Square-rigger," said Hardin. "Must be a training ship. Can you count the masts?"

"Three." Her eyes were phenomenal, but untrained. She could see farther than he could, but not as much. As the Swan drew near enough to make out detail, Hardin thought of his father. He would be over ninety if he were

158

alive. Nearly eighty years ago he had sailed ships like that. It moved past, too far to make out its name, a ghostly stack of sails, blue in the distance, pointing the red where the sun had been.

Ajaratu asked if he was hungry and brought up a tray of cheese and cold canned meat. When it was dark, they sat beside each other and drank coffee and talked. It had been an easy three weeks, despite the long distance they had sailed, with gentle weather. Neither was tired, and in this tropical July weather they had taken to supplementing three or four hours of cabin sleep with naps on deck.

At the end of a comfortable pause, Ajaratu suddenly asked him why he had stopped practicing medicine. He gave her his standard answer: He had become too busy designing medical instruments.

"But I wonder if you took up instrument design out of interest or as a way to leave medicine?"

"Both," he said honestly. "I found that I liked the definite *yes-no* aspects of engineering more than the artistic *maybe* of medicine. Do you know what I mean?"

"I know that medicine means *maybe*."

"It's hit or miss," said Hardin. "I missed once and it kind of got me."

"Patients die," she answered. "It's their nature."

"Mine didn't die. But she went through hell because of me. For years. She was a friend. A nurse I had known for a while. I didn't exactly treat her at first, it's just that she started coming to me because she didn't get any satisfaction elsewhere. She was a black woman."

"Is that why you're comfortable with me?"

"I think that I'm comfortable with your blackness because you are. I guess that's because you're African. You seem glad of what you are."

He felt her shrug beside him. There was an edge in her voice when she spoke. "That doesn't make me any more authentic, you know. I just happen not to be a welfare patient in a New York City emergency room. What happened with your friend?"

"She was nervous, overweight, unable to sleep, and suf-

159

fering gastric disorders. She'd had the condition since she was eighteen, and every doctor she went to told her she suffered hypertension—which is common among American blacks—or she needed psychiatric help to get to the source of her anxiety.

"I ran every test in the book. Nothing. She finally decided to do something about it herself. She'd been studying Zen and yoga and chanting and she decided she could use her heightened awareness to, as she put it, 'look into her body.' She looked in and she saw thyroid. Finally I ran everything again and she was right. You know what?"

"Graves' disease."

"A young woman's disease. You're a young woman. You remembered that out of the thousands of diseases you read about in school, but I forgot. It was advanced and the thyroidectomy didn't work, so she's got to take pills for the rest of her life."

"Doctors' errors are more telling than other people's."

"I like things clear. That's why I like sailing. What the ocean wants, the ocean gets. And if you feel the need to be absolutely right about something, you can polish your navigation. You can do everything right, strictly according to procedure, on the ocean, and it'll still kill you; but if you're a good navigator, at least you'll know where you were when you died."

"You're absolutely crazy, Peter."

"It's true," he laughed. Then, as if the word "died" had pricked his memory, he stopped laughing.

Ajaratu quickly changed the subject.

"But your navigation seems so haphazard. You'll say our course should be one hundred and eighty-four degrees and then you sail one eight five."

"It's easier to sail a big point on the compass. You know, easier to read. You have to remember that a sailboat naturally wanders—the winds push it sideways and the waves shove it—so you have a built-in error anyhow. You can try to sail one eight four, but why not admit ahead of time that you're going to sail, at best, within five degrees of the course you want? Your plotting is approximate. That's what dead reckoning is all about. Approximate speed, approximate current, and approximate compass bearings give you an approximate course. When you have to know exactly where you are, you ask your chronometer, and the sun and the moon and stars. They don't lie."

Ajaratu stretched out on the cockpit seat and looked at the night sky. It was pitch-black now, studded with stars. "I can't get over how they are different colors," she said. "Is that red one Rigel?"

"Betelgeuse."

Hardin sat on the floor of the cockpit and guided her finger across the diamond of Orion. "Reverse the initials. Betelgeuse, red, and Rigel, blue. What's the orange star?"

"Aldebaran."

"Good. And the brightest one?"

"Sirius."

"There's Vega. And that's Capella, the goat. See her kids?"

"Yes."

He got the sextant and took three sightings on each of the four stars, measuring their angles of altitude. Then he went below and looked up the average of each of the measured angles in the Nautical Almanac. He worked out his position on the chart, then turned out the red chart table light, and rejoined Ajaratu in the cockpit. He thought she was asleep, she was so quiet, but she spoke after a minute.

"Where are we?"

"Where we should be. . . . Are you cold? Want a blanket?"

It was very dark, but he saw her arm blacken a line of stars as she raised it from beneath her head and touched her body.

"It's so warm," she said. "I forgot I'm still in this swimsuit. Feel my skin. See how warm?"

Hardin extended his hand, pale in the star light. She took it in hers and pressed his fingers to her belly. "See? Warm."

"You're shaking."

161

"Oh?" She held his hand to her trembling form.

"Ajaratu?"

"Yes?"

"You are very, very lovely."

"Do you think so?" she asked in a small voice.

"I do. And you're very young and—"

"Are you preparing an excuse?"

"No. . . . I just . . . I don't know what to say."

"I do," she said. "I think I fell in love with you the first time I saw you."

He felt a morbid loyalty to Carolyn, as if she were still alive and he would kill her if he broke the bond between them. He said, "I feel cast in the role of older, wiser seducer."

"Older wiser seducer? Haven't I the right to want you? Did it ever occur to you that *I* would seduce *you*, take you from your wife?"

"No. You're a very young and sheltered religious woman."

"Therefore?"

"Well, are you?"

"Yes. All of those things. What about them?"

"They make me responsible for you."

"I was right the first time," she said, sounding hurt. "You've prepared an excuse."

"You flatter me," he replied, wondering if she could soften him; the thought of losing his hate was frightening.

"Flatter you?" she said angrily. "You're not talking to me, Peter. You're having a conversation with yourself." She stood up and started toward the companionway, then stopped and stood still for a long moment. After a while, she sat back down and cradled her head to her knees. She said, softly, "There is going to come a time between us when I demand things of you, Peter. You had best know that. I won't always let you be."

Two days, thought Hardin. He'd drop her in Monrovia in two days. He'd be all right when he was on his own again.

As if she could read his thoughts, she said, "I might

162

pursue you." She laughed. "That would be quite something. There you would be, making radars and thermometers, and who should appear on your doorstep in New York City but a tall, black doctor from Africa. Whatever would you do?"

"I would like to see you in New York."

"Perhaps you will."

Hardin chuckled.

"What?" she asked.

"You'll hate me, but I was thinking about a cartoon. A couple embracing under the stars on a summer night in the country, and the woman is saying, 'I know you'll call me in New York, but could I hold your watch?' "

Ajaratu put her mouth to his ear. Her breath was warm. She said, "I shall faint outside your office. Passersby will bear my body to your workbench. You will put down your soldering gun and revive me, like a good doctor."

The Swan heeled. She buried her bow and the wake grew suddenly louder. The wind was rising as the land, cooling in the night, exhaled over the sea. She heeled further, burying her lee rail in the black water.

Ajaratu disengaged the self-steering and took the helm while Hardin replaced the genoa with a smaller jib. He thought that the excitement which had risen between them had cooled in conversation, but he was wrong. As he stowed the genoa, his mouth grew dry thinking of her.

The land breeze brought cloud, which blotted out the stars. He felt Ajaratu's hand on his cheek. "I can still see you," she whispered, caressing him tentatively. "You glow."

Hardin shuddered. Her hand passed over his jaw and her fingers trembled on his mouth. He parted his lips and touched his dry tongue to her palm. He moved toward her, feeling clumsy, blind in the darkness, his mind numb. Her shoulder touched his and she pressed against his chest and she was liquid in his arms and he felt like scaly, rusted iron.

Her lips found his. She kissed him, then buried her face in his neck. He reached for her, caressed her silken skin, felt excitement in spite of himself, and with it ease. He played his hands gently over her body, felt in the dark for her face and lifted it to his mouth and kissed her long and deeply.

Together they lay down on the cockpit seat, their lips locked, their legs entwining. She tasted of cinnamon, he thought, and when he unhooked her bikini top her breasts swelled against his fingers as firmly as her velvet tongue entered his mouth. Her hands grew less tentative and moved emphatically over his body.

He tensed as they glided down his belly. Then he stopped her.

"What's wrong?" she breathed.

He said nothing as he stared into the black night, his eyes and mind filled with Carolyn, his body empty.

"Peter?"

"I'm sorry," he muttered.

There was a long silence, broken only by the noise of the boat ghosting through the water. When Ajaratu spoke, her breathing had returned to normal and her voice was calm.

"I'm sorry, Peter."

She touched his face. He jerked back, too late to stop her from feeling his tears.

"Oh, I'm so sorry. Oh, you poor thing."

"Sorry to disappoint you," he said bitterly.

"It's my fault."

He stared at the dark for several minutes. "What?"

"You don't disappoint me. I wanted too much. I wanted to take, but I couldn't give."

Hardin waited, but she said nothing more. "What?" he repeated. "What do you mean?"

"It's all right, Peter," she said, her voice lightening artificially. "It doesn't matter."

Confused, but sensing that she was even more confused, Hardin said, "Would you please tell me what you're talking about?"

"Some other woman will help you better than I can."

164

It took a moment for her words to sink in. When they did, he sat upright. "Oh, for Christ's sake! You think I can't because you—Oh, for Christ's sake!"

"I thought I could excite you."

Hardin exhaled loudly and looked up at the black sky. The cloud was thinning in spots, and clumps of pale stars shone down. He could see her silhouette move as she replaced her bikini top. He felt reprieved. It was over and he and Carolyn were still intact.

"Would you like a cup of tea?" Ajaratu asked. She brushed past him toward the companionway and paused at the hatch, waiting for an answer. He could barely see her outline in the dark, but something about the stiff and awkward angle at which she held herself told him that she had lost her knowledge of her own grace. He saw her maimed by his failure.

He rose to his feet. She waited. He approached her, then reached hesitantly to comfort her and embraced her like a child. She stood still and listened wordlessly while he patted and stroked her back and tried to explain that his inability to make love was no fault of hers. After he finished, she rested her head on his shoulder.

"I suppose I believe you," she said, touching his arms, rubbing them with her fingers. "But I'm still very sorry that I can't be the one to help."

Hardin drew her closer. "Thank you," he whispered. "I'm sorry too." They clung tightly and gradually his mind began to blank out all but the comforting touch of her hands on his arms and his own hands on her back. Her skin felt as soft and smooth as warm satin.

Like a far-off light that appears on the horizon without prelude, he felt a tiny core of desire where there had been nothing. It spread rapidly into his thighs. He moved against her and pleasure tumbled through his body.

"Ajaratu."

He crushed her body to his, her mouth to his mouth, driven by a powerful desire too strong for art or skill or thought of anything but the taste of her mouth and the

165

sleek firmness of her body. When at last he released her, he laughed aloud. "Disregard everything I said."

She laughed with him, breathlessly, and pressed closer. "Perhaps I *am* the one," she murmured.

Hardin bent his head and kissed her breasts, slowly and lovingly, searching for her excitement. Then he caressed the long beautiful insides of her thighs until she moaned with delight, and, drawing her with him with touches and kisses, he led her down the companionway to his berth.

He awakened in a panic.

A noise. The shipping lanes.

He was in his berth. Ajaratu stirred beside him, her hands reaching sleepily. He slipped off the berth onto the settee, then down to the sole and felt his way across the cabin and darted up the companionway.

There was still cloud. The night was black as coal. He saw no lights. The Swan was sailing comfortably, on course. He trimmed the luffing jib and the self-steering and went below as the noise repeated.

The radio. He'd forgotten to turn it off after eight o'clock.

A muted squawk from the earphones. Not loud, but different enough from the boat sounds to catch attention. He sat at the chart table and put on the headset. It was Miles, broadcasting on his own direct link radio. He had made initial contact several days before to report that LEVIATHAN was scheduled to off-load at Bantry Bay and Le Havre and might take two more days at a third port, depending upon the market.

Tonight, he said, "Kilo, Uniform, Xray."

They were using international alphabet flag code for privacy. LEVIATHAN was *Zulu*, which really meant shore stations. Hardin was *Hotel*. Miles was *Mike*. Startled, Hardin focused the navigation light on the flag-and-pennant chart above the chart table. His memory was correct.

"Repeat," he said, pressing the transmit button.

Miles's signal was the same. "Kilo. Uniform. Xray."

Kilo, stop instantly. Uniform, standing into danger. And Xray, stop your intention. A redundant, unmistakable "Cancel, cancel, cancel."

Hardin dropped code. "Why?" he asked, stabbing the voice button.

"Xray, Xray, Xray!"

"Why, dammit?"

He heard Ajaratu stir on the other side of the thin bulkhead. She called his name in her sleep. He glanced around the edge of the nav station and saw her turn over in the berth and face the other way.

"Why?" he whispered into the microphone.

A staccato drilling sound interrupted Miles's reply. The Russian radar interference. It rattled like the coins in a blind beggar's cup. He waited, fuming, while it chattered in his ears. What the devil was Miles talking about?

The night Miles had boarded him in the channel, Hardin had refused to accept his coy reference to a democratic state in need of a new weapon.

"You mean Israel?" he had shot back.

Miles had smiled. "Is there anything else you would like to know?" He listened, his smile undisturbed, while Hardin aired his suspicions. Then he had answered him with a single phrase. He wanted Israel to regard oil tankers as "targets of opportunity."

What if, he had asked, Israel demonstrated to the oil-producing nations and their economic allies, the consuming nations, that the crude-carrying tankers vital to their mutual existence were vulnerable to acts of terrorism on the high seas?

"They'd blow you off the face of the map."

Not Israel *per se*, Miles had retorted with heavy irony, but uncontrollable Jewish terrorist groups. "The whole world is willing to believe that the Black September doesn't really represent Palestine, just because they are Palestinian and draw support from Palestinians, and seek refuge in Palestinian camps." He had nodded at the cabin sole which concealed the weapon. "You pose a serious threat, Mr. Hardin."

167

"I'm not Jewish."

"Your wife was Jewish," said Miles. "Do you remember the Hebrew name you were given when you married Carolyn in Rabbi Berkowitz's study on East Sixty-eighth Street?" He nodded impatiently. "Yes, we learned something about your life. Do you remember your Hebrew name?"

"Chaver Israel."

"Friend of Israel," Miles translated. "It's fitting that a friend of Israel would inspire other Jews to seek out targets of opportunity. Don't you think?"

"Two thousand oil tankers a month round the Cape of Good Hope," Hardin had protested. "You can't stop the flow of oil."

"We can certainly disrupt it," Miles had replied. "And what more dramatic demonstration of that ability than sinking the biggest ship in the world. LEVIATHAN—"

"No!" Hardin had shouted. "It's not yours. It's mine. It's my loss, my fight, and my revenge. Leave it alone."

"It will be yours, Dr. Hardin. All I offer is the one thing you can't do yourself. Surveillance. I'll tell you a half day in advance exactly where the ship is. She's yours to sink. Your victory."

"I'm not looking for a victory."

Miles had chuckled. "That's fortunate. Because we'll claim it privately, regardless of whether you accept our help. In fact, Dr. Hardin, perhaps we could arrange it so you wouldn't be implicated. Perhaps you won't be a fugitive."

Hardin had replied, "All I want to do is sink it."

"Then let us help."

The Russian woodpecker stopped abruptly. Hardin turned up the volume and strained to hear through the hiss of the headphones. He glanced at Ajaratu, barely visible in the red glow of the chart light. She was fast asleep, her body instinctively braced against the Swan's gentle heel.

Miles's voice came in loud and clear. "Xray."

"Why?" snapped Hardin. "Did Zulu sail?"

"Yes. They found you out."

Hardin's mind raced. They would try to dodge him. "So?"

"They've taken a helicopter."

Hardin pressed his fingers to his temples and tried to think. Could he attack at night? No. Distances were too deceptive in the dark. A dull ache grew in his stomach.

"How did they find out?" he asked, knowing it mattered not at all.

"Similar to the way we did. Sorry."

Miles sounded genuinely compassionate. Hardin said nothing. The airwaves hissed in his ears. After a while he stopped trying to find a way to blame the Israeli for what he knew was his own carelessness in Germany. He wondered, if he had it to do again, whether he could have killed the soldier who sold him the weapon, to keep him quiet. He shuffled through the charts in the drawer beneath the table.

"Still there?" asked Miles's voice.

"I'll call in a week," said Hardin.

"What for?"

"I've got to think about this."

He turned off the radio and headed for the sail bins.

12

Captain Ogilvy's legs ached. They were thin beneath his tailored uniform and they felt as if they were sheathed with lead that weighted every step and squeezed his calves and thighs. The pain gnawed at his concentration, but he refused to leave the bridge while LEVIATHAN was still in close quarters.

He had last slept twenty-four hours ago at dockside the afternoon before sailing. While the ship was moored, his first officer was in charge of off-loading, his second of laying out their course to the Gulf, and his third of directing provisioning. On the high seas he trusted them to stand their watches. But whenever the ship maneuvered in heavily trafficked areas like the English Channel, the Cape of Good Hope, or the Quoins at the entrance to the Persian Gulf, he and he alone commanded LEVIATHAN. The others were good sailors, but only he understood the dimensions of the ship's momentum.

His legs were always the first to protest the long watches. Arteriosclerosis, the doctor had told him. Insufficient blood to the extremities. Pills to open the arteries did little more than flush his face. He had installed a proper commodore's chair on the bridge, just after and starboard of the helmsman. A big swivel device. But it wasn't like driving a bloody car. He couldn't just sit there. Not when he had to keep hopping up and down to view the radarscope and press his face to the bridge windows, and run out on the wings to get a look aft or abeam.

Forget the anticollision computer, the satellite navigation, and all the rest of the electronic aides. When your ship had to pick her way through a crowded channel like a plow horse in a barnyard, you didn't con her from an armchair. Not likely. You ran your bloody arse off just to see where she was.

Though he had been born the child of a laborer and a kitchen maid, Ogilvy affected the manners and speech of an upper-middle-class Englishman. Talent and ambition drove him from his obscure west-country town. He had been accepted, against virtually impossible odds, at Dartmouth after he had learned that British naval officers were expected to speak differently from seamen. The habits he had taught himself stuck; he might refer to a subordinate's colossal error as a balls-up or something that annoyed him greatly as being ruddy, but his officers rarely heard him utter the bloodys and arses that crewed his thoughts.

He puttered about the bridge, willing his legs to behave, extending his stay miles beyond necessity, reluctant to break off the grueling effort. Finally, when Brest was far astern and fifteen hundred miles of open Atlantic lay between LEVIATHAN's bow and the Madeira Islands, he turned to his chief officer, who was on watch.

"She's yours, Number One. Good night."

"Thank you, sir. Good night."

"I thought the off-loading went well."

"Thank you, sir."

"I hope our friends in Le Havre don't hear of it."

"Sir?"

"They might feel we were discriminating against them, don't you think?"

The chief smiled wanly. They had spilled two hundred gallons in the French port when a coupling parted. Ogilvy chuckled and left the bridge. He liked the sudden thrust to keep his officers alert and, though his chief had sailed with him for six years, thought it best to remind him of his responsibilities.

His personal steward, a frail Indian, drew his bath and laid out his pajamas, moving about the cabin with the swift quiet motions of an Afghan hound. After he bathed, Ogilvy lay in his comfortable double bed with the curtains drawn and a cup of hot chocolate at his side. Spasms of relief rippled luxuriously through his legs as he prepared for a solid twelve hours of sleep. His chief knew his habits and he would not be disturbed for anything less than Emergency Stations.

Channel markers, running lights, and the speckled sweep of the radarscope flashed before his eyes and he heard over and over the bearings repeated by the helmsman. He sipped the cocoa and waited for his mind to surrender command and leave the bridge. He was sixty-three years old and he knew how to be patient while natural processes ran their course.

The helicopter pilot wandered up to the bridge to watch the sunrise from the highest point on the ship. He hurried through the bridge house, ducking past the helmsman, and went out on the port wing, where the view was best and he wouldn't be in the way.

The size of the ship still amazed him. If the U.S. Navy had any smarts, he thought, they'd underwrite a few of these babies and build them so they could be converted into aircraft carriers. Set up a double-purpose merchant marine like the Russian Navy's.

Shoot to kill.

Bruce's last words still echoed in his brain—and forget what Bruce had said about Ogilvy. Bruce was his real boss. The pilot shivered. He had the right to blow the guy's head off. Like the war, only better. This guy didn't have any gooks backing his hand. A goddamned turkey shoot.

He shivered again, but for a different reason; whenever he started to feel good, he remembered the crash. His eyes wandered from the rising sun to the distant Bell Ranger. He hadn't completely lost his nerve, but this was his first job since the crash in Texas, and he'd taken it only because it meant flying over water.

He wouldn't be wearing this Halloween face if he'd ditched in the water instead of trying to save his passengers. No passengers on this job; just him and the craft and the gun. He tore his eyes from the helicopter and looked at the sea, rehearsing the emergency landing drill: Head for the water; lay her on her side just before she hits; climb out and start swimming.

He'd almost turned back from the hospital in Southampton, but the guy started screaming. The pilot rested his gloves on LEVIATHAN's vibrating rail and watched the waves for a long time.

The wing decks were wet with morning mist, and it was still chilly, when the third officer came on watch at eight o'clock and asked if he wanted a cup of coffee. The pilot stepped gratefully into the warmth of the bridge house.

The young men talked, leaning on the varnished wood rail in front of the bridge windows, watching the sea. The third had a wife—a bride of five months—in England. Wives were not welcome on LEVIATHAN, as they were on most oil tankers; Ogilvy's preference. The third's wife resented the fact that he would sail with Ogilvy anyway.

172

The helicopter pilot had a girl friend in Dallas. She was a flight attendant with ninety-percent-off flying privileges and she had promised to join him in Arabia.

"Do you think you're going to Arabia?" asked the third officer with a knowing smirk. "I've been in the P.G. sixteen times and the most I've seen of Arabia is a white line on the horizon. LEVIATHAN loads offshore."

The pilot's face twisted into a grin—prompting the third to wonder if his girl friend was from before or after his accident. "But I got a ticket off here." He nodded at the Bell Ranger. "Maybe I can wangle a leave and catch up."

"Maybe if you get chummy with the Old Man."

"He's got as much use for me as a cowman has for sheepdip."

The third nodded with studied sagacity. "Not an easy man to get close to," he intoned. "We've had some good chats, though. I think he rather likes me."

"What makes you think that?"

"We served together in P and O. He asked me along when he took LEVIATHAN."

"What's P and O?"

While the third explained about the Peninsular and Oriental Steamship Company and the positions he hoped to hold in it some day, a seaman came onto the bridge to relieve the man at the helm. The new man noted the course and speed and confirmed that the sea ahead was empty of obstacles and that the automatic pilot was functioning, then sat behind the yoke, which was moving slightly, controlled by the computer's invisible hand. The two helmsmen exchanged covert grins over the third officer's ambitions.

"It just hit me what this thing looks like," drawled the helicopter pilot. He tapped the glass, indicating the green decks beyond. They were bisected by gray pathways and the central catwalk, and scattered with dark pipes, black winches, towers, fire stations, and yellow valves. "It looks like a goddamned oil field."

"I wouldn't know," said the third.

"Yeah, right, you don't get off the boat. Well, I seen a

173

lot of 'em down home and that's what this thing looks like." He stared at the sea and shook his head. "I can't believe the son of a bitch is moving. Jesus! I know dirt farmers who built castles when they found less oil than in this thing in their back yard. And a guy in a sailboat wants to sink it. I'll be damned."

"Quiet!" hissed the third, glancing back at the helmsman.

All morning he'd been trying to devise a way to suggest that the Old Man tell the crew before they learned it as rumor. The helmsman gazed at the bow.

The pilot whispered, "It's crazy, man."

"Well, perhaps he is."

"You don't sound worried."

"It's as you said. One man."

"*And* one rocket. Pretty hard to miss a target this big."

"From the deck of a sailing yacht?"

"Maybe you've never seen a TOW. A nine-year-old with bifocals could hit this thing with a TOW."

"Well, I guess that's why you're along."

The pilot picked up one of the binoculars that sat on the wooden rim beneath the big square bridge windows and scanned the water.

"Hey! Look there."

The third looked where he pointed. A white dot on the horizon, dead ahead.

"That's a sailboat," yelled the pilot, bolting toward the chart room on his way to the lift.

"Disengage the autopilot!" cried the third.

A screaming thunderous racket tore Ogilvy out of his sleep. Incoming fire, was his first thought. It whisked him back forty years to a wartime Atlantic and he had his feet on the deck before he realized his error. The deck was thickly carpeted, not the cold wet steel of convoy stations.

The racket faded. Memory returned. He'd been up a few hours in the middle of the night, then back to bed, and he was groggy with sleep. He threw open the heavy curtains and looked out on LEVIATHAN's gigantic deck. The helicopter. It was ranging ahead of the ship. He rubbed his eyes and looked again. He saw a sail at ten thousand yards.

He put on his robe and rode the elevator one level to the bridge. 0930, said the chart room clock. His third officer was on watch, leaning on the rail under the bridge windows, drinking coffee and intently watching the helicopter. Ogilvy glided silently behind him.

"What the ruddy hell is going on, mister?"

The third stiffened to attention, put down his coffee mug, and slowly turned. He paled when he saw Ogilvy's expression.

"Sir?"

"Who authorized that takeoff?"

"He said he saw a sail, sir."

Ogilvy picked up a pair of binoculars. The helicopter was darting over the water, closing with the white sail on the horizon. The captain focused the glasses. Immediately, he banged them down and pointed a shaking finger at the radiophone.

"Raise him."

"Sir?"

"Immediately!"

"Sir!"

The third raced to the radio and made contact.

"Tell him to return to the ship."

"He says he's circling for a closer look."

"He is to return immediately!" shouted Ogilvy.

He stalked onto the bridge wing and watched the helicopter circle and grow large in the sky, while the distant *clip clop* sound of its main rotor gave way to the whine of turbine. The aircraft clattered to the deck. Ogilvy waited until the deck gang had secured it and the pilot was walking slowly toward the bridge tower. Then he switched the bridge telephone to public address.

"Pilot!" His amplified voice echoed grimly about the ship. "Report to the bridge!"

He waited, fuming, his body still aching with weariness

175

despite the long sleep, until his third ushered the pilot onto the wing.

"Where were you going?"

"Checkin' out a sailboat," he replied jauntily. Ogilvy noticed the anxious flicker of his eyes behind his sunglasses.

"Checking out a sailboat, did you say?"

The pilot shifted his feet. "Yeah. Like I'm supposed to."

"Pilot," Ogilvy said softly. "You will wait for permission from me or the senior officer of the watch before you leave this ship. Is that clear?"

"Yep . . . but, Captain . . ."

"But?"

"But if it's an emergency. If that guy is coming for us, do you want me to waste the time asking for permission?"

Ogilvy pointed at the sail. LEVIATHAN was catching up rapidly and the yacht was close enough to make out some detail. "Describe that yacht to me, mister."

The pilot shrugged. "It's a sailboat."

"Does it have any distinguishing features?"

The pilot squinted in the bright light. "Yeah. It's white. It's got a red sail in front."

"That is the spinnaker," said Ogilvy. "A headsail in the bow. It is attached to the forward mast. There is a second mast aft. Do you see that, Pilot?"

"Yep." His lips quivered in an apparent smirk.

Ogilvy continued as if he didn't notice. "That second mast is forward of the tiller. Do you see that?"

"Yeah. I saw that up close. Can't tell from here. You got good eyes, Captain."

"That is a ketch," said Ogilvy. "Repeat after me. Ketch."

"Hey, now come—"

"Ketch," Ogilvy said icily.

"Wait a—"

"Ketch."

The pilot wet his lips. "Okay. That's a ketch."

176

"Two masts, you ruddy nincompoop. A ketch. Hardin's boat is a sloop. One mast. One jib. Get me paper and pencil."

The pilot extracted a pad from the breast pocket of his nylon flight jacket. Ogilvy snapped it out of his gloved hands and drew a triangular profile with his gold pen.

"One mast, one mainsail, one jib. Sloop. And when you see one you ask permission to leave my ship. I'll not have some damned fool hopping off my foredeck whenever he takes it into his head to have a little jaunt."

He stormed back to bed, but he couldn't sleep.

The helicopter was a stupid way to protect LEVIATHAN. The crew would find out soon that something was wrong, which would get them worked up and nervous every time the damned thing took off. Bad enough they'd sailed in blood with the galley steward maimed by the mooring cable. There'd be no peace on this voyage until the helicopter was tied down and the pilot confined to his quarters. Ogilvy smiled. That bloke was in for a surprise when they reached southern waters.

Foolishness. Hardin was a minor threat at best. How in blazes did he think you could sink LEVIATHAN? Probably shared the popular delusion that an empty crude carrier was a gas-filled bomb awaiting a match. But every tank was so heavily inerted—the oxygen forced out by engine exhaust—that you could drop a burning house in and watch it go out.

One rocket against a ship a third of a mile long. The man was mad, or a fool. Not that a hit wouldn't do damage, which was why he had devised a simple, fool proof defense. Too simple to bother explaining to James Bruce and his lot at the company.

He donned his robe and slippers and rang his steward for tea, which he took into the office of his three-room suite. An oversize chart on one of the paneled walls showed the eleven-thousand-mile tanker route around Africa—the seas between Europe and Arabia. The North

Atlantic Ocean. The South Atlantic Ocean. The Indian Ocean. The Arabian Sea. The Gulf of Oman. The Persian Gulf—LEVIATHAN's waters.

Ogilvy had all the facts, all the times and all the distances in his mind, and now he grease-penciled them on the chart's plastic overlay. Hardin would have known LEVIATHAN's date of departure almost to the day by reading the marine journals. So why had he left England three full weeks ahead of the tanker?

In the answer was Hardin's plan.

Ogilvy had inquired closely about the yacht. It was much more important than the man's motivation and the range of the weapon, and the way he parted his hair. It was a fast boat; Hardin was likely to be competent and he had a woman to spell his watches, so one hundred fifty miles a day seemed a likely speed. Three thousand miles in three weeks, four thousand in four, the extra week being LEVIATHAN's cruising time to the target area.

The tanker routes were well known. They were obvious on any decent chart and it was clear that around the bulge of West Africa they became quite narrow where the ships cut close to the coast to save fuel costs. Ogilvy drew an oval around the tanker routes between points three and four thousand miles from England. The oval encompassed the bulge of West Africa. Included within the thick black lines were Dakar, the capital of Senegal; Freetown, Sierra Leone; and Monrovia, Liberia.

Within that oval, Hardin would try to attack. It explained his departure date. It was a narrow, easily surveilled hunting ground. And it offered an escape route— South America was only eighteen hundred miles away.

Ogilvy picked up dividers and uttered a small, private sound of satisfaction. The man was on a sailboat, for pity's sake. Nine knots maximum. Maximum. Six and seven much of the time. He didn't need a helicopter.

13

Ajaratu woke during the night. Hardin's overhead luminous dial clock said four. The boat was pitching and she was cold. She reached for Peter—remembering. Her body felt liquid, deep, and brimming. She tasted him in her mouth and smelled him on her hands. He wasn't there. A sail crackled sharply overhead like pistol shots. It invaded her memories and confused her.

Then the sound stopped and the boat lunged forward and stopped pitching and she realized that he had adjusted the rig. Trembling with cold and anticipation, she crawled into his sleeping bag and waited for him to trim the steering gear and come back to her. She awakened again at dawn, curled in a tight ball with her hands between her thighs, still alone. The boat was heeling. It sliced through a wave and spray plumed past the window.

The teak cabin was yellow-gray with first light. She found the parts of her bikini, put them on, and draped one of his work shirts around her shoulders. Then she shook out her hair with her fingers and went up to the cockpit.

Hardin was standing squarely behind the binnacle with both hands on the wheel, his eyes on the sails, his leg muscles flexing with the boat's motion. Bracing herself against the sharp heel, Ajaratu edged toward him and kissed him shyly. He reached around her and cranked one of the winches.

"You look like an old man," she said. "Your hair is white."

His face was caked with salt spray. She waited for a reply, got none, and looked around. Waves were lapping the Swan's lee rail. The stern wake poured furiously be-

179

hind them and the boat seemed to leap across the troughs.

"What's that?" she asked.

There was a third sail between the main and the big genoa, rigged like a jib from a new stay between the mast and the forestay.

"Staysail," said Hardin. "I rigged it last night."

"Why?"

"Speed. But it's not working too well; it's robbing the genny. That's the trouble with a sloop. On a ketch you've got seventeen places to hang a sail, but it just doesn't work that way with one mast."

Ajaratu nodded uncertainly. She had never seen the Swan strain so. What had been a broad and comfortable platform on the sea had become a tilting, racing sliver, cutting the water like an angry knife.

"Would you like coffee?"

"Please."

She edged back down to the galley. She tied the coffee-pot to the gas range with an elastic shock cord and braced herself against the stove as she measured the coffee. It was getting low. When they got to Monrovia, she would help him shop to provision the Swan for the crossing to South America.

Tears splashed onto the pot and sizzled away. It wasn't the leaving. She wouldn't shed those tears until after he had gone. But why hadn't he said anything about the night? She thought she had pleased him. She knew she had. She alone couldn't have felt such pleasure.

She poured the brewed coffee and climbed the companionway with his cup. The Swan was leaning way over. She looked at the water racing past and admitted what she had known since she had awakened. Hardin was driving the boat, racing for Monrovia, rushing to put her off, chafing to be alone.

He took the coffee with a quick nod.

"Would you like me to spell you?" she asked.

"Thanks." He moved aside so she could stand where she could see the binnacle, tapped the compass, and said, "One eighty on the nose."

The boat was close-hauled and it took her several minutes to adjust to the feel of it. It kept trying to turn into the wind and the wheel required more than the usual restraining pressure to stay on course.

Hardin corrected her twice—sharply the second time—before he sat and took a sip of his coffee. Soon he put it in the gimbled holder and cranked the staysail winch. Though he was no longer steering, his eyes were still restless on the sails. Ajaratu spread her feet on the slanting deck and gradually got used to the wheel. It tugged like something alive, but it took less strength than concentration to control it.

Hardin stood abruptly. Her eyes shot to the compass. She was afraid she'd gone off, but he said, "Head upwind a hair. I gotta drop the staysail. It's not pulling worth a damn."

She let the Swan go up. Hardin winched the sail in, ran forward, lowered it, and stuffed it down the forehatch.

"Back to one eighty!" he yelled as he went down the hatch to stow the sail. When he returned to the cockpit, he adjusted the sliding snatch block through which ran the genoa sheet. His eyes were busy, flicking from sail to sail, to the water, to the telltales, to the sky, and back to the sails. A luff rippled the main. He winched it out.

"Wind's shifting north."

"We're flying!" she said.

"And it's dropping off, dammit."

"You look tired."

"I'm fine." His eyes shot to the top of the main. "Watch the sail. It's telling you you're off."

"Sorry."

She brought the Swan back to one eighty. What was he doing? Why rush? What harm in a few days together? She brought her fingers to her throat, remembering the things they had done last night. Her cross was gone.

She laughed. "Do you want to hear something funny?"

"You're heading up."

"Sorry." She corrected, then spoke. "Do you remember

181

that you said I was religious? We broke the chain for my gold cross."

Hardin glanced from the straining staysail. His eyes met hers and for just a moment they softened his face in a way she had never seen.

"Thank you for last night."

Her heart flew. "Did you . . . ? I thought you were sorry."

He searched her face and brushed her lips with his, making her tremble. "I'm only sorry that it's not another time and another place."

"What other time?" she murmured.

"Any other time." He looked away.

"Did you see my cross?" she asked.

"No. It's probably in the berth." His attention returned to the sails.

The wind continued to shift toward the north, dropping in strength, until the main and the genoa were boomed far out and the Swan's speed grew slower and slower. When it was almost dead astern, Hardin said, "I'm going to try a spinnaker."

Ajaratu took the helm and followed the orders he shouted from the foredeck. After lowering the genoa jib, Hardin attached the spinnaker halyard to the big light sail, fastened the spinnaker pole, clipped on its sheets and guys, and quickly hoisted it opposite the main. Returning to the cockpit, he pulled the pole aft.

The sail filled like a balloon. The boat seemed to lift out of the water as the straining nylon bulged ahead of it. Hardin cast a triumphant glance at the boiling wake.

Ajaratu was captured by his excitement and the boat's powerful response. It surged through the sea, and because the wind was astern, it moved quietly, the only sound being the bow wave and the bubbling trail astern. It seemed to go faster and faster as the white sun rose in the limpid tropical sky. Even when the day grew hot and the water flattened, the Swan still flew.

Hardin controlled the spinnaker sheets. Its very size

182

made it delicate and he watched it closely, surveying its billowing surface, measuring the wind, testing, evaluating, accommodating.

Ajaratu became absorbed in the Swan's rhythm; she began to feel a mystical kinship with the sails and the lines, knowing almost ahead of time what to do to drive her best, when to ease off, when to take in, when to steer with the helm, and when to guide her with the sails.

They ran for hours, rarely speaking, married to their tasks, lost in the lifting, driving speed. At last, as the lowering sun yellowed like old paper, Ajaratu began to tire. Her concentration lagged.

"One eighty," snapped Hardin. "Steady."

"I have to eat," she replied. "You should, too."

Hardin said nothing.

"Can we ease off for a while? Let me make something to eat."

"I'll take her," he said. "Just be ready to come running if the wind picks up. It feels like it's going to."

She went below and again she worried that he regretted making love with her and wanted her gone, off his boat, out of his life. The boat rolled unpleasantly with the spinnaker and, as she had the coffeepot, she tied down the kettle to heat water for soup. She trimmed mold from the bread's crust, unwrapped some cheese, and cut up their last apple. The fresh food was almost gone, nothing left but the rows and rows of cans.

Suddenly she felt she had been at sea too long. She wanted to see land, to smell soil. She thought of a green salad fresh from the kitchen garden. Crisp lettuce and icy radishes. It was the rolling, she decided. The constant side-to-side motion was depressing.

While she waited for the water to boil, she tidied up his bunk and looked for her cross. It wasn't in his sleeping bag. Nor was it on the settee beneath the berth. She knelt on the settee, gripping the edge of the bunk, and laid her cheek on the foam cushion and tried to think of a reason not to cry.

183

Her cross glinted on the cabin floor. She crawled under the table, but when she tried to pick it up she found that the chain was caught in a crack in the floor.

It was time to douse the spinnaker.

The wind was rising quickly. He called Ajaratu. She didn't answer. Probably in the head where she couldn't hear. A strong gust caught the sail, pulling the Swan forward in an awkward lunge. He decided not to wait for her.

He engaged the steering gear, slacked the spinnaker guy, and started forward, snapping his safety harness around his torso and connecting it to the center line. As he reached up to release the spinnaker pole, the wind filled the headsail, even though he had slacked the guy. There was too much pressure on the pole to move it. He yelled for Ajaratu. The wind whipped the words away.

He hesitated, afraid to lower the bellying sail because if it fell ahead, the boat would run it over. Better to spill the wind. Fast. It was blowing hard. He raced back to the cockpit, slacked the spinnaker guy some more, and started to winch in the leeward sheet. It was too late. A powerful gust whipped the crest off a wave, wetted his face, and banged into the sails.

The spinnaker blew apart with a thunderous report.

Hardin gaped at the split nylon flapping like a pair of pants on a wash line.

"Son of a *bitch!*"

He leaped forward and caught the flailing spinnaker pole before it broke its mast fitting, secured it in its niche beside the cabin, then lowered the torn sail in stages, struggling to keep the billowing mess out of the water. When he had it down, he steered back to one eighty, set the self-steering, and stormed below to see what the hell had happened to Ajaratu.

The kettle whistle was shrilling and the steam had beaded drops of water on the teak cabinet doors behind the stove. Ajaratu was kneeling on the cabin floor. For a second he had the crazy thought that she was praying. Then he saw the floorboards heaped to one side. She was staring into the open pit of the bilge beneath the dining table. She faced him, her eyes wide with disbelief.

"What are you doing?" asked Hardin. He turned off the gas jet and the kettle quieted.

"I was trying to find my cross," she said in a choked voice. "The chain was stuck in a crack."

Hardin approached the bilge and looked in. She had pried the top from the wooden crate. He supposed he would have too if he had seen the U.S. ARMY stencil. The rocket was a deadly-looking cylinder, its thickness awesome, its purpose unmistakable, dark and evil as a lie.

"Are you mad?" she breathed, still crouching over the hole.

Hardin stared down at her, his hands working at his sides. Was this the price of letting go? Retribution for betraying Carolyn?

"It's madness!"

"No," said Hardin. "It's not madness."

"What is it then?" she asked loudly, rising and advancing on him, searching his face with anxious eyes. "Suicide?"

"It's my life," said Hardin. "Not yours. But no, it is not suicide. Now get up on deck!"

She planted her feet firmly and stared back at him. "Can you rationally say that you don't care about the lives of the people on that ship?"

"They'll have time to get off."

"Are you quite sure?" she said witheringly. "Or did you just think of that?"

"I don't have to convince you, Ajaratu. Take the helm. We're close to the shipping lanes." He knelt on the cabin sole and began replacing the floorboards. She stood over him, unmoving.

"If just one man doesn't get off in time you'll be a murderer."

"They'll get off."

"You don't realize what you're doing, Peter."

He looked at her coldly. "The helm."

She stalked up the companionway. Hardin finished re-

185

sealing the rocket crate, then went out on the foredeck to untangle the spinnaker sheets. The fore guy jammed in its eye fitting and he crouched at the stem, struggling to free it. It didn't matter about the spinnaker. He had another— and besides, it was an awfully big sail to fly alone. The Swan fell off a sea. The bow plunged and Hardin lost his balance. He had to drop the force guy and hold fast to the lifelines.

"Wear your safety harness!" Ajaratu yelled from the cockpit.

He ran to the cockpit where he'd left it. Even in light seas, he had drummed into her, wear the harness whenever working near the edge.

"Sorry," he said, as he buckled it on. "I forgot." He looked at her. She sat stiffly beside the helm. It sounded so stupid. She called him a murderer and he apologized for not wearing his safety harness. She returned his look with smoldering eyes.

"What do you want?"

"Nothing. It's funny. You hate me, but you want me to be careful."

"Do you think I could sail this bloody boat alone?" She burst into tears. "Please. I don't hate you. Listen to me, Peter, please."

Hardin sat beside her, surprised by her tears. She had been a cool, almost forbidding presence at her hospital, and unceasingly cheerful aboard the boat, but now she was dissolving like a child. Her body heaved and shuddered. He took her in his arms.

She pressed her face to his chest. "We've shared so much. I can't believe you're the kind of man to do such a thing."

Hardin gripped her shoulders, held her at arms' length, and forced her to meet his eyes. "Now listen to me. That ship destroyed everything I cared about."

"Care about new things," she demanded. "Care about living."

"Not until I'm through with the past."

"It's not for you to finish the past. It's done."

186

"It's not over."

"A man can't proclaim when a moment is over."

"The hell I can't."

"But vengeance is God's right, not yours."

"I was waiting for Him. Next you'll tell me that LEVIATHAN stomping my boat into the ocean was an act of God."

"Perhaps it *was* an act of God."

"Well you just consider this a reaction of man."

Her face set in hard lines and the tears stopped. Hardin stood up angrily. The boat was suddenly very small. He started forward to put up a headsail, then he grabbed her shoulders again.

"I'm going to tell you one more thing. You take it any way you want. I thought I was going crazy. Nightmares were tearing my head up. I was dying inside. Right up to the moment I knew for certain the one thing I had to do was sink that monster."

"Have you no doubts?"

He drew her closer. "I was afraid to make love to you. I thought you might soften me."

"Did I?"

"No. You made me a lot tougher."

"How?" Puzzled.

"You reminded me how happy I'd been."

She contemplated his face, searched his expression. "If I were on LEVIATHAN, would you still—"

"It wouldn't make any difference."

"What?"

"You'd get off with the rest of them."

"How can you be so sure?" she asked, her eyes probing his.

"You have no idea how big it is. It's not going to sink like a stone or vaporize. It will take a long time to die."

"You're out of your mind, Peter. If it's that big, how can you possibly sink it?"

"I know its flaw."

"You'll be killed."

"That's not part of my plan," he said with a small smile.

Ajaratu pulled away from his hands.

"What if I try to stop you?" she asked. "What would you do to protect your vengeance?"

Hardin stared at her.

"Would you kill me?"

He smiled coldly. "I've figured that out. I'm putting you in a dinghy at the Monrovia harbor and then I'm taking off like a bat out of hell."

"And what is to stop me from reporting your intentions?"

"Somebody beat you to it. They're hunting for me with an armed helicopter."

"How do you know that?"

"I know it."

"Then it's over anyway. You can't do it."

"Maybe."

"What are you going to do?"

Hardin gave her a thin smile. "So you can turn me in?"

She shook her head angrily. "I didn't say I would."

"I can't take the chance."

"What if I give you my word?"

"I'd suspect you were humoring a madman."

She brushed by him and disappeared down the companionway. He ran up the genoa and pushed the Swan to make up the speed lost since the spinnaker blew. The trade wind—unusually far south according to the Sailing Directions—blew steadily stronger, and occasionally the Brookes and Gatehouse speedometer showed an incredible ten knots.

Ajaratu returned to the cockpit. She was silent for an hour. Her face was devoid of expression, turned inward. Hardin watched the speedometer needle's fits and starts. He wondered if the instrument's propeller shaft was worn. He would check the speeds against the distance covered between sun shots as soon as he got another long run with the wind astern.

"Look," he said suddenly, leaning over the leeward side and pointing at the bow.

She hesitated before following his lead, but an involuntary cry of pleasure escaped her lips when she saw the trade-wind rainbow dancing in the gossamer spray of the bow wave.

"It's beautiful."

The colors were as distinct and pure as the light in a crystal prism. The rainbow blinked like a channel marker, appearing, disappearing, reappearing, scattering shafts of yellow, green, and blue that blended and fanned in radiant half circles as the spray rose and fell with the sharp bow.

"Look!" Ajaratu gasped.

The rainbow turned red—a color as deep and rich as a cardinal's cape.

"It looks like blood."

Hardin gazed somberly into the rainbow. It was as if the sea were bleeding when the Swan cut it.

"Do you have a plan?" she asked.

"What do you care?"

"I don't want you to be killed."

"Neither do I."

"I won't allow it," she said angrily. "I'll stop you."

"You can't. I told you they already know about me."

"Yes I can."

Hardin looked at her. Her mouth set primly and her eyes were deadly serious.

"How?"

"I'll make my father use his influence with the Liberians, the Ivory Coast, Guinea, Sierra Leone, the Senegalese, and Ghana. They'll catch you and impound your boat."

"Did it ever occur to you," Hardin asked, "that I might wrap a chain around your legs and drop you over the side?"

"Like a slave?"

"Stop being stupid."

"I feel a slave to you," she said softly. "But I know you wouldn't hurt me."

He looked at her coldly. If she thought that, he couldn't protect himself. "What do you think, we're in love because we screwed in the starlight?"

She hit him with the nearest thing at hand. It was the binoculars, and the right front lens caught him under the eye. He reeled back, clutching his face, too shocked to react. Her lips bared her teeth and she raised the heavy glasses to swing again. Her eyes were wild. Hardin brought up his hands to block the blow. Blood ran down his cheek. When she saw it, she hesitated, her arm in midair, and her lips slid trembling into place.

"Oh, God, what did I do to you?"

Hardin automatically put the Swan back on the course she had left when he released the helm. Astonished by her ferocity, he stared at the blood his palm left on the wheel. "Christ."

"I hurt you."

"I'm okay."

She lowered the binoculars. "I'm sorry. I never did a thing like that in my life. I never felt such anger."

"I didn't mean that," said Hardin, gingerly touching his cheek. "I'm sorry I said it."

She spread his fingers and examined the cut.

"I want to come with you," she said matter-of-factly.

Hardin looked at her. Her rage gone, she seemed very young, very vulnerable, very much the soldier's daughter raised in the convent. He said, unable to think of anything else, "What?"

"I'm coming with you."

"No way."

"I'll spell you. I'll keep you strong. Isn't that why you let me come this far?"

"Forget it."

"You *have* to take me."

"Oh no I don't."

"Yes you do. I know you won't kill me. But you know I would make my father catch you. So you have to take me."

Hardin stared at the water. She went below and returned with the small first-aid kit. When she had cleaned and taped the cut under his eye, he said, "Please, Ajaratu. Leave quietly at Monrovia."

"Anything but that."

190

"Go home and start your clinic. Go to school; do what you planned."

"I don't care about those things."

"Then find something you do care about."

"I have." She met his eye and Hardin had an awful feeling that she was less confused than he.

"Don't you have any doubts?" he asked.

"None."

"Would you really turn me in if I put you off at Monrovia?"

"I will."

Hardin shook his head in dismay. "Jesus Christ—listen, you better think about this. It's going to be very hard. You'll hate me in a week and hate yourself in two. And you'll hate the boat and the water and by then it will be too late to stop. We'll pass Monrovia tomorrow. You have until then to decide."

"I already have decided," said Ajaratu. "Where are we going?"

"Winter."

14

LEVIATHAN neared the Canary Islands the fifth morning out of Southampton.

Captain Ogilvy called his second officer to his office and without comment instructed him to make an unusual alteration in their normally undeviating course.

The second's brows rose and he looked at the Admiralty chart on the wall behind the captain's desk. Ogilvy casually rearranged the framed photographs of his wife, a woman he enjoyed more in her letters than in the flesh, and their daughters, whom he knew mostly from holiday cards, weddings, and announcements of grandchildren.

His desk faced the door. Beside the chart was a big window that offered a clear view of the vast green deck and the sparkling sea ahead of the bows. The office was furnished in the modern style of corporate grandeur, expensive leather chairs, deep blue carpeting, paneled walls and gold draperies. Had it not been for the ceaseless vibration that caused the captain's gold pen to walk across the polished desk top, it would have seemed that the white-haired executive and the youthful assistant standing before him were conducting business in an office tower high above a busy city.

The second officer looked again from the written course to the chart. His broad, open face was clouded with puzzlement. Ogilvy seemed oblivious that his number two was juggling conflicts.

Navigation was the responsibility of the second officer. Taking account of sea conditions and weather reports, he had to plot the most economical route for LEVIATHAN to sail. With transportation costs of well over a million pounds for a round trip between Europe and Arabia, every mile and hour saved represented enormous gains. Conversely, every mile and hour wasted brought harsh inquiries from the Company and a reminder that the expense of a hundred miles squandered might equal a second officer's yearly salary.

Should he question the captain's orders or bear the responsibility later for not raising the obvious objection of expense? You just didn't know with Captain Ogilvy. Sometimes when he was getting bored on a long run, the Old Man deliberately set you up for ridicule.

Ogilvy prodded him, his voice tinged with irritation. "Is there something on your mind, Number Two?"

"It will cost about seven hundred miles, sir."

"Twenty thousand pounds," Ogilvy agreed.

The second nodded doubtfully, screwed up his courage, and ventured, "It may run more like thirty thousand, sir."

"Thank you, Number Two," said Ogilvy, dismissing him.

The second officer's tensed shoulders sagged almost imperceptibly. He had pulled it off, aired his objection, and not suffered retaliation. But as he backed out of the door, Ogilvy called after him, "Perhaps you'll find a way to minimize the expense."

Bloody hell! He hurried up the single deck to the chart room behind the bridgehouse. The Old Man had trapped him after all. He had probably already worked out the new course and knew to the penny what it would cost. If he didn't duplicate the captain's calculations, Ogilvy would ride him for a week. He dreaded going to dinner without a solution.

He worked until noon, when his watch began, pausing just before for a quick plate of curry brought to his chart table by a Pakistani steward. Then he took the bridge from the third officer, shot LEVIATHAN'S midday position with the sextant, confirming the cool, silent lights of the satellite navigator, and spent the rest of his four-hour watch devising ways to cut the cost of skirting the leeward edge of the Cape Verde Islands.

He fed several schemes into the ship's computer, which had access to LEVIATHAN'S bunkerage, ballast, and engine performance, as well as weather, current, wind, and wave-height reports on the millions of square miles of ocean that would affect conditions on their route. The weather maps coiling out of the facsimile machines showed a deep depression forming in the Drake passage—the ragging storm-spawning waters between Antarctica and South America's Cape Horn. They'd be hearing from that one on their new course if the South Atlantic high didn't stall it.

By the end of his watch, he had settled upon a plan he could bring to dinner. He took a swim in the ship's pool, then had a nap to set him up for his night watch.

Whenever LEVIATHAN was steaming routinely on the open sea, there were two seatings in the officers' mess. The younger men—engineering and electrical juniors, thirds, and seconds, the radio officers, and the deck third, whose watch began at eight—dined at seven o'clock, while their seniors—the captain, the chief engineer, and chief electrical officer, and the desk second—gathered in Ogilvy's office for cocktails.

They dressed for dinner because Ogilvy was still at heart P and O and foremost among the old British line's traditions was Red Sea rig, officer's dress for tropical climates. They wore open short-sleeved white shirts—despite the frigid air conditioning—with gold-braided shoulder insignias, black cummerbunds, and dress slacks. Ceremony, Ogilvy had once explained to the second officer, was a shipboard necessity. Without it, isolation from the strictures of the land might breed disorder among the kind of men who had chosen the illusory freedom of the sea.

Ceremony also divided the tedious days aboard the automated ship into bearable blocks of time, each with specific expectations, functions, and conclusions. The second had awakened from his nap at six-fifteen, showered and shaved and dressed leisurely, timing his preparations so he would have to hurry the last few minutes not to be late to Ogilvy's cabin.

The sixty minutes allotted to cocktails was time enough to receive a cocktail from the steward, sip a third of it while inspecting the captain's prints and antique charts, chat up an officer he hadn't already talked to that day, settle down in an armchair for a natter with a couple of others, then rise for a second drink, which he finished just as the dinner chimes rang.

The officers made their way slowly down a broad stairway two decks to the dining salon, talking in twos, following the captain. At ten past eight they sat to soup and sherry. Immediately, the meal was interrupted by the late arrival of the chief officer, who had just been relieved at the bridge. The stewards scurried about him, bringing hot soup, filling his sherry glass, and the dinner began in earnest.

Ogilvy—his white hair gleaming, his shoulders heaped with braid—presided over the second seating like the lord of a great country house. He dominated conversation with stories of his gunboat days in the Persian Gulf and convoy

194

duty on the North Atlantic, peppering his remarks with acerbic comments on men he had served with during his long career. As the meal progressed, he shifted to the various versions of current events which he received on his radio as LEVIATHAN steamed down the North African coast.

Egypt was asking for a new conference; the Israelis had better be careful, said Ogilvy. The Arab's word was not the honest bargain of the Europeans. The black African states were accusing South Africa of maintaining concentration camps. They have to protect themselves, said Ogilvy. He offered a solution. The white government should put it squarely to the blacks. If they don't like the system they can return to their homelands. But if they stay, they have to take it as it is. North Sea oil production was still increasing. It perplexed Ogilvy. On one hand, it was a relief to see the trade balance back in proper order. On the other, with all that easy oil money propping up the economy, what was to convince the British workingman that he still had to improve his output, which had fallen to disgraceful levels.

His officers regularly nodded assent, but rarely replied except when he asked a direct question. The stewards, their jackets as white as the spotless table linen, unobtrusively shuffled china that bore the seal of LEVIATHAN—a charging black whale, its head raising a gold wake, its flukes pointing the sky. Only the absence of women and the low, modern tile ceiling belied the fact that the senior officers were not in the first-class dining room of a passenger liner.

The second officer tried to eat sparingly of the lavish meal, conscious of a fold of flesh which was developing beneath his chin like a pink beard. He drank a little of the white wine with the fish course, and only pretended to sip the red with the meat. Ogilvy would ask about the new route over coffee and he wanted a clear head. He avoided the potatoes and the second helping of meat which the steward tried to press on him, but he succumbed to his apprehension and nervously buttered a large roll. He was rehearsing his report in his mind and reaching for a second roll when Ogilvy suddenly addressed him.

"What did you come up with, Number Two?"

The stewards were already clearing Ogilvy's place and the officers had been eyeing the captain expectantly, waiting to be led to the wardroom. Since dinner talk was usually of inconsequentials and rarely touched upon ship's business, they exchanged curious glances and sat back to hear the second's reply. He wiped his mouth, took a sip from his crystal water goblet, and detailed LEVIATHAN'S new route.

The officers looked surprised.

"Well, done," Ogilvy said heartily. "It sounds quite ingenious."

"Thank you, sir."

The captain suggested a slight alteration on the third day, but the second knew that the Old Man was pleased. He found himself looking forward to coffee and a good, stiff brandy in the wardroom.

"A dogleg?" asked the chief electrical officer. He was new this voyage, a replacement standing in for the regular chief.

"Exactly," said Ogilvy with a disdainful smile.

"Why?" the new officer asked boldly, and the second waited for an explosion. Although the chief electrical officer and the chief engineer held pay and company rank equal to the master, as was typical on modern ships, Ogilvy brooked no challenge to his supremacy at the dinner table.

The Old Man liked a young staff that would give him old-fashioned respect, and his regular officers, pleased with high rank at a young age, did nothing to annoy him. The second knew he was unusually young to hold his ticket, but Ogilvy had shepherded him through the ranks since he'd discovered him as a cadet at P and O.

The replacement was a man in his forties, and having suffered years of deck insult before electronics was recognized as an important part of the ship's equipment, he

196

took great relish in being his own man. His question caused Ogilvy's smile to turn cool.

"For the simple reason," the captain said, "that the man who intends to attack this ship will do so off the bulge of west Africa. Somewhere between the Canaries and the Ivory Coast."

The officers nodded carefully. This was the first indication that Captain Ogilvy gave serious weight to the threat, and they had allowed his casual attitude to be their own.

Ogilvy laughed. "Chap's in for a bit of a disappointment. What?"

The second officer laughed with him, and the first smiled thinly, but the new man wouldn't let it go.

"How do you know where he intends to attack?"

Ogilvy frowned. He clearly didn't like the new man, and the second officer, who feared the captain and tended to seek safety in his prejudices, willingly shared his distaste for the electrical chief's sloppy appearance and his outspokenness. He was thirty pounds overweight, his hair was shaggy, and his dinner kit was disgraceful, as if the ship's laundry couldn't keep a chap's clothes in tip-top shape. He made no secret of the fact that he had a good job offer from Decca and might leave the sea to work for the electronics firm.

He said he missed his wife and he admitted to a peculiar affliction. After years as a merchant officer, he had suddenly begun to suffer seasickness. The doctors told him it was psychosomatic, but several days out he had asserted loudly that LEVIATHAN seemed a cure. She sailed steady as a rock. He had said he'd like to sign on permanently if he didn't join Decca.

Ogilvy replied to his question about Hardin with chilly deliberation.

"Having assessed the sailing characteristics of his boat, the time he left England, the weather, tides, currents, and winds along this coast, and his apparent intention to track LEVIATHAN with radar, I have reached the inescapable conclusion that he could attack only in the sea-lanes off the west African coast."

197

"How is that, Captain?"

"He hasn't the speed to chase us," Ogilvy said with ice in his voice. "Therefore, he must lie in wait. With only a few hours' warning from his radar, he has to attack where he thinks we will be. In a heavily traveled sealane. Also, there is some psychology at work here. Along the bulge, he will be quite close to South America. That seems the logical place he would try to escape to."

"I must say I doubt that," said the electrical chief.

"Really, Sparks?" asked Ogilvy, reddening. "Perhaps you would offer us your wisdom on the matter."

"I don't know about wisdom," he replied, his brow knitting briefly at the "Sparks" dig. "But I don't believe that if the man is a loony he's worrying about escape."

"You are quite right," said Ogilvy. "You offer little wisdom." He turned to his other officers. "If this doctor were a simple madman, he would have sailed into Le Havre and fired his rocket while LEVIATHAN was moored to the oil pier like a tethered goat."

The second nodded vigorously as the captain's eyes raked from officer to officer and skewered his.

Ogilvy repeated his thought. "The fact that he did not attack in a harbor where he had no chance of escape indicates that he is carefully planning his escape."

"What if he had another reason not to attack in a harbor?" asked the electrical officer.

"Such as what?"

"I don't know. Perhaps it didn't fit his plan."

"If you think of it," said the captain, rising from the table, "do inform us."

"But you have to come back this way. For how many voyages will LEVIATHAN avoid this coast?"

"When LEVIATHAN next sails this coast," replied Ogilvy, "Hardin will be in custody. Every port from Las Palmas to the Gulf of Guinea has been alerted, but I imagine they'll nab him in Lagos. The Nigerian woman will take him there. You see, your Africans are a tribal lot. They go home when they're afraid. Coffee, gentlemen?"

"You're killing yourself," said Ajaratu.

Hardin's cracked lips tightened. He looked around with heavy eyes. The tropic sea lay limp and white beneath a sun so diffused by humid air that it seemed to fill the sky. Thick damp heat shrouded the boat and blurred the horizons. They hovered close and so it seemed he would sail forever on a small but endless pond.

"Let me take her for a few hours," said Ajaratu. "Get some sleep."

Hardin shook his head. The squint lines which arrowed toward his eyes had grown deeper as he drove the Swan south. He said, "The wind's coming around. I want to use it. You sleep. Relieve me later."

She went below reluctantly and when she was gone he swallowed a handful of vitamins and a heavy dose of amphetamine—his third in three days. By the time the wind had shifted, as he had expected, toward the northeast, the drug was singing in his brain. He hadn't used speed since he had interned, but he had remembered to concentrate on his purpose before he swallowed it. If he hadn't, he might have spent the next twelve hours gaping through thick clouds at an imaginary star.

With the wind almost dead astern, he rigged a whisker pole and boomed out a big jib—a reacher—opposite the genoa. Then he lowered the mainsail, lashed the boom, and returned to the helm. The Swan ran powerfully behind the pull of the double headsails. It was a classic self-steering rig—the kind you could leave untended for days in the tradewinds—but he was fighting for speed, and for speed he had to tend the wheel and the sheets and steer a perfect course.

Fifteen minutes later the wind dropped somewhat and he went forward and slacked the jib halyards to belly the sails so they would catch the lighter wind. In half an hour he was back on foredeck, tightening the halyards, because the wind had risen. It held steady through the sunset, and he dozed, despite the drug, until a terrible banging started at the bow.

It was dark. There were no stars. He raced to the mast

and found that the reacher had dropped the whisker pole and spilled its wind. He repositioned the pole, returned to the cockpit, and cranked the sheet. The sail bellied, then collapsed again. His eyes had adjusted to the dark and he saw that seas hitting aft on the port side had slued the Swan upwind. He put her back on course and adjusted the self-steering to compensate for the wave action.

The Swan sailed well for half an hour. Then the wind swung abruptly due east. He doused the reacher, stowed the pole and the sail, unlashed the boom, and raised the main. The east wind spawned new seas which set up a fierce cross chop with the swells from the previous wind, and the Swan began shipping spray. Hardin shrugged into his foul-weather jacket and dozed at the helm, his two-week beard dripping water.

He awakened with a start. The Swan had slowed. He looked at his watch. Four. It was pitch-black and the wind had shifted back to the northeast. He sheeted out the main and the genoa. Every bone ached for sleep, but he knew he would do better with the reacher. Cursing his decision to buy a sloop instead of a ketch or a yawl, he forced himself to boom out the big headsail and lower the main. Only when he sank exhausted at the helm, and saw the speed indicator reading eight and a half knots, did he admit that the advantages of numerous sail options on a two-masted boat were exaggerated. They might make you think you were doing more for speed, but the Swan was going faster than any ketch he had ever seen.

He woke again before dawn. Heavy seas were slamming the sloop broadside, knocking her off the wind. He doused the reacher, raised the main, and set a new course. Southeast, into the seas. The next time he awakened, the sun was warming the back of his head. The seas had subsided, so he put her back on a southerly course. He looked blearily at the empty ocean and decided it had been a pretty good night.

The sky promised another blazing tropical day. One of the last they would see.

They had crossed the equator three days ago and the fifth parallel of latitude yesterday. Ascension Island was six hundred miles to the west, the coast of Africa—the mouth of the Congo River—a thousand miles east. Ahead lay the South Atlantic Ocean, and astern was LEVIATHAN, steaming toward the Cape of Good Hope at more than twice his speed, regardless of wind, current, and storm.

Ajaratu came on deck. "You were supposed to wake me," she said accusingly. "I slept all night." She took his face in her hands as if to kiss him, but she examined it and said, "You've taken quite enough pills for several days. Your eyes look like marbles."

Hardin showed her the course. Then he went below and collapsed on his bunk, too tired to wash the salt from his face.

Something shook the mast and Ajaratu's scream tore him from his sleep. He stumbled up the companionway. The boat was sluing upwind. A gusty force 5 had kicked up whitecaps. The genoa had slipped its sheet and tangled in the shrouds and was slamming its stainless steel clew against the mast, banging from side to side and threatening to rip the main. Ajaratu was inching forward atop the coach roof, reaching for the lethally flying clew.

"Don't!" he yelled, flinging himself forward and pinning her arm an instant before she could touch the flailing sail. He pulled her away, and waited until the Swan had turned more to the wind before grabbing the heavy clew. A gust slammed the genoa and it almost dragged him off the coach roof. Ajaratu lowered the halyard and together they secured the blowing sail.

He showed her where the steel clew ring had snapped. She marveled that such a thick piece of metal could break. Hardin replied that there wasn't a piece of gear aboard that wouldn't, pushed long and hard enough. They raised another genoa and he spent an hour sewing a new clew ring to the damaged sail. Then he went back to sleep.

At noon the heat drove him out of the cabin. Groggily, he came on deck, dangled a small bucket over the side,

201

and poured warm seawater on his head. He checked the way Ajaratu had trimmed the sails. Then he shot the sun and fixed his position.

"Where are we?"

"Two thousand two hundred and three miles northwest of Capetown. We might make it."

She started to speak, hesitated. Then she said, "I was about to say, 'God willing,' but that's a bit much considering the circumstances. Isn't it?"

"That depends whose side He's on." He stretched out in a sliver of shade cast by the billowing mainsail. Hot sun grazed him on either side, but Ajaratu steered so steadily that the shade patch barely moved. Her eyes flicked from the sails to the compass to his face.

"You're tempting fate talking that way."

Hardin propped himself up on one elbow. "We've sailed over four and a half thousand miles nonstop—two thousand miles in the last eleven days—we're alive and the boat still floats. We've already tempted fate."

"Go to sleep."

The mainsail was luffing slightly. He worried that it had stretched from hard use. Ajaratu trimmed it before he could speak.

"Sleep."

Hardin slept.

"Monrovia?" howled the helicopter pilot. He cocked his head at Ogilvy like a bird hearing the hawk's rush. "What the hell am I gonna do in Monrovia?"

"Frankly, young man, I don't care if you sell your helicopter for a handful of trinkets and go native. LEVIATHAN has no need of you."

"I don't even know where Monrovia is," the pilot protested.

"Number Two will give you your course and the ADF frequencies."

"But Captain Bruce—"

"Is not master of this ship. Begone, sir."

Ogilvy stood on the wing and watched the bosun escort

202

the pilot to his aircraft. The machine buzzed away until it was an empty space in the hazy eastern horizon.

"Number Two."

"Sir?"

"What's his ETA?"

"Fifteen hundred."

Ogilvy looked at his watch. Two hours. Another hour to tell the Liberian office he'd been sacked. "I'll be in my cabin when the Company calls."

The second officer thought he saw a chance to ingratiate himself with the captain. He said, with a collusive grin, "Shall I have the bosun dismantle the shortwave aerial, sir?"

"Whatever for?"

The second's grin faded. "The, uh, fittings are, should be inspected, sir. Maintenance . . ."

Ogilvy regarded the young officer with a chilly expression. "When you attain your own command, Number Two, you will learn why a ship's master answers to none but God."

The second swallowed. "Yes, sir."

Ogilvy stared, his face like stone. Suddenly he broke into an unusual, warm smile. "You'll also find, Number Two, that under such conditions you will rarely dodge a question."

The call came while Ogilvy was dressing for dinner. As LEVIATHAN was an hour behind Greenwich time, James Bruce must have been called back to the London office from his house in Surrey. Ogilvy stared out the window at the soft tropic sea while he spoke. His steward waited with his uniform shirt, his eyes averted from the captain's pale, white torso.

"Yes, Captain Bruce."

"Cedric. The Monrovia office reports that your helicopter pilot landed there this afternoon."

"Thank you, Captain Bruce. I'll note such in the log."

"Will you stop calling me Captain Bruce, Cedric?"

Ogilvy's smug voice hardened. "I'm done with the helicopter. I steered around Hardin. He's in my wake."

"You can't know that."

"We're at sea, Bruce. I know it."

"They're mad as hell here, Cedric. You've gone too far this time."

"It was damned foolishness carrying that helicopter. It was a menace to my ship every time it flew."

"LEVIATHAN's as stable as an airfield," snapped Bruce.

"Cold comfort for the helicopter in a force eight."

"The winds aren't too strong for the helicopter that brings your fresh meat from Capetown."

"That's a twin-rotor Sikorsky built for the job and piloted by two chaps who know their business. There's no comparison with that motorized mosquito you tried to burden me with. The freight helicopter is once on and once off, and my crew deserves its mail and decent food."

"The Company wants you to take it back."

Ogilvy's voice turned harder still. "If that aircraft lands on LEVIATHAN, I will lash it down and put the pilot in irons."

"Cedric."

"Do you believe me?"

After a short pause, Bruce said, "Yes, Cedric, I believe you, but I don't know if it will wash with the directors."

"Tell the directors that I located the source of the fuel contamination that nearly caused LEVIATHAN to drift aground in the Solent. Tell them I repaired it. Tell them my maintenance checks unearthed a second frozen mooring winch. Tell them I repaired it. Tell them I've patched three dozen steam leaks in the engine room. Then tell them that the helicopter is useless in heavy weather. And if those boardroom commodores ask why I expect heavy weather, you might remind them that LEVIATHAN is bound for the Cape of Good Hope and July doesn't mean summer down there."

Hardin dreamed he was sledding. It was cold. The sled skidded over rough snow, the runners hissing, the wooden frame creaking. Birds circled above his path and shrieked for a conclusion he couldn't predict. The sled leaped a hillock and careened down a steep slope. He hurtled toward a black wall at the foot of the slope, unable to stop the sled. He turned. The wall turned with him, surrounded him. It was everywhere. He yelled his fear.

"Peter!"

Ajaratu. He was on the boat. Oddly, there was a blanket over him. He opened his eyes. The sky was gone. Ajaratu sat at the helm, one hand on the wheel, the other on his shoulder. She was wearing foul-weather gear. Hardin ran his hand through his hair. It was soaked. He sat up and stared. The top of Swan's mast was lost in thick fog.

"Jesus. Why didn't you wake me?"

"You couldn't do anything."

"How long did I sleep?" He rubbed his eyes.

"Four hours," she answered quietly, staring into the fog. "It's happened so fast, Peter. As if it had been lowered onto us. Or leaped out of the water."

"We've reached the South Atlantic," said Hardin.

"It's got suddenly cold. And then the fog." She sounded frightened.

"It'll lift." He glanced at the compass. They were on course, close-hauled into a wet southeast breeze. The surface of the sea was calm, but every few moments a swell from the southwest rolled the Swan sharply, as if something in the water had seized the keel and given the boat an experimental shake.

The sea was quiet, but there were sounds of life even though they were hundreds of miles from the nearest island. They heard the lonely cry of a single bird somewhere in the fog and surface life close to the boat—a mammalian snorting. Hardin cocked his ears toward the wet, fleshy, bubbling noise and scanned the thick fog for the ominous mass of a surfacing whale.

"It's so strange," whispered Ajaratu.

Hardin shivered.

"Winter?" she asked.

"Soon," he replied, softly, as awed as she was by the eerie silence and the clinging mist.

He went forward and rigged a staysail. The boat responded with another quarter knot as it edged into an invisible sea.

The South Atlantic was a huge and empty ocean. After the fog lifted, they sailed for days in isolated frenzy, speeding between remote horizons—distant convergences of the blue sky and the darker sea unmarred by smoke or sail. In vivid contrast to the oppressive white haze of the tropics, the air was fresh and crisp and cooler, and the sky so clear that it seemed if they looked hard enough they might see through the color to the black space beyond.

The water was strangely unriled, calm, but not calm, because under its smooth surface the big swells continuously undulated from the southwest. Hardin watched them soberly. They were a record of the seas toward which he was steering and a promise of what he would find when he got there.

There were calms and there were gales, and the gales—forty-knot winds that raged for hours at a time—blew with increasing frequency. Since the winds were primarily from the direction they were heading, southeast, Hardin had to beat against them and that cost time. Rather than tacking toward the African coast where the winds would be lighter, he decided on a dogleg. Close-hauled, he bore west of Capetown, gambling that he would catch westerlies farther south.

He became obsessed with a fear that LEVIATHAN would beat him to the Cape of Good Hope, round the tip of Africa, and steam safely toward the Persian Gulf at twice his best speed. He drove the Swan as hard as he could, sailing on the edge, on a precarious line between the boat's limits and disaster. His heaviest genoa—a sail too stiff for ordinary use—would take enormous punishment. In gales he flew the powerful jib long after instinct clamored to douse it; and when the Swan heeled at too steep an angle for efficiency and began spilling the wind, he reefed the main and let the big headsail keep pulling, despite the risk of a knockdown.

They were entering their sixth week at sea, and Ajaratu was becoming capable of handling the boat in any conditions. When exhaustion drove Hardin to his bunk, he replaced the genoa with a smaller jib and a staysail. If sail changes were necessary while he slept, Ajaratu could handle the two smaller sails by herself.

He came on deck one morning after a good sleep. It was blowing a strong gale. The sea was rolling and spray hissed from the crests. Ajaratu, her face etched with fatigue, looked apprehensively at the genoa he had dragged up the companionway.

"It's getting worse," she said.

"Get some sleep."

"It's blowing too hard for that sail, Peter."

"I can handle her."

He clipped his safety harness to the lifeline—they were wearing them routinely now—dragged the genny past the coach roof and the mast, and hanked it onto the forestay. Ajaratu was steering close to the wind. She headed up to ease the pressure on the jib. He dropped it and ran up the genoa, and the Swan heeled sharply when Ajaratu went back on course. Hardin lowered the staysail and dragged both jibs back to the cockpit and down the companionway, because too much water was coming over the bows to open the fore hatch.

He had just come back up to the cockpit and closed the main hatch when the gust struck the genoa. It knocked the Swan on its side before he could attach his lifeline.

Hardin fell out of the cockpit, over the coaming. Flailing out, he gripped the mainsheets, but before he could save himself he was into the cold water up to his waist. He heard Ajaratu's frightened cry cut short. He saw her head in the froth beside the boat, then a wave folded over it and she was gone like Carolyn.

He struggled toward the helm, seized the wheel, and, turning around in the cockpit, searched for the sheets, which were underwater. The mast lay on the sea; the sails had filled with waves, but any second the weight of the keel would start to pull her up; and when she came, he had to release the sheets before the wind knocked her over again.

The mast started to rise. He found the jib sheet and yanked it free of the jam cleat. The sails whooshed out of the water and the Swan righted with a rush, rolling back and forth, and pitching violently as Hardin hauled on Ajaratu's lifeline.

She broke surface, gasping. He pulled her into the cockpit, which was full of water. She took the wheel and he clipped on his lifeline and raced to the mast. The heavy genoa was flapping with the fierce wind. He lowered it as fast as he could, gathered the sail out of the sea, and hauled it back to the cockpit.

Ajaratu, still gasping and coughing, watched him with smoldering eyes.

"I'm sorry," he said, pouring the water out of the folds of the sail. "You were right."

She steered downwind, filled the main, and put the boat back on course.

The days ran together. He knew them only by his sun shots and the numbers in the Nautical Almanac and his penciled halting line, south, south, south on his chart. He continued to veer from Capetown, but he had to go with the wind and trust that the westerlies would push him east.

Sometimes the wind died, becalming the Swan in a pocket of air as hot and still as the tropics. But while the sails flapped emptily and the lightest spinnaker dropped like wet laundry, the boat wallowed in misery on the ceaseless swells, invisible crestless waves that worked beneath the surface—lifting, dropping, spawned in conflict, hidden like resentment, racing from distant Antarctic storms toward the open bays and fragile harbors of southwest Africa.

Once they saw a ship's smoke. Hardin immediately lowered the sails and took down the radar reflector. He was a wary outcast, fearful that they might report his position. It was the only ship they saw, because they had sailed far

208

west of the shipping lanes in their quest for the wind. And while it was a relief not to have to stand alert for ships, it was lonely. Ajaratu didn't seem to mind, but Hardin finally succumbed to the solitude. Using his false call sign, he radioed Miles via the long-range international radio relay station at Capetown. The Israeli made contact at dawn.

He asked Miles for LEVIATHAN's position—it was a hundred miles west of its usual route, a lucky break—but what he had really wanted was to hear Miles's voice as proof that he and Ajaratu and the Swan, battling ever-worsening seas, still existed, and had not, by a quirk of navigation, sailed into a dream sea at the edge of the world.

15

The chief electrical officer lay awake in the dark, gripping the edge of his mattress, wondering what had changed. The skin on the back of his neck prickled and he reached for the light switch.

"Christ," he breathed aloud.

LEVIATHAN was rolling.

The ship leaned to one side, then the other—a barely perceptible motion, but startling for its very existence. He had been aboard twelve days and this was the first she had budged from a plane as flat and straight as the horizon.

The weather satellites had been right as usual; the southern storm that had spawned below Cape Horn and was racing across the South Atlantic was a big one to build such swells so far from its center.

LEVIATHAN was rolling more acutely when the breakfast bell sounded, and the long crosswise corridors in the accommodations tower were rising and falling like seesaws. On his way to the dining salon, the electrical chief climbed a steepening incline that slowly leveled off until it was flat. Moments later, he was loping down a hill.

His sense of smell seemed unusually acute when he finished breakfast; the sausage grease reeked strongly and his coffee tasted sour. Too late, he recognized the familiar signs of worse to come.

He hurried up to the bridge wing for fresh air. It was colder than the day before. To the west, far, far away, great unmoving anvil-top black clouds loomed like solid rock. The air was clear and very cold, the water deep blue, almost black, and the sunlight fell from a wintery angle, darkening the water and offering little warmth. The smooth surface of the sea undulated like gelatin as row after row of buried swells filed out of the southwest and rolled the high and empty LEVIATHAN with ever-crescent ferocity.

He lay down in his cabin, knowing he had to get up to take his subordinates' reports. It was heavy with the odor of furniture oil. He closed his eyes, took a deep breath, and stood up to go on watch. His stomach heaved and he bolted for the bathroom.

The rolling grew worse, and the next evening, when he felt recovered enough to attempt dinner, the stewards had dampened the tablecloths to stop the plates from sliding.

Captain Ogilvy asked how he felt. He sounded genuinely sympathetic, but the electrical chief attributed it to the general lightening up that had come from giving the mad doctor the slip and knowing they would pass Capetown in four days. The long, seventeen-day first leg would be over; they'd be in the Gulf in two weeks.

After dinner the talk turned to the weather. The engineers and the subordinate electrical officers retired, but the electrical chief stayed on with Ogilvy and his desk officers to speculate on the route of the storm.

Ogilvy dispatched a cadet to bring the latest weather and wave charts from the bridge, and when he had, the officers spread them out on the wardroom coffee table and grouped around while the captain led a discussion of probabilities. He drew their attention to the isobars, which showed that the depression had continued to deepen as it moved rapidly east, from a point five hundred miles below the tip of South America to its latest recorded location fourteen hundred miles due west of Capetown.

He traced the route across each of the charts with a thick, wrinkled finger. Then he said, "The South Atlantic high didn't slow it one whit. Now, for some reason, it's stalled."

"There's a powerful high at the Cape," said the first officer. "Ten thirty millibars."

"I think it will stay where it is until we've passed, or perhaps swing north," said the second.

The first officer picked up a satellite photograph and examined the enormous cloud swirl.

"Trouble?" asked the chief electrical officer.

"Trouble?" Ogilvy pointed at a wave chart. "They've reported ten-meter waves at its center—thirty-five feet—in addition, of course, to the swell. On another ship I would say you have to respect the sea's power and assume that indeed there might be trouble." He tossed the map to the table. "This is Leviathan. The storm will cost nothing but bunkerage. You might want to run up the fuel figures, Number Two."

"Yes, sir."

Tinkling musically, the empty coffee cups slid across the polished table toward the wardroom's curtained stern windows. Ogilvy smiled as the second officer reached to stop them.

"She's pitching," he said. "You're seeing a rare event on Leviathan, Sparks. Enjoy it."

The bow rose a degree or two, then fell away the same small measure, and the electrical chief had a curious feeling that the other officers were gladdened by the reminder that they were indeed aboard a ship, a tender vessel influenced, albeit marginally, by the movement of the sea. He thought, as he had often since he had boarded the tanker, how young they were.

The first officer telephoned the bridge and spoke to the third, who was on watch. "The swells are holding west," he reported, "but the wind is shifting south." Normally dispassionate, even he seemed excited by the prospect of a storm.

"The advance guard," Ogilvy proclaimed.

The chief electrical officer was of the generation between these young officers and Ogilvy, the generation that bridged the old and modern, the rigid and the casual, and having served on many ships in many oceans, had seen enough captains to know how the tyrannical old bastard got his way. But who would master LEVIATHAN when the Old Man had gone?

Ogilvy stared down from his full height at the charts and JAX radio facsimile weather and wave printouts on the coffee table. Abruptly, he swept them aside.

"The storm will move," he announced. "Across the Cape."

No one asked him how he knew.

That night the pitching worsened, and by dawn the regular rise and fall of the bows made the whole ship tremble. The electrical chief slept badly—not sick, but in suspension, waiting when the bow rose for the drop to follow. His hands tightened each time LEVIATHAN reached the apogee, rearing high to smash the rollers like a relentless battering ram.

Finally, at dawn, he gave up on sleep, dressed warmly, and went to the bridge wing, where, at first light, he leaned into a bitter-cold wind and watched the grand liftings and stately plummetings of the great blunt bows. They flung clouds of spray that dumped tons of water on the front third of the ship each time LEVIATHAN plunged into a trough and raced on to pummel the next wave.

Great breaking combers covered the ocean's surface in mighty rows two hundred yards apart, each row separated by a frothy field of white water. The wind was strong, and when a sudden wave rose higher than the rest in a long trough, the wind knocked it down for its impertinence. He walked to the edge of the wing and looked over the side. Here in the lee the water was smoother. He strained to hear the breaking waves, but heard only the wind rushing past his ears as Leviathan charged into it at a heedless sixteen knots.

Movement caught his eyes, and he was startled to see a giant albatross a few feet away, riding the wind beside the ship and watching him with an unblinking yellow eye. The bird was enormous, its wingspread ten feet at least, and he noticed that its far wing drooped lamely and its head and neck were strained with weariness. He guessed that it had been mauled by the storm, and he stepped away to encourage it to land if a rest was what it wanted.

The albatross floated closer to the railing and reached tentatively for the gray metal with its webbed feet. One suspicious eye remained fixed on the electrical officer.

"You're all right," he murmured. "I won't hurt you." He glanced at the bridge house to make sure, but the helmsman sat by the wheel staring at where the autopilot was taking him.

The bird's feet clamped tightly around the railing and it tried to fold its wings. The right wing collapsed into its resting place, but the left stuck half open at a stiff and awkward angle. The albatross flapped it, as if to try again, but the wind tore at it, unbalancing the bird. Too late, it opened the other wing to steady itself.

The wind wrenched the albatross from the railing. Fighting to fly, struggling frantically to mate its wings to the turbulence around the ship, it was swept up and back.

Its instincts were good. It didn't resist the air, but tried to float with it, and it cleared the thicket of wires and antennas on the mast. Then its stiff wing betrayed it and the bird was blown hard against the tall starboard funnel. Cartwheeling like a kite without a tail, it plunged toward the water.

The electrical officer leaned far over the edge of the wing and watched the albatross thrash helplessly in the bubbling wake. He stared astern long after the white of its feathers was lost in the riled water, angered by the loss, blaming the giant ship.

Ogilvy came onto the bridge wing and stood beside him.

213

He wore a high-collared greatcoat and a milky-white silk scarf at his throat.

"Good morning, Sparks. There's something—"

Bristling, the electrical officer cut him off.

"Captain Ogilvy, I'd like to remind you that Levia-THAN's electric plant produces enough kilowatts to power a fair-sized town. On your bridge electronic equipment pinpoints your position to an inch, anticollision radar tracks every ship in a sixty-mile radius, meteorological instruments observe every weather disturbance in the hemisphere, and your telemetry gear allows you to communicate with anyone in the world."

Ogilvy looked bemused. "What exactly is the purpose of this inventory?"

"Just this, Captain. Since the functioning of these instruments is my responsibility on this voyage, I would prefer that you not call me 'Sparks,' which somehow implies that I divide my time between fiddling with a shortwave radio and changing light bulbs."

Ogilvy offered his blandest smile. "Then you're probably just the officer to inform that as we steam into a major storm, the electronic bow-pressure indicators have all failed."

The chief electrical officer felt his jaw drop. "All of them?"

"Every last one."

"When?" Schematics and circuit plans raced through his head. Where Ogilvy saw the steel plates and members that formed the ship's hull, tanks, and decks, he saw miles and miles of copper wire and coaxial cable connecting the thousands of components of the electronic and electrical systems without which the ship would be a drifting hulk.

Ogilvy chuckled. "No need to look so upset, Sparks. It's not really that important."

"Not important?" he asked incredulously. "Without those sensors, how can you possibly know the effect of the seas on the bow? It's five hundred yards from the bridge."

Ogilvy stopped smiling abruptly. "I've been at sea fifty

214

years, sir. Long before they cooked up radar, much less bow-pressure indicators. I know the effect of the seas on my bows, thank you."

"I'll have it repaired immediately."

"I also know better than to depend upon electrical wizardry in salt air. This isn't a laboratory, it's an ocean."

The electrical chief had heard that litany time and time again in the past fifteen years. He offered his own in return. "Electronics is merely a way of making the ocean smaller."

"A bigger ship is the only way to make the ocean smaller," retorted Ogilvy.

The chief electrical officer hurried into the bridge house and took the elevator fifteen levels down to the control room. It was sound-proofed and air-conditioned, but the floor trembled from the engines. His seconds and thirds were huddled around the computerized failure-trace system, eyeing the electronic wave patterns that cantered across the test-instrument oscilloscopes.

"Why wasn't I called?" he demanded, swiftly scanning the computer-generated formulas on the CRT screen.

"We couldn't find you, sir. We've got it under control."

He bit back an angry retort. LEVIATHAN's crew were a clannish lot and they'd made it clear that they put little trust in an outsider. He asked what had happened.

"It looks as if the telemetry system isn't functioning."

"Bloody hell," said the chief.

The pressure sensors measured sea forces on certain key bow plates. The information was fed up a coaxial cable from the bottom of the ship to a microwave transmitter on the forward deck that relayed it back to the tower. It was a one-in-a-million breakdown. The fact that the transmitter was working despite the data-signal loss meant that the failure was probably in the jumble of cables and connectors where the pressure sensors' signals joined in a sealed junction box a hundred feet below deck, deep at the bottom of a crude-oil tank.

"We've already got volunteers to go down."

"I'll go myself," said the chief. "Have the forward

tanks deinerted. I want an oxygen mask and a radio-phone link to the deck."

He donned a boiler suit and a slicker and rubber hat. Then, accompanied by his subordinates, he went on deck, climbed onto the fire-station catwalk, and began walking toward the spray-sheathed bow.

Secretly, he wished he had let one of the younger men who had volunteered do the work, but he didn't know them and he wanted the repair done right. If the system went down again when the tanks were full, it would be out until they off-loaded in Europe, because, unlike the situation on a freighter, there were no access tunnels in LE-VIATHAN's huge hull. The only way to reach the junction box that mated the bow sensors was to descend into the hellish silence of the empty oil tanks.

The spray poured from the sky like a salty rain as he neared the bow. The lifting and plunging was much more pronounced at the forward end of the ship, because as LE-VIATHAN reared to shatter the sea it pivoted from the stern. A deck gang had preceded the electrical officers and the yellow-coated sailors were grouped around an open man-hole just behind the forwardmost bulkhead.

The electrical chief gazed down at the steel ladder that disappeared into the black hold of the ship and thought wistfully of a desk job at Decca. The slow rise and fall of the bow would make it difficult to hang on to the ladder. He stripped off his hat and slicker and slung a backpack of tools and components over his shoulders.

The bosun gave him a special hard hat with a miner's light and a radiotelephone headset built in. An oxygen mask was dangling into the hole, to be lowered beside him in the event that he descended into a gas pocket. The in-ert gases, which were supposed to prevent the tank from exploding, had been pumped out already, but there was no guarantee that an oil puddle, missed in the tank clean-ing, might not create a gas pocket that would asphyxiate him. The hat, the light, the telephone, and his shoes were all rubber covered to reduce the chance of sparking an explosion in the temporarily air-rich, deinerted tanks.

216

He squeezed his bulk through the manhole and began the long climb down. The air stank of crude and was deathly still compared to the wind and spray above. He counted fifty steps down the narrow ladder that tilted to and fro with the ship's movement, and stopped to rest.

It occurred to him that nowhere but the sea would an engineer with his experience be risking his life to make a nuts-and-bolts repair. Looking up, he saw a tiny circle of light that was the manhole. A shadow moved over it— one of his men, he thought wryly, wondering if the new boy had plunged to his death.

He turned on the light. The beam shone on gray metal. Everywhere he moved his head, the light showed the dead gray color of a bottom fish. He resumed his descent into the empty crude tank and a rumbling sound began to echo. Twice he passed through horizontal dividers, interior decks trod only by the oil. Then he was in the deepest tank, a tall narrow space that descended to the bottom of the ship. The rumble was louder. Black circles showed in the gray—oil inflow ports, the mouths of the thousands of pipes that honeycombed the million-tonner's hold.

He reached the bottom, grateful to be off the ladder, and felt through his rubber soles the source of the rumbling. LEVIATHAN's belly shook gently each time the ship smashed a big roller. He followed his light to a massive steel member, located a small door at chest height, telephoned to double-check that the power was off, unscrewed the fasteners, and removed the door.

The junction box was partially filled with crude oil. It spilled out as he stripped away the broken gasket and stuffed it in his bag. The oil had touched the lower rows of SC coaxial connectors, but apparently none had penetrated the threaded couplings because they were designed for severe environment. He unscrewed several and shone his light into their sleeves, confirming that their seals had held, then widened his search.

It was the main coupling. The high-power LT inch-and-a-quarter connector had been breached. The corrosive oil had ruined the contacts. He cut the male and female parts from the coaxial cable and crimped on replacements.

The telephone headset erupted with a happy shout. "Contact!"

Quickly he put a new gasket on the door and resealed the junction box. Gathering his tools into his sack, and making sure that he had left nothing behind, he climbed the ladder back to daylight, where his subordinates greeted him with a new warmth. After showering the stink of the oil out of his hair, he changed into warm clothing, found Ogilvy on the bridge, and reported the malfunction repaired.

The wind had freshened. Ogilvy said nothing for a while. Then he nodded at the sea.

"Weren't you the chap who suggested that the man on the sailboat might attack somewhere other than the bulge of Africa?"

"I didn't see how you could be so sure, Captain."

"Look at that."

Fierce lines of rollers marched implacably through the flashing whitecaps that leaped in their troughs. Spray, whipped from the crests by the wind, skidded smokily across the gray water like fine snow blowing over ice.

The sun moved behind gathering clouds. The waves seemed sharper, the water darker. Jagged peaks rose on the horizon like distant mysteries, fearsome, remote, but filled with the menace that they might come near. The water looked cold and forbidding, the mist penetrating, the sea like an undulating stone overlaid with a white net of spray and torn crests.

"I would remind you," said Ogilvy, "that we stand two hundred feet above the water. Can you imagine what these seas would look like from the deck of a thirty-eight-foot sailboat?"

The Swan battled two oceans as it swung east-southeast toward Capetown and dared the advance storm winds with double-reefed mainsail and a heavy jib. There was the ocean of the great, widely spaced rolling swells—Cape rollers—marching from Antarctic seas to the tip of Africa.

218

The giants were breaking now. Their tumbling crests seethed with foam. They chased after the Swan, lunged at her starboard quarter, lifted her high as Hardin spun the wheel to keep her from broaching, and raced ahead with mechanical regularity.

The second ocean was between the rollers, and there the Swan fought her worst battles. The wind whipped it to a fury, and though the sun glowed through the high cloud cover, it was often impossible to see from one steep wave to the next through the loudly hissing, smoky mist blown from the spiky crests. The Swan pounded from wave to trough, plowing, smashing, heeling, and pitching. A roller lifted her momentarily above the chaos—eased her passage even as it tried to turn her sideways and capsize her—then returned her to the cruel chop and the blowing spray.

The great rollers had been nourished by the storm that was driving the Swan's barometer ominously lower, but the seas between them were the children of the wind. The wind filled the air with a thick, blowing mist. The mist was often impenetrable and made the cockpit misery. It was cold and wet, and clogged the nostrils and stung the eyes, and it worried Hardin more than the wind and the seas and the oncoming storm. He'd come this far in the Swan seeking rough conditions where they wouldn't think he would attack, but what he feared was being unable to see LEVIATHAN through the spray. He would have to get very close.

Miles Donner knew the growth of the seas by the weakness of Hardin's radio signals. He had been manning the transmitter on the top floor of an old office building in Limehouse for four days since Hardin had unexpectedly broken silence. He was a thousand miles west-northwest of the Cape of Good Hope, driving east-southeast toward Capetown in heavy seas. He wanted LEVIATHAN's position and heading.

As Donner tracked LEVIATHAN in the days that followed, Hardin's signal grew more and more erratic, fad-

219

ing in and out, silencing for minutes at a time. It wasn't a matter of distance or atmospheric attenuations, Donner's radio operator explained, but rather the result of the aerial on Hardin's mast dipping beneath the steepening crests. When the signal was strong, it carried the heavy roar of the ocean.

Since the convulsion the Mossad had suffered, Miles Donner had created an informal network of friends and helpers within and without the intelligence organization. They included Mossad people like Grandig in Germany, sympathetic English civil servants, and a number of El Al airline personnel. He worried about the danger of fragmenting the Mossad, but felt the initiative was necessary if Israel was to launch bold and creative espionage efforts. It was this private network that he used to track LEVIATHAN.

An El Al navigator who was also Mossad had a contact in the United States. She worked in a map room at Strategic Air Command headquarters. She observed LEVIATHAN on the spy-satellite television and radar maps. The giant ship was easily distinguished from the smaller shadows and blips sprinkled around the African coast, but only an interested observer would have noticed that the tanker was slightly west of its usual route.

Once a day, the woman at SAC relayed the tanker's position. When she was off duty, Donner and the El Al navigator employed the services of an English meteorologist who had access to weather-satellite pictures of the South Atlantic. By the end of the second day, the navigator was able to plot the remainder of LEVIATHAN's likely course using the information received, the ship's known speed of sixteen knots, and its destination.

Donner drew that line on a South Atlantic chart and then had the navigator plot the tanker's likely position at hourly intervals. They drew a second line indicating Hardin's east-southeasterly heading. The lines crossed at eleven degrees fifteen minutes and ten seconds east, and thirty degrees, twenty-nine minutes south—a point in the South Atlantic five hundred miles northwest of Capetown.

Hardin reported that he was making five or six knots. If

220

he could hold that speed, calculated the navigator, Hardin would reach the vicinity of the target area half a day ahead of LEVIATHAN. Even through the static and the roar of the seas, Donner could hear the elation in Hardin's voice.

The El Al navigator was less sanguine. While Donner watched, he muddied the clean precise point of intersection by adding swirling lines to the chart, penciling in the progress of the Antarctic storm. Inexorably, the falling barometer, the rising wind, and the burgeoning seas were creeping up on Hardin.

They were pooped suddenly.

Hardin was at the helm. Ajaratu was climbing the companionway with a thermos of hot soup. He saw surprise in her face—an expression of utter disbelief—and he turned to look back. He never made it around. With a crash that shook the boat and a deluge of bitter-cold water, a giant sea buried the stern.

The wave slammed him against the wheel, his arms tangled in the spokes. His head smashed into the binnacle. Then the wave pounded him to the cockpit sole. He came up swimming, thinking he had been swept overboard, but he was only in the flooded cockpit.

Ajaratu was gone. She hadn't yet fastened her safety line. Hardin floundered out of the cockpit and looked down the companionway. She was sprawled on her back in the water on the cabin floor. He started to help her, but the Swan lurched heavily, bow down, throwing him against the hatch.

The boat was lying beam to the seas, her mainsail swinging madly over the water, her jib sheets tangled. A big roller was bearing down on her.

Hardin slammed the latch shut and dove for the helm. She answered grudgingly. He locked it far over and hauled in the main. Then he steered her stern around to the oncoming sea, staggered forward on the leaping deck, and untangled the jib. He set the self-steering and raced below.

Ajaratu was sitting wedged in the corner of the galley,

cradling her left forearm, her eyes shut. She gasped, "I think it's broken."

"How's the rest of you?" He knelt beside her, his teeth chattering.

"All right, I think."

He pulled off her foul-weather parka and cut away her sweater. Draping her bare shoulders with a dry blanket, he examined her arm in the glare of his biggest flashlight.

"Simple fracture?" she asked, her voice trembling with pain.

"Looks that way. There's no bruising."

"Thank God." She smiled tightly. "I don't fancy a closed reduction by a doctor who doesn't practice."

"Will you accept a splint?"

She tried to smile again, but her ash-gray lips wouldn't hold it. She nodded and shut her eyes again.

He splinted her arm with a thick magazine, electrical tape, and rubber shock cord. Then he helped her to the settee, stripped off the rest of her wet clothing, wrapped her in blankets, and eased her up into his bunk.

"I'm so sorry, Peter. I won't be much help to you now."

"We'll do fine." He wedged pillows around her so she wouldn't roll, and strapped her in with the safety belts. Her mouth was tight from pain. He gave her an injection of morphine and covered her with another blanket. Her eyes began to cloud as she watched him towel dry.

He knelt on the settee and kissed and caressed her until the drug put her under. Then he worked the bilge pump behind the nav station. It took an hour of steady pumping to empty what the sea had driven through the open hatch.

Ajaratu was fast asleep when he was done. He counted her pulse. It was stronger than before, indicating she was beyond the danger of severe shock. He started the engine to run the generator and tried to radio Miles. The deepening seas were blocking his signal. He had the same problem with the loran, but he managed to receive a position signal while the boat teetered on a high crest.

Donner's navigator wrote in the wave heights. Five meters (sixteen feet) then six, and seven. Two days before intersection seas of twenty-five feet were being reported in the area and all shipping was being warned away from the middle of the South Atlantic to the coast of Africa. The navigator replotted the point of intersection because Hardin's speed had dropped to four knots, and Donner radioed the revised course. Hardin had to sail more southerly to meet LEVIATHAN, closer to the storm.

"Do you think he'll make it on time?" said Donner.

The El Al navigator knew Hardin only as a reedy voice on the radio and a pencil dot on a very large chart. He tossed the most recent wave-height report onto the stack.

"Time will be the least of his problems."

"He won't reach the ship?"

"He won't reach anything."

16

Pursued by tumbling seas, the Swan ran before a cold gale. Mountainous rollers chased after her, breaking in gigantic crests hundreds of feet long, frothing and foaming with an unearthly roar.

They were shifting from the southwest to the west, directly astern Hardin's course to intercept LEVIATHAN. He thought that was a good break, at first, because the only way to survive their awesome power was to hold the Swan's stern to the advancing rollers so she would rise with them before they broke over her. But when she climbed their steel faces, her sleek racing hull betrayed her.

She was simply too fast. As her stern rose with each

following sea, her bow angled down toward the bottom of the trough, her speed accelerated, and she rushed along the steepening slope so fast that she was in danger of ramming her nose under water and pitchpoling end over end.

He had to slow her. He took down the storm jib and, to reduce windage, refurled the main stormsail more tightly around the boom and replaced the self-steering vane with the smallest one he had. It had little effect.

Bare-masted, the Swan still raced, so he brought up his heaviest line—a one-inch nylon anchor rope—bent a big loop in the end, weighted it with one of his spare anchors, a heavy plow, and trailed it over the stern. Dragging deeply, the long, thick, weighted line slowed her by a knot.

He broke out more lines and streamed them. While searching the stern lockers for something to weight them with, he came across the torn cargo net he had found in Rotterdam. He tied it to his last one-inch nylon and let it out two hundred feet astern.

It was night when he had finished. Heavy clouds blocked the stars, and only the glow of the seas breaking around the stern relieved the blackness. The trailing lines and the net had slowed the boat enough to give him some control. He set the self-steering and went below to rest.

Ajaratu was asleep, breathing regularly. It was oddly quiet in the cabin. The rumble of the sea was muted, the hiss of the crests muffled. He needed dry clothing, but he needed nourishment more and he didn't know how long he could stay, so he strapped on the galley safety harness and boiled water and made a concoction of tea, bottled lemon juice, and honey. He drank two mugs of the hot syrupy liquid, then brought some to Ajaratu and raised her head to the mug. She swallowed groggily and fell back to sleep.

A humming sound began to reverberate in the cabin. It was the wind on the stays, blowing harder. He looked at the barometer. The needle was sinking. It dropped farther in the time he took to strip to the waist, towel dry, and put on his last dry sweat shirt, a heavy wool sweater, and his foul-weather parka. Not knowing when he would next

224

have a chance to eat, he ate several spoonfuls of honey and peanut butter, gnawed some blue-molded cheese, swallowed a single amphetamine, and climbed back to the cockpit, timing his exit from the cabin so that the boat was clear of a breaking sea when he opened the hatch.

He took the helm just in time. The wind, which was gusting to sixty knots, began marching around the compass. It wasn't long before the seas responded. Quarter waves, cross seas, eddies, and breakers opposed the Swan. Running blind, Hardin saw many of them too late to steer away. They covered the bows, staggering the boat, and swept over the sides, flooding the cockpit, soaking him again and again. But always, the thrust of the storm-whipped Cape rollers was dominant. Hardin stayed all night at the helm and in the end, when the wind had settled down to a steady gale from the west, he was alone with his first enemy.

Dawn broke, weary gray, and the rollers were bigger than ever, tall as houses, and traveling fast. Here and there they flung secondary higher waves to the sky like pincers reaching for giant birds. And they were getting steeper, pushing the Swan too fast again. She was pitching bow down, threatening to tumble.

The rumbling, growling seas were still building, nearing heights and steepness that no yacht her size could survive. A wave broke over the stern, drenching him, filling the cockpit. Before the drains could empty it, she yawed, coming beam to the sea. He tried to steer her back, but she responded sluggishly, impeded by the trailing warps.

With a calm that surprised him, he began to admit that it might be the end. Though her hull was intact, and her rigging still erect, she was reaching her limits. He was determined to hold on as long as he could, for he hated that LEVIATHAN would escape, but death did not frighten him. He had concluded that bargain when he had declared war on the tanker.

He regretted that death should take Ajaratu. He wanted to go below and comfort her, so that she wouldn't die alone in the cabin, but he couldn't. To abandon the wheel would be a kind of suicide, to deny survival, a hastening of the event.

A massive sea towered over the sloop. He fought the wheel, pulling her around. One of the streamed lines snapped at the cleat, releasing the cargo net. The stern turned to the sea, and Hardin saw that another had parted in the night. Now only two were holding her back. She accelerated and buried her bow at a steep angle.

Green water engulfed the deck from the bow to the mast. Then the sea behind broke and crashed onto the stern, flinging Hardin across the cockpit, smashing his knees on the seats. For several moments, as he struggled in the water, he saw nothing but the boom and the mast. The Swan was entirely underwater. The bow rose, and then she surfaced, low in the stern, yawing, beam to the rushing sea.

Hardin dragged himself to the wheel and fought to bring her stern back. The boat turned too slowly. An enormous wave bore down on her. It caught her at an angle, half on the beam, half on the stern. She heeled until the mast seemed horizontal and the spreaders were poking a wave top. A second crest clawed the sky, hastening to finish her. This was it.

But the sloop skidded on its side and surfed ahead of the looming wave. Startled by her sudden burst of speed, and unable to stop her, Hardin waited for the bow to submerge for the final time. But instead she raced the wave until, gracefully lifting her stern, she let it pass under her.

Hardin steered her stern-on to the seas again. Again the bow submerged, buried to the cabin. Haltingly, staggered by the tons of water, the Swan struggled to surface. Hardin looked back and his stomach clutched. A bigger sea was rocketing after him, and behind it a great shaggy comber—a freak—almost twice as tall as the monster it was following.

The Swan sped forward, dragging the lines like broken harness, desperately lifting her stern, pointing down the stormy mountain. She started to slip under, cleaving a deeper and deeper bow wave that began to curl over her decks.

Hardin tried to steer her out of the dive. But, underestimating her speed and spooked by the freak sea which was rising like a cliff, he made the mistake of oversteering. Before he could correct, she had heeled sharply. Her bow lifted, and in an instant she was surfing on her side, heeled far over, skidding ahead and then over the pursuing crest. He was trying to figure out what had happened, when the shadow of the second gigantic comber fell darkly on the sea.

The Swan tried. Gathering speed, she began lifting her stern to the towering monster. It carried her high, so high that Hardin caught a glimpse of the miles and miles of raging sea. But the higher she climbed, the more steeply she pointed down and the faster she went.

The crest began to curl overhead and Hardin knew it would finish the job, turning her over and slamming her down on her mast. The nylon lines streamed taut from her stern, as tightly as if they tied her to the bottom of the ocean, but not tight enough to stop her lethal acceleration.

Suddenly, he understood what the Swan had shown him: The waves were driving her forward at great speed, but whenever they hit her stern, at an angle, she heeled, drew her bow out of the water, and skimmed on her side. He realized, to his astonishment, that the heeling boat was actually safer the *faster* she skimmed, because the greater her speed, the more slowly and with less force the waves driving her passed under her.

He turned the wheel, heeling her; his heart leaped as she leaned over and extracted her bow and lay on her side. Locking the rudder at a slight angle, he fumbled a clasp knife out of a zippered parka pocket, opened the six-inch blade, and slashed at the lines. Strand by strand he cut their tenacious hold on the boat, sawing with both hands until they parted.

The Swan surged forward. Unbound, she raced upon the wall of the wave, climbing as it caught up with her. The speedometer needle spun to its limit and the boat leaned on her side and skimmed the water like a surfboard. She attained the peak. Water bellowed around her and spilled into the cockpit, but the next moment she was sliding safely down the backside of the comber.

He was back in control. Unencumbered by the dragging lines, the Swan responded quickly to the helm as he piloted her over the rollers, letting them pass under at a slight angle. By allowing the sea to plot the route instead of resisting, he became, if not its master, a tolerated partner.

But after half a day, when the sea and wind gave no sign of abating, despite the lightening sky, Hardin's exhilaration began to fade. The seas, as large as ever, were regularly breaking over the Swan. As she was tight, and her small cockpit drained quickly, it posed no danger to the boat, but he was battered brutally.

He was drenched to the skin, bitter cold, and his strength was going. He was having difficulty holding the wheel. At first he thought it was jamming, then he realized he didn't have the power in his arms. He needed warmth, dry clothing, and food, or he would quite simply die of exposure.

His mind began to wander. He let the boat out of his hand and it came to near disaster by taking the seas too much abeam. The second time he nodded out, the wheel clipped him on the jaw, waking him, and he realized he had to go below before he passed out.

He rigged the smallest wind vane on the self-steering and set it to hold the stern at a twenty-degree angle to the seas. Then he waited, his hands hovering over the helm, to see if the self-steering would duplicate his method of protecting the boat from the rollers.

The Swan surfed along several waves with little difficulty, and it looked as if Walter could handle it as long as the seas stayed as uniform as they were now. There was a risk that they would change suddenly, but in the shape he was in, he had no choice.

He waited for a sea to break, and when it had he quickly opened the hatch, scrambled down the companionway, and slid it shut. Then he fell down the last couple of steps and sagged to the deck, luxuriating in the void. It was dim and chilly in the cabin, but there was no spray, no wind, and the noise of the sea was muffled. He closed his eyes.

But he shouldn't waste his chance. He forced himself not to sleep. Without standing, he pulled off his soaking clothes. The parka, the sweater, the sweat shirt. His pants, underwear, and socks. Still slumped against the companionway, he found a dry towel in the drawers beneath the chart table and rubbed his cold skin. He dried his hair and his face and only then did he stand.

He put on dry pants and turtleneck sweater, socks, and slippers, and hung his least-wet foul-weather gear by the companionway in case he had to go up in a hurry. Ajaratu was still sleeping. The straps had held her well, and her splinted arm was in place. He straightened her blankets and worked his way across the heaving cabin to the galley, where he boiled water and filled a big mug with a triple dose of packaged soup, and left the stove on to heat the cabin.

Bracing himself on the sette across from Ajaratu, he sipped the hot liquid and marveled at what was probably the most luxurious moment of his life. He was alive when he had expected to be dead. He was dry and he was warm and his belly was filling, all because a thin skin of fiberglass stood between him and the South Atlantic.

Ajaratu stirred. Hardin mixed another mug of soup and brought it to her. He undid the straps, lifted her head and brought the mug to her lips. She drank several mouthfuls, then smiled at him.

"How you doing?"

"Much better. That was quite an injection. I still feel it."

"No pain?"

Tentatively, she raised her splinted arm with the other hand, and winced. "Not too much." Favoring it, she

229

propped herself up on her good elbow, automatically drawing the blankets over her breasts. Then she took the mug of soup and drank deeply. Her eyes settled on a window and she froze with the mug to her teeth.

A wildly breaking comber was filling the sky. The Swan leaned over and surfed. "What has happened?" she breathed.

"We're still alive."

"You look exhausted." The Swan heeled again. She rolled against the outside bulkhead, instinctively shielding her broken arm. "Walter?" she asked doubtfully.

"He's doing a pretty good job."

"Come in with me," she said. "You should sleep."

"Can you stay awake in case it gets worse?"

"Yes. I've had plenty of sleep." She raised the blanket and pressed against the bulkhead, making room for him. "Come in."

Hardin crawled in beside her and put his face on her shoulder. Made clumsy by her arm, she worked his sweater up to his shoulders and pressed her warm skin to him. Hardin suddenly wanted her very much and she didn't seem the least surprised.

The Swan clawed out of a deep trough up onto the crest of a roller and the loran readout screen flickered alive with a line-of-position number. Hardin located the LOP on the latticed loran chart and marked it. The sea passed under the boat and she plummeted beneath the range of the paired radio pulses before he could get a reading on a second LOP. The signal-loss indicator lighted and the screen blinked out.

Hardin waited anxiously while the Swan crossed the trough. He had tried to fix his position by a sun shot at noon, but though it had glimmered through the cloud, the seas were too chaotic to establish the horizon. It had taken an hour of carefully applied stove heat to coax the dampness out of the loran.

He watched the readout with weary eyes as the Swan started another climb. He'd slept for several hours, but a

230

cold, wet hour on deck fitting the bosun's chair and flying the storm jib had left him exhausted. The screen lighted.

The same LOP appeared. Hardin tensed, silently begging the Swan to stay atop the crest until he received another signal. Just as she began her descent, the numbers changed. He turned to the chart and found his fix where the two lines of position intersected.

Triumph welled in his chest.

They crossed astride a thick black line he had penciled earlier. LEVIATHAN's course. He had reached this empty dot on the ocean ahead of the tanker. With luck, he had time to prepare.

"How's your arm?"

"I can steer," said Ajaratu.

"No heroics. Tell me ahead of time if you can't handle her. Or don't want to."

"Tape my arm."

She sat on the engine box and braced her legs against the boat's rolling. Hardin helped her peel off her sweaters. The chill air brought goose bumps to her breasts.

He had already fashioned a new splint from a thin sheet of fiberglass, and now he anchored her forearm protectively to her chest with surgical tape. When the limb was immobile, he helped her on with her sweaters, a foul-weather parka, and a heavy life jacket, and then, on sudden impulse, pulled a stainless-steel mixing bowl from the galley cupboard.

"What is that for?"

He wrapped a heavy towel around her head like a turban and placed the bowl over it. "In lieu of a crash helmet."

"I must look like an idiot."

A slack grin loosened his face. His heart was pounding wildly. "If a wave sends you flying like they did me, you've only got one hand to protect yourself." He worked the parka hood over the bowl and tightened the drawstrings. "Beautiful." He felt giddy.

"You should wear one, too."

"I can't," he replied soberly, trying to focus on the things he had to do. "It would get in the way of the sights."

Her gaze slid toward the open bilge.

Hardin shrugged into his own parka. It was damp and cold. In the zippered pockets were his knife, penlight, flashlight, cable cutters, pliers, and a screwdriver. A block and tackle was draped from the companionway, the line carefully threaded through the pullies. A canvas sling hung from its lower hook.

By its sound in the rigging, the wind was rising. He got the radar antenna from the aft cabin, tied a piece of line between his wrist and the mounting, and carried it up the companionway. Before he opened the hatch he reached down and cupped Ajaratu's chin in his fingers. He was back in control. She held his gaze when he spoke.

"You got me here and I thank you. I can do the rest alone."

"I want to help you."

"Let's go."

He opened the hatch, took a faceful of cold spray getting out, started the engine to drive the generator, then dragged the antenna to the mast. Reeling about the deck, which leaped and bucked like a frightened horse, he climbed onto the boom, worked his legs into the bosun's chair, and began hauling hand over hand on the tackle. Four feet of line spilled from the multiple-pulley system for each foot he hoisted himself. Ajaratu coiled it in the cockpit.

The mast swayed violently, swinging him off the coach roof—starboard over the water, back to port. The seas plucked at his legs. The Swan buried her nose. His side-to-side arc stopped abruptly. The lines fetched up and slammed him into the mast; he twisted frantically to protect the antenna, which dangled from his wrist.

The bow climbed out of the water, but before he swung aft, he hooked his arm between the mast and a halyard—the topping lift—and held it in the crook of his elbow. The wire steadied him like a track as he pulled himself higher. He rested at the spreaders, thirty feet above the boat, and watched the South Atlantic play sullen host to a winter storm.

The sky was as gray as the water; the giant rolling combers still marched from the southwest, and the rising wind was beginning to repeat its earlier maneuver of flattening the seas between them. Hardin resumed hoisting himself with grim satisfaction. He would have a clear shot from the top of one of those rollers.

When he was secure at the masthead, he swabbed out the fitting with an oily rag and inserted the antenna. Then he guyed the light chicken wire and aluminum through which the wind shrilled thinly, removed the watertight plugs from the electrical connectors, and joined the antenna to the circuitry that protruded from the mast. Ajaratu waved that the radar showed a signal, and Hardin quickly lowered himself to the deck. The radarscope was next to the racing instruments above the companionway.

Ajaratu was excited. "Is that it?" She pointed at a white-green flower in the outermost circle. It was on top in the noon position, dead ahead.

Hardin cupped his hands over the screen to block the gray daylight and looked closely. The radar showed a fuzzy picture in the first two circles. That was expected. The jury rig wasn't designed for short-range resolution. Beyond those circles, which represented the closest ten miles, pinpricks of light appeared and faded.

The bright-green flower began to wilt.

"It's only a big sea," said Hardin. "See? It's fading."

Ajaratu crowded close, gripping his waist to support herself. Hardin braced his arms over the closed hatch and cupped the screen so she could see. The Swan climbed a high roller and the outer circle blinked other distant waves, but nothing as steady as the echo signal from a steel ship.

"Beyond our range," said Hardin. "Watch the scope. I'm going to jink her." He transferred Ajaratu's safety line to a handrail, and snubbed it short to give her something to brace against.

233

Then he took the Swan off self-steering and guided her back and forth among the seas, pointing her bow from east to north, performed with the rudder the sweep ordinarily done by a spinning radar reflector. Several times Ajaratu thought she saw something, but each time the target faded. Though she was less than ten feet away, she had to shout for him to hear above the roar of the water and the blaring wind.

He gave it up after a while. LEVIATHAN wasn't near enough yet. That the radar wasn't working or that the ship had already passed he couldn't allow himself to think. It must have slowed for the giant seas.

The sky was darkening in the west. The wind began hinting a shift to the south. It was dancing one way, then the other, too capricious yet to affect the seas, but sufficient to play havoc with the storm jib and fox the steering gear. Hardin helped Ajaratu to the helm, secured her safety line, and put her on a northeast course. If the storm was intensifying, his only chance was to intercept LEVIATHAN as soon as he could.

He propped the boom in its crotch, then rigged the block and tackle from it and lowered the canvas sling back through the hatch. Going below, he slid the hatch cover closed against the rope to keep out the blowing spray. Then he manhandled the wooden crate out of the bilge and dragged it across the sole on a blanket.

The Swan heeled sharply, surfing on a comber. Hardin yanked his feet out of the way an instant before the crate crashed into a bulkhead. He removed the lower companionway steps, jammed the crate against the engine box, levered off the top, and worked the canvas sling under the weapon. Then he hauled on the tackle until the lines angled tightly between the boom and the weapon and forced the hatch cover to slide open. A roller rumbled under the boat and an errant prong surged into the cockpit and down the companionway. The cold water poured down Hardin's chest.

He heaved on the block and tackle. It was rough going

until the weapon cleared the engine box. Then the Dragon hung perpendicular to the boom and rose freely. It gyrated with the boat's motion, however, and gouged large splinters out of the aft teak bulkhead.

Hardin scrambled onto the engine box and blocked it with his shoulders while he hoisted. He face was level with the Brookes and Gatehouse instrument panel. He glanced at the radar screen. Still nothing. The speed indicator beside it registered eight knots. The needle spun to eleven as the Swan lunged down a slope. They were rocketing too fast under the storm jib. The wind was rising and he knew he should take it down, but first the weapon.

He heaved on the line. The long pull up the mast in the bosun's chair had taken a lot out of him and his arms were numb. The Dragon swung away before he could stop it and it shifted in the sling, threatening to fall out. Gripping the tackle in one hand, he wedged his shoulder under the weapon. One hundred fifty pounds slammed into his collar bone. The pain was blinding. He straightened his legs and heaved with all his strength. The Dragon settled properly into the sling. Gasping with pain, he continued to haul the tackle.

"It's getting bad again," yelled Ajaratu. Hardin said nothing and she watched with fathomless eyes as the black cylinder slowly emerged from the cabin.

Hardin pulled until it had cleared the hatch. Then he closed the cover, lowered the weapon onto it to get some slack, and shifted the block and tackle to the end of the boom. Now when he raised the Dragon, it swung over the front of the cockpit. He knelt on the crossbench behind the hatch cover and carefully lowered the weapon until it touched his shoulder.

He removed the lens caps and peered through the binocular sights, his heart pounding as much with excitement as exertion. The crosshairs bisected the top of a Cape roller and, quite abruptly, the Swan was a very potent piece of machinery.

He covered the lenses, tied off the tackle, and looped

a line from either end of the four-foot cylinder to deck cleats so the weapon wouldn't swing. Ajaratu's eyes were on him. He turned and met her gaze, prepared for resistance. He saw none. Only resignation—then something else, excitement, he thought, but she looked away before he could be sure.

The wind continued to flatten the waves between the rollers. He took it as an omen for success. Visibility was getting better—at least when the rollers carried him above the turmoil—and he thought that if the wind held at this force—just below a strong gale—and didn't shift and rile a bad cross sea, and if LEVIATHAN came before dark, he had a decent chance.

"A light!" cried Ajaratu, bracing the wheel with her leg and pointing at the radarscope.

Hardin cupped his hands over the screen.

Outer edge of the inside ring. *Too close.* Upper quadrant. Twelve o'clock. A bright-green light. A wave? A glitch? It faded. But when the bow rose it blossomed again. Hardin stared—his excitement mounting—gauging its intensity, willing it not to be a wave, gradually realizing that a wave couldn't last so long, praying it wasn't another ship, but knowing that they were fifty miles west of the shipping lanes to Capetown and that if it was a ship, it could only be LEVIATHAN.

How did it get so close? Perhaps the storm was too much for the radar. The light was nudging the second ring. Ten miles—less than an hour away. He backed away from the screen and joined Ajaratu at the wheel.

"Yes?"

"Yes."

He took the wheel and used the bright light on the radarscope like a compass needle to sail toward it. It glowed more and more brightly as the sky darkened from north to west. He held it dead center, steering toward the tanker. The lessening distance between them was symbolized by the light dot's progress toward the center of the scope.

The wind began to howl in the rigging, building the rollers but still smoothing the seas between them. Hardin shifted course only to tuck the Swan's stern safely over the tops of the rollers. Then he lined the light up again and sprinted through the broad trough ahead of the next looming sea.

"Thunder," said Ajaratu, cocking her head and peeling open her parka hood. She closed it quickly against the cold.

Minutes later Hardin heard it too. A deep, single report like thunder dead ahead, but no lightning brightened the gloomy sky nor lanced into the worsening seas.

Without warning, the wind swung around to the northwest. The Swan was blown back, staggered by the sudden change. The radarscope went dark. Hardin shoved past Ajaratu to check the set. He ducked instinctively as a shadow passed overhead. It was the radar antenna. The wind had ripped it off the mast.

A dark line closed on the bow, and seconds later driven sleet lashed the boat. Hardin groped his way back to the wheel and bowed his head with Ajaratu, huddling from the stinging missiles. The thunderlike noise sounded again and again, louder than before, borne on the shrieking wind, closer and closer like the din of retreat heard in the rear lines with ever more frightening clarity. The sleet thinned, turned to bitter-cold rain, stopped.

Hardin looked back and saw a tremendous comber traveling rapidly from the southwest. Its crest began to crumble, spilling tons of white water ahead of it, catching up with them at a frightening speed.

Gripping the wheel with both hands, he tried to hold her into the wind to take the roller from behind. The crest loomed high, threatening to curl over and drop on the Swan, but she rose with it, climbing, struggling up and up, and finally reached the crest, where she wallowed like a wood chip in the rushing foam, high above the raging sea. Miles away, mountainous waves serrated the horizons.

Hardin stared.

A massive black shape rammed through the swirling chaos.

LEVIATHAN.

Bow on and close.

17

Black against the sky, crowned in white spray, the oil tanker shattered the towering seas, goring the combers, straddling the troughs, driving implacably through the storm that mauled the sailboat in its path. Livid smoke stood above the unmistakable silhouette of its twin funnels. The wide bow climbed heavily out of the water, poised at a steep angle, then dropped like a trip hammer.

A thunderous report echoed across the turmoil.

The Swan plummeted down the backside of the roller, deep into a boiling trough, and Hardin lost sight of LEVIATHAN. He steered frantically through chaotic cross seas, heading for the next roller.

Ajaratu leaped onto the deck behind him and, gripping the backstay, shouted directions from her high perch. He steered as she said to and the Swan was suddenly climbing as if in the slings in a boatyard. Then she was atop the roller, surfing on the thick, white crest. Hardin steered to keep her up and tried to estimate the distance to LEVIATHAN.

Machinelike absorption possessed him, focusing his senses on the black ship. The sounds of the sea faded. He was dimly aware of Ajaratu crouching beside him, ready to take the wheel. His eyes felt like binoculars, clear and steady.

It was as if he had a range finder in his brain. He knew as surely as tossing a ball where he would fire his rocket.

238

In four seconds the Swan would slip from its perch. Three hundred yards to port a gigantic breaking roller was plowing across the sea. LEVIATHAN was two rollers beyond it, but the ship would cross those two in the time it took Hardin to reach the first. He looked for a path through the turbulent trough—a path to his shot. He had sailed six thousand miles to be there for five seconds.

The Swan teetered off the crest. No longer able to see LEVIATHAN, Hardin steered downwind as the roller rushed past, then close-hauled across the trough, dodging the spiky seas that leaped around the Swan like the walls of a living maze. He heard thunder when LEVIATHAN bombarded its first roller, and knew that the Swan was crossing too slowly because he wasn't yet halfway across. Risking a narrow passage between two waves about to collide, he steered farther off the wind. The Swan accelerated, but a sea buried the bow and for a second white-green water mounted the foredeck. He feared she wouldn't come up, but she flung the water off like a dirty blanket.

When the growl of the roller grew to a roar and it was looming overhead, Hardin showed Ajaratu a route up the writhing slope.

"Stay on top as long as you can."

She took the wheel without a word, and her eyes, large in her drawn face, locked on the roller. Hardin unlashed the Dragon, knelt beneath the weapon, and let the barrel nestle onto his shoulder.

He removed the lens caps, quartered the sea in the crosshairs, set the range finder for three hundred yards, and blended his body with the weapon. The roller drew near. The Swan began lifting. He swung the muzzle until he was aiming ahead over the port side, and made certain that the fiery exhaust wouldn't jet back at Ajaratu.

The bow sloped sharply. They were halfway up the roller, lifting fast, racing to get to the top before it fell on them. The Swan started to yaw as the water grew violent. The roller's surface was disintegrating, turning to chaos. Ajaratu worked the wheel with one hand and her knee. The boat straightened, still rising.

Hardin heard the thunder of LEVIATHAN hitting its second crest. Then the Swan surged to the top of the roller and the sea spread before them and LEVIATHAN filled the sights.

Its massive bow climbed ponderously toward the sky. Hardin fixed the bulbous prow in the cross hairs. He reached for the trigger switch, aiming for the waterline. The setup was perfect. The monster was rearing, baring the whole of its prognathous bow.

Ajaratu screamed a warning.

The black in Hardin's sights turned milky gray. A craggy second crest toppled over the first, piled tons of seawater on the Swan, and smashed him to the deck. The Dragon spun wildly and the muzzle raked his temple as he fell under the icy water.

Somersaulting about the cockpit, he crashed into the boom, the wheel, the winches. Pain stabbed his face. Something sharp gouged his kidneys. Ajaratu catapulted into him. He closed his arms around her and held on with all his strength. Suddenly his lifeline wrenched his chest and he felt himself being dragged through the water.

His lungs burning, he held Ajaratu with one arm and tried to swim to the surface. His lifeline held him. Panic welled into his mouth. The Swan was sinking, dragging him with her. He clawed at his parka for his knife. The zippered pocket wouldn't open. His fingers were numb. Then his face was out of the water. He took a mouthful of brine, gagged it out, and pulled Ajaratu back when a wave plucked her away.

The Swan was slamming up and down in short fierce waves, smacking the water, threatening to smash their skulls. Hardin tugged Ajaratu's lifeline to make sure it was still attached.

"You okay?" he shouted.

She nodded, her teeth chattering. The water was much colder than the air.

"I'll go first."

He pushed away from her, kicked toward the Swan,

gauged the rise and fall of the pounding hull, gripped the toe rail when she was at her lowest, and dragged himself under the lifelines. The jib was snapping like a machine gun. He reached over the side and hauled in on Ajaratu's safety line. When the boat lurched toward her, she slithered snakelike under the lines, despite her bound arm, and clambered into the cockpit, where she collapsed on her back and lay gasping, her face painfully contorted.

The boat was in a trough. The big sea that had broached them had vanished to the east, and the next giant roller was roaring toward them. The sheets were trailing in the water. The wheel spun in crazy circles as the wet sail flapped and the boat wallowed helplessly, bereft of way. Snagged by its sights, the Dragon dangled from the sling, banging its muzzle on the deck.

Hardin hesitated, torn between saving the weapon and manning the wheel. The sea won. The weapon was useless without the boat. He stopped the wheel with the friction brake, then put it hard over and waited for eons for the sloop to put her stern to the seas. The jib, partially tangled, banged full with a maverick gust. The bow responded, the Swan took way, and the stern slowly wheeled toward the threatening roller.

He locked the wheel, leaped over Ajaratu, and tried to lift the Dragon back into the sling. Lashing the front of the cockpit, splintering the teak cross seat, it was too heavy, too wet and slippery and unwieldy to control. He reached to lower it with the block and tackle.

Ajaratu cringed, her eyes round with terror, and he thought, fleetingly, that he had never seen her scared before. He looked up. The sky was black with LEVIATHAN.

The oil tanker lumbered atop the crest like Hardin's nightmares, looming over the Swan; the wave's upward flow was lifting her to LEVIATHAN even as the ship was flattening the crest and descending upon the sailboat.

And, as in a nightmare, Hardin couldn't aim his weapon. The broaching sea had hopelessly tangled the block and tackle. He struggled furiously, heaving the muzzle up at the passing hull by brute force, his whole will concentrated on firing.

Blood thundered in his ears, blotting out the roar of LEVIATHAN's passage through the storm. He saw red. A quiet, cool voice deep in his mind told him he couldn't sink LEVIATHAN with this shot. He wouldn't listen. He burned to inflict damage, to maul and maim, to rip a hole in the monster, to punish.

"No!" screamed Ajaratu.

"It's mine," yelled Hardin.

"No," she screamed again. "You'll kill us!"

She gestured frantically at the back of the rocket launcher. The exhaust was jammed against the cockpit coaming. Were he to fire, it would explode in his hands.

Hardin nestled his face to the sights. It didn't matter. The rocket would launch regardless, and at such short range he didn't have to be alive to guide it. The wall of the ship was yards away; he could see the hull welds. He fumbled for the trigger switch. Movement intruded on his field of vision. Motion different from the passage of the hull atop the crest, or the leaping water, or the heavings of the Swan. Ajaratu was coming at him, swinging a ten-inch bronze winch handle.

There was time to fire before she hit him, but the look on her face brought him back to sanity. He scrambled aside. The winch handle grazed his ear. Hardin seized her wrist.

"Okay, I'm fine. Let's get out of here." He released her and pushed her toward the helm.

Ajaratu stared at the winch handle, then up at the hull rushing past.

"Move!" he roared. "Right rudder. It'll crush us."

LEVIATHAN and the Swan were still on parallel courses, heading oppositely. The wave was still drawing the Swan up while the ship was still settling down. Hardin could see its bottom plates.

He planted his feet and stood ready to try to fend off, but as LEVIATHAN descended upon them he wondered if

242

it might be more sensible to haul the inflatable life raft from under the cockpit seat than to try to soften the collision. He waited, transfixed, with the boat hook in his hands, too battered by fear and shock and too exhausted to make a new decision.

Exactly as it had when it had run down *Siren*, LEVIATHAN had stolen the wind from the Swan. The jib swayed uselessly, and the rudder seemed to have no effect. The Swan refused to budge more than twenty feet from the tanker.

"Play the wheel," Hardin shouted, but Ajaratu stood still, her eyes closed, her head bowed.

"Stop praying and steer!" he bellowed.

A quarter wave detached from the great Cape roller supporting LEVIATHAN and forged ahead, growing rapidly larger. Ajaratu steered the Swan's stern over it and it swept the sloop away from the main roller. It disintegrated in seconds, spilling the Swan deep into a trough a hundred yards from LEVIATHAN.

The oil tanker steamed past, its square stern curling an enormous wake out of the sea like a giant plane gouging a thick pungent wood shaving from a soft board. The wake united with the shattered roller, and the combination raced after the Swan like a falling building.

"Inside!" Hardin yelled. He locked the steering wheel and dragged Ajaratu around the swaying rocket launcher to the companionway. Shooting glances over his shoulder at the perpendicular sixty-foot wave, he fumbled the hatch cover open. Ajaratu scrambled below. The wave thundered closer. He dove after her and slammed the hatch shut.

"Grab ahold."

He clambered into his bunk—the smallest, most protected space in the cabin—and pulled Ajaratu in with him. The monster reared. The cabin darkened in its shadow. The Swan fought to attain the crest, but the wave was too steep and too chaotic—multifaceted—to provide a slope to climb. Her bow pointed the ocean floor. The wave curled over the Swan and for a long, dark moment the boat sailed in a cave of water. Then the crest collapsed. And the Swan tumbled onto its bow, end over end, until her mast pointed down and her keel to the sky.

18

A steel toolbox caromed through the main salon, splintered the fore cabin door, and hurtled the length of the boat back to the stern cabin. Hardin and Ajaratu slammed into the berth's ceiling.

Appendant to the crashing, banging din of objects falling and breaking and the thunder of the rampant wave, a grinding, wrenching sound shook the Swan—the diesel engine shifting on its bed. Hardin held his breath, waiting for it to shear its bolts and plummet through the roof.

Water-dimmed light shone through the upside-down windows and hatch covers. She righted suddenly, dragged around by her seven-thousand-pound keel. They sprawled from the berth space and everything that had fallen to the ceiling cascaded about them. Their heavy foul-weather gear protected them from the broken glass, but Hardin cut his hand as he tried to stand.

She flipped again, end over end, and landed upside down. The Dragon smashed the Lucite hatch cover and a torrent of icy water gushed in.

The water surged over the broken crockery, rattling like surf on a pebble beach. Hardin and Ajaratu floundered ankle deep on the ceiling of the wrecked salon waiting for the keel to right the boat again. But the new weight of the water ballasted the upside-down hull, steadied it in the heaving backwash of the giant wave, and stiffened its resistance to the keel. The light dimmed and the water tugged at their knees.

244

"We're sinking," said Ajaratu, her voice calm. Her free hand bit fearfully into Hardin's arm.

"She'll turn over," he said, his mind screaming for the next roller. It was their one chance of turning upright, but where was it? It seemed like minutes since the boat had pitchpoled. Then, with sudden horror, he remembered the way LEVIATHAN had flattened the ocean after it had run down *Siren*. How long before a roller disturbed the wake and nudged the Swan?

"Peter?"

"I'm here." He drew her close to comfort her. It was nearly dark.

"I love you."

The cabin grew quiet but for the echoing lap of the rising water sloshing from bulkhead to bulkhead. The Swan began to descend quickly.

"Peter? Tell me you love me."

The boat sank lower, but the water in the cabin did not rise correspondingly. They were dropping into a trough.

"*Lie to me! Please.* Tell me you love me."

"A wave," Hardin cried. "Hang on, she's going to throw us."

The boat climbed abruptly, heeled onto her side, and lurched upright. A torrent thundered in the broken hatch cover. Hardin lost his grip on Ajaratu and pitched headlong into the waist-deep water. Pummeled by floating floorboards, he surfed across the cabin and regained his feet under the spewing hatch. Then the Swan floated sluggishly out of the giant sea. Light flooded the cabin and the torrent stopped. Something slammed hard against the hull.

"Ajaratu!"

"I'm here."

She half walked, half swam out of the forecabin. Hardin had already taken his cable cutters from his parka. He started up the companionway shouting orders and dodging the Dragon, which hung through the shattered hatch, swinging wildly as the boat rolled with sharp, abrupt motions.

"Get me a jib and hammer and nails. And get pots and buckets."

Ajaratu struggled back toward the fore cabin, heading for the sail bins. The thing pounding the hull banged again with a brutal jolt.

"No," Hardin shouted. "Tools first!"

He climbed fearfully onto deck, the panic of his voice ringing in his ears.

The damage was total. The seas had swept the Swan's decks clean, leveling her mast, tearing away her helm, ventilators, bow pulpit, and lifelines, their stanchions and most of the toe rail they were welded to. Her boom lay across the coach roof, ripped from the mast, but pinioned to the boat by the antitank rocket in the cabin.

Like a whirlwind which can drive a straw into an oak, the sea had been capricious. Incredibly, it had plucked a deeply seated genoa halyard winch from the coach roof, while a foot away the spinnaker pole still rested securely in its fastenings.

The mid and fore hatches had held, which was why they were still afloat. The after stay and the port shroud had parted, but the forestay and the starboard shroud hung tautly over the side, and as the sea rolled her, the jagged foot of the aluminum mast reared out of the water and shook the Swan with a blow to her bow.

Hardin raced forward on the pitching deck, crouched near the stump where the mast had twisted apart, and severed the starboard shroud with the cable cutters. He went for the forestay, but as he knelt, he looked back, alerted by a deep rumble. Another Cape roller was after the wallowing Swan; he had no safety line. But if she was thrown against the mast again, it would hole her.

He worked desperately to cut the forestay, leaning over the bow to reach beyond the heavy chain-plate fittings which were too thick for the cable cutters. The stay parted with a bang. Then the halyards and sheets fetched up tightly between the mast stump and the sinking aluminum shaft.

The Swan began to lift with the roller—heavy and reluctant. He cut the main halyard, the genoa halyards, the spinnaker halyards, the spinnaker pole lifts, and the flag halyard. He looked for the topping lift, but it had already parted. A single line hung over the side abreast the cockpit. The jib sheet. He stumbled aft, and cut it.

The mast was gone, but the roller was upon them. He leaped down the companionway, yelled to Ajaratu to hold on, spied the dining-table top floating in the waist-deep water, wedged it into the hatch, and standing on the engine box, tried to brace it with his back. The Dragon shoved at his legs as the boat pitched.

The roller curled over the Swan and buried her. Hardin held fast for several seconds. Then the pressure of the water was too much and it flung him aside and poured in. When the wave had passed, the Swan was much lower in the water. Ajaratu grabbed Hardin's parka and hauled him upright.

"Your toolbox is in the sink. The jib is on the stove. What should I do?"

"Bail. Throw the water into the cockpit. I'll help you as soon as I cover the hatch." Stuffing his pockets with hammer and nails, Hardin folded the jib into a triple square, dragged it up on deck, and spread it over the gaping hatch. Covering the entire area from port to starboard including two holes where the ventilators had been, he lay flat over the Dacron to keep the shrieking wind from blowing it away. Then he nailed it to the teak decks. First the corners, then edges, driving nail after nail, stopping only when a comber drove him below, then resuming the work on the patch. Water spouted fitfully from the small space where the washboard had been as Ajaratu bailed into the cockpit, which drained back to the sea.

The block and tackle was hopelessly tangled and there was no way to lift the Dragon out of the cabin. Hardin lashed the boom to several deck cleats, then secured the antitank weapon with rope to keep it from banging them while they bailed the waist-deep water.

They bailed through the night, struggling to stand upright as the hull wallowed drunkenly in the storm-driven seas and their exhausted bodies cried for sleep. They rested briefly at every hundred buckets. Midway through their fourth hundred, Ajaratu scooped an unbroken honey jar into her pail. Greedily they poured the thick sweetness into their mouths.

Ajaratu suffered the most because she couldn't relieve the strain by switching arms. Several times Hardin tried the bilge pump, but the debris in the bilge clogged it. They worked past dawn until, despite the fact that breaking seas had often poured under the patch, the water was too shallow to scoop with buckets. What remained was a black and noisome soup of seawater, engine oil and battery acid, floating food, clothing, books, charts, blankets, and tools.

Hardin cleared the bilge-pump intake again and Ajaratu crouched beside it and strained the water with her fingers while he pumped until his arms and back were burning and his heart felt it would explode. He straightened up and leaned against the Dragon, which hung in the sling like a dead shark.

Ajaratu sagged against the engine box, her head drooping to her chest. Hardin picked her out of the slime and sat her at the chart table. He cupped her chin to get her attention. "Find the storm jib and all the line you can get and come up."

She stared vacantly.

"Fast."

"I don't know if I can," she mumbled.

"You better. We're not out of it yet."

He pushed her toward the fore cabin and went on deck. The wind had subsided slightly, but the seas were running as high as before. He found the emergency tiller in a cockpit locker next to the life raft, used its attached wrench to open the rudder-shaft cover in the cockpit sole, and fastened the tiller. To his relief it moved, which meant that the rudder had survived the violent tumbling.

Ajaratu passed up several coils of line. Hardin told her to pile mattresses under the Dragon, and when she had he cut the tackle, letting it drop to the padding and freeing the boom, which he fitted with lines and a halyard. Then, with her help, he raised the aluminum pole and lashed it to the mast stump by wrapping it round and round with nylon line. He guyed it fore and aft and to either side, then hoisted the storm jib to the top of the jury rig and, numb with exhaustion, took the tiller as the sail filled and the Swan stopped rolling.

Ajaratu gingerly turned the sodden pages of the *Sailing Directions for Southwest Coast of Africa*. It was five days since they had pitchpoled, and they were drifting into Table Bay, Capetown's broad open harbor which spread beneath the improbably level and aptly named Table Mountain.

" 'During the winter,' " she read, " 'when northwesterly winds occur, a current sets into Table Bay from the northwestward.' " She closed the book, marking the place with her thumb.

"We'll need it," said Hardin, eyeing the short sails—a jib and a miniature main on a jury-rigged boom made from the spinnaker pole. They barely pushed the Swan to steerage in the light, cool breeze.

His sextants were smashed, as were the radio and loran. With no idea where the storm had blown them, he had navigated roughly by the sun, wanting nothing more than to sail east until they reached land. Table Mountain, rosy purple beneath a stunning lavender-blue sky, an unmistakably giant mass shouldered by the conical Lion's Head on one side and the rugged Devil's Peak on the other, had been the first land they had seen.

Now, as northwesterly rollers, final legacy of the storm, began carrying them toward the mouth of the Bay, he was thankful that among the few things they had rescued along with the invaluable Sailing Directions was his passport. He would need a lot of help from the American Consulate —despite what trouble they had for him regarding the Dragon—to get Ajaratu safely out of South Africa.

The storm had purged him of his hate for LEVIATHAN and he was left with a single, vivid image of the great

249

ship bludgeoning the seas like an iron club, the same seas which had nearly killed him. He was grateful to be alive, and he was humbled. But the sea had shown him that in humility there was strength, strength that had come from tasting fear, from having flinched, from knowing with utter certainty a power greater than his own. As a sailor he had always accepted the might of the sea. In LEVIATHAN he had seen its master.

The revelation left Hardin less peaceful than empty. It would be a long time before he wanted anything again. He would start simply. He would get Ajaratu safely out of South Africa. He would repair the boat. He would sail away. Where, he didn't know and didn't care.

The Swan drifted deeper into the bay, borne more on the current than by the wind. The white buildings of Capetown, gleaming in the sunlight on the distant shore, looked like breakers crashing at the foot of Table Mountain. Five miles across the bay, stone breakwaters formed a harbor, which was better protected than the outer anchorage. Hardin scanned it with his binoculars, searching for a small private cove or marina where they might repair without having to contend with the authorities.

Merchant shipping docks occupied the south, large basin behind the breakwaters. Ajaratu read aloud from the Sailing Directions. There was mention of a yacht basin behind the Duncan Dock. Hardin could see the cranes and pneumatic grain loaders of Duncan Dock, but a high, dark jetty blocked the yacht basin from view. They agreed that it would be too close to the center of Capetown. The glasses swept the coast northward beyond the basins. He saw some industrial plants, a fishing harbor, and the suburbs of Capetown. He decided to sail farther into Table Bay, as long as the current carried them, then come about and sail up the coast until he found a small yard.

He had been unable to start the engine, even though a check showed it hadn't shifted very much when the boat had pitchpoled. It was worth another try. He gave Ajaratu the tiller and went below and worked the hand crank. It coughed hopefully after a few minutes. He pulled harder, and it rumbled to life. Elated, he went back on deck, took the tiller, and engaged forward gear.

The propeller shaft thumped loudly. He choked the engine with a disappointed groan. "Shaft's bent. Son of a bitch." He closed his eyes and let the sun bake his face. It was low in the north, a winter sun, but it felt good. He had been so cold and wet so long that he wondered if he would ever be warm again.

When he looked again, the Swan had halved the distance to the harbor jetties. The buildings were distinct now, as was the broad, shallow slope where the city rested between the water and the sheer base of Table Mountain. He saw warehouses on the jetties which formed the narrow-mouthed Victoria Basin and the vast Duncan Dock to the north of it.

He stared at the dark mass in front of Duncan Dock. He had thought it was a jetty, but a tall white structure towered over one end, leaning at a steep angle no building ever stood.

"My God," breathed Ajaratu. She handed him the glasses.

Hardin twirled the focus wheel. The soft edges crystallized.

LEVIATHAN.

Its bow was smashed.

The front of the ship was deep in the water. The stern was high. The propellers were exposed, their colossal blades gleaming like drawn swords. The ship was surrounded by tugboats and lighters, and white streams of water spewed down its black hull like mountain waterfalls.

Hardin steered closer, bearing ahead of the bows, which he inspected with the glasses. They were crumpled from the waterline to the decks, and he marveled that its crew had made it to safety. Workmen were erecting scaffolding around the bows. The rumble of big pump engines drifted

251

across the water and red sparks cascaded from dozens of points as welders and torchmen cut away the smashed plates.

Hardin put the Swan about and began beating up the coast. He had seen a launch heading toward him from Duncan Dock.

"Reception committee," he said to Ajaratu.

Her eyes flashed, but they both knew they were in for a tough time with the South African police.

"Go below," said Hardin. "If they're just being helpful, I'll tell them we don't need any."

Her mouth set tightly as she went into the cabin. Hardin looked straight ahead, as if sailing a thirty-eight-foot sloop with a twenty-foot mast were an everyday occurrence. The launch pulled alongside and slowed, its engine burbling softly.

"Hardin!"

Festooned with cameras, film cannisters, lenses, and light meters, Miles stepped nimbly aboard and greeted Hardin with a probing smile. His men, stocky blond youths, made fast to the Swan fore and aft, then stood watchfully by their lines. The launch speeded up several knots, bearing the Swan with it. Miles nodded with satisfaction.

"I had a feeling that you'd end up here, if you made it. My people said it would be likely with the Benguela Current slowed by the storm." He smiled again. "Of course, they also said you wouldn't make it."

"I made it," said Hardin.

Donner glanced the length of the battered sailboat. "Just."

He looked at Hardin. Deep lines scored his face. His eyes were red, his bearded cheeks sunken. He had lost weight and his arms, corded with long, stringy muscles, were too thin. The hand that gripped the tiller where the elaborate helm and binnacle used to be had the dry, fleshless look of a claw. He seemed in shock, oddly indifferent. Staring straight ahead, he spoke.

"I want you to get Ajaratu out of the country."

252

"Already arranged," said Donner. "Is she below?"

"Yes."

Donner climbed down the companionway. The once-beautiful salon was a shambles. Ajaratu leaned against the dining table, her arm in a sling, glaring defiantly at the hatchway. She looked surprised when she saw him, recognizing him but not remembering why.

"Good afternoon, Dr. Akanke. My name is Miles. I will take you home."

She stared.

He extended a finely manicured hand. "We must hurry. They may have seen you coming into the Bay."

She brushed past him, went up the companionway, and spoke to Hardin. Donner took a quick look around the cabins, assessing the damage, then returned to the cockpit, where Hardin was explaining that Donner would do as he said.

"What about you?" she asked.

"I'll take care of him," said Miles. "We must hurry, Doctor."

He took her arm and guided her onto the launch. His men were getting nervous. At any moment the security-conscious South African Railways and Harbors Administration might send a patrol boat across the bay to investigate this rendezvous between a private launch and a dismasted yacht.

Like the King's Jews of early Europe, Israelis often acted as unofficial messengers in modern Africa between bickering states, black and white. The system had grown out of Israeli agricultural and technical aid, engineering projects and trade, and military training programs. The Mossad had taken its opportunities, along with the technicians and merchants, and, all things considered, it had a decent organization in South Africa. But the worst way to strain secret contacts and friendships was to run afoul of zealous functionaries who had the power to arrest before strings could be pulled.

One of Donner's men draped a long, hooded raincoat over Ajaratu's shoulders. Donner was struck by her regal bearing and his hands strayed toward his camera, knowing a picture. The weary lines the ordeal had carved on her face heightened her beauty and gave it character beyond her years.

She looked at Hardin and their eyes locked. He stood and leaned over the cockpit coaming and took her hand. "Thank you, Ajaratu. I wouldn't have made it without you."

She nodded silently and glanced astern at the black bulk of LEVIATHAN, listing steeply.

It was a stiff good-bye, Donner thought, like defeated generals exchanging farewells over broken swords.

Hardin sat back down at the tiller, the woman's eyes still on him. "Will I see you?" she asked.

"Yes."

"When?"

"Soon."

"Please," said Donner. "We have to go."

"Peter?" She smiled thinly. "May I hold your watch?"

Hardin removed his battered Rolex without a word, leaned over the coaming, and slipped the expansion band around her wrist. He kissed her hand. She combed her fingers through his hair for a moment, then stepped into the launch's cabin and sat down and stared at the deck.

Donner snapped his fingers. His helmsman handed the wheel to another and stepped onto the Swan. "Leslie will help you to a mooring up the coast," said the Israeli. "I'll come back for you."

Hardin looked at LEVIATHAN. "Are they repairing it, Miles?"

"Yes."

"Get me a mast."

BOOK THREE

19

"Where are you going?" Miles asked.

A week had passed, and Hardin had recovered enough strength to supervise the refitting of the Swan. They were alone in the Afrikaner boatyard owner's office.

"North."

Miles smiled wryly and refilled their teacups from a pot on a popping wood stove.

"East or west?"

Hardin regarded him with faint amusement; he was keeping his plan to himself, but the Israeli never stopped trying. "Can you spring for lift on a freighter to Durban?"

"East."

"That's where they keep Durban."

"I assume you've had your fill of Cape rollers?"

"Yes," said Hardin. "And that's a very tough thousand miles around the Cape in winter. You'd save me two or three weeks."

"What's your rush? LEVIATHAN's laid up for a month."

Hardin shrugged. Six or seven weeks was more like it, he had learned in the pubs where the shipfitters drank. It was reassuring to know things Miles didn't. "Can you arrange it?" he asked.

"Of course, but I'd rest easier if you'd give me even a general idea of your intentions."

"It won't work that way."

Miles frowned petulantly and Hardin, who didn't want to anger him, put his cup down on the scratched wooden desk and looked the Israeli in the eye.

"Let me explain something, Miles." He pointed out the multipaned window to where the Swan rested on a cradle. "When I get out there on that boat again, I'm stuck. I can go anywhere in the world that the wind will take me. I can even go a lot of places that the wind doesn't want to take me. But only at eight knots. A hundred sixty, a hundred seventy miles in a good day, working hard. That's about twelve minutes in a plane. Do you get what I'm saying?"

"Obviously, at any given moment you are trapped within a small perimeter, but I fail to see why you can't—"

"Like a fish in a barrel," said Hardin. "All I can do is hide the barrel. Therefore, I'm telling nobody where I'm going. Two nights out of Durban and I'm my own man."

"But you need me."

"I want the exact hour LEVIATHAN leaves Capetown. And that's all."

"As well as a ride on a freighter . . . repairs . . . provisions . . ."

"Helpful, not necessary."

"What would you use for money? You're wanted for questioning by the United States Army. You can't very well use your American Express card."

"I'm a doctor," Hardin said. "I can walk into the lowest dive in this town and get a thousand bucks for sewing up a safecracker who got shot by a guy who wasn't supposed to be home."

"This is going to cost more than a thousand dollars," Miles groused.

"I'll give you a letter of payment to my lawyer in New York."

"No, thank you."

"I didn't think so."

"And don't treat any criminals. This is a police state in case you hadn't noticed. In fact, the sooner I get you out of here the better off we'll all be."

"Put me on a ship," said Hardin. "I'm grateful for your help and I'm not telling you where I'm going."

"I'm not sure I can allow this," said Miles. "I may have to review my options."

"You go review your options," said Hardin, wearily climbing to his feet. "I gotta work on my boat."

258

The Swan was lifted from Table Bay by a deck crane and lashed to a solid cradle amidships, and the freighter immediately got underway. Donner had arranged to return on the pilot boat, so he stood beside Hardin and watched with him as they slid out of Duncan Dock and slowly by LEVIATHAN. Listing, as it still did, it resembled a sheer-sided rock promontory more than a ship.

Hardin's lips curled sardonically and his eyes stayed on the stricken ship until they were beyond the breakwater. Then, as the pilot boat came alongside, he thanked Donner formally and promised to keep in touch on the new radio. Donner had the disquieting feeling that he was laughing at him.

"Good luck, Doctor," he said, taking his hand.

Hardin held on for a moment and Donner felt something solid in his palm.

"You keep forgetting I'm an electrical engineer," Hardin said with one of his rare and easy smiles. He opened his hand.

Donner found a small piece of metal in his palm, the electronic tracking device he had fastened to the top of the mast so he would know where Hardin sailed.

"Don't apologize," said Hardin. "I wouldn't believe you."

The freighter belonged to the Polish Ocean Lines. Hardin slept as much as he could and forced himself to eat large meals. He was a long way from recovered and still tired easily. Few of the crew spoke English, which made it easy to keep to himself.

Miles had given him a couple of letters from Ajaratu. He opened one the third day out, and read it several times.

Dear Peter,

I hope you will come to your senses, but I do not expect it. Your senses, of course, are the problem. I fear you will let them drive you to a violent, lonely

259

death. You are a man possessed by the past, a lover without his love—my tragedy as well as yours.

Forgive my morbid tone. I mean to persuade you, not add to your unhappiness, but I miss you terribly already and it's been but a week.

Here the ink changed from blue to black and she dated it a day later. Her mood was different.

Thank you for your watch; and for your friend Miles, who removed me from the clutches of the South African racists in a most ingenious way. I'll tell you about it sometime. A word of caution: Having seen him operate, I would not want him for an enemy.

Here I am being morbid again. Peter, please, please consider again what you are doing to yourself. There are moments I hate myself for not knocking you over the head and sailing you straight to Lagos. Is that why you never taught me how to navigate? But you did, didn't you? You taught me so many things, I can't remember them all.

I love you. Protect yourself.

Ajaratu

In a postscript she added,

I am determined to end this letter on a happy note. Here it is: You are a passionate and tender man. I want both. Come back to me when you can.

He folded it carefully, slipped it with the second letter, unopened, between the stained pages of the Swan's log, and put them from his mind. Four days after they left Capetown, and greatly rested despite a rough passage around the Cape of Good Hope, he had his boat offloaded in Durban Harbor. He set sail and beat right back out the breakwater into the Indian Ocean.

He put far out to sea to avoid the strong Agulhas Current. Then, two hundred miles east-northeast of Durban, he found water in the bilges. Not a lot, not as much as many wooden boats would have had in such choppy seas, but much more water than he had ever seen in the Swan. The hand pumps emptied it easily, but when he checked again hours later, the bilges had again begun to fill.

The Swan was a different boat now, almost as if she knew she had been beaten. She carried a wooden mast because the proper aluminum mast couldn't be obtained on such short notice, and while Hardin liked wood, he would be chary of driving her as hard as he had in the South Atlantic.

It was a simple matter to pump every four hours, but between times, when he wasn't tending the sails, he looked for leaks. He plugged a suspicious joint in the forepeak where the deck met the hull, but the water persisted, even after seas were no longer splashing over the bow.

The real problem, he concluded, was that pitchpoling two or three times—he didn't know which—had knocked the hell out of her in ways and places that couldn't be seen. The result was that the Swan had been reduced to equal footing with more ordinary boats, prey to material weaknesses which had never before concerned her. Hardin, used to babying the twenty-year-old *Siren* and several wooden boats before her, was not especially disturbed.

And she was still as devilishly fast.

Five days after leaving Durban, she was kiting east of Bassas da India, an island midway between Mozambique and the island of Madagascar. The wind held and he tore up the Mozambique Channel, covering the four hundred miles from Bassas da India to Ile Juan de Nova in a breathtaking two days.

He skirted east of the blue sheer-sided volcanic mass of Anjouan—one of the Comoro Islands—and, leaving the green waters of the Channel, steered northeast into the Indian Ocean and up the East African coast.

Tanker traffic was heavy on this route, and he often saw

several VLCC's at a time. The blundering ships dominated the sea lanes, their presence a constant threat to lesser traffic. For safety and concealment, Hardin altered course a few degrees to the east. Angling farther and farther from the coast, he sailed out of the mild southern African winter back into equatorial heat on the beginning of a two-thousand-five-hundred-mile voyage to the Arabian summer.

The weather stations reported that the southwest monsoon was holding longer than usual this year, but it was late August already. Hardin was still a thousand miles below the equator, and September was the transition month when the powerful winds abated, then wheeled about and stormed back down from the Arabian sea. He hoped to catch the tail end of the monsoon going north, or at least the brief calm between them, and he pushed the Swan hard, fearing what would happen if the winds turned too soon.

What happened was worse. After a week and a half of steady wind, he was suddenly becalmed in the Indian Ocean, a hundred miles north of the equator and far to the east of the shipping lanes. The wind stopped abruptly The sea flattened, and the burning sun spread an eye-searing haze over all he could see.

It was utterly silent. Even the creaking of the self-steering and the *tap-tap* of the halyards on the mast had ceased to sound. There were no waves, no swells, not a ripple. The Swan stood as still as a cup on a glass table.

When it looked as if the calm might last for a few hours, he went about the business of the boat, pumping the bilges, cleaning the galley and the head, straightening up the cabin, airing his bedding, his eye occasionally drifting toward the water, waiting for a change.

It grew hotter, the air heavier. He rigged an awning over the cockpit and shed his shirt, and then his shorts for the comfort of a loincloth made from a light, absorbent towel.

The next morning, having slept on deck where it was

262

cooler, he saw the soap and dinner scraps that had washed down the galley drain still floating beside the boat.

The greasy slick stayed there for days.

He crawled around the stifling bilges on another fruitless search for leaks. The calm would have been a good time to check the hull from underwater, but despite the heat he resisted going over the side because he feared sharks.

The same frightening image always came to mind. He would be working underwater, concentrating on the hull. A dark torpedo shadow, longer and thicker than his own body, would hurtle out of the depths. Before he could move, it would seize him.

As if called up by his imagination, a shark surfaced one evening. Easily a third the length of the Swan, it thrust its head out of the water and watched him watching it. It made a few passes, which caused the boat to move for the first time since the wind had stopped. Then it dove to deeper water and never returned. Hardin gazed longingly after the fish, hungering for motion.

To fill the heavy hours, he did dozens of useful, nonessential jobs. He was tightening the fittings on the engine box when the thought came to him that his screwdriver handle was actually a circle of levers—an infinite arrangement of levers bearing on the fulcrum of the screwdriver shaft, separated by an infinite number of triangular spaces.

He wondered, could every tool be reduced to the simple components of lever and fulcrum? A wrench? Obviously a lever, the nut it turned the fulcrum. Pliers? Two levers. The pistons in the engine? The idea seemed to break down. Maybe they distributed power through levers. He couldn't concentrate.

He dozed in the thick heat until he was drugged by sleep and sun, and decided to use the engine. It was a matter of time versus fuel. He motored on and off for several days, searching for the fringes of the monsoon, until his fuel was gone. He cursed his stupidity. Now he had no way to maneuver but the wind, no way to power his radio but the batteries, and no way to recharge the batteries.

He didn't know when he first noticed the triangles, but one day he realized that his boat was composed entirely of triangles. His eye traced the triangles of the stays and the mast. The forestay angled from the tip of the bow to the top of the mast, forming a triangle of stay, deck, and mast. The back stay formed another. The shrouds made triangles above the spreaders.

The biggest triangle was the limp mainsail, majestic in its boldness, daring to fill its triangular space with white Dacron while the stay triangles encompassed nothing more than air. The jib was another bold triangle.

There were many others, on deck and below: the smaller triangles of the bow and the pulpit; the forepeak, the companionway, the propeller shaft, the coach roof; many others.

The stitches in the sail's seams contained thousands. Had sailmakers discovered triangles accidentally or had they known the secret all along? The answer could be in the weave of the cloth.

He inspected it minutely, but no matter how he turned the cloth he couldn't find them. The sailmakers had kept the secret for their own advantage. Somewhere, deep in the weave, he knew the triangles existed.

He ran to the sail bins. Of course!

The triangles were hidden in the heavier sails. He pulled a storm jib from its bag, but quickly threw it aside in disgust. They were too clever to hide their triangles in that sail.

The heavy spinnaker. This was a sail of secrets—so big and ballooning round in the wind—appearing round instead of its true shape, the shape of a triangle.

He dragged the sail on deck, spread it over the boat from mast to helm, and crawled over it on his hands and knees, his face bent to the rumpled nylon. As night fell he collapsed on the cloth and sobbed with frustration. The sailmakers had hidden their triangles with ferocious care. He would never find them.

He slept on the sail. The next day—he had lost count of what day—was stifling hot at dawn. He awakened groggily and splashed warm seawater on his face. He wanted coffee, but the business at hand was too important to wait.

He removed the eyepiece lens from his binoculars and used it as a magnifying glass to scrutinize the weave of the sailcloth. At noon, despite the infernal sun, he arrived at an important realization. The spinnaker was a ruse.

And he had been stupid enough to fall for it, even when the true answer was right in front of his eyes, hanging on the mast. The main. Of course, the main. There he would find the triangles. He shoved the fake spinnaker into the water, thinking he was lucky to have found it was false now, instead of when he needed it. Then he held his improvised magnifying glass to the main, his heart beating faster in anticipation.

He was right. The cloth was full of triangles, a veritable storehouse of them. He laughed loudly. He had cracked the sailmakers' secret. He felt giddy with triumph. He hadn't realized that he possessed such power. Then it struck him that a man with the power to beat the sailmakers, the cleverness to plumb the secrets they hatched in their hidden lofts, such a man could make mincemeat of the calm.

And then, blindingly, the solution came. The great revelation. The ultimate knowledge. Ironically, it had nothing to do with the triangles or the sailmakers' petty secrets. No. This was knowledge of the gods. LEVIATHAN knowledge.

This was the way it worked.

He had known it all along, of course, he just hadn't needed it before. This level of knowledge was part of you, not something you could learn. You knew it, or you didn't.

He gathered the boat's kerosene lamps in the salon, and heaped the settee cushions on the dining table. Unhurried, secure in his certainty, he lifted the chimneys out of the kerosene lamps, wrapped the glass in towels, and stowed them carefully in the cupboard beneath the galley sink. Then he unscrewed the wick holders and wiped each wick dry as he removed it from the bowl. Careful not to spill any oil, he laid them in the sink because he realized that he hadn't the time to stow them individually now. The power was coming.

He upended the lamps and emptied the bowls onto the cushions. The cabin reeked of kerosene, but it didn't matter. His plan would take care of that. The wind would air it in seconds, even as it filled the triangular sails and drove the Swan north to the monsoon.

He took a match from the watertight bottle by the stove, laid it beside the striking strip, and went on deck to inspect the sky. It was frightening how clever they were. The sky was the same dull blue it had been forever. There was absolutely no sign of the enormous power stored so close by, waiting for the right mind to release it.

He climbed down the companionway, chuckling to himself. Like everything else in life, it was so simple. All you had to know was how to signal the power and the power was yours. He struck the match and carried the flame to the table. He was laughing. He knew the signal.

Cedric Ogilvy dangled the medal by its ribbon and tossed. It landed among the papers on his makeshift desk with a tiny thud. Lloyd's of London had cited him for Meritorious Services. A company director had actually flown out to present the award.

Meritorious Services? He was a proud man who enjoyed the symbols by which Britain rewarded exceptional deeds—he had his share of decorations from the war—and yet he felt cynical about this one. To be sure, he had saved the insurance brokers a pretty penny. Millions of pounds. That made him Lloyd's hero, even though the South African newspapers were still savaging him weeks after he had defied the Capetown harbor authorities who tried to block him from Table Bay.

The medal had landed on a letter of congratulations from the Company. He didn't believe them. He'd had the most peculiar suspicion that they were disappointed that he had saved LEVIATHAN. With the present glut of both oil and crude carriers in the world market, LEVIATHAN was less of a profit maker than they had hoped. To wit, practically giving away that last shipment to the Fawley refinery rather than bringing it back to Arabia marked *Sorry, no takers.*

"In conditions where another Master might have abandoned his vessel," the Lloyd's citation read, "Captain Ogilvy stood fast and brought his charge to safe harbour."

It was like running a bloody blockade, Ogilvy thought grimly. They had all but fired across his bows . . . there had been several moments when he hadn't expected to see this bridge again. The afternoon they had neared the storm, when the sky was darkening with the southern winter, his second had asked him to come to the bridge.

LEVIATHAN was heaving the seas skyward as she plunged through the Cape rollers. The second wanted him to see the bow-stress indicators. The steel plates were suffering heavy pressures. He ordered two-thirds speed.

Ogilvy had monitored them for a while, matching the instrument readings with the ways his mind and body responded to the ship. Despite the thunderous boom each time the ship battered a roller, he was not yet concerned. After many bow failures tanker designers had learned a thing or two, and LEVIATHAN's bluff bow was a much stronger affair than those of lesser ships.

Nonetheless, with the seas worsening, he had decided —reminiscent of wartime—to eat dinner on the bridge. His steward treated it like a ruddy picnic, spreading a feast of finger food on a silver tray beneath a bridge window that had a screen cleaner so that Ogilvy could watch the seas while he ate.

The full storm hit at 2100 hours. He ordered speed cut from two thirds to one half and, using the short-range radar to spot the freak waves which were rearing above the gigantic rollers, he began a maneuver never before done on LEVIATHAN: He conned LEVIATHAN around the waves, weaving among them like a ten-thousand-ton freighter.

Had she been an ordinary ship she would not have survived. In all his years at sea, Ogilvy had never seen a storm its equal. It had had four thousand miles of ocean to build in, and it had used every mile to advantage.

At midnight, when he thought it couldn't get worse, the shriek of the wind tearing around the bridge house suddenly doubled in volume. The ship heeled under the new impact, and for the second time that night LEVIATHAN did something it had never done before. Ogilvy ordered the helm put down, and the ship ran before the storm.

At dawn, when they drew dangerously close to land and he was forced to order a southerly turn, a big sea did the first damage. LEVIATHAN staggered—he hadn't believed it possible that such a mass could be staggered—and the needles on the bow-stress indicators shot into the red and stayed there, knocked out by the impact.

Ogilvy had no way of assessing the damage. The entire forward two thirds of the ship was inaccessible until the storm ended. There was no interior passage to the bows, and anyone who stepped on deck or even climbed the fire-station catwalk would be swept away.

Again the ship staggered; the impact shivered the deck and Ogilvy didn't need a damage report this time to know that the bows were collapsing. He ordered the engines reversed to spare the thin bulkheads that formed the forward tanks, but before LEVIATHAN's forward momentum could be stopped, a third sea smashed the bows, inflicting, he discovered later, the worst damage of all.

Like the baron of a besieged castle, cut off from his counterattacking armies, he waited, blind and ignorant, guessing the worst as the ship began to sink. Engines reversed and all pumps running, he backed away from the storm, stern to the seas like an ant dragging a crippled victim to its nest.

Old-fashioned discipline and seamanship had saved the day. His crew had worked like bloody blacks to dike the fire room. Had it flooded and they lost power, LEVIATHAN would have foundered. When the storm eased, he wheeled her about and backed toward Table Bay.

It was then that the radio had exploded with South African protests. LEVIATHAN was too big. LEVIATHAN threatened Capetown. Ships over three hundred thousand tons deadweight were expressly forbidden to enter the harbor. The drydocks were too small. They couldn't effect repairs. If LEVIATHAN sank in the approaches she would block the harbor.

Ogilvy was outraged. To refuse aid, to abandon his ship and men to the elements, was the ultimate example of the venality of the landsman. Ironic, it was, that those with the securest position on God's planet were the least charitable. He ignored the protests and continued backing the tanker at a painful crawl toward Table Bay while the bows sank lower and lower. The storm rollers were still crashing into the bay, and they had a tricky passage across the harbor until they dropped anchor off Duncan Dock.

Ogilvy anchored the ship for two reasons. It was as close as he could get the deep-draft ship to the repair facilities; but more important, he had placed the ship in the busiest part of the port so that it would be to the South Africans' advantage to repair it as quickly as possible to clear the way.

He picked up the medal again and smiled slightly. The port captain had threatened to arrest him. But it was too late. *Fait accompli.* His ship was saved.

His officers had returned to England until the repairs were completed, but Ogilvy had stayed aboard LEVIATHAN with the skeleton crew. He felt closer to the behemoth than ever before. Day after day he sat alone on the bridge in a high leather chair watching the work on the distant bows. What was it the Chinese said? Save a man's life and you were responsible for him forever. The same, he imagined, with a ship.

The match flared out.

Hardin stepped back to the galley, removed a second match from the bottle, put back the stopper, and lighted the match. The flame stood tall. He walked slowly across the cabin, shielding the flame from the breeze of his movement, and held it above the cushions. It flickered, leaned forward, and went out. A thin plume of smoke raced over the waiting pyre.

Patiently, Hardin turned to the galley for another match. Cool air whiffled down the main hatch and fanned his face. He paused uncertainly. He hadn't yet signaled the power. Then the boom creaked overhead and the words in his mind began to sound like the torment of a stranger.

As if in a trance, he climbed onto deck. He saw the spinnaker lying in the water, its clew caught on a stanchion. Automatically, he hauled it aboard, spilling out the water. Overhead the main crackled. The boom ran out to starboard. Hardin cleated the sheet.

A little wake bubbled astern. Catspaws rippled the water. A gust riled the smooth spots between them, and the Swan burbled upon a small white bow wave.

The radio gave him the time, the date, and the weather reports. The wind was the leading edge of an intense high-pressure system that was chasing up the Indian Ocean after the receding monsoon. He remembered the empty fuel tanks and shut the radio. No engine, no generator, no way to charge the batteries. His last log entry was four days ago and it ended with a meaningless jumble of words and symbols.

He was deposited quite suddenly the next day in the hot, damp, hazy monsoon. The great moving air mass drew the Swan within itself, and its powerful winds propelled the sailboat over large rolling seas, which moved as steadily and predictably as the wind, offering great speed for little risk.

Blowing spray and dense humidity soaked everything, and only the constant wind filling the paired headsails was consolation for the misery of the damp heat. Water gathered everywhere—on the decks and fittings, inside and out. It dripped from the ceilings, soaked the bedding, slicked the cabin sole, saturated his charts, drenched the biscuits, and weakened the batteries.

They were going. The tugs were alongside, the crew gathered from the pubs and brothels of Capetown, the officers flown in from England and Bahrain, the fuel bunkers filled, the galley provisioned.

Ogilvy's new chair stood almost amidships the bridge, directly in front of the windows just starboard of the helmsman's line of sight. Seated, the captain was as tall as when he stood. He used the wooden ledge beneath the windows as a deck.

"Yes, Number Two?"

"The pilots are aboard, sir. We're ready to sail."

"Send them to me."

LEVIATHAN was pointing north, up the coast of the exposed bay. Bloody useless anchorage—how many nights had he lain in his cabin while LEVIATHAN, tethered by her anchors, rolled abysmally on the northwest combers that disrupted the harbor like football rabble trampling a village green.

The pilot, a big false smile on his round face, stepped toward him, his hand extended. His assistant grinned behind him, equally blond and round faced.

"Not to worry, Captain. We'll have her out in two shakes of a lamb's tail."

Ogilvy remained seated, his hands in his lap. He had never liked the South Africans' siege mentality, and the refitting of LEVIATHAN had confirmed his prejudices. They never stopped worrying about their precious coasts, and they hated the oil tankers almost as much as they feared the blacks who were going to push them into the sea.

He gave the pilots a hostile glare, then exercised a captain's prerogative.

"You, sir," he addressed the senior pilot. "You will stand right here and answer my questions, if I have any. I'm quite familiar with your harbor, having negotiated it

271

without a ruddy pilot in a gale and having lived in it
aboard this ship long enough to know its channels."

The pilot started to open his mouth.

"Number Two," cried Ogilvy. "Prepare to get underway."

He walked onto the starboard wing to supervise weigh-
ing the anchors. Tugs scurried beneath the hull, and spec-
tators gawked from the outer breakwater of Duncan Dock
and from small boats that were buzzing around LEVIATHAN
like flies.

She shuddered to life. Her propellers churned the water,
roiling the harbor's gray bottom mud. She turned majestically, shook off the tugs, and steamed toward the open
sea.

20

El Al's Nairobi–Tel Aviv flight took to the air and the
young Israeli in the next seat asked Miles Donner if he
was a tourist. He wore khaki pants and a faded bush
jacket and he regarded Donner's expensive clothes and
cameras with open hostility.

"I have business in Jerusalem," Donner said gently.

"Are you British?"

"Yes," said Donner. His eyes were glazed with exhaustion; he had been about to go to bed for his last night in
Capetown when the orders had come to report to Mossad
headquarters. Eight-hour flight to Nairobi, three-hour wait
at the airport, and now six more to go. Then across Israel
and face the music without sleep. He would drink wine
and try to sleep on the plane. And not worry about the
reason for the sudden call.

"Are you a Jew?" asked his companion. He had the
open, assured, almost arrogant manner of a Sabra.

"Yes," said Donner. "What were you doing in Nairobi?"

The man grimaced. "Agricultural advisor. Twelve months in the bush."

"I imagine you'll be happy to get home."

He replied with a Mediterranean shrug. "Have you been in Israel recently?"

Miles nodded.

"I hear it's worse. The prices." Again the shrug. Then his dark eyes flashed angrily. "Of course prices wouldn't bother you."

Donner laughed. "When did you ever meet a wealthy Englishman?"

That got a big grin from the Sabra's bold mouth, but his sun-tanned face turned cold when he spotted Miles's expensive watch. "Do you send trees?" he asked bleakly.

Miles thought of the Palestine of his childhood, when the gardens were oddities—new oases in the desert or remote islands in the sodden marsh. He met a lot of young people like this Sabra in the Mossad. Life was hard in Israel, still, but no longer harsh, and now the young poor resented the older rich.

The Sabra stared at him, waiting an answer.

"Forests."

Donner had to suppress his excitement while the jet liner bumped across Lod Airport. As a British photographer on assignment, his cover would not include joy in homecoming. He let the Sabra do it for him. Before the plane stopped, the young man was out of his seat, his face split by a big grin, his eyes wet.

"Shalom," said Donner.

"Shalom!" said the Sabra, tearing down the aisle ahead of the other passengers.

Donner used his British passport, then escorted his bags through customs like the legitimate passengers and boarded a bus to the center of Tel Aviv. With the continuing migration of Jews from North Africa and the open air shops and restaurants they favored, the city was looking and smelling more and more Eastern Mediterranean, more Arab than European. He checked into the Hilton, showered, stole an absolutely vital two hours of sleep, telephoned Weintraub, and took a city bus some five miles to the Mossad. He rationalized the sleep. If it had been a genuine emergency, there were ways to meet him at the airport without exposing his cover.

Well before the bus stopped a hundred fifty yards from the ring of buildings encircled with heavy wire-mesh fencing, it contained only Donner. Around the outside of the fence was a wide, clear, flat space. Donner walked past the sun-baked earth to the single gate, showed a pass, and went around the massive circular block of main buildings to a smaller structure in back. The Mossad lived frugally, but it had its own security, including closed-circuit television and electronic sensors.

The headquarters staff were as casual in the presence of command as any Israelis, but after he had passed the third checkpoint and was deep in the restricted areas, the young men and women stood to acknowledge him as he passed their desks. His escort ushered him into the Chief's office and there the courtesy ended.

The Chief was a balding, painfully thin man ten years Donner's senior. His khaki shirt was too big for his emaciated chest, and inappropriate to his dead-white skin. He looked Donner over with unconcealed distaste.

Zwi Weintraub was with him. Weintraub was a veteran of the Irgun terrorist cadres of Partition times, and Donner's friend and mentor. Red-faced and plump, he embraced Donner warmly. Hard muscle slid beneath his flesh. He said to the Chief, "You remember Miles?"

"Vividly." In 1973 the Chief had been a field agent—his cover a philology chair at a German university—when both he and Donner independently had unearthed details of the Egyptian-Syrian attack plans. Two simultaneous sources had seemed too much for the Mossad intelligence analysts. They had suspected a plant and hesitated, and the philologist had, correctly and unfairly, blamed Donner for the fiasco. It was a rare lapse of logic. He was still essentially a professor, a devout believer in procedure and academic clarity.

"Hello," said Donner. "Congratulations on your appointment."

"I'm not so sure that the Service needed an aging field agent at its head," the Chief replied stiffly. "We will see if congratulations are in order in the months to come."

"Congratulations on your personal achievement, then," Donner amended with a smile.

"You rate personal achievement too highly, Donner. Your attitude leads to things like this plan you've concocted with Weintraub."

Donner raised a gently admonishing hand. "The fault is mine. My plan."

"I thought so." The Chief glanced at Weintraub. The old man returned a placid smile.

"What do you think of it?" asked Donner when he saw that Weintraub wasn't going to reply.

"Lunacy," snapped the Chief. "We are a legitimate nation and legitimate nations do not underwrite piracy on the high seas."

"Our legitimacy is still questioned by our enemies," Donner retorted.

"You would make us new enemies."

Weintraub frowned and his face lost most of its innocuous roundness. "It is a good plan," he said seriously. "It is bold, and yet it represents low risk to us, and it just might succeed brilliantly."

"Even if it were all that," replied the Chief, "it would be the kind of special operation that belongs to The Unit. Not to a station head or a field agent."

"The Unit didn't think of it," said Donner.

"It is to be terminated."

Donner was stunned. He had expected argument, but not outright condemnation. He turned to Weintraub. Zwi smiled reassuringly. "Miles's plan," he said, "is on this afternoon's agenda. The Ministers' Committee for Security and Foreign Affairs will decide."

The Mossad Chief looked angry. The Committee consisted of the Prime Minister and his top ministers and advisors. Weintraub was a member, as was the current head of the Mossad. The old man had taken an internal policy decision out of the Chief's hands.

"All right," he said. "It's best we settle this right out. Then we can take up the matter of your independence." His eyes held Donner's for a long moment, then dropped to the papers on his desk. Weintraub motioned to Donner —it was time to retreat diplomatically.

He threw an arm around Donner's shoulders as they strolled out of the building into the sun. "Don't worry about him," he said expansively. "I won't let him bother you no matter which way this goes."

Donner nodded unenthusiastically. "No matter which way this goes" sounded like thin support. They entered a canteen in the Defense Complex—the same place, he recalled with sad irony, that he and the new Chief had waited the night before the '73 war, each nursing his information like melting ice cream, hoping the Mossad would read it the way he did. Weintraub ordered tea and asked about England. Donner dragged him onto the subject of Hardin. The old terrorist kept talking away from it until Donner realized that he was embarrassed that the decision was out of his hands.

"They won't approve it, will they?"

Weintraub shrugged. "Putting it to the Committee was the only way to go over his head. I've already talked with some of them. You've got a reasonable chance."

"How did he find out?"

"He's after you, looking for things."

"But not even my staff knows. Only my closest—"

"I'd look out for your friend Grandig, if I were you."

"How do you—"

Weintraub smiled. An hour later, a young Air Force officer came to the table with a telephone message. Weintraub was expected at the Prime Minister's offices deep within the military compound.

Weintraub bustled through the heavy security like an

old lion oblivious to his half-grown cubs. "They'll like you," he said. "You'll see."

The meeting room was dominated by a long table. The Ministers' Committee for Security and Foreign Affairs were already seated. They were busy-looking men with tired eyes, lined jowls, and sagging mouths that turned down at the corners, as if their faces had been maimed by a thousand frustrations. Most wore the ubiquitous open-collared shirts and shapeless slacks of Israeli public life, and Donner felt like a stranger in his elegantly tailored tropical suit and silk tie.

He sat at one end of the table, his expression composed, while Weintraub introduced him in colorful terms. His mind seethed. He could see by the way they listened that Weintraub was the Committee's resident character, their last touch with the old heroics. They heard little good news in these times of fragile peace, and nothing dramatic. There was in their tentative patience hope for a brief amusement.

Gloomily, Donner recognized that his mentor had slipped unwittingly into obsolescence. He noted their quickened interest, however, when Weintraub referred to his British photographer cover, his London club membership, his Curzon Street address; Donner had often experienced the love-hate feelings of former British colonials, and he knew how to use them to his advantage. They still harbored old memories of English snubs and felt somehow vindicated when offered the chance to hire a tame Englishman.

"Good afternoon," he said, standing, and speaking in his crispest tones. He thanked Weintraub and the Committee for their time, remarked how pleasant it was to visit Israel again, and then launched into his plan briefly and forcefully.

"I propose a simple plan to counter terrorism by pressuring the governments that support terrorists. We shall support *Jewish* terrorists who attack targets of opportunity. The targets of opportunity will be the oil tankers that deliver Arabian crude to Europe."

Their eyes lighted. They could imagine how the oil producers would abandon the terrorists they were financing. And they could see how European nations that often let terrorists escape Israeli agents would clean out the cells and safe houses where attacks were plotted. He thought he had them convinced.

Then doubt clouded their eyes. They exchanged uncomfortable glances; one of them took the easy way out. He asked the Chief what he thought of Donner's idea.

"Madness," said the Chief. His bony mouth snapped shut and he waited until someone else asked him to expand upon his opinion. "Because our strongest allies, our best friends, are dependent upon that oil. Germany, Sweden, the Dutch, the United States. We can't risk their anger. It would be like a hitchhiker stopping cars with land mines."

"Drech!" Weintraub said cheerfully, stepping in before they could laugh at the Chief's unexpected joke. "It is a brilliant idea. The threat alone will do it."

"You can't threaten without doing it at least once," replied the Chief.

"Exactly," said Weintraub. "That is what Miles has done. He's set the wheels in motion for a very convincing demonstration."

"What have you done?" asked the Prime Minister, quieting the Mossad Chief with a quick gesture.

Donner explained about Hardin.

The Prime Minster listened expressionlessly. When Donner had finished, he turned to the Mossad Chief. "Why didn't you tell me about this?"

"I only just learned it."

The Prime Minister turned to Donner. His horn-rimmed glasses usually hid his eyes. Now, looking straight at him, Donner was surprised by the fierceness in his ordinary face. He was looking at a fellow killer.

"Do I understand that you created this plan on your own?"

"Yes, sir."

Weintraub interrupted. "I was kept posted on the progress, Mr. Prime Minister."

The Prime Minister spoke without taking his eyes from Donner. "But you are no longer active in the Mossad, Zwi. You are now a member of my cabinet with certain security duties that do not include espionage. Why did you not pass this information to the Mossad?"

Weintraub looked pained. The Prime Minister didn't wait for an answer. "For that matter, Donner, why didn't you report to your superior?"

Donner answered carefully. No one in the room looked amused anymore. "There was nothing to report yet. The man made all his own arrangements."

"But you procured his weapon."

"No. He got it himself. That's how we discovered him, as I mentioned."

"What did you do?"

"I offered to radio the location of the ship. He accepted my offer mainly to get rid of me."

"Does he know who you are?"

"He guessed—it doesn't matter. He's fanatically devoted to sinking the ship. It's all he cares about. He does not think of himself as working for Israel."

"And your only involvement was radioing messages about the ship?"

"Until Capetown that was true."

The Prime Minister glanced from the concerned faces of his advisors to the death's-head of his Mossad Chief, to Weintraub, and back to Donner. "What happened in Capetown?"

"Miraculously, Hardin survived the same storm that nearly sank the ship. I suspected he might."

"How?"

"There is a tenacious quality about him. I had—"

"Intuition?" the Prime Minister asked scathingly.

"Yes, sir. I arranged to remove his companion from the tender mercies of the South African police and—"

"What companion?"

279

"A young Nigerian woman named Ajaratu Akanke," said Donner, looking at the minister for African affairs.

The man raised his brows. "Brigadier Akanke's daughter?"

"Yes."

"I thought she was in England."

"She went with Hardin."

The African affairs man smiled broadly. "Wonderful. Akanke can be a good friend." His smile faded. "Why didn't you inform me?"

"Security," said Donner. "I was waiting until the project had reached completion. General Akanke agreed to delay his thanks."

"Security?" snapped the Prime Minister. "Who else knows of what you've done?"

"No one, including Akanke. I told him nothing of my connection with Hardin. I then helped Hardin outfit his boat in Capetown and I arranged passage, discreetly, for him and his boat to Durban so he could avoid the heavy seas off the Cape. He was in rather poor shape."

"And what is he doing in Durban?"

"He sailed out of Durban the day he arrived."

"Where?"

"I don't know."

"Well, what does he intend to do?"

"Sink LEVIATHAN."

"Where?"

"Somewhere between Durban and Arabia."

The Prime Minister glanced at the wall maps. After a long pause, he said, "That is four thousand miles. Where is he now?"

"I don't know. I radioed when LEVIATHAN was ready to sail. He hasn't answered his radio. I would guess either the Mozambique Channel or Ra's al Hadd. Most likely the Channel. He needs a restricted area."

The Prime Minister's eyes turned opaque. "Would you step outside, please? We'll call you."

Weintraub gave him a worried nod as he stood up and left the room. An attractive young woman soldier brought him tea while he waited. Eventually, they called him back.

Only Weintraub, the Mossad Chief, and the Prime Minister would meet his eye. The others stared at the table. Then Weintraub shrugged slightly and spread his hands as if to say he was sorry. The Prime Minister spoke.

"Your friend Zwi Weintraub has convinced us that you have acted in a bold tradition. Nonetheless, the Committee fears that the risks involved are greater than the possible gains. We veto your plan."

Donner shook his head angrily and spoke with nothing to lose. "There will come a time when you will wish you had the weapon I've tried to give you. Sometime when you need a threat."

"Thank you for coming here," the Prime Minister said stiffly.

"What about Hardin?"

"We'll stop him," said the Mossad Chief.

"No!" Donner said emphatically.

The others stared at him.

"Zwi," said Donner. "Please."

Weintraub stood up.

"Let Miles cover his own tracks. It's his right."

"It's a little late to talk about his *rights*," said the Chief. "We can't have any more mistakes."

Weintraub smashed a fist to the table. "It's his right, Mr. Prime Minister. And he doesn't make mistakes. He's the best you have."

21

The monsoon rampaged into the high coastal mountains of southeastern Arabia and ricocheted across the Arabian Sea toward the Makrān shore of the Indian subcontinent. Hardin left it behind as he rounded the tall light and radar tower on the sandy cape of Ra's al Hadd and entered the Gulf of Oman.

The change was as abrupt as slamming a door. It was hot, the water flat. In the space of a few miles he sailed from tumultuous seas to a stagnant pond. He bagged the heavy headsails that had borne him the last sixteen hundred miles and boomed out a light spinnaker. The Swan ghosted northwest two miles off the increasingly high and barren rock cliffs of the eastern Arabian coast.

She was crusted with salt. There was no more blowing spray, but the air was still humid; and in spite of the heat, which made the perspiration pour from Hardin's body, it would be days before the pale sun rid his bedding, clothes, and food of the pervasive mold that had grown in the constant moisture.

The dampness and the petty annoyances of weeks alone at sea had worked insidiously against his spirit, distracting him, grating his temper, so that small problems—like the need to constantly adjust the self-steering gear, which was slipping from wear—took on disproportionately large dimensions; bigger problems—the leaking hull—loomed enormous. The beating she had taken in the monsoon seas had aggravated the condition, and his imagination, whetted by solitude, conjured vivid pictures of the cabins filling and the Swan plummeting to the bottom with him trapped inside.

Ironically, the land also unnerved him. He had been all but a week of the past three months at sea, sailing deep and open waters, and the presence of a nearby coast was vexing—an obstacle and a danger.

The wind stopped in the afternoon and the sails hung slackly. The rocky coast was barely visible in the haze off the port side. To starboard, miles distant, moved the ghostly gray-black shape of an oil tanker heading for the Strait of Hormuz, the mouth of the Persian Gulf. At times, as the afternoon broiled hotter, several were visible at once, a menacing parade seen softly through the gauze of the humid airs.

He heard an insistent wail and, combing the shore with

282

binoculars, spied a red stone minaret in a tiny village. The call to prayer came loudly over the still water. He had seen several settlements along the shore where rivers and inlets trickled into the gulf. Most seemed too small and primitive to sell diesel fuel, nor did he have currency for the Sultanate of Oman, whose shores these were. The Sailing Directions named the Rial Saidi as the coin of realm and mentioned that the Sultanate had close ties with Great Britain. He wanted to buy fuel, but he was afraid.

Sur, up the coast, was a small port, but there he ran the risk of discovery. It was doubtful that many private yachts sailed these waters, and the Swan would be noticed and remembered. Port authorities would demand visas and bribes and probably forward his passport number to the nearest American consulate. Worried, and torn by indecision, he waited for wind.

The sails began to flap. But the breeze was out of the northwest, dead ahead. He raised the genoa and sailed close-hauled north. When he reached the edge of the shipping lane, he came about and tacked back toward the coast, consulting the Sailing Directions for water depths close to shore. The wind, the northwest *shamal*, grew stronger.

He beat against it through the afternoon, tacking between the coast and the channel. He was on a tight port tack when a big red-hulled double-ended Persian Gulf boom dhow appeared ahead on the horizon and crossed his bows. The Arab *lansh* was running with the wind, driving hard out of the northwest, her high lateen sail billowing like a scimitar-shaped cloud. Her sailors, a dozen hawk-nosed swarthy men, gaped at the trim white sliver of the Swan as they lumbered past.

The air cleared somewhat in the evening. He saw occasional stretches of flat land between the shore and the hills. They were shaded with the green hues of farms or orchards, but they would end abruptly as the cliffs and promontories shot up again and the land became barren. Another dhow passed him just before dark, hugging the coast as he was to avoid the giant oil tankers.

283

He sailed through the night, dozing on the tacks, waking to come about, trusting his finely tuned internal clocks to rouse him before he sailed too close to the land or the busy sea-lanes. Three months ago he would have considered it a foolhardy stunt, but he had done almost nothing but sail the Swan in that time and he knew things about it he himself hadn't known before.

The wind died in the morning and a thick mist settled over the water. As he was safely midway between the shore and the shipping lanes and there was no current, he wrapped himself in a storm sail for protection from the chilly damp mist and fell asleep in the cockpit, knowing that the sails would rouse him if the wind picked up.

He awakened with his scalp prickling danger and peered into a thick fog. He heard the muffled grind of a marine engine. He couldn't tell from what direction it was coming, but it was getting unmistakably louder. Now it sounded astern.

The high raked bow of an Arab dhow parted the mist.

Hardin leaped up, shouting at the lookout perched atop the jutting stempost. The Arab yelled his astonishment in a high-pitched frightened voice and gesticulated frantically toward the stern of the speeding *lansh*.

Hardin braced for the collision. The dhow was so close he could see a little model airplane mounted on the bow like a figurehead. The clattering din of a diesel engine revving in reverse raced to a high whine. Twenty feet away, when he and the lookout were staring into each other's faces, the high bow slued around and the freight vessel slid past, circled slowly, and stopped beside the Swan, which was bobbing in its wake.

Its sail was furled around a massive yard that lay on the deck like a long, ruffled snake. It was high sided and heaped with cargo: crated washing machines and refrigerators, bales of figs, cotton, and dates, some motorcycles, and an old black Mercedes Benz. What had appeared to be mounds of canvas began to stir, and the crew—a ragtag sun-blackened group of men and boys in turbans, headcloths, and robes—emerged from their makeshift beds and gathered to stare.

A big man, the captain by the quality of his robes and the sound of his voice, stormed out of the square aft deckhouse, shoved between two sailors, and loosed a torrent of outraged Arabic at Hardin. His face was bronze. Black stubble shadowed his chin, and his eyes, black and flashing and separated by a massive hooked nose, blazed angrily.

Hardin waited until he paused for breath. Then he pointed at his slack sails. The Arab's face darkened. Hardin tried a friendly smile; diesel exhaust hung in the wet air.

"Hello," he croaked. He hadn't spoken in five weeks. Clearing his throat, he called again. "Hello!"

The Arab captain beetled his brow and turned to his crew. Several minutes of animated discussion were punctuated by gestures at the Swan's sails. Finally, after a white-haired old man pointed at the dhow's lowered yard, the captain turned back to Hardin.

"Salaam!"

"Salaam," said Hardin.

The captain stretched his arms at the size of his boat. She was over seventy feet long and must have displaced a hundred tons. Then he grinned and held out two fingers to remark upon the Swan and outcome of a collision.

Hardin grinned back. Conscious that both he and the captain were fast running through their store of universal gestures, he pointed at the pipe stack that was thrusting blue-black engine exhaust above the *lansh*'s wheelhouse.

"Diesel?"

"Diesel," the captain repeated proudly. *"Taali!"*

Diesel—*Taali*? Hardin smiled and nodded admiringly, searching for a word for fuel.

"Taali!" the captain reiterated, motioning Hardin to come aboard.

Taali—come. Hardin hesitated, wary of boarding the Arab boat.

The sailors tossed a hemp line to Hardin and hauled the Swan closer until it rubbed alongside the reddish hull. Hardin climbed onto the cabin roof, took their extended hands, and pulled himself up to their deck. His own hands and arms, burned by the months at sea, were nearly as dark as the Arabs'. For a long moment they looked each other over.

The dhow crew were of all ages. Some sported fierce moustaches, others were clean-shaven, or bristling like the captain. Hardin relaxed. Beneath their exotic clothing they were workingmen and sailors.

The captain finished inspecting him, then announced with a broad happy smile, "English!"

"American."

The smile faltered. "American?"

"Do you speak English?"

"Oh, yes. Once. Enough. Long ago more. Hello, pound, trade." He searched his vocabulary. His face lighted. "Diesel."

He led Hardin through the stacked crates of cargo to the wheelhouse. It was a small square structure of painted wood and glass near the stern. A helmsman squatted patiently at the wheel, puffing on a hookah. Acrid tobacco smoke wreathed the cabin.

The captain pointed toward the back of the wheelhouse, down through an opening in the deck where an old Cummins 4–71 chugged in neutral, tended by a boy with bony wrists and red-rimmed eyes that teared in the oil fumes.

"Diesel fuel?" Hardin asked.

The captain regarded him gravely, digesting the question. Then his eyes lighted and he shouted loud orders. A sailor scrambled over the side and bent a towline to the Swan's bow. Hardin decided it would be too complicated to stop him. The captain shouted down to the engine room. The boy engaged a large lever and the engine engaged with a low whine. Another shout and the chugging quickened. The helmsman twirled his spokes. The sailors holding the towline played it out and the *lansh* was underway, heading northwest, dragging the Swan after it like a new toy.

Hardin asked where they were going and pointed at the old compass screwed to the wood in front of the helm. A sextant lay beside it with a shattered horizon glass. The captain pulled a dog-eared chart from a bunch rolled up in a slot above the wheelhouse windows and smoothed it out on a crate outside the doorway. First he pointed at the Oman coast, established their position twenty miles southeast of Muscat, then pointed at the capital city itself.

Hardin felt a stab of panic. By gestures, head shaking, and finally holding his finger at a point several miles past the harbor, he tried to explain that he didn't want to go into the port. As his meaning dawned, the captain looked mildly incredulous. He was a coastal trader, bearing goods from dhow harbor to dhow harbor, and Muscat was the biggest port between Sur to the south and Khōr Fakkān at the foot of the Musandam Peninsula, a hundred eighty miles to the north.

He waved his hand over the chart. Where then was Hardin going? Hardin pointed beyond the top of the chart. The *lansh* captain pulled out his other charts, patiently unrolling one after another until Hardin satisfied him by pointing to Kuwait. He looked past Hardin's worn shirt, shaggy hair, and cutoff khakis to the obviously costly Swan and nodded his understanding. Kuwait and a wealthy American were an obvious combination.

He took Hardin through his cargo, pointing casually at the car and refrigerators. Then the sailors unfurled bright Persian carpets on the wooden deck. Hardin exclaimed over the splendid colors and knelt to feel the knots that corrugated the undersides.

The Arab gestured with upturned fingers. Did Hardin wish to buy? Hardin held out empty hands and shook his head sadly. Beyond his means. The captain took his unwillingness as a bargaining stance and shrugged with a knowing smile. In the course of the haggling that followed, his English improved remarkably.

But as he began to unroll more rugs, casting them over

the deck with a graceful flourish, Hardin interrupted with his original question. "Fuel?"

The Arab looked blank. "Diesel?" How much interest did an engine warrant? he seemed to be thinking.

"Taali," said Hardin, motioning toward his boat.

The captain shouted at the helmsman, who called down to the engine room. The diesel slowed, and as the boom drifted along on momentum, the sailors hauled the Swan alongside. Hardin climbed down to the cabin roof and took the Arab's arm as he followed.

The Arab watched with interest while Hardin demonstrated the lifting power of the main halyard winch by lowering the main partway, then raising it tight to the masthead. Below deck, he marveled over the lavish and compact galley. He turned the knobs of the stove, and struck a match, but the burners would not light. Hardin showed him the empty Calor gas bottle. The captain called up to his dhow and moments later a berobed sailor handed down a fresh gas container. Hardin thanked him and hooked it up. Together they lighted the stove. Then Hardin removed the companionway steps and opened the engine box.

The Arab nodded appreciatively at the little two-cylinder engine. "Good."

"Diesel," said Hardin. What the hell was the British word for fuel? "Petrol."

The captain threw up his hands, mocking his incomprehension.

"Petrol!"

Hardin nodded vigorously.

The captain looked up through the open hatch and spoke to the sailors who were leaning over the side of the *lansh,* watching the proceedings. A length of hose was lowered from the dhow to the Swan. Hardin inserted it in the chrome fuel input on deck, the captain waved, an order was relayed by shouts, and moments later the hose quivered as a hand pump went to work in the depths of the *lansh.*

The transfer completed, the captain invited Hardin

aboard his boat for tea. Hardin offered him South African pound notes to pay for the fuel, but the Arab waved it away, and reiterated, "Tea."

Hardin took a small wooden box from his chart table and went with him. The *lansh* started forward again, tugging the Swan along, and the entire crew with the exception of the helmsman and the lookout on the bowstem took a tea break. Most of them squeezed into the old Mercedes, closed the doors and windows, and filled the car with blue smoke.

Hardin, the captain, and a boy who turned out to be his son had their sweet black tea sitting cross-legged upon a red carpet atop a packing crate marked MACHINE PARTS. The boy had a battery-powered tape player. The Rolling Stones played softly while they talked.

The captain's English continued to improve with use. He said it was a language he had learned as a boy on his father's dhows when the English colonial administrators still controlled the coast and dhow harbors between Kuwait and East Africa. He remembered them fondly because the English had supported free trade. Since then, he complained to Hardin, the dhows had fallen on hard times; the fleets had been decimated because the independent states that had succeeded the colonies impeded trade with high taxes and bureaucratic restrictions in every port from Muscat to Socotra to Lamu to Mombasa.

Hardin gathered that now the dhow men lived a somewhat renegade life where a portion of their trade had to be smuggled past greedy customs officials in order to make a profit, and government administrators were their worst enemies. The captain scowled darkly and compared them to the crocodiles that infested the rivers of East Africa.

"Bite, bite," he said, pantomiming their jaws, and grinning broadly at Hardin when his son laughed.

The fog began to thin and the propellers of the model airplane on the jackstaff, which had been freewheeling in the breeze of forward motion, stopped when the wind blew from astern. The captain wet his finger, looked at the hazy sky, and rose with apologies. He shouted orders, and watched his men gather around the heavy hemp rope which was attached to the long yard.

"*Kaus*," he said to Hardin, pointing to the southeast, naming the wind. "*Inshallah*." God willing. He opened his hands to Hardin, offering the choice of a continued tow. Hardin shook his head.

"*Kaus*," he repeated. The Swan's sail was fluttering. He presented the wooden box to the captain. The Arab opened it and reverently lifted the black and mirrored sextant from its velvet cradle. His eyes feasted upon it. He tried a fix on the sun, which was a softening white ball in the hazy sky, but the horizon was still too indistinct.

"*Moni*," he apologized.

Hardin knew from the Sailing Directions that *Moni* meant the dust clouds that obscured the sky almost every summer day. They blew sand from the desert, cut visibility to a half mile or less, and lowered the ceiling to a few hundred feet. He was gambling that they would continue into September.

The captain carefully replaced the sextant in its box and laid it on a ledge in the wheelhouse. *Hands off* was the obvious message he snarled in Arabic to the helmsman and the sailors who were watching. Then he dived into his hold and reappeared with a prayer rug, which he pressed into Hardin's hands. Hardin examined it in the pale sunlight. It was hardly a fair exchange. He felt like a thief. Then the captain ordered the Swan pulled alongside. He took Hardin's hand in his and stood by until he was safely aboard.

Hardin heaved the hemp line back to the dhow. The Arabs' diesel stopped chugging. Silence gathered around the two boats like another mist.

The sailors put their weight to the thick halyard, several climbing halfway up the mast as they hoisted the massive yard to the wind. Slowly, jerkily, the white lateen sail carved a higher and higher slice from the pearly sky. The patched canvas filled, straining ahead of the mast, bending the thick yard.

290

The Swan and the dhow sailed side by side on the quickening breeze until Muscat appeared beyond a sudden opening in the rocky cliffs. Then they veered apart as the Arabs made for the city and Hardin continued up the coast, pointing the distant Strait of Hormuz.

It occurred to him that he didn't know the vessel's name. He thought of Carolyn. Right now they would be talking about the Arab sailors. He had noticed that their engine was a Cummins and that their giant yard was made of three separate timbers. She would know who the old man with the white hair was, and whether the captain liked the Rolling Stones or just put up with his son's taste.

He manned the cockpit bilge pump and pounded away on it until he was gasping painfully in the humid heat, still trying to remember her face.

22

"This Nigeria!"

Ajaratu Akanke spread her hands over her desk in mock exasperation, sympathizing with Miles Donner for the delays he had suffered at the hands of the Lagos airport immigration officers.

"The British left seventeen years ago and the civil servants who took their posts still think that a clipped accent and a clean white shirt are badges of competence." She smiled. "Tell my father if you want revenge and he'll post the man to the swamps of Warri. He still talks about the way you rescued his daughter—when he isn't raging about my escapade."

Donner chuckled. "He did seem to have a temper. How've you been? Are you happy to be home?"

"Certainly. There's such excitement here. I imagine

291

you felt such a spirit in Israel when your country was born."

"I was in England. I missed the fun." He assessed her with quick eyes. "Your arm is healed?"

"Perfectly."

"And you've got the best clinic I've seen in Africa."

"It should be," she said with a smile. "It's in Lagos's wealthiest quarter."

"I think your father wants you within easy reach."

Ajaratu fell silent. She glanced at her appointment calendar. It was a heavier-than-usual day, but still nowhere near as trying as a single hour of intern duty in London. Finally, with a tentative smile, she asked the question that hung between them.

"How is he?"

"I was hoping you could tell me," said the Israeli. "I gave him your letters. I thought he might have written back."

"I've heard nothing."

"The last I know he sailed from Durban."

"Did you radio?"

"I broadcast every night at eight, Greenwich Mean Time, as agreed. I think he may have acknowledged a week ago when I radioed LEVIATHAN's departure and Persian Gulf ETA. I'm not sure. His signal, if it was his, was very weak. As if his batteries were down or heavy weather was attenuating his signal. It's just possible he was in the monsoon."

Ajaratu said, "I've been hoping for a telephone call that he's come to his senses."

"Do you think that likely?"

She shook her head. "No."

"Do you think he's unbalanced, Dr. Akanke?"

"No."

"What do you think he's going to do?"

"I'm afraid he is going to sink LEVIATHAN or die trying."

"Have you any idea where he might attack?"

Ajaratu looked out her window at the white office towers of downtown Lagos.

"I have no idea," she said. "Why do you ask?"

Donner replied, "If something has happened to him I want to know where to look."

"Something like what?"

"Shipwreck. Grounding. Native attack—forgive the expression." He said the last with a teasing smile designed, she thought, to put her at ease. "You know what I mean. I think he may need help."

"Or he may want to be left alone."

"Perhaps," Donner said casually. "Of course, we'll know the answer to that very soon."

"How?"

"LEVIATHAN sailed from Capetown last week. She is slated to arrive at the Gulf in four days. If, a week from now, when she has loaded and left, she hasn't been attacked by Hardin, we can assume he either needs help or is lost at sea. Unless he's planning to hit her full, in which case—"

"He wouldn't do that," she said firmly. "He would never sink the ship when it carried oil."

"How exactly does he plan to sink LEVIATHAN? From what angle would he shoot?"

"He wouldn't tell me. Besides, if he is lost, what does it matter?"

"Only that the precise manner in which he meant to sink the ship might indicate the *place* he intended to do it, and that would give me a clue as to where to find him. If he needs help."

"And if he doesn't?"

"I'm afraid his lack of radio contact means he does."

"But you said that is because he has weak batteries."

"Weak batteries indicates no fuel to run his engine to recharge them. And no fuel indicates he was becalmed and had to run his engine. He might still be becalmed."

"That would be wonderful," said Ajaratu. "LEVIATHAN would avoid him and when the wind came he would sail into port and, I hope, contact you or me. Frankly, I hope it's me. I want another chance to talk him out of it."

"Do you really?" said Donner.

"Of course. It's madness."

Donner toyed with the edge of her desk. Abruptly he met her eye. "I've been less than candid, Dr. Akanke."

"In what way?"

"It's my intention to stop him from attacking LEVIA-THAN."

She asked why.

Donner looked away. His voice was subdued, as if he were embarrassed. "I have new orders," he said, obviously resenting them. "I am not to allow Hardin to sink that ship."

"You have orders to stop him?"

"Yes."

Ajaratu again turned her gaze to the window. Her fingers caressed the gold cross at her throat. "Perhaps I can help," she said.

"How?" asked Donner.

"You said that you radioed LEVIATHAN's departure time."

"Yes."

"Peter will call to confirm the ETA."

"Perhaps."

"He will," said Ajaratu. "He's not the kind of man to ignore anything that will help him get what he wants. When he radios for the ETA tell him that LEVIATHAN has been delayed, and let me speak to him. I'll try to persuade him to drop it."

"Do you think you could?"

"I know I'll have a better chance with him than you would. We know each other very well."

"Maybe it would help," Donner said doubtfully.

"It would be best," said Ajaratu. "I'm sure . . . Tell me something, though. What will you do if he doesn't call?"

Donner nodded as if he had given considerable attention to that possibility. He replied, smoothly, "If that happens, I'll ask my people to enlist the aid of local authorities around the Mozambique Channel, Ra's al Hadd, and the Strait of Hormuz."

294

"Why there?"

"The sea-lanes are narrow in each of those places, which makes them likely spots for him to launch his attack."

"And the local authorities in Mozambique and Arabia would stop him on your say?"

"Yes."

"Why would they do that?"

"We have good friends in Africa. How do you suppose I got you out of Capetown?"

"But *Arabia*?"

Donner smiled. "Neither we nor the Arab states can afford to be unremittingly bellicose. It is occasionally in both our interests to cooperate."

"Would they hurt him?"

Donner smiled easily and looked her straight in the eye. "No. I will make it abundantly clear that he is to be observed from a safe distance until I get there. Or should I say, *we* get there? You do intend to come with me?"

"Of course." She looked at her watch. "Excuse me, I must clear my schedule. I'll be right back." She hurried out the door, smoothing her white skirt around her hips. She made a telephone call at her receptionist's desk. Then she returned to Donner.

Moments later, there was a knock at the door. Ajaratu went to it, opened it, spoke briefly, and shut it. Her hand on the knob, she spoke softly to Donner.

"The police have come for you."

Donner half rose in his seat. "Why?"

"I've told them that you are a psychotic and that you have threatened the lives of several prominent leaders including my father. You'll be taken to a hospital for observation. I've asked the police to be gentle so long as you behave. I'll see that you're treated well."

"Kind of you," said Donner, sitting back down. A small smile played on his lips while his eyes darted from the door to the windows and back to the door. "How long am I to be . . . observed?"

"I'll arrange your release after Hardin sinks LEVIA-THAN."

"I thought you wanted to stop him."

"Not at the price of his life," said Ajaratu. "You'd stop him at any price and he's too determined to let himself be taken gently—I just want to keep him alive. That's the only reason I helped attack LEVIATHAN, and it is why I am stopping you now." She smiled sadly. "I love him."

"I have no desire to hurt him," Donner protested.

"But you would," said Ajaratu. She opened the door and two burly men in khaki uniforms came into the room and fanned out with their hands hovering over unbuttoned holster flaps. Donner carefully raised his hands, his eyes flickering from one policeman to the other.

They frisked him roughly, found nothing, gripped his arms, and started to march him out the door. Ajaratu was struck by how small and ordinary he looked between them. "Boys," she said, in the manner in which Nigerians of position addressed men who worked for them, "he's sick. Don't hurt him." Then she handed each a five-naira note to buy his wife a present. Grinning broadly, they walked Donner out of the room.

Ajaratu stared at the door, musing over what she had done. She would have her hands full freeing Donner in two weeks and getting him out of the country without her father finding out about it. She might have gone too far. But if she had let Donner leave, she would have been cosigning Hardin's death warrant.

23

Piloting with binoculars, compass, charts, and the Sailing Directions, Hardin sailed close beside the steep and barren island-studded Musandum Peninsula to avoid the oil tankers. High empty inbound ships plowed ponderously north to the narrow Strait of Hormuz. Outbound, steaming south, they glided deep in the water, brimming with crude.

When he reached the Strait, he abandoned the safety of the coast and sprinted six miles across the traffic lanes toward the islands of Great and Little Quoin, the rocky sentinels at the entrance. It was a nerve-wracking maneuver made worse by the killing heat and the dust haze which cut visibility to less than a mile.

He sailed blind, navigating by compass, guessing the speed of the powerful tide, and dodging the oil tankers that moved in and out of the Strait as relentlessly as the cogs of a machine.

A helicopter droned through the murk. He waited, his scalp prickling. Iran had a naval base at Bandar 'Abbās, forty miles north, and regarded the Strait of Hormuz as its charge. For that reason he had already removed his radar reflector. The helicopter dipped below the ceiling for an instant, then vanished.

The haze lifted slightly and he saw an island with a tall light tower on its southern end. Little Quoin. The bulk of Great Quoin loomed to the south. Little Quoin was a mile and a half west. The tide had pushed him farther east than he had imagined. He took a bearing a second before another dust cloud slammed across the water, and steered for the island through a frothy chop.

Little Quoin rose vertically out of the water. Sailing past its east and southeast walls, Hardin searched for the landing shown on his chart. It was a low finger poking the water. He approached slowly, not knowing whether the navigational aids on the island were attended. The finger turned out to be a low, stone wharf.

The wharf was the only sign of man on the narrow shelf of land to which it was attached. The Sailing Directions promised six feet of water alongside. Hardin dropped his sails, started his engine, brought up an anchor, and turned the Swan until she was standing thirty yards off the pier, bow out. Then he set the anchor, ran reverse propeller for a moment, and played out the line as she drifted in. When her stern was four feet from the end of the wharf, he snubbed the anchor line. Then, carrying a stern line, he jumped from the cockpit to the wharf and tied it around an old brass cleat. The hot stones seared his knees. They were the first land he had touched in six weeks.

The Nigerian police manacled Donner to a ring on the floor in back of the Land Rover. One sat with him while the other drove through the glittering center city away from Ajaratu's clinic toward the outskirts of Lagos. They passed from a European ambiance of new glass-and-steel towers intermingled with older colonial structures to an American-inspired superhighway that slashed through a burgeoning industrial park.

Donner felt like a fool. The silly bitch had foxed him. He briefly analyzed his mistake and decided that he must have sounded too anxious. No. It was forgetting that she had been on the boat with him through all that first voyage. All that rigmarole about the radio must have rung untrue.

What to do? A sick man couldn't very well ask the police to take him to his friend General Akanke. A madman couldn't ask his jailers for anything. She'd really put it to him.

The highway ended abruptly at a construction detour, and moments after gliding at seventy miles per hour the Land Rover was bouncing through a shantytown between tin-roofed packing crates, gin dens, and open markets. The dirt roads were fouled with garbage and muddied here and there by water gushing from broken water mains. Ragged indigents squatted beside the road and slept in the alleys. Children played in the mud puddles, and soldiers, red-eyed from drink, slouched at the larger intersections.

The police drove as fast as the rutted roads would allow, regained another modern highway, and shortly pulled up at the emergency entrance of a modern hospital. They took Donner's money, but left him his wallet. Then they hustled him in, supervised his manacling to a chair, and left.

Hours later he was taken to a psychiatrist, a young Nigerian who spoke Oxford English and hung his university degree beside a framed map of London. He read the brief hospital report to Donner, which stated that he had made threatening statements against political leaders, and asked Donner if he understood the gravity of such charges. Donner, still manacled, said he did. Then he asked if he could telephone his family in London.

The Nigerian scanned the rest of the report. "That won't be necessary. Dr. Akanke has instructed the British Embassy to notify your family."

"Thoughtful of her," said Donner. "Nonetheless, I would prefer to call them myself."

"No need," said the psychiatrist, closing the issue. "Tell me a little bit about yourself, Mr. Donner."

They conversed casually for several minutes, during which Donner mentioned the names of a couple of prominent St. Bart's psychiatrists. The young man had read their books and was impressed. "You must be a wealthy man to afford their treatment."

"They're just friends," said Donner. "Now, sir. Could we accept, for a moment, the hypothetical point that I am *not* a psychotic. Hypothetically. Can we do that?"

The doctor nodded. "Hypothetically."

"Thank you. Now let us assume that Dr. Akanke stumbled into matters she can neither appreciate nor comprehend. Can we assume that?"

"For the moment."

"Thank you. Let us finally assume that *you* will understand those matters when a disinterested third party explains them. Can we assume that?"

The psychiatrist shook his head. "We have no disinterested third party."

"One telephone call."

"Hypothetical?" the psychiatrist asked with a smile.

Donner smiled back. "Not if you want a real third party."

The psychiatrist spread his hands on his desk and made

a triangle with his thumbs and forefingers. Staring into the triangle, he asked, "Am I supposed to think that you are clever?"

"Not especially," said Donner, "but just a trifle more clever than a man who publicly threatens the leaders of a country he is visiting—one telephone call will settle your doubts."

"All right." The doctor dialed the telephone and held the receiver to Donner's ear. When the ringing stopped, Donner spoke the names of the hospital and the doctor. Then he said, "You can ring off now."

"Is that all?"

"You may as well put me in a cell now. But if you go out, sir, I strongly advise you leave word where you can be reached."

The land seemed to shift under his feet as Hardin took his first tentative steps around the narrow shelf. Shells and soft sand at the edge of the gray, uninviting water quickly gave way to a barren stretch of dust and rocks behind which rose the almost sheer face of the island's cliffs. A steep path, cut like the straining folds of a tied drape, ascended the yellow stone to the light tower on the brink. It was hot, much hotter than on the water, as if the rocks stored the sun's heat and fired it back in concentrated bursts.

Hardin confirmed that he was alone, then searched the brown, dry base of the cliff for a spring to replenish his dwindling water supply. Finding nothing but dust, sparse blackened shrubs, and insects, he started up the cliff path.

It was a slow, laborious climb, complicated by his sea-attuned sense of balance, though rusty iron handholds and railings were imbedded in the stone wherever it was particularly steep or dangerous. As the fittings were old and the path seemed untrodden recently, Hardin supposed that repairs and maintenance of the navigational aids were effected from helicopters instead of boats.

He reached the summit, where a hot wind swirled dust devils around the masonry base of a steel tower. As expected, he found a helicopter landing pad—a white circle cleared among rocks—and other signs of modernity—a generator shed protected by steel shutters and massive padlocks, and a heap of motor-oil cans—indicating regular visitations by the keepers of the light. Atop the tower, which was guyed with steel cables, was the light—its mirrored reflectors blazing in the pale sun—and above it the quiet arm of a radio-beacon antenna.

A ladder clung to one side of the steel tower. Hardin climbed fifty feet—halfway to the top—and looked down at the misty cloud cover that had hidden him from the helicopter. It was thinning and he could make out the Musandam Peninsula that separated the Gulf of Oman from the Persian Gulf, and some of the nearby islands. The rest he knew from the charts.

Iran lay forty miles across the inverted-U-shaped strait to the east, north, and west. The United Arab Emirates were south. The Gulf of Oman narrowed at the foot of this island and turned west into the landlocked Persian Gulf. The Gulf was the monster's home and the Strait of Hormuz was its only door.

It was a perfect trap. LEVIATHAN had to pass Hardin in the narrow sea-lane. He even had an escape route. Southwest, out through the broad Gulf of Oman, and beyond the Arabian Sea to the limitless Indian Ocean.

He climbed down the tower and the path to the base of the cliff and made a second inspection for signs of human activity. Again he found none.

Satisfied that the island was safe, he returned to the Swan and celebrated his landfall with a canned cinnamon cake and some evaporated milk.

After eating, he swept the close horizons with his glasses to check that no boats were approaching. Then he lay sweating on his bunk and tried to sleep. The boat was steady for the first time since he was becalmed. Accustomed to compensating for pitch and roll, Hardin tossed and turned in restless anticipation of movement that did not come and, tired as he was, he could not sleep. He waited an hour, got up, and again scanned the water.

301

The haze was lifting, as it had every evening he had been in Arabian waters, but the heat was just as bad. Six or seven miles to the south crouched the faint outline of Jazirat Musandam, the island at the tip of the Musandam Peninsula which marked the south side of the narrow entrance to the Strait.

He watched the double procession of oil tankers and conjured a vivid scene in his mind. In two or three days LEVIATHAN would bloat the inbound procession. Twice as wide as the others, higher, longer, it would lumber toward the Strait, filling the narrow passage like a rogue elephant roaming the single path in a village of flimsy huts. He saw himself in the middle of the channel, the bow of the monster quartered in his weapon's cross hairs, waiting until it was very close.

Darkness fell. Curtaining the ports and the transparent hatch covers, he lighted an oil lamp and went out on deck to be sure that no light showed. He returned to the sweltering cabin, pulled up the floorboards, heaved out the Dragon, and went over it carefully, checking the electrical circuitry. Miles's people had cleaned the weapon and pronounced it operational. The battery tested low, and he replaced it with a spare mercury cell.

"I'm not political," said the psychiatrist.

"Sensible."

Perspiration beaded the black man's upper lip. He helped Donner into his jacket, which the Israeli had draped neatly on the cot in the barred room where he had waited, and watched anxiously while he buttoned his collar, replaced his belt, and knotted his tie.

"I've been told to take you to the airport."

"Do you know Dr. Akanke personally?"

"No sir. . . . We've met."

"As far as I am concerned, this matter is closed. You will hear nothing more of it and neither will she."

"What about the person who telephoned me?" asked the psychiatrist.

302

"He will say nothing. He is her father's colleague, not his friend."

Hardin pumped the bilges, as he had done four hours earlier, and discovered that the Swan had leaked as much sitting at her mooring as she had underway. Then he started the engine to power the radio. The exhaust echoed loudly off the stone pier.

It was ten minutes before eleven—eight o'clock GMT. The lights of the tankers passed solemnly to the south. Green lights on the empty inbound ships and red on those heavily laden and heading home.

Miles came through via the long-range station at Kuwait. Apparently he had guessed the Gulf. Or maybe he was trying the Mozambique Channel at the same time.

"Golf-Mike-Hotel-November," said Hardin. "Golf-Mike-Hotel-November."

"Thank you, GMHN," said the Kuwait operator. "Go ahead, please, NHMG."

"Kilo-Uniform-Xray."

"What?" yelled Hardin. Stop instantly, standing into danger, stop your intention. The same message Miles had sent two months ago off the Liberian coast.

Miles repeated over and over until Hardin broke in. For a moment, as each transmitted, neither heard the other. Then Hardin broke through.

"Why?"

"Zulu returned to Capetown."

"What?"

He had heard, but couldn't believe.

"Repeat," said Miles. "Zulu returned to Capetown. Repeat. Zulu returned to Capetown."

"When?" It didn't seem possible. It couldn't be.

"Over a week ago. I tried to tell you, but you haven't received my signals."

"What happened?"

Once Miles had radioed that LEVIATHAN was sailing from Capetown bound for Hālūl Island in the Persian Gulf, Hardin had stopped using the radio.

303

"The bow gave way again," replied Miles. "Off Durban."

"Why didn't they go into Durban?"

"I don't know."

That didn't make sense. Why Capetown when Durban had bigger drydocks? "How badly is it damaged?" he asked.

"They say it will be months before she sails," replied Miles. "Where are you?"

Hardin's mind was spinning. Months? Where could he hide for months? Where could he get the boat repaired? Where would it be safe to get food and water? He quailed from the prospect of so much time alone on the boat. The radio hissed in his ears; he barely noticed that every few moments the static was interrupted by faint bursts of a staccato tapping sound. The fear of solitude came as a surprise. He thought of Carolyn.

"Where are you?" Miles repeated insistently.

Maybe the Israeli could help again. "I need a place to lay over and refit. I'm exhausted and the boat is sinking under me."

"Of course you can't stay. Are you safe for the moment?"

"For the moment."

"Where exactly are you?"

"On an island."

"In the Strait?"

"Where can I go?" asked Hardin.

After a short pause, Miles said, "Perhaps I could help you in India."

"That's a long way from here."

The signal was weak, but it carried the smile in the Israeli's voice. "We haven't too many friends in Arabia."

"How about a ship in the Indian Ocean?"

"No."

"What about one of those fruit carriers?"

"Would you please be specific? Just give me your position and I'll get back to you."

"Are you positive that Zulu's going to be laid up so long?" Hardin asked doggedly.

"Yes! She's a frightful mess. I saw her myself this afternoon. She looks worse than before."

"You're in Capetown?" He had assumed Miles was in England.

"I flew here as soon as I heard. Give me your exact position and I'll make contact tomorrow on a secure channel with our usual code."

Hardin's hand had begun trembling. His body filled with an aching weariness. Bitterly, he thought of the weeks he had driven the Swan, racing to reach the Strait ahead of LEVIATHAN. He couldn't believe that the ship had faltered again. What was getting in the way each time he tried to kill it?

"Okay," he rumbled into the microphone. "Call tomorrow. I'll wait here."

"Give me your position so I can use the secure channel."

"Hold on."

Overwhelmed with disappointment, he felt the corners of his mouth commence the crumbling breakup of his face. He sagged over the chart table like a drunken man. Tears filled his eyes. He hated the radio, hated Miles. He had to be alone with his grief. Shaking his head violently and taking a deep, temporarily steadying breath, he spoke into the microphone.

"Okay . . . longitude—"

The earphones rattled softly.

"Yes?" prompted Miles. "Go on. There was interference. It's over."

The faint tapping sound was gone, but it echoed in Hardin's ears like clanging bells. He snapped off the transmitter and stared at the radio. *The Russian radar tests.*

Miles had lied. He was in England.

Slowly, in a trance, Hardin removed the headset. His mind picked up speed as the alarm bells grew louder.

What had he said to him? Did he give away his position? Did he name the island? Was his signal being traced?

He rose from the chart table and started up the companionway, moving faster and faster with each step. Miles had lied; and he had asked for his position. His *exact* position, as if he were setting him up.

A hot breeze riffled the water and stirred the thick night air. He retrieved his stern line, and hauled up the anchor.

The first patrols raced into the Strait moments after he fled Little Quoin. Thinking they were helicopters, he scanned the dark and overcast sky while the whine of their jet turbines drew rapidly closer. No lights flashed overhead, but the sound grew louder. The whine deepened to a howl, then a thunderous roar.

Hovercraft.

A pair of the high-speed air-cushion attack boats closed swiftly from the north. Searchlight beams bristled from their sleek, low hulls, darting over the wave tops, slicing the night. In their backlight, Hardin saw heavy machine guns, rocket launchers, and spinning radars.

They came straight for him—a hundred feet long and lightning fast—skimming the water on air-cushion squalls of froth and spray like a band of desert horsemen riding clouds of billowing dust. His diesel was shuddering at full throttle, but the Swan was turning six knots to their fifty. A searchlight skipped the waves like a flat stone, seeking the sloop's white hull.

Miles had screwed him beautifully and he'd done everything to help but hold his coat. He'd let the Israeli keep him on the air, milking his grief and fear until the Iranian radio operators had homed in on his signal. The Hovercraft closed. A quarter mile, three hundred yards, two hundred yards.

They broke formation and veered apart. Hardin waited for the flat hulls to settle to the water as they slowed, but they came swiftly, their speed undiminished, and he felt a new fear. They were going to strafe him. He spotted the machine gunners hunched over their weapons, the backwash of the spotlights gleaming on their helmets.

His mind screamed to go over the side, but he was paralyzed by fear and disbelief, frozen to the wheel. They were on him with a whoosh and a roar; he'd be dead before he heard the guns. Then they were past, one on either side, and howling toward the island behind him.

The Swan tossed in their wakes. Hardin gasped at them, trying to blink their white glare from his eyes, realizing gradually why they had missed him. It wasn't luck. With a wooden mast and her reflector dismounted, the fiberglass Swan was a negligible radar target. The Hovercraft crews, trained more in technology than reality, depended primarily on their radar and had miscalculated the blinding effect of their own searchlights. Had they charged blacked out, the gunners and lookouts would have spotted the white Swan at the range they passed.

He looked astern with his binoculars as he fled. Lights blazing, the Hovercraft circled widely in opposite directions, then converged upon the high dark shape of Little Quoin Island, executing a pincer movement that closed on the stone wharf where he had tied the Swan. Whatever their other deficiencies, the Iranians were impressively good at signal tracking. Their lights danced over the wharf, the beach, and the backdrop of the cliffs. A harsh chorus of electronic bullhorns crackled across the Strait as uniformed sailors leaped ashore with rifles and machine pistols.

Hardin steered for the middle of the shipping channel, altering course again and again to dodge a number of boats whose lights were converging on the island behind him and the oil tankers which steamed past, oblivious to the hunt.

At any moment someone would take charge of the chaotic operation and conclude the obvious. When that happened, the flotilla would fan out on a sector-by-sector search from the Musandam Peninsula to the coast of Iran.

Already lights were circling around Little Quoin as if the naval craft were clustering, awaiting assignment.

Hardin drove the Swan as fast as it would go. The northern tip of the Musandam Peninsula was a maze of islets and coves. Jazirat Musandam, the island at its tip, was less than four miles away. If he could make it there, he would have a good chance of weaving back down the crenelated coast and out to the safety of the Arabian Sea. He steered south-southwest, toward the lower end of the island.

The night resonated with the throaty rumblings of marine engines, the whine of the Hovercraft, and the buzz of helicopters. The sound of his own diesel would never be heard in the searchers' cacophony. He neared the Peninsula. Two more miles. But in the next mile, lights began to appear ahead—beads of light strung together on the beams of searchlights—as the hunters anticipated his break for the rugged coast.

Hardin swung left, back toward the shipping channel, pointing the Swan's bow toward the empty blackness east of the lanes. Then he cut his engine and drifted, reluctant to commit to the new course. There was no concealment but the night on those broad open waters, no place to hide from the Iranian Navy which patrolled the east coast all the way to Pakistan.

At daybreak, the morning haze and the desert dust clouds might hide him, but would they hold? The barometer had climbed steadily all day and was still rising last he looked. High-pressure systems were common here late in September, and if one did move into the Gulfs, the clear winds would blow his cover away like the wispy smoke of a snuffed-out candle.

A minesweeper knifed through the water close enough for Hardin to see its silhouette against the sky. It veered across his bow, its searchlights just missing him, and raced to fill a gap in a string of lights that guarded the Peninsula. Halfway there, it disappeared behind the blackness of an outbound ship.

He hesitated in the midst of the traffic lane, torn between

the temporal safety to the east and the immediate danger to the west. Then the outbound ship began to pass him, several hundred feet away, slowly blocking his view of the hunters. Hardin stared at it, trying to make out its dark form. It was moving very slowly. He accelerated the engine and steered toward the ship, an idea flickering in his mind.

She was an oil tanker, but much smaller than the behemoth VLCCs and ULCCs that ruled these waters, no more than thirty thousand tons. And she was old. Very old. Her gracefully raked funnel and her midships bridge blotted handsomely proportioned dark shapes out of the night sky. But it was her languorous pace that drew Hardin to her side. Her engine worked with a tired thumping wheeze as she started her long journey home at less than six knots.

He steered into her gentle lee and crept forward until the Swan was riding comfortably just inside the dark ship's low bow wake. Then he eased back his throttle. The Swan slowed to the same speed as the throbbing tanker, pointing directly into the wind which scraped the curling crest off her bow wave and played it over Hardin's face in a cool spray.

He was safe in the shadow of her flaring bow until dawn—at first light, before her helmsman noticed a mast where there shouldn't be a mast, he would sprint the few miles to the coast and find a hiding place until it was dark again. He expelled a deep breath. Already the sounds of the search craft were fading astern as the old tanker plodded away from the Persian Gulf.

He was safe. His hands began to shake and his stomach churned in a delayed reaction to his fear. For the first time since he had entered the Gulf of Oman, he felt cold. Then a new thought began to gnaw at his mind. If LE-VIATHAN was laid up at Capetown, why had Miles set the Iranians on him?

24

"We will load one million tons of Bul Hamine crude at Jazirat Hālūl."

Captain Ogilvy's amplified voice echoed through the corridors, the dayrooms, the engine room, the mess, and the bridge, and on the deserted decks where the monsoon wind blew spray from the crashing wave tops.

The crew responded with a relieved sigh. The new sea berth east of the island of Hālūl offered ample maneuvering room for LEVIATHAN to connect easily at the loading buoy. There was a price for safety, however. The sea berth was a remote outcropping of pipes and hoses on the crude-slicked surface of an empty sea; and Hālūl Island was fifty miles from Qatar. There was no canteen, nor even a place to exchange the ship's movies.

"We will discharge at either Bantry Bay or Le Havre," Ogilvy concluded. "That will be all."

Damned shame not knowing whether it was Bantry or the French port. His men had a right to know where they were going; a precise destination was a better focal point on a long voyage than a question.

He shut off the P.A. and stepped out on the bridge wing, anxious to watch the low coast of Ra's al Hadd grow large on the horizon. The damp following wind stank of the ship's smoke, and the rails dripped spray and condensation.

The monsoon was running late this year. He thought how that must have wreaked havoc in India. What a way that lot lived, laying about doing not-all, just waiting for the rain.

It would be hot in the Gulfs when they rounded the corner. He had less than an hour of bearable weather left on the bridge wing. Then for five days—two in, a day to load, and two out—he'd be trapped in the air conditioning, the doors and windows screwed tighter than a submarine.

"Sir?"

It was his second officer and he knew better than to bother him while he was taking the breeze.

"Yes, Number Two," he snapped irritably.

"Radiophone, sir. Company channel."

"What the blazes do they want?"

"I didn't—"

He continued to stare at Ra's al Hadd. Let them stew. They'd already sent loading orders; now what did they want? Finally, he took a last deep breath of the salty wind and walked to the bridge house. The radio officer had routed the call to one of the telephones by his new chair. Ogilvy had taken to spending hours in it every day, to the consternation of his navigational officers who had to cope with the Old Man's eye on them throughout their watches.

It was James Bruce in London. They exchanged chilly pleasantries, their last confrontation still rankling. Then Bruce said, "He's at it again."

"Who is at what again?"

"The doctor."

"Hardin?"

"Yes."

"West Africa?" asked Ogilvy, irritated that Bruce would try to foist another helicopter on him when he rounded the Cape.

"No," said Bruce. "The Iranian Navy chased him at the Quoins."

"*The Quoins?* How in hell did he get there?"

"The same way that he got to Capetown," said Bruce. "He sailed."

Panic knotted Ogilvy's stomach. "When was he in Capetown?"

"About the time you arrived."

"How do you know all this?"

"I'm not going into it on the air," said Bruce. "But we

311

have various sources. The same who alerted us the first time."

"Why didn't he attack in Capetown?"

"We don't know. He might have been disabled."

"Are you telling me he came into Table Bay after the storm?"

"Apparently he did."

Panic of another sort rippled through Ogilvy. He dispelled it quickly. The sea was arbitrary. Hardin was undoubtedly a very lucky man to have survived, but he had no special powers.

"Where is he now? Is he hunting?"

"Not now, he isn't. He's running."

Ogilvy laughed sarcastically. "One man in a sailing yacht gave the slip to the Iranian Navy?"

"It was night. But they think they're driving him your way."

Instantly, Ogilvy switched to the bridge telephone. "Number Two!"

"Sir?" The reply came fast. The second was watching from the starboard wing.

"Post men at the bow and masthead."

"Yes, sir."

"The man on the sailing yacht."

"Yes, sir. . . . Do you suppose he will attack, sir?"

"Not if your lookouts keep a weather eye," Ogilvy snapped.

"Yes, sir."

The charts of the remainder of his voyage passed through his mind like filmstrips. Narrow traffic schemes. Target areas. The Quoins was typical of Hardin.

"Are you there?" asked Bruce on the radiophone.

"Yes. What are you doing about him?"

"The Iranians and the Saudis will provide sea and air cover until they capture him. You should be seeing the first of them any moment."

"Bloody marvelous," Ogilvy replied heavily. "Two wog air forces chasing one bonkers yachtsman. I'll be lucky if one of them doesn't prang into my hull."

312

"This is an open channel," Bruce said stiffly. "Please mind your tongue, Cedric."

"Is there anything else?"

"No. Just don't worry, Cedric. You'll be safe as houses. I'll contact you as soon as they capture him."

"*If* they capture him."

"They will. . . . One thing, Cedric. The Iranians might request that you heave to until they do."

"Not bloody likely," snapped Ogilvy.

"Now be reasonable," Bruce said primly.

"Hardin can't set up a shot if he's on the run."

"Try not to provoke them, Cedric."

"There's a high coming in tomorrow. They'll have him as soon as the sky clears. There's no need to stop." He cradled the phone.

The radio officer approached his chair moments later.

"Excuse me, sir. Shall we call in to Doha?"

"Yes. Get your ETA from Number Two."

Ogilvy went out on the bridge wing again and stood watching Ra's al Hadd. A flock of helicopters approached in formation and buzzed the ship with an infernal racket, which, Ogilvy assumed, was meant to be reassuring. They bore Saudi Arabian markings. He stared stonily ahead, ignoring the grinning fool who hovered beside the bridge tower and waved as if he'd just won the Battle of Britain.

Hardin had certainly chosen a poor place to be hunted. Both the Saudis and the Iranians cast greedy eyes on the Persian Gulf and its approaches; they would blanket the area. Out here the Iranians wouldn't challenge the Saudis, but farther in clouds of aircraft, from their base at Chāh Bahār across the Gulf of Oman, would descend in a demonstration of their control of the strategic strait. A grim smile wrinkled Ogilvy's lips. If they put their Navy into the search, there would be less of them to pester crude carriers with their pollution checks.

His mouth tightened. What a horrifying lot to be hunting a man. Hardin had no idea what he was in for. Once when he had been in the Gulf, long ago, before the war, he and another foolhardy young officer had gone ashore in mufti at Al Jubayl; it was during Id al Fitr, the end of Ramadan, the fasting month. The Arabs had caught one of their number drinking some whiskey, which was forbidden by Moslem law, and Ogilvy had been an unwilling witness to a savage public flogging. Pinned near the pillory by the bloodthirsty mob, he had seen and heard it all—the victim's screams, the sighs in the crowd, the fierce odor of sadistic excitement, the blood—but the thing that stuck in his mind and marked him forever was the awful sound of the lash. It made a noise like ripping cloth as it tore through the man's flesh.

It had left Ogilvy with a hatred of the Arabs he had never lost. The Iranians noisily insisted they were not Arab, but if half one read in the newspapers was true, they were just as bad with their secret police and their torture chambers. Hardin was in for a bad time whichever side caught him. Damned fool.

25

Hardin raised his spare sextant to the pearly sky and measured the angle between the molten white sun and the pale horizon. He marked the time—a minute and forty seconds after noon—then crouched under the storm sail awning he had rigged over the cockpit and pored through the fine-print tables in the Nautical Almanac with eyes that burned from fatigue. He couldn't work at the chart table because the temperature in the cabin was one hundred twenty-five degrees.

Though the Swan was plowing west-southwest at six knots, its passing created no cooling breeze, merely a sluggish stirring of the thick, gritty air. Fine dust hung everywhere, layering the decks and coating Hardin's skin, the inside of his mouth, and his burning eyes.

314

He took a swig of warm water from the Thermos, swirled it around his mouth, and swallowed. Then he finished his calculations and confirmed what his watch and the Swan's speedometer had already told him. Having motored at top speed for the thirteen hours since he had reversed course and abandoned the safety of the old tanker, he had penetrated eighty miles into the Persian Gulf.

The euphoria he had felt after his escape, his impulsive doubling back, and his undetected thrust through the Strait had evaporated in the white heat of morning. His head ached from the heat and the constant grinding of the diesel engine. His back hurt from sitting so long, pains lanced his shoulders, and with the exhaustion that weighted his body came the doubts.

He was low on fuel again, almost out of food, the loran was shot—a victim of the oppressive humidity—and he was in desperate need of sleep. The Swan was leaking badly. But even if he could find a way to rest and even if the Swan could be repaired, he had no hope of escape. The six-hundred-mile-long boot-shaped Gulf was surrounded by land. The narrow Strait of Hormuz, the only way in, was the only way out.

This was not the challenge he had taken. When he had first known that he had to sink LEVIATHAN, he had accepted the likelihood that he would lose his existence as Peter Hardin, but with the oceans of the world before his boat, he hadn't doubted that he would find some sort of life somewhere. Even when he had learned about the helicopter and had raced to the southern seas, he had held no illusions—within the limits of his experience and imagination—about the endurance that the long, brutal voyage would demand. But then, too, his fate had been in his own hands. He would endure. Similarly, the ambush at the Quoins had offered a good chance to escape in the confusion.

But now there would be no escape, only death. And the bitch of it was he didn't want to die, had never intended to

315

die, and every fiber of his being was crying out against death, crying to put the boat about again and sneak back out the Strait when night fell.

He sat a long time, nodding over the wheel, blinking at the compass, ransacking his predicament for a decent withdrawal. He was lightheaded from fatigue; he had no charts because he had never considered pursuing LEVIA-THAN into the Gulf; and his single ally had betrayed him to the Iranian Navy. If he turned around now, he would be miles out in the Gulf of Oman before dawn.

And yet: The Sailing Directions that covered the Gulf of Oman included the Persian Gulf, and while they were intended only to supplement charts, they still listed courses, dangers, and the positions of ports and islands including Hālūl. Miles couldn't hurt him any more than he had already, and no one, including the Iranian Navy, knew that he was deep inside the Persian Gulf.

Pressing on, Carolyn would joke through clenched teeth on difficult days. He scooped a bucket of warm Gulf water and poured it over his head. Then he drank fresh water, swallowed a handful of vitamins and food supplements, and pumped the bilges for ten minutes.

He turned the radio on full volume and tuned it to the frequency listed in the Admiralty Guide for the coastal radio station operated by Shell at Doha; the Sailing Directions instructed vessels bound for Hālūl to report their estimated times of arrival and the amount of cargo they required.

The dust united with the humid haze and the low clouds to form a dense canopy that hung over the Swan like hot cotton. He could often see as far as a mile when the wind roused the haze, but the ceiling stayed low, pierced only by the white sun, and though he sometimes heard the *buzz-thump-thump* of helicopters, he saw none. The radio blared a medley of accented English as ships from all the world rounded Ra's al Hadd.

He went below to check the bilges. The heat was appalling; his temples began to throb as if a thick, knotted rope were twisting around his head. He noticed that the barometer was rising rapidly. If a dry, northern *shamal* was coming in, it might disperse his cloud-and-dust cover before nightfall. He couldn't worry about it. He was a few miles south of the tanker routes, and at present that was all he could do to stay out of sight. When he got nearer to Hālūl, he would look for a place to hide until it was time to kill LEVIATHAN.

The heat pounded on the boat like sand dropped from a steam shovel, and Hardin drowsed despite the rattle of the engine and the intermittent ear-piercing crackles from the radio. Suddenly, he awakened to a new sound. An English voice, muddied by weak reception, was trying to raise the Qatar coastal station.

"H-O-Y . . . H-O-Y . . . H-O-Y. This is Sierra-Quebec-Foxtrot-Bravo . . . Sierra-Quebec-Foxtrot-Bravo. . . . Hotel-Oscar-Yankee . . . Hotel-Oscar-Yankee. This is Sierra-Quebec-Foxtrot-Bravo to Hotel-Oscar-Yankee. Do you receive me, please?"

Hardin flung himself down the companionway. Sierra-Quebec-Foxtrot-Bravo, SQFB, was LEVIATHAN's call sign.

"Hotel-Oscar-Yankee. Hotel-Oscar-Yankee. This is Sierra-Quebec-Foxtrot-Bravo calling Hotel-Oscar-Yankee. Do you receive me, please?"

He had switched to the earphones and was fine tuning the receiver before he realized that the cabin floor was wet.

Water gleamed in the grooves between the floorboards, and here and there puddles crinkled from the engine's vibrations.

LEVIATHAN turned the corner of Ra's al Hadd and the sea changed with an abruptness that startled Ogilvy as much now as it had the first time more than forty years ago. The water flattened like gelatin. The heat rose twenty degrees; and the wind died. Soon steep cliffs marked the coast they would follow, and ahead the hazy Gulf of Oman glared like an oven seen through smoked glass.

Ogilvy fixed his binoculars on the speck of white that was the lookout on LEVIATHAN's bow—an English sailor wearing a hat for protection from the hot sun. He picked up the bridge wing phone and spoke to the bosun. Moments later a sailor pedaled a bicycle forward on the shimmering deck. He relieved the lookout, who returned to the bridge tower.

The new man was Pakistani, because Ogilvy believed that eastern men were less affected by the heat than westerners. At his feet was a Thermos jug of iced tea, issued by Ogilvy's orders, to preserve him in the baking heat so he would stay alert. Overhead a new lookout, also carrying a Thermos, was climbing the mast between the twin funnels. Both men would be relieved in an hour.

Visibility was several miles, and every few minutes a helicopter could be seen hanging on the horizon like a Christmas-tree ornament. But the only sails on the sea were lateens, ageless shapes as common to the Gulf of Oman as the rocky promontories on its coast. Could Hardin dart out of one of those rocky coves? It wasn't likely. LEVIATHAN was seven miles offshore and helicopters had her in constant sight.

Ogilvy returned to the comfort of the air conditioning, retired to his cabin, and ordered lunch. He ate slowly, pausing between courses to lean back in his comfortable desk chair, wondering about Hardin and his obsession. The man was a renegade, a traitor to his healing profession, an outcast by choice. There were people like that. Radicals, criminals, fanatics. All outsiders, all having in common a perverse hunger to linger beyond the circle of human warmth.

He smiled. The dining steward thought that he was happy with the iced melon, but Ogilvy was teasing himself with a strange insight. In a rare moment of introspection he had included seamen—and their captains—in the lonely clan of voluntary exiles.

Concluding his lunch and his thoughts simultaneously, the captain climbed into bed for his last rest in many hours. The exacting business of navigating the crowded Gulf and loading the oil was about to begin. He would have little relief until he was conning LEVIATHAN past these shores in the opposite direction, deeply laden and homeward bound.

He picked up his bedside telephone and called the bridge for a report on the search and the air cover. Nothing; the Arabian helicopters were still sweeping the water ahead of LEVIATHAN. He cradled the telephone reflectively. Was it possible they were making a big mistake?

He lay awake in his darkened cabin pondering and playing the charts through his mind again. He felt he knew Hardin. He had seen the way the man had waited at the pub, listening, watching, then attacking. He liked setting traps. And to have survived the storm that had disabled LEVIATHAN and kept going showed he was a man of extraordinary determination, lunatic as he might be.

Ogilvy dialed the telephone.

"Radio Room, Second Officer—"

"Get me Captain Bruce in London." He dressed in ten minutes it took to place the call. Bruce came on with assurances. The Iranians promised to have Hardin very soon. Ogilvy cut him off.

"A fiver says he doubled back."

Hardin stared at the wrinkled puddles. How long had he slept? Why hadn't he noticed the sluggish feel that the extra weight gave the Swan?

LEVIATHAN's radio operator was still hailing Doha. "Hotel-Oscar-Yankee. Hotel-Oscar-Yankee. This is Sierra—"

Hardin ripped off the earphones and yanked the jack to reactivate the loudspeaker. "Foxtrot-Bravo calling Hotel-Oscar-Yankee. Hotel-Oscar-Yankee. . . . Do you receive me, please?"

He raced onto deck, began working the big hand pump in the cockpit. Clear water poured from the outlets in the transom. The radio fell silent. Hardin pumped, lifting and dropping the plunger with mechanical regularity. Sweat glistened over his body, trickled down his brow into his eyes. His heart pounded more and more rapidly. He switched hands. His arm was aching.

The radio snapped aloud again, the voice obliterating the softer beeping of morse code. "Hotel-Oscar-Yankee. Hotel-Oscar-Yankee."

Crouching beneath the awning, flinching from the sun, he switched hands again. Somewhere, beneath the waterline, the hull had opened wide. It was probably around the propeller shaft, but he couldn't find the leak and work on it until she pumped out.

His whole body and concentration were married to the beating up-down-up-down of the pump. Raise the plunger, lower the plunger. Raise-lower, up-down. Over and over and over in the killing heat. A roaring in his ears began to drown the sound of the engine. He could hear his blood surging through his head, racing to carry oxygen from his straining lungs to his throbbing brain. Up-down, up-down, up-down.

"Sierra-Quebec-Foxtrot-Bravo. Stand by just a moment, please."

A new voice. Accented English.

"How do you receive me?" asked LEVIATHAN's radio operator.

There was silence.

Hardin leaned over the transom. The bilge water still looked clear. It hadn't sat long. He dragged himself back to the pump. When he looked again, it was the same. He pumped some more.

"Sierra-Quebec-Foxtrot-Bravo," said the accented voice. "This is Hotel-Oscar-Yankee. Doha Coastal Station. Good afternoon. Is that LEVIATHAN?"

"Lima-Echo-Victor-India-Alph—"

"Yes, LEVIATHAN," interrupted the Doha operator. "We've been expecting you. How are you today?"

"We're well, thank you. Is that Ahmed Shied?"

"Yes, LEVIATHAN."

"Gordon MacIntosh here. Good to hear your voice again."

320

"And yours, my friend, after all this time. Did you have a pleasant voyage?"

The bilge stream spouted air and Hardin sank to the cockpit floor, quivering with exhaustion.

"Very pleasant," said the radio. "Have you been well?"

"Very well, thank you."

"I'm glad to hear it."

"Say again, please. I'm losing your signal."

"I said, I'm glad to hear it."

"I can't make you out, LEVIATHAN. Say again."

"I'm glad to hear it."

"Please switch to channel eight."

Hardin forced himself to his feet and stumbled into the broiling cabin to tune the radio to the new frequency. LEVIATHAN and Doha were just reestablishing contact when he did. As their chatter resumed, he returned to the cockpit, switched off the engine, and looked around the water. The low swells were the same sullen gray, but the cloud canopy seemed to be thinning.

He went below again, removed the companionway steps, raised the engine box, and peered into the water swirling in the bilge. Stretching full length on his stomach, he dipped his hand in the water and probed the slimy bottom, crawling aft, feeling under the engine bed and finally behind it. The boat drifted silently, the cabin grew hotter as it slowed, and the engine, which had been running wide open since last night, ticked and pinged and exuded the stink of burned oil.

He felt around the gland where the propeller shaft speared the bottom. The radio conversation between LEVIATHAN and Doha continued unabated as the operators traded news and salutations. Abruptly, the Arab asked, "And what of this crazy man?"

The Scot replied, "The Old Man said he didn't want it nattered about on the air."

"We'll catch him soon," said the Arab. "Do not worry, my friend."

A chill that had nothing to do with the Arab radio operator's empty promise strolled down Hardin's spine. He felt pressure on his fingers like the solid-inside-a-liquid thrust of an underwater inlet in a swimming pool. It was a handspan in front of the shaft, and it felt enormous.

He played his fingers over the hidden flood, estimating the size of the hole. The engine must have shaken open a crack from the pitchpoling. Would it split further?

"What is your ETA?" asked the Doha operator.

"ETA twenty-two hundred tomorrow. Repeat: LEVIA-THAN ETA Hālūl twenty-two hundred tomorrow."

His mind racing, his fingers stroked by the unseen torrent, Hardin listened to the Scot and the Arab sign off.

Twenty-two hundred. Ten o'clock at night. Good for cover, bad for aim. He wished the Dragon had an infrared scope. Thirty-four hours from now; less than a day and a half. Move!

He plugged his twelve-volt electric drill into the outlet on the switchboard above the chart table and carried it, his tool box, and a bag of wood scraps to the cockpit. The boat, stopped, was rocking gently in almost flat seas, and the heat closed on it like a vise.

He drilled four holes through a small piece of oak six inches square and three quarters of an inch thick. The holes angled into the wood an inch from each corner. Then he dragged brass flathead wood screws over a bar of soap, lubricating their threads. Movement caught his eye. He glanced over the side and recoiled with stomach-wrenching horror.

A fat yellow sea snake with a body as thick as his arm slithered on the Gulf's placid surface. It raised its head inquisitively as it approached the Swan. Twin nostril flaps quivered on its snout. Unblinking eyes took in the hull. Its flat rudderlike tail flipped sideways, the snake's soft, sinuous movements turned swift and jerky and it struck the boat.

Terrified that it would climb up the side, Hardin yelled and swung at the snake with a boat hook. He missed, just grazing the blunt head, but before he could pull the pole from the water, the sea snake struck back angrily, fanging the boat hook and coiling its six-foot body around it. The aluminum tubing quivered in Hardin's hands, conveying the serpent's muscular spasm.

Hardin wrestled the pole away and the snake dove out of sight. Gasping for breath, his skin crawling, he saw that other snakes swarmed the water. Some swam lazily past, others like the first seemed more inquisitive.

He was afraid that they would slither aboard and follow him into the cabin. Never entirely easy with what lived in the water, he was in the grip of a fear that threatened to paralyze him as completely as the sea snake's ghastly bite. He walked the decks, heedless of the leak and the dispersing mist, armed with the boat hook, lashing out at any that came close.

That they were poisonous—far more deadly than land snakes—he knew too well. He'd treated a United States Navy officer who'd been bitten while skin diving in the South Pacific. They were closely related to the cobra. There was no serum for most of them. Their bite was painless—a neat injection through a pair of slender fangs—but death was slow and inevitable. After several hours the legs were paralyzed, then the eyes closed and the jaws locked. Convulsions in two or three days, paralysis of the diaphragm, then respiratory failure—none of which repelled Hardin as much as the hideous sight of the fat bodies slicing through the water. He couldn't believe that they couldn't climb aboard the boat if they wanted to.

The macabre joke of it saved him. If he watched the sea snakes long enough, the Swan would sink. It would take a day or so, but they would still be in the water when the boat went under. So he had to turn his back on them while he patched the crack.

He looked up and saw no danger. Ominous patches of gray-blue mottled the overcast sky. As the barometer had indicated, clear air was moving over the Gulf. He gathered his tools and the wooden patch and hurried below.

Prone on the sole, aft of the engine, he spread his tools within easy reach and dipped his hands into the bilge water. An image of a snake, no less vivid for its irrationality, flickered through his mind. It had come down the forward hatch and swum the length of the bilges, squeezing through the drainholes that connected them. Or it had entered through the split itself, sucked in by the pressure of the leak. He glanced over his shoulder, half expecting to see a thick, yellow body sliding down the companionway.

Fear and the heat were stifling his breath; there didn't seem to be enough air this low. He forced his mind to the repair. The bilge had already filled four inches since he had pumped.

He crammed caulking into the split and drove it deep with a caulking iron and hammer. Then he felt with his fingers. The water still flowed. He shoved in more of the thick, rubbery compound and hammered the caulking iron until the flood stopped. Waiting a minute, he felt again. When he was sure the compound was holding, he went on deck.

He cooled off and rested. Then, casting an anxious eye at the thinning overcast, he pumped her dry and returned to the bilge and sponged out the remaining water.

He slid the oak patch under the propeller shaft and seated it in the caulking. There was a slight belly in the fiberglass, so he took the plate out and planed the bottom edges. When he repositioned it, it sat snug and flat on the bottom of the boat.

He drilled starter holes in the fiberglass through the holes in the oak. Then he inserted the screws, bearing down hard as they turned through the oak and bit into the hull. Using his largest power-grip screwdriver—and recalling his realization when he was becalmed that the screwdriver handle was really an infinite circle of levers—he twisted each screw tighter and deeper, alternating from one to the other, until a thin line of caulking compound squeezed out between the patch and the hull.

Nauseous from the heat, Hardin fled to the cockpit and collapsed beneath the awning, his head roaring, his stomach turning, until gradually, buoyed by the job done, he regained his strength. The sky was much clearer. In places, open patches glowed distinctly blue in the sunlight.

Several snakes drifted by, sunning. One, lacing its way past the boat, lowered its scaly head and drank the salt water. Another turned its black, lidless eyes toward a sudden breath of burning air that ruffled the Gulf's gelatinous surface, and then, quickly followed by the others, dove simultaneously into the turbid water.

Hardin tore his eyes from them and looked at the horizon.

He was astonished by how much clearer and more distant it had become. He could see black oil tankers parading in the north. Ahead, dark billowing smoke smudged the western sky where waste-gas fires flared atop offshore oil wells. Beneath the smoke, drilling rigs and well derricks dotted the Gulf like fence posts on a prairie.

A second puff of hot wind fanned his cheeks. The water rippled tentatively. A low black squall line appeared in the northwest, between the oil fields and the tankers, and spread wider and darker. Steep, dark anvil-topped cumulonimbus storm clouds rode above it.

Hardin was watching blearily, trying to muster a response to the swiftly advancing squall, when a bubble-top helicopter pounced out of the sky like an angry wasp.

Preceded by an oblong shadow which grew quickly longer and wider, a big twin-rotor helicopter with Persian markings swooped low and lighted on LEVIATHAN's starboard landing circle. A young Iranian naval commander descended from the aircraft and strode jauntily toward the bridge.

Overhead, a flock of Saudi Arabian helicopter gunships circled like jays raging at a hawk in their nest. The Saudis had been escorting LEVIATHAN—darting between the giant ship and the land, searching coves and river mouths—when the Iranian had suddenly appeared from the east, flown through their formation, and descended to LEVIATHAN's deck, asking clearance from neither the ship nor its escort.

Captain Ogilvy sat seething in his chair on the bridge, watching the trespasser walk his deck, hating everything the binoculars showed. The Iranian's pressed and starched blue uniform glittered with garish service ribbons and the vulgar sort of decorations the wogs passed around like a packet of cigarettes. His hair was thick, black, and shiny. Dark-green sunglasses in the United States Air Force mode covered his eyes, and a small automatic pistol hung from his hip. He seemed impervious to the heat that baked the decks as LEVIATHAN began its voyage up the Arabian coast. Ogilvy snorted an oath: The upstart carried a swagger stick.

The Iranian officer had established two points. Iran could patrol the entire Gulf of Oman as well as the Persian Gulf. And the Iranian Navy would board any merchant ship it pleased. Ignoring the seamen Ogilvy had ordered to meet him, he continued into the tower and appeared, moments later, on the bridge.

"Good afternoon, Captain," he said, approaching his chair.

Ogilvy surveyed him with a cold eye. "Not only have you violated the sanctity of this ship, sir, you have also jeopardized international relations by challenging Saudi Arabian sovereignty."

Puzzlement crossed the Iranian's lean, gray-dark face, then anger. He spoke English with an American accent.

"The Iranian Navy is here to help, Captain. We don't need any lectures from an English subject on matters of international relations."

Ogilvy purpled. "Seventy-five years ago," he said, rising to his full height, "long before you were born, young man, *British* subjects brought order to this territory. We stopped your warring and bickering, we established free trade, and we even charted your waters. You can learn a thing or two from British subjects, sir."

LEVIATHAN's helmsman raised a hand to cover his smile and the second officer wondered for a wild moment if the Iranian's savage expression meant that he would draw his

326

pistol. The man flushed darkly, but Ogilvy spoke again before he could respond.

"What is your business here?"

"We are pursuing this man Hardin," said the Iranian after a long pause, apparently willing to change the subject. "We must ask you to stop your ship until we capture him."

"He's in the Persian Gulf," said Ogilvy.

"No, he did not enter the Persian Gulf. He fled in this direction."

"Then why haven't you captured him?"

"He is one man on a small boat. The Gulf of Oman is large and the Musandam coast is riddled with hiding places. We will have him shortly. In the meantime—"

"He's not here," Ogilvy repeated. "He's in the Gulf."

"He can't be," said the Iranian. "We blocked the Strait."

"You were all looking the other way," said Ogilvy. "And in the dark you missed one man on a small boat. He foxed you by doing the unexpected."

"Why are you so sure he is in the Gulf? Why not the Makrān coast?"

"I know he is in the Gulf because I know the man."

"There is no escape from the Gulf."

"Escape matters less to him than sinking LEVIATHAN."

"You're playing a hunch," said the Iranian. "Just a guess."

"I am right," said Ogilvy. "You're wasting your time searching the Musandam Peninsula."

"Perhaps," the Iranian conceded patiently. "But until we *know* that, we must ask you to stop."

"No."

"LEVIATHAN is threatened, Captain Ogilvy. You can't risk your ship and crew on a hunch."

"LEVIATHAN has a schedule to keep," Ogilvy replied. "The Saudis are doing a good job of covering us. We'll be quite safe, thank you."

"And what will happen at night when the helicopter pilots can't see?"

327

"It doesn't matter," said Ogilvy. "Hardin is in the Gulf."

The Iranian commander shook his head briskly. "I'm sorry, Captain, but I have orders to stop your ship until the threat is past."

The Englishman stared disbelievingly. The Iranian crossed his hands behind his back and rocked on his heels. Ogilvy's expression turned thunderous. His lips tightened, his brow knitted, his nostrils quivered. The second officer took a step toward him, alarmed that the captain might suffer a stroke. Ogilvy chased him with a glance.

His voice trembled with emotion. "LEVIATHAN *will not stop.*"

"We command you to stop for your safety."

Ogilvy glanced out the port windows. A grim smile gladdened his face. "You are in the territorial waters of the Sultanate of Muscat and Oman," he said crisply. "A bit out of bounds, what?"

"If you won't stop now," said the Iranian, "we will board you in our own territory for pollution checks. I can guarantee you, Captain, it will take many days to inspect a ship this size. Many days."

"That's extortion!" Ogilvy shouted.

"It's for your own good."

"Let me tell you something, young man. I know what is best for my ship. Get your helicopter off my foredeck." Ogilvy stalked across the bridge and buried his face in the radarscope.

The Iranian followed him. "I'm warning you, Captain. We'll hold you for weeks."

Ogilvy straightened up from the scope. His face white with anger, he pounded the console.

"I'm not some Chinaman on a ten-thousand-tonner you can push around. This is LEVIATHAN. I am Captain Cedric Ogilvy. And when I inform the world that you dare blockade my ship, you'll wish you'd never heard of me."

The Iranian opened his mouth, but Ogilvy cut him off. "You people have been getting rather cheeky with your shiny new navy, and the merchant shipping community is getting mighty fed up."

"These are our waters!" the Iranian shouted back.

The two men glared at each other oblivious of the gaping helmsman, the second officer, a cadet at the course computer, and an Indian steward with a tea tray.

The VHF radio broke the silence. The second officer picked up the handset. He turned to Ogilvy. "It's the helicopter. They're calling this man."

The Iranian reached for the phone. Ogilvy nodded and the second released it. The Iranian listened. His mouth tightened and he handed the phone back to the third.

"Well, Captain, it seems you were right."

"Yes."

The Iranian smiled sardonically. He removed his sunglasses, revealing a pale untanned mask around his eyes. "An Aramco company helicopter pilot has spotted Hardin's boat in the Gulf, sixty miles east of Jazirat Hālūl."

The helicopter hung at mast height, fifty feet to starboard. The pilot, vaguely visible behind the Plexiglas bubble, raised a glinting object in both hands and Hardin, panicked by the suddenness with which it appeared, braced for the shock of a bullet.

Forcing his mind to action, he leaped to his feet and waved as if asking for help. Then he saw the binoculars in the pilot's hand and realized that the helicopter was a private aircraft, not military. His relief was short-lived. The craft circled the Swan for a closer look and he saw the company name—Aramco—on the tail. The oil companies were hunting, too.

Sickened by his helplessness, Hardin watched the pilot draw a radio mike to his mouth. Unbidden, an angry yell, a wordless *no,* leaped from his throat. The buzz of the hovering aircraft smothered it. Aramco would receive the message in minutes and pass it on to the Iranian Navy. How long before their high-speed attack boats were racing over the Gulf?

The water bubbled and boiled beneath the helicopter's

whirling blades. The pitch of the rotor sounds lowered abruptly. The airship tilted its transparent nose and shot away to the south. It dwindled to a small black dot and Hardin stared until it disappeared. Warm air brushed his back. He turned around and saw the reason the pilot hadn't lingered.

A dark shadow with teeth of snowy white. The squall filled the sky from horizon to horizon; black clouds rode a frothy, leaping sea. The air pressed upon his body. The heat was abruptly searing. He gasped for breath, his heart pounding. Dark streamers and ragged masses of cloud shot ahead of the squall line like thrusting lances. Vivid lightning played over its face. The next wind blast was cold. The heat dissipated magically, replaced by a gravelike chill. Overhead, the Swan's rigging began to hum.

Hardin raced to close the main and mid hatches, dropped down the bow hatch and brought up a storm jib, which he hanked to the forestay and raised seconds ahead of the raging white line. He was halfway to the wheel when a massive gust screamed through the rigging and bellied the stormsail like a balloon. The Swan tried to turn before the wind, but the full force of the squall hit before she was about and heeled her sharply.

Hardin tumbled off the coach roof, smashed into a lifeline stanchion, and fell between the stainless steel cables. His head ringing from the impact, he wrapped his arms around the stanchion and kicked the water, seeking purchase where there was none. The mast spreaders dipped toward the lacerated swells. The wheel spun wildly, a flicker of spokes inside a blurry chrome circle.

Hardin pulled himself back through the lifelines and scrambled into the cockpit. He rescued the wheel and secured the jib sheet. The Swan righted and raced downwind, crashing from wave to trough in choppy ten-foot seas, smashing southward like a roller coaster where moments before there had been calm.

A burst of hailstones raked the deck like machine-gun fire. He bowed his head to protect his face and tried to steer a course, and he prayed that the squall would last long enough to put distance between himself and the place where the helicopter had seen him.

He had read and reread the Sailing Directions this morning. A half dozen times since dawn, trying, in the absence of charts, to make pictures from the carefully worded descriptions and warnings.

Ahead, south, was the Great Pearl Bank, a region of shoals, islands, rocks, strong tidal currents, and coral reefs. It extended over most of the great bight in the southern part of the Persian Gulf that was bordered by the Trucial Coast in the east and the Qatar Peninsula in the west.

Jazirat Hālūl, LEVIATHAN's destination, lay fifty miles from Qatar on the northwestern rim of the Great Pearl Bank. The oil-loading island was almost due west of him, but the squall was driving him south.

He waited for a relatively smooth spot between the choppy seas and tried to jibe about and head west, but the waves pushed the Swan toward her lee side. Her bow swung south again and the jib slammed back with a vehemence that threatened to shred the Dacron. He tried several more times to jibe about and point west, but the seas, piling high before the northern squall winds, kept beating him south—away from Hālūl and toward the Pearl Bank.

"I told you he'd be in the Gulf," Ogilvy crowed. He barked a harsh laugh and a broad smile creased his pink face. "Did they catch him?"

"I don't know," said the Iranian, preparing to leave. "The report was sketchy. Our ships are proceeding there. We should have him within hours."

"Of course," Ogilvy said sarcastically.

The Iranian commander started toward the chart room door and the elevator beyond. He paused as if to say something, then seemed to change his mind. Ogilvy watched him go. He was tempted to needle him about their argument, but he felt expansive because he had been proved so dramatically correct. On impulse, he followed the Iranian and caught up at the elevator.

"I'll walk you to your helicopter."

"No need," the Iranian said stiffly.

"My pleasure. I could use a breath of fresh air."

"It's hot. You'll be sorry you left your air conditioning."

The heat hit like an open furnace as they stepped onto deck. For a moment Ogilvy reconsidered the long walk out and back, but he could hardly withdraw the courtesy, so he kept the pace slow and chatted him up, confirming, as he had suspected, that he was one of those American-trained sorts who'd been in the States for university and military training, served aboard their fleet, and now shuttled back and forth every time the Yanks invented a new weapon to sell the Shah. The Iranian fell silent as they trudged toward the helipad. Ogilvy gazed ahead, admiring the length of his great ship, thinking about Hardin. Would he be relieved, when he was captured, that it was over?

The sky ahead looked slightly clearer than it had earlier. That meant a *shamal* was building in the northwest. Storms today, and tomorrow the Gulf would be crystal clear. And much less humid. Thank Allah for small favors, what?

He couldn't remember how he had stood the pre-War Gulf patrols without air conditioning. His shirt was wet and beads of perspiration streamed down his cheeks like tears. He'd bathe and get back in bed as soon as the wog was gone.

They exchanged polite good-byes and Ogilvy glanced astern while the Iranian climbed the big aircraft's boarding stairs. The walk out was always worth the inspiring view back. LEVIATHAN's mighty bridge structure was an awesome sight, its twin funnels marking the sky like the towers of a giant suspension bridge.

"Captain?"

"Yes?"

He looked up. The Iranian had slid open a window and

thrust his head out. "The copter that spotted Hardin lost him in a squall."

"Can I presume that you'll catch him before we arrive tomorrow night?"

Unexpectedly, the Iranian grinned. "To be sure. You may proceed as you are."

Ogilvy said nothing, refusing to rise to the suggestion that LEVIATHAN moved at Iranian will. The rotors began to whine into motion. Ogilvy pounded the side of the airship with his open palm. The Iranian opened the window and looked down. The blades ceased.

"What is it, Captain?"

"Tell your people to look on the Great Pearl Bank. He'll hide among the reefs."

"I'll keep it in mind, Captain. It's a good point."

"Tell me something," said Ogilvy, ignoring the Iranian's anxious-to-be-off expression. "Will you hand him over to the Americans or try him yourself?" He saw himself mirrored in the Iranian's sunglasses; the reply was chillingly oblique.

"I suppose if we knew for sure he was American, we might. Of course, we wouldn't know if his passport were lost in the struggle, in which case we would hand him over to SAVAK."

"SAVAK?" said Ogilvy. "It's hardly a matter for the secret police."

"We will take care of the problem," replied the Iranian. "The oil producers have nothing to worry about. Nor do the shippers."

26

The compass card skittered crazily, spinning like the dial on a fat man's scale, but turning inexorably southward as once again the Swan fell off the wind. The squall had driven her south for hours. South, when Hālūl was west. South, toward the Great Pearl Bank. South, until Hardin was lost.

Finally, regardless of the hammering seas, he tried again to come about and beat into the shrieking, howling, northwest wind. The steep-sided waves attacked her bow, staggering her, driving her back. He trimmed the storm jib and the abbreviated mainsail—reefed to the extra storm slabs sewn by the Fowey sailmaker—and searched for a workable mean, a compromise between the thrust the wind gave the boat and the choppy seas it heaped in her way.

Clouds of spray lashed over the bow. Green seas broke on it, burying it to the mast. The water sizzled under a new fusillade of hail that drummed across the cabin and dropped an inch of stinging ice beads into the cockpit. Hardin's face was slashed raw where his ragged beard didn't protect.

Then a sharp wave slapped the starboard bow and the Swan was around, clinging to a starboard tack. For a long moment the pummeling seas held her dead still. Her stiff storm sails crackled uselessly. Hardin sheeted them out, inch by inch, until she began to gain headway.

Then he yanked her back.

The compass hung at 285—fifteen degrees north of west—and at last the Swan moved slowly forward, forward toward Hālūl, farther and farther from where the helicopter had found him.

He maintained the 285 course for an hour. Then the wind shifted to the northeast and he was able to steer even closer to the north. The Swan tore swiftly through a roiled cross sea, gaining the distance lost. Hardin ran up a bigger jib.

He was elated. After endless, numbing days of light airs and oppressive heat, the sloop was flying like a bird on cool winds. Setting the self-steering, he went below to check the bilges. An acceptable amount of water sloshed about. The patch was holding.

The sky seemed brighter. The Sailing Directions had noted that most Gulf storms were of short duration and this one looked as if it might be dying; the wind had eased slightly, even though the seas seemed as roiled.

A strange sound layered over the howl of the wind and the slush of breaking wave tops. It was coming from dead ahead, a soft, muttering thunder unlike a boat or a plane; it sounded like breakers, but he was at least sixty miles from the coast of Qatar and probably thirty from Jazirat Hālūl.

Concerned, he went forward and stood on the plunging bow, one hand wrapped around the forestay, the other shielding his eyes from the rain and spray. He scanned the stormy murk, then belatedly snapped his safety line to the stay, angry for letting himself be so distracted. Something white showed in the gloom. His scalp prickled.

He ran for the wheel.

Two hundred yards ahead, a glistening white line split the gray water like a leer on a dirty face. The seas were breaking on a reef. He had blundered into the Great Pearl Bank.

The Swan bore down swiftly on the lethal outcropping.

His hands on the wheel, Hardin hesitated. The part he could see was the least dangerous; the rock and coral could extend underwater in any direction. He turned upwind to take way off the Swan. If she hit at the five and a half knots the speedometer indicated, she'd rip her bottom out.

Close enough to see cracks in the coral where the water sluiced back to the sea, Hardin steered into the biggest waves to stop the Swan faster; then he lowered the main and stood on the bow, which rolled and plunged like a speared shark, and tried to fathom the extent of the reef.

On a clear day, according to the Sailing Directions, the reefs were easily discernible, but at this moment neither the dark sky nor the riled water let him see the underwater portions of the jagged rock and coral in his path.

The Swan held her head to the waves and drifted slowly astern. Hardin shivered, remembering a typically understated caution in the Sailing Directions: "It is not safe to be underway after dark when near or within the reefs." It would be night in two hours.

He cursed himself for failing to see what the exceedingly choppy seas had meant; the steepness of the waves had shown him he had entered shoal water, but he had been blind. He shivered again. He had been on the Banks some time; he had actually come upon the reef from the south. How close had he come to grounding already?

Coral to port!

In his mind, Hardin heard a thin wail from aloft—the lookout's alarm his father mimicked in a tale of running a square rigger through the treacherous reefs of the Tuamotu Archipelago in a South Pacific typhoon. Puckering his eyes, he could just make out, to the left, another long, low-lying shadow. As the wind blew him nearer, he scanned its contours, searching a way around.

The one ahead was disappearing as he drifted astern. He heard a new growl of breaking water, steadied himself on the pitching foredeck, and searched for the reef. He had coral ahead and coral aport. It was either turn tail or try to claw to starboard on a close-hauled tack.

Coral astern! Again he heard his father's reedy cry.

A small piece showed, a single wicked prong, surrounded by what looked like a gigantic rolling comber but was actually the storm seas breaking on a submerged reef that extended hundreds of feet to either side. He had sailed into a three-sided box, a coral canyon. It was a miracle he hadn't struck bottom on the way in. And it would take a miracle to beat out against the northeast wind.

He hoisted the main again to its stormsail height and put the Swan on a port tack. The sails filled. She stopped pounding as the wind steadied her against the chaotic shallow-water chop, and began to run east out of the box.

Coral to starboard! She was yawing south. The waves were driving her to the right, shoving her toward the underwater reef. He brought her about, put her on her starboard tack, and tried to steer for open water. The wind drove him west.

Coral dead ahead! He came about again. Would the engine help? He was loath to risk the pounding the propeller shaft would give the patched crack. The wind pushed him back.

Coral astern! He changed course and tried again and again to beat against the wind, but as earlier, the seas kept driving her back. *Coral to starboard! Coral to port! Coral dead ahead!*

He had thought he had made it that time, when a fourth reef suddenly grinned ahead. The hell with it. He put the helm over, jibbed about, and ran for the deeper water inside the coral box. Then he put her head to the wind, and tossed his heavy plow; the anchor line dropped thirty feet before it began to lie diagonally. Plenty of water here, but what was a hundred yards away?

The Swan tugged the anchor, pulling it, and the line reverberated as the steel bill bounced along the coral. He played it out farther until it gripped something and stayed put. When he was sure it would hold, he readied a spare, then noted the bearings of the reefs ahead and to port.

The anchor kept her bow to the waves and stabilized the plunging, pitching hull. Hardin opened some cans of fruit and fish and ate them in the cockpit, ignoring the pelting rain, one eye fixed on the reefs, waiting for the first hint that she was dragging.

The sky was brightening and the wind began to drop. The rain tapered off to a drizzle. The light got better and the waves began to subside to a post-storm swell.

With luck, the coral he had encountered was a far northerly outcropping on the edge of the Great Pearl Bank. With luck, few shoals and patches lay between him and the deeper waters to the north. With luck.

The drizzle stopped abruptly. He went below and checked the chronometer. Less than an hour to sundown. He shouldn't have eaten. It made him tired. He felt his weariness undermine his ability to make decisions. He saw himself too willing to ride at anchor and wait for something to happen.

It wouldn't work that way. He'd never get out if he waited till dark. He was too close to LEVIATHAN now to blow it with a cautious move. He had to take a chance.

Locking the rudder dead center, he rerigged the jib sheets so he could control them from the foredeck. He lowered the main and hauled up the anchor. Then, bracing his legs against the pulpit rails and standing on the tip of the bow, he looked down into the water and steered the boat with the jib.

He headed between the big northern reef he had first seen and the scattered outcroppings to the east, seeking the outlines of their underwater prongs. The water seemed opaque, then the bow would rise or a swell would flatten and he could see into it. A dark shape loomed ahead. He tightened the jib sheet. The Swan sailed around it. A shoal patch showed light sand. He guessed it was ten feet under, and sailed over it. The water deepened and he saw nothing.

Then a ridge of stone peaked almost to the surface, just below the level where the diminishing seas could break on it. He slacked the sail and the Swan wallowed to port. He guided her along the ridge, looking for an opening. It ran for three hundred yards, than vanished abruptly into the belly of the sea. He sailed over the cut and headed north.

The air was turning humid again, and the wind and waves continued to ease. But while the clouds were sifting apart, thinning, making it easier to see the reefs, a sunset glow in the haze to the west told Hardin that night was only minutes away.

A jagged barb of broken coral appeared four feet under the surface. He saw it too late, heaved on the jib sheet with aching hands, and held his breath. The Swan glided toward it, over it, frighteningly close. Her fin keel touched. Hardin gripped the stay, waiting for her to pivot on the reef and smash hard. She trembled free.

He spotted no coral for ten minutes. Was he out of the reefs? Or was he grazing over them, blind in the thickening dusk? He strained to penetrate the water. Suddenly

338

the horizons lifted like a curtain and he could see for miles ahead.

Lights glittered in the north on oil derricks, drilling rigs, and steaming tankers beneath a canopy of clouds and gas-flare smoke. The butt of a pale, weak sun slid into the Gulf and the leaping flames of the burning gas flares cast a ruddy glow over the darkening sky.

Awed by the brilliant electric array that stretched from east to west as far as he could see, Hardin let the Swan stand into the wind, and got his binoculars from the cockpit. The lights squiggled white and yellow; his hands were shaking with exhaustion. He steadied the glasses against the forestay and focused to infinity.

He was on the rim of the Great Pearl Bank. The reefs were behind him. Hālūl was somewhere to his left. Ahead, north, was the tanker route passing through the lighted oil fields.

On the edge of those sea-lanes was a remarkably bright cluster of golden lights. It looked to be a giant oil platform high above the water and widely surrounded by smaller rigs and derricks, some of which were horizontally connected by lighted pipelines. A big Hovercraft, wallowing in the swells, entered Hardin's binocular field and stopped outside the platform. Helicopters circled above.

As the red night deepened, the electric lights and gas flares shone brighter. The dying wind stirred the humid air with whiffs of burning gas. The water reflected the rusty glow of the sky and the faint sounds of engines were everywhere.

Hardin scanned the hellish scene, looking for a place for the Swan. These were producing oil fields, the monster's lair, the reason LEVIATHAN existed. He was alien. His boat too small, too white in this place of red water and black steel. Behind him, on the Great Pearl Bank, was the shadowy form of a dark island, enticingly close.

27

Six anxious men gathered in a conference room atop
Wellhead Number One, a ten-hole oil-pumping platform
thirteen miles north of the Great Pearl Bank in the
middle of the Persian Gulf. The room was incongruously
luxurious. Enormous picture windows edged with thick
drapes formed the outer walls between the low ceiling and
the thickly carpeted floor. A lavishly stocked bar occupied
one corner, an elaborate communications console the
other. The big windows shone golden light into the red
Gulf sky, topping the platform with the crown of gold that
Hardin had seen from twelve miles away.

Number One belonged to a consortium of Kuwaiti,
Iranian, Saudi, and Swiss shareholders and was, as such,
as close to neutral territory as the six men could find in
the Persian Gulf. The oil fraternity considered Hardin a
threat to all and the managers of Number One had
willingly lent their facility to the men who were hunting
him.

The Iranian naval commander who had landed on
LEVIATHAN and crossed swords with Captain Ogilvy had
been hunting Hardin for twenty hours, and the fatigue that
etched the pale skin around his eyes showed him to be
somewhat older than he had seemed to Ogilvy earlier in
the day.

His Saudi Arabian counterpart was also in uniform, but
he wore the khaki of the Air Force. The Arab was a slight,
wiry man with glittering eyes, and whenever he mentioned
Hardin, he spoke his name as if he were discussing
dangerous vermin.

An unlikely pair observed from the back of the room.
One was a tall, swarthy man with a hawk nose who wore

the flowing white robes and headdress of a Qataran prince and sipped a glass of orange juice. Beside him was a short, pale, plump-faced American in a white shirt and a narrow black necktie. He drank scotch on the rocks and perspired heavily although the room was air-conditioned to a deep chill. Their eyes flickered in unison to whoever was speaking, and they watched warily, as if, at the first sign of danger, they would crouch back to back like legionnaires in hostile territory.

The American was the terminal manager of the Hālūl Island depot; the Qataran, his boss, the operations director of the Qataran oil company, which owned the depot. Occasionally they interrupted the discussions to point out that the storage tanks and loading arms of Hālūl were of equal importance to the ship LEVIATHAN; finally the American ventured the opinion that the Iranians and the Saudis seemed to care less about Hālūl than their own honor.

James Bruce hushed him with a warning glance. They had enough trouble already without antagonizing the military men. He had just flown in from London into Bahrain by Concorde; the oil company that had chartered LEVIATHAN had ferried him to the platform. Exhausted by the long journey and battered by the noise of the helicopter, he had trouble concentrating on the byplay between the Iranian and the Saudi, and he had turned to the sixth man in the room—an Englishman, thank God—for assistance.

Miles Donner had been very obliging. Before the others arrived, he suggested that Bruce nap for half an hour. Gratefully, Bruce let himself be taken to a comfortable bed in a nearby stateroom. Donner had wakened him an hour later, explaining the extra half hour by saying nothing of importance had occurred. He gave him a cup of thick black coffee, and when Bruce reappeared in the meeting room, Donner poured him a stiff whiskey, which set him up very nicely. He still had trouble concentrating, but he felt confident that Donner would look after his interests.

He didn't understand entirely what Donner was doing

341

here. Apparently he was some sort of representative of Israel, and that nation's secret service had discovered that Hardin was at it again. But in some odd way he had practically taken over the strategy session. He seemed to know a lot about Hardin, and he used his knowledge as a buffer between the Arab factions.

Bruce gazed out the wide picture windows at the dull yellow patch where the sun had set. Above and around it the sky was taking on a ruddy glow, as it did every night in the Gulf oil fields where the burning gas flares painted the night sky more vividly than any sunset.

Sixty feet beneath him an enormous Hovercraft tossed in the rough seas. Sleek and new—British built in Southampton—it was heavily armed with surface-to-surface and surface-to-air missiles, deck cannon, and machine guns. The Iranian had arrived on it moments before with a grand flourish of reverse propellers, which hadn't concealed from the master mariner's eyes the Hovercraft's glaring deficiency: It was a bloody pig in rough seas. God help the Iranians if they ever had to fight in a storm.

The Saudi had come by helicopter. Three helicopters, to be precise. His had landed. Two escort craft, bristling with weapons, circled the wellhead continuously. They were relieved every fifteen minutes as pairs of the gunships shuttled the two hundred miles to Saudi Arabia to refuel.

Miles Donner paused in his conversation with the Iranian, drew the Saudi officer close, and got the two men talking. Then he disengaged slowly, like a man backing away from a precariously balanced addition to a heaping litter basket, and motioned Bruce to the bar. He mentioned lightly that the denizens of the opposite shores of the Gulf mixed as reluctantly as oil and water, and poured the company captain a fresh drink.

For a moment, Bruce thought he might be getting sloshed, but he reckoned he could handle one more, and it was very soothing. He was surprised by the way the Arabs took to Donner. None of the scorn you would have expected them to show for a Jew. Donner seemed to guess his thought.

342

"The men of the Gulf states are much more reasonable than some of Israel's other neighbors," he said with a smile. "We have something in common."

"What is that?" asked Bruce.

"We both have a lot to protect."

"What are they arguing about?"

"Ostensibly," replied Donner, "they are discussing their claims to the Persian Gulf. In actual fact, they are arguing that they are Arabs and Persians, about which they have been arguing since the dinosaurs put their feet in the air and turned to oil." His smile dimmed. "It might be amusing if Hardin weren't still out there. They wasted the last hour of daylight debating jurisdiction— Excuse me, Captain. I've got to sort them out again."

He hurried across the big room, neatly dodging the managers of the Qataran oil company, and stepped between the Arab and the Iranian with a suggestion that they three study the area charts and plot a cooperative search pattern. Simultaneously, the two officers said they had to speak with their aides, who were standing by aboard their staff vehicles. They picked up telephones at opposite ends of the communications console and spoke rapidly in their own tongues while Donner spread the charts of the Hālūl oil fields on a conference table.

The Saudi reported that the helicopter pilot who had spotted a yacht in the Gulf had been shown photographs obtained by radio-facsimile machine from the Nautor boatyard in Pietarsaari, Finland. He was sure he had seen a Nautor Swan 38.

The Iranians weren't so sure. While they had a sizable force patrolling the Hālūl fields in the dark, they were still combing the coves and bays of the Musandam Peninsula in the Gulf of Oman. The parties agreed on one fact: Tomorrow's weather boded well for them. It would be a clear day.

"That means that Hardin will have to hide," said Miles Donner, leading them to the conference table. "Where?"

Unlike most of the dispassionately printed Admiralty charts, those for the southern bight of the Persian Gulf were ablaze with colored ink. The Great Pearl Bank was studded with shoal warnings, islands, and known reefs and overlaid with reminders that the area was not thoroughly charted; but beyond the reefs, for twenty-five miles either side of Hālūl, the charts had the frantic look of color coded electronic circuitry as they warned mariners of the sea rigs, wellheads, exploration buoys, mooring sites, submarine pipelines, floating pipelines, barge routes, and loading buoys that posed hazards to navigation in the oil fields.

"There," said the Saudi Arabian Air Force colonel. He pointed at the thicket of drilling operations. "He'll hide among the boats and barges to make it difficult to see him from aloft."

"No," said the Iranian. "He must hide from boats as well."

"Where then?"

"Here." The Iranian traced the Great Pearl Bank with his swagger stick. "Within the Banks and no more than thirty miles from the sea-lane to Hālūl."

"Why?" asked Donner.

"Two reasons. There are many, many small islands, all uninhabited and protected from deep-draft patrol boats by the reefs. If I were on a little sailboat I would anchor in a cove beside white sand and cover my boat with a white sail. You'd have to get next to me to distinguish the boat from the glare of the sand." He smiled at the Saudi. "And you'd never see me from the air."

"And would your sail protect you from heat sensors?" the Arab asked scornfully.

"The sail would reflect as much heat as the sand," the Iranian snapped, too quickly.

"Nonsense," said the Arab.

Donner sized up the two men. The question of the heat sensors was a good one and the Iranian didn't know the answer. They couldn't afford the luxury of finding out tomorrow. "What was your second point, Commander?"

"I spoke with the captain of LEVIATHAN personally this afternoon. He predicted that Hardin would be in the Persian Gulf before we received the helicopter report. He knows the way the man's mind works."

"Did he say where he would hide?" asked Donner.

"Yes. He said he would hide on the Banks. He said to look in the reefs."

"The reefs won't hide him from air surveillance," said the Arab.

"The islands would and even the reefs might. How long did it take you to find your downed Bell Huey last month? Four days? Five days?"

The Arab flushed. "It was partly submerged."

"The Gulf is big," Donner said diplomatically. "Very big. Which is why, my friends, our best chance may be to combine our efforts in an air-sea search of a single area."

"Very big," agreed the Arab. "Vast as the desert."

"But Hardin is restricted by his speed," said the Iranian. Spreading his thumb and forefinger like calipers, he straddled Hālūl on the chart and moved his hand eastward in a sixty-mile swath along the sea-lane. "Eight knots at best under sail. Six under power. Thirty miles maximum in four hours. He can't afford to stay too far either side of LEVIATHAN's route. He can't hide on the Qatar Peninsula, for instance, or deeper than thirty miles into the Pearl Bank."

"Do you agree?" Donner asked the Saudi.

The Air Force man nodded reluctantly, then turned his answer to make the conclusion his own. "Our helicopters are already concentrating on this route."

"Perhaps," said Donner, his voice soft, his manner easy, "perhaps we should concentrate on *one* side of the route."

"Perhaps."

Donner rubbed his chin and pretended to study the chart. "Perhaps the Pearl Bank is the most logical place for a small boat, as the captain of LEVIATHAN suggested."

"There is no place to hide north of the route," said the Iranian.

"There are the oil fields," said the Saudi.

"But they are busy places," said Donner. "The workers there are already on the lookout for a sailboat. There are men on rigs and barges and *lanshes* all over those waters, night and day. Besides, it is not a place . . ." He searched for a word to describe the grim industrial scale of the oil fields, the filthy waters and the putrid air. "It is not conducive to a small boat. Not compatible with a little sailing yacht."

"It is no place for a sailboat," the Iranian agreed.

"We must consolidate our effort," said Donner. "Can you recall your units from the Musandam Peninsula?"

"If we can use them to search the Pearl Bank," said the Iranian.

"But you don't know those waters," protested the Arab.

"What about the pearl hunters?" asked Donner.

"Of course," cried the Arab. He nodded excitedly at the Iranian. "We will give you our pearl hunters and fishermen to show you the way. They know the reefs and the coral."

"Wonderful," said Donner.

"Thank you," the Iranian said thoughtfully, and Donner guessed that he was wondering how many Saudi spies would be among the pearlers to garner information about Iran's sophisticated navy.

"I'll have them rounded up immediately," said the Saudi.

"We'll have to wait until dawn," said the Iranian. "We can't search the reefs at night."

"If I may suggest . . ." said Donner.

"Yes, my friend," the Saudi said expansively, pleased, it seemed, with the bargain struck.

"There is one thing we can do tonight," Donner said softly. "Send your aircraft aloft with searchlights. Sweep the reefs along here." He pointed at the chart. His voice hardened and, for an instant, thought James Bruce, there was no question that the mild-looking Israeli with the upper-class English accent had taken full charge of the hunt.

"Force him to keep moving. Don't let him sleep. Drive him. He's fagged out already. Perhaps when morning comes there won't be much of him left."

28

The violent roar of high-speed marine engines shocked him awake. He leaped to the hatch, his mind clinging to sleep, his stomach paining from fear. A shadow raced across the oil-field lights and the flat wake of a planing hull bubbled somewhere past the Swan. Before the clamor had dwindled to an echoing rumble, the shadow vanished in the red darkness.

The sky had brightened in the hour since the sun had set. A ruddy glow stretched east to west between the Swan and the northern horizon, stoked by the gas flares blazing atop the sea rigs. The night was red with the flames— some near, some far—that flickered like the watchfires of warring giants. Reflecting the fireballs, the Gulf rippled bloodily as if they had washed their swords in it.

The night was hot, as hot as the day had been before the storm, so hot that it seemed the flames heated it as the sun did the day. The seas had calmed. A hot north breeze, reeking of burned gas, did not disturb them. The Swan still stood between the oil fields and the dark island, fixed by the north breeze and the south-setting current, much as he had left her before he had dozed off at the chart table with his head on the dog-eared Sailing Directions.

He pumped some seawater into the galley sink and rubbed the warm liquid on his eyes. It smelled of oil. Then he resumed reading the section marked CAUTION:

> Vessels are warned to keep outside of an area about 14½ miles offshore from eastward to south-southwestward of Jazirat Hālūl, due to the existence of drilling rigs, oil-well structures, mooring buoys, and numerous submarine pipelines.

Three oil fields have been established in the vicinity. . . .

Hardin had come out of the Pearl Bank at the southeast end of a chain of rigs and wellheads that extended for nearly twenty-five miles to Hālūl Island. The oil men would be working night and day. He scanned further, re-read the section several times, and tried to force his exhausted mind to sponge up details.

> A bank with a least mean depth of 10.4m (34 ft.) lies about 17 miles southward of Jazirat Hālūl. A 90-foot abandoned and unlighted oil rig is charted in the shoalest part of this bank. A LIGHT is shown and a FOG SIGNAL sounded from each of several drilling structures. . . .

No problem; draft out here wasn't a worry.

He set a small jib, but left the main furled. The headsail would pull him quickly enough and he could see better without the big mainsail blocking the sky. There was a considerable amount of helicopter and airplane activity on the south horizon and he caught glimpses of their searchlights raking the water.

A white sail was a hell of a target for a searchlight. He tied a line to the tail of the jib halyard and ran it back to the cockpit where he secured it within easy reach. Then he put the Swan on a broad starboard tack.

For the first time in three months he wasn't concerned with speed. He was close to the sea-lanes—the tanker lights told him that—close to LEVIATHAN's route—two hours' run at worst—but first he had to find a hiding place. A place to stash a thirty-eight-foot boat for twelve hours. A place he couldn't describe. A place he didn't even know existed. A place he would find more readily plodding at two or three knots through the crimson darkness than if he were racing. Time was against him, however. He had less than ten hours of night left to search the oil fields.

348

The Iranian naval commander and Captain Ogilvy were blue-water sailors, deep-sea modern-ship men, and each made the same mistake about the Nautor Swan and the man who owned her. She displaced 16,120 pounds—under eight tons—and weighed less than a few links of LEVIATHAN's anchor chain. Fully loaded, she could sail in water seven feet deep. And yet she was a deep-water boat, a miniature ship with a fixed keel, and Hardin feared grounding no less than they did.

Faced with the grim alternatives of reentering the Great Pearl Bank or sailing into the noxious oil fields, Hardin saw no real choice. He no longer voyaged from coast to coast. He had made his break from the land, which he had come to see more as an obstacle than a destination. Deep seas were his haven now. Shallows were anathema, the last place he would go for refuge, and he would have sailed through burning water rather than risk the Swan's hull on another reef.

He neared the edge of the oil field, and burning water seemed to be what waited. Flames rimmed the sky, dulling the electric lights on the sea rigs to pale, white dots, and the stench of gas grew so strong that he feared he would be poisoned by the wind.

A giant fireball leaped fitfully from the top of a sea rig a mile away, wrestling with the night, strangling the dark. It silhouetted closer rigs and threw their tortured shadows on the water like the victims of a jail-yard riot. Hardin steered away from the flare, afraid that the light of its thrusting flames would reveal his presence to a tow crew passing close ahead.

They were pulling a long string of pontoon-supported pipe that looked like the fleshless backbone of a dinosaur. The tugboat, the turban-topped figures of the deckhands, and the skeletal pipeline etched sharp black lines on the fiery backdrop of sea and sky, and only when the tug moved beyond the range of the fireball did its green and white running lights escape the grip of red.

Hardin waited until the hollow rumble of the tug engine faded into the darkness. Then, quickly, he sailed the bright waters, holding his breath until he had reached the next dark patch, an area of several miles around and devoid of activity. From the darkness, he saw planes sweeping low on the horizon.

He pointed the Swan toward the big platform he had seen when he had first emerged from the Pearl Bank. Its gold crown still glowed warmly and it glistened with hundreds of electric lights that crusted its spindly legs, lined its upper decks, and shone in its windows. He closed within a half mile and watched as a pool of light suddenly filled on the roof and a twin-rotor helicopter settled into it.

A number of boats were darting to and from the platform. He released the extended jib halyard and dropped the sail. A boat tore past, unseeing, and faded into the night. Hardin raised the jib again and proceeded northwest into a forest of drilling rigs.

That this was a new field was apparent by the gangs of men working on the rigs. Some of the towers were under construction. Others, completed, shook with the ceaseless rocking of the drilling arms. In the distance, a single pillar of fire marked the sky. Hardin moved through the rigs, veering from lights, hiding from men, seeking the shadows.

The hot breeze was from the south now—it had been shifting every few moments—and he didn't hear the workboat's engine until it was alongside. Roustabouts sat on the stern, sagging with weariness. Perspiration glistened on their naked torsos and reflected the reddish sky. Hardin doused the jib again. The workboat swung across his bow and entered a lighted channel. Hardin left the jib down and started his engine, relying on the almost constant murmur of machinery to block the quiet exhaust of the Swan's diesel at half speed.

Ahead was a brightly lighted pumping derrick. He steered north of it. The wind, which had shifted again astern, brought the hollow airy sound of a tugboat coming up behind, hauling high empty barges and closely followed by a second tow.

Hardin swung the Swan south, but before he could get on a new course to take him past the derrick, on which a work gang was unloading a freight boat, a push-tow barge and tug loomed ahead. Hardin swung north again and cut his engine. He was in the center of a two-hundred-yard-wide stretch of water between the oncoming push tow and the overtaking barge pulls. Ahead, dead center, were the workmen on the derrick.

He looked back and growled a curse. Forging past the barge tows was a big dhow under sail—utterly out of step in the macabre drilling field, a visitation from another place and time—that threatened to run the Swan down from astern.

He thrust the throttle forward and steered toward a slot between the barge tows and the derrick. As he drew near he could see the men laboring in the damp heat, heaving crates and drums of wire and hose onto the loading dock where others humped the material toward an open freight elevator.

The tug towing the barges was pulling alongside, fifty yards away, a dim crenellated shape against the distant gas flares. Hardin glanced back and timed his passage by the derrick to share it with the dhow. He speeded up. The men loading stopped and, as he had hoped, stared the other way at the unlikely sight of the wooden ship.

Hardin slowed his engine to make less noise. When he was fifty yards from the derrick he saw a red glow in the shadows behind the loading dock—a laborer was sneaking a cigarette. He turned lazily toward Hardin, staring at nothing.

On the other side of the derrick, the dhow cut across the path of the oncoming push tow. The push-tow helmsman screamed his outrage. The return abuse from the dhow's wheelhouse drew hoots of laughter from the men on the derrick. The laborer peeked around the corner where the shouts were emanating.

The laughter stopped. The laborer sat down again with his back to one of the massive legs that speared through the loading dock. He took a deep drag on his cigarette, blew the smoke in the air, and looked out at the water.

Hardin cut his engine. Distant sounds took its place. The Swan sliced along on momentum, approaching the laborer's field of vision. He was no more than a hundred feet away, so close that Hardin could see that he was not an Arab, but European, with light hair and a muscular body overlaid with fat. His head lolled to his shoulders as if he was drifting to sleep.

Astern, Hardin heard the second tow coming up. Would the barges distract the man, or wake him, or create a dark backdrop which would make the white Swan even more visible?

She was almost past the derrick, but slowing markedly. Then the laborer turned his head so that Hardin was once again about to drift into his field of vision. The tug's long barge line crept by to starboard.

Hardin pulled the throttle all the way back and nudged the starter button. The engine gave a quick grind, but didn't catch. He eased the throttle forward a notch, trying to start quietly. Again it wouldn't.

The wake of the barge line was advancing behind him. He set the throttle at the normal start position and waited while the diagonal wave caught up. At the moment it lapped over the exhaust port, he hit the starter. The engine caught and the rising wave muffled the sound.

Hardin throttled back, engaged the prop, and eased away from the derrick. He looked back. The cigarette glow brightened, then arched after him as the man flipped his butt into the water. He stood and stretched, still staring. Hardin felt as if his eyes were boring into the Swan. The man stopped in midstretch, his arms held high like a referee's signal.

The son of a bitch saw him.

Hardin hit the throttle. The Swan shot forward. The laborer grew small astern. A second man appeared from around the corner of the loading dock and gesticulated angrily. Casting a final glance over his shoulder, the laborer scurried back to work.

He let his breath out with a long sigh and pointed the

Swan toward the next fireball four or five miles away. It was a split flame and it lunged at the sky like a reptile's tongue. Numerous oil derricks sprinkled the distance. Those near towered higher than the Swan's mast; their shadowy frames reminded Hardin of the empty girders of half-built skyscrapers. Those far were stubby black marks at the bottom of the fiery sky.

He raised the jib and cut the engine.

The Swan glided into water that quivered with the flamboyant sheen of an oil slick. The floating crude glossed the surface and shone like a liquid mirror, trapping the light the way soft tar might hold a dancer's feet, retarding the reflections, making each ray pirouette so slowly as to bare everything. Colors separated, sharpened, multiplied. What had seemed red became many reds—a bleeding rainbow—scarlet, cherry, ruby, wine, magenta, copper, brick.

The spilled crude had an oddly pure smell, sharp, stinging the nostrils, but less noxious than the stink of the burning gas. It left a murky line on the Swan's white hull. Something flickered against the boat. Hardin jumped back, startled. The dying sea snake struck again, rolled belly up, and sank.

Hardin passed a half mile south of the lunging split-flame fireball and found another flare to steer by. The oil tankers in the north seemed closer. A dark form, inbound, blanked his steering mark. He turned several points south, still pointing north of west, to avoid converging with the tanker route, and crossed a broad, dark empty stretch devoid of rigs and wellheads.

Something white gleamed to port. He watched it with his glasses. Breaking water. A reef. Too close to the Pearl Bank. Spinning the wheel, he turned ninety degrees and headed north on a beam reach, his feet tingling for the sudden rupture of coral against his hull.

Hardin maintained the new course until he had crossed the sea-lane. The flow of ships would be a better barrier between him and the reefs. He found a new flare and steered west.

Two young men took off from bases on either side of the Gulf. The Arab was flying a Royal Saudi Arabian Air Force jet-turbine helicopter. The Persian was at the helm of an Iranian Navy landing Hovercraft, an amphibious vehicle designed to deliver a pair of battle tanks to the enemy coast.

It carried no tanks today, only a crew of spotters with binoculars and radar scanners, and consequently it often topped its cruising speed of sixty-five miles an hour. Whenever it did, the increased dynamic pressure—the pressure of forward motion—threatened to overwhelm the pressure of the supporting air cushion. The pilot was experienced, and he was enjoying the game of driving his craft to the brink of stability, stepping over, and skittering back.

He and the Arab met just north of Dās, a small island fifty miles southeast of Hālūl. They were on converging courses, the Hovercraft skimming the water on a luminous froth, the helicopter flying at wave-top level, its searchlights blazing. Each saw the other at the same time. Each recognized a denizen of the opposite shore. Neither would give way.

The only witness to the fiery explosion was the pilot of an Arabian spotter plane and he reported, his voice shaking with rage, that the Iranian craft had deliberately rammed the Arab helicopter. Rumor raced across each force's radio airwaves, and before the commanders prevailed, several exchanges of gun and rocket fire had occurred.

Miles Donner did all he knew to patch up the temporary alliance. Now he stood with his back to the conference room and stared out the graying windows, waiting for the sun. Bruce, the Englishman, was asleep on the couch. The managers of Qatar Oil had retired to staterooms, and the only other people in the room atop Wellhead Number One were the Iranian commander and the Arab colonel.

The Iranian, his eyes weary, sat like stone while the Arab raged. Only once did he respond in any way and that was with a single glance, so filled with hate, that even

354

the Arab seemed to realize that another word might cost him his life.

The Arab stormed to the door, opened it, announced that his forces were going to search the oil fields.

"He's in the Pearl Bank," the Iranian said evenly.

"He can't attack from the Pearl Bank," said the Arab. "We will stop him."

"You've got to find him first."

"We will find him."

Donner turned around and decided to make a final try. "We really ought to concentrate our forces in one place."

"Then search the oil fields," said the Arab.

"He's not there," the Iranian said firmly. "He's in a cove someplace, in the shadow of a cliff, or camouflaged on a beach."

"We will spill no more blood on the Pearl Bank."

"Tell your pilots to look out for the derricks or they'll be spilling a lot more blood," said the Iranian coldly.

The Arab slammed the door. Moments later his helicopter thundered off the roof. It circled the wellhead, and for a terrifying instant Donner thought he would strafe them.

Dawn came to the Gulf like a banked fire. The red sky slowly grayed; the flames seemed to flicker down to glowing coals, then white ash. A leaden mist rose from the water. A morning star shone overhead and promised a clear day.

It found Hardin, hollow eyed, southeast of Hālūl, and still searching for a place to hide his boat. The wind had dropped to a light breeze and he was on an open stretch of water, miles from the next oil-rig cluster. He raised a spinnaker. The sail ballooned.

The Swan ghosted northwest, rolling in the light sea. Hardin heard helicopters. Their noise faded, only to be followed by others, which also passed, unseen. The sky began to lighten in the east and turn pearl with the coming sun. Half an hour more and the Swan would be very visible.

355

A gas flare billowed from a group of rigs ahead, but now in the morning light its smoke was more apparent than its flame. Hardin muttered a curse. He had just cleared them when he saw a single rig, a mile ahead. He would have to douse the spinnaker to dodge it.

He was on the foredeck, stretching to reach the spinnaker pole, when he noticed something different about the oil rig. It showed no lights. No tenders bobbed about it, nor did he see any motion of drilling or pumping machinery. He got the binoculars and scanned it carefully.

A thought, or a memory, was nagging at his mind. He headed the boat upwind, let the spinnaker collapse, secured it so it would not suddenly fill, and went below to check the Sailing Directions. He skimmed the section on Hālūl, not sure what he was looking for, but more and more convinced that he remembered something of value. His eyes stung with weariness, and the typeface blurred repeatedly.

"Jazirat Hālūl . . . Great Pearl Bank . . . Radar Target . . . A light . . . reef . . . tide rips . . . path . . . CAUTION . . . LIGHT . . . FOG SIGNAL . . . Obstructions . . . Anchorage . . . Sea berth." He went back, knowing he had passed it. "CAUTION . . . oil fields . . ." He found it! "A bank with a least mean depth . . . *a 90-foot abandoned and unlighted oil rig is charted in the shoalest part of this bank.*"

He steered downwind and filled the spinnaker and pointed the Swan at the distant tower. Then he ran below, his exhaustion forgotten, and brought up two long nylon lines. He dropped one of the coils in the stern and the other on the bow.

The tower was closer now. The first rays of the sun lighted its top. Quickly, Hardin doused the spinnaker and started the engine. The rig was a hundred yards off now and he probed it with the binoculars.

It was definitely abandoned, derelict, empty, and it had about it the air of another age, a reminder of a century past, like the smelter chimneys that Ajaratu had shown him above the played-out tin mines of Cornwall. It was probably less than ten years old, but it held the same promise that never again would man endeavor anything on this spot of the earth.

Rust streaked the black girders and a quick sail-around revealed that anything of value that could be moved, including its lower cross beams, had been taken off. Nothing remained but the structure itself—an elongated pyramid—four massive legs that sank to the bottom of the Gulf and rose sixty feet, naked, to a steel lacework that looked more graceful the higher it climbed.

It was impossible to fathom what waited beneath the oil slick inside it. He went in easy, feeling his way with his boat hook. The Swan glided into shadow, past the leg, which was festooned with cleats and jagged metal fittings. Hardin attached a line and walked it astern, then played it out. Diagonally, the distance from leg to leg was almost sixty feet longer than the Swan—and Hardin let her continue until her bow was almost hitting the far leg. Then he snubbed the stern line and hurried forward to tie the bow.

He let out ten feet, secured it, and returned to the stern, where he pulled up the slack until the boat was riding easily between the legs, which bore a high-tide mark four feet above the water, and for which he allowed extra line. Then he looked up.

The mast had cleared the lowest crosspiece by six feet, but inside, the tower rig towered another thirty or forty feet above it to a massive cross formed by two huge girders from which the drilling apparatus had been suspended. Blue sky showed through the four quadrants around the cross, and sunlight illuminated it with golden shafts.

Moments later, the sun came over the horizon and it warned Hardin that on this day he would have no shelter from haze and dust and mist. Worried, he drew on strength he hadn't believed he had left, inflated the rubber dinghy, and rowed out fifty yards. From that distance, he was shocked to see that the Swan was clearly visible: Her white hull gleamed ghostly through the shadows, and as she rose and fell on the gentle swell, her chrome fittings glinted like mirrors.

An aircraft engine muttered an approach. Hardin pulled on the oars. The engine got louder, closing quickly. He rowed as fast as he could, accidentally forcing the flexible blunt nose under a wave top, half filling the boat. Seconds after he regained the shadows of the old rig, a light plane buzzed past at wave height a mile away.

Breathing heavily, Hardin gripped the Swan's gunnel and pondered how to camouflage her. The sails were all white, so he couldn't drape her, and he had no paint to darken her hull. He shipped the dinghy's oars, tilting them outward so as not to drip oil on the handles.

The oil.

He scooped a handful off the water and smeared it on the Swan. It left a black stain, streaked with white where the calluses on his palms rubbed through the viscous paste. He brought up another handful and repeated the process. Soon he had a patch four feet long from gunnel to boot, as dark as the water. He wiped his hand as clean as he could and climbed aboard the Swan for the mop.

While he was below, he turned on the radio and dialed VHF Channel 16, the communication link between incoming ships and the cargo facility on Jazirat Hālūl. He set the volume loud enough to hear it while he worked on deck, then proceeded to dip the mop into the oil slick and swish it along the hull, painting from stern to bow on the starboard side. When what he could reach was covered with the thick brown-black crude, he got back into the dinghy and wiped the underside of the raked bow. Then he started on the port side.

The radio blared intermittently as tankers from Europe and Japan radioed estimated times of arrival and cargo requirements. Hālūl assigned berthing pilots or anchorage instructions, and a sound picture emerged of a large busy terminal juggling sea berths and loading time to operate at peak capacity.

There was no shortage of crude floating around the Swan. For every mopful that Hardin lathered onto the hull, another flowed close to replace it, as if the abandoned rig were oozing the stuff at a steady rate. He finished the port side, climbed back onto the Swan, and coated the white work—the cockpit coaming, the ventilation cowls, and the sides of the cabin trunk—and dabbed oil in the light-reflective Lucite hatch covers and windows. Then he draped a navy blanket over the shiny wheel and steering pedestal and removed the white sails which were furled on the boom and bagged at the foot of the forestay. He smeared oil on the stainless steel safety lines and pulpit and on the aluminum boom.

He rowed out again on the dinghy and checked the boat from every angle. At fifty yards she looked as dark as the shadows in which she was moored. Except at the stern. There, her transom gleamed as white as if she were docked at the New York Yacht Club, spruced up for a Sunday sail. He hadn't been able to bring himself to cover Carolyn's name.

It was too white. Probably visible at a mile. He rowed back under the rig to the transom. Slowly, reluctantly, he smeared oil on it with his hands, carefully delineating a neat and reverent rectangle around the space where her name resided. He became obsessed with outlining it perfectly and, in a stupor of sleeplessness, painted the transom over and over until the roar of a passing boat snapped him back to consciousness. He waited, immobile, until it had gone.

Then he stared at the black letters in the little white box that was all that was left of Carolyn. The space he had left her still gleamed in bright contrast to the camouflaged hull and he suddenly heard her speak to him as clearly as if she were sitting in the dinghy, wrinkling her nose at the smell of the crude. Her voice rang in his mind, alive with laughter.

"Don't blame me if they see you."

A trembling smile ruffled his lips. He blew her a kiss and smeared her name with oil.

As a final precaution he blackened the orange dinghy. Then he climbed back into the Swan and rested in the cockpit. He needed sleep desperately, but until he heard confirmation of LEVIATHAN's exact arrival time, he couldn't turn off the radio.

It spoke periodically, jerking him from his half doze, startling in the clarity of close-range signal strength. He stayed awake during one long exchange, watching the sky. The master of a Japanese 333,000-tonner was angrily demanding that the island's ULCC sea berth be opened to him as he had brought his Ultra Large Crude Carrier to the Gulf two days ahead of schedule. The biggest sea berth was reserved for LEVIATHAN, which was due in that night.

Hardin stared at the sky, waiting for the Japanese master's reply. LEVIATHAN was coming, but he had to know when. Maybe the angry captain would provoke the information. He did not; the airwaves became silent. Hardin spun the channel selector. Most of the chatter was in Arabic. Several of the higher frequencies were very busy and he guessed it was the Iranian Navy and Arabian Air Force craft he kept seeing in the distance. He was almost too tired to worry, but it looked as though they had laid on a full-scale hunt.

When he saw movement on the Pearl Bank, he scanned them with his binoculars. Iranian boats were plying the shallow water four or five miles away. He braced the powerful glasses to clear the image. The boats were shallow-draft launches that looked like modified pleasure cruisers, They cut deep wakes. Their decks were lined with uniformed sailors, some holding rifles, others searching the water with binoculars. A curious sight caught his eye.

On the bow of each boat was a turbaned figure clad in robes that billowed in the slipstream. They were signaling with their arms, and each time they did the boats changed course. Locals who knew the reefs, was Hardin's guess. The contrast of their robes and headgear to the sailors' uniforms reminded him of American cavalry entering hostile territory under the guidance of an Indian scout.

The radio nudged him awake. A quick exchange in Arabic. It reminded him to return to Channel 16. He did, then lay awake, tense, his mind racing, worrying, wondering if they would stop the ship until they found him. Or would they give up? He had not been sighted, he was sure, since right before the storm. They might suppose he had perished. Then he worried about the laborer in the oil fields. Had he seen him? Had he reported it? He might have, to explain why he wasn't working when the foreman caught him.

The sky was the clearest he had seen since he had entered the monsoon weeks before. The *shamal,* of which the storm had been the vanguard, had brought clear and marginally cooler and drier air. The temperature still hovered around ninety degrees, though, and clarity on the Gulf meant five miles visibility instead of one. The wind, more a sea breeze than the desert airs which had blown from the east and west, was steady at ten knots from the northwest. If it held, he'd run before it and let it blow him straight to LEVIATHAN.

The sun stretched toward its noon apex and the heat deepened. Strange mirages teased Hardin's weary eyes. Blurred specters, giant cloud ships, sailed upside down across the sky. The mirages, soft mirror images of tankers invisible ten miles away on the sea-lane, paraded in orderly procession. One after another they budded on the southern skyline, fattened as they neared, flowered above, and dispersed in the north like winter-dead leaves.

The menacing whine of approaching helicopters intruded on the almost peaceful, lulling mutter of the distant patrol boats. A formation of three—black dots on the horizon—was heading toward him. The dots grew large and bright; Hardin watched apprehensively.

The helicopters were a hundred feet above the water. They would pass fairly close to the rig. Suddenly they banked in unison, descended on a nearby cluster of sea rigs, split up, and buzzed each rig individually. Then they regrouped and came at his.

Hardin dived into the cabin; they might be using infrared heat sensors. He crouched by a window, wondering if his camouflage would work.

Then he remembered the mooring lines—two nylon lines, one at the bow, and one at the stern—gleaming as

361

white and shiny as only synthetics could. He had forgotten to blacken them with oil.

They descended, squatting in the air, fat bodied and ungainly looking despite their startling speed. At a half mile their bubbles were visible, then their guns and the shadows of the soldiers manning them. They closed to two hundred yards.

Abruptly, they wheeled and shot away in the direction of a Hovercraft, which had suddenly appeared in the distance speeding toward a group of derricks.

Hardin stayed in the cabin, his mind swimming, watching the helicopters overtake the Hovercraft and chase past as if it were a race. They buzzed the derricks and continued on before the Hovercraft arrived.

He waited until they had vanished in the north. Too weary to wonder why they had broken off—merely grateful—he finally left the broiling cabin and lay down in the cockpit and listened to the radio.

The sun perched on the center of the steel cross of girders atop the sea rig. It shimmered white, like a ball of molten glass. Slowly it moved west and one of the girders shadowed Hardin's eyes. When he looked next, it was beyond the frame of the derrick and he knew he had slept for half an hour.

His mouth was dry. He went below and pumped a cup of water from the pantry sink spigot. He drank it, drew another, and another. On the third, the pump pedal felt loose and air mingled with the water in the spigot. He had reached the end of his supply. Somewhere along the line he had ceased to conserve water, he couldn't recall when. Rummaging through the cupboards, he found a bottle of Soave and two small bottles of Perrier, which he put in a net bag and hung over the side after clearing the oil with the mop. He would go out in style.

"Come in Hālūl. Come in Hālūl."

Hardin recognized the rich voice of LEVIATHAN's Scottish radio officer. He eased into the chart-table seat

362

and switched to the headset. The Hālūl operator acknowledged the call.

"Please arrange berthing pilot at twenty-four hundred."

"Berthing pilot twenty-four hundred."

Hardin looked at the chronometer. A little less than twelve hours. The monster had rounded the Quoins and was in the Gulf: now he could sleep. It was too hot in the cabin so he hauled his foam mattress into the cockpit and closed his eyes and tried to stop thinking.

29

Black and massive as the night, LEVIATHAN sped toward the setting sun and loosed a rending whistle blast at an old baggala dhow. The engineless two-masted *lansh* was strugging to beat westward against the stiff *shamal*; it surrendered its course and tried to scurry away from the overtaking tanker.

LEVIATHAN steamed on, ramming a broad wake through the gentle swell. A plume of black smoke trailed from each funnel and mingled over the froth astern like thick and lethal flukes. The smoke dispersed in the wind, but long after the ship had passed, its bow wave caught the running dhow. The sailors saw it curling after them and clung to their cargo and rigging. The wave rolled the Arab boat brutally, shifting crates, threatening her ancient wooden yards, her creaking masts and hemp lines, and shaking the wind out of her patched sails.

Captain Ogilvy stared ahead, heedless of the consternation in LEVIATHAN's wake. He stood on the bridge wing, watching the glow on the horizon, scanning the water. He had two lookouts on the masthead, two on the bow, and a man glued to the radar. The bridge phone rang. Ogilvy answered.

The Saudis were on the radio. They reported that it would soon be too dark for effective air surveillance. As Hardin had not been found, they suggested that LEVIA-THAN heave to until morning. Ogilvy replied, curtly, that he much preferred to be a moving target, and hung up. Then he called the second officer, whose watch it was, and asked him to send the bosun.

The bosun was a short, wiry Irishman with the glint of pride in his eye that made a seaman a leader.

"Evenin', Captain."

"Bosun. I want all the furniture from the wardroom and the crew's mess stacked on the helipads."

"Sir?"

"Make a real mess out there, and do it quickly."

The bosun tossed a salute and left the bridge wing at a fast trot. Minutes later, Ogilvy saw him urging a pair of deck gangs toward the helicopter landing pads with tables and chairs.

After several trips back and forth, they had cluttered the pads. Ogilvy picked up the wing phone and switched to the public address system. His voice echoed across the vast decks. "Bosun! Strew those hoses about. Muck up those open spaces." The men darted to do his bidding. Minutes after they had finished, and while the fading light was still strong enough for him to see the bows, a big helicopter appeared in the west and closed quickly with the ship.

"Floodlights," Ogilvy ordered on the phone.

They flared on, bright white, illuminating the green decks like a lighted ball field. Ogilvy watched the heli-copter circle, lower, then stop abruptly in midair. He reached the bridge phone. "Connect me to the helicopter."

It was the Iranian Navy commander. James Bruce had reported earlier that the man was in charge of the search for Hardin.

"Yes, Commander?" said Ogilvy.

The reply was patient. "Apparently, Captain Ogilvy, you don't wish me to land."

"I've had a bellyful of comings and goings for the last

364

two days," said Ogilvy. "LEVIATHAN will board her berthing pilot at twenty-four hundred hours."

"Unfortunately, sir, we haven't found Hardin yet and we can't permit you to go any farther until we do."

"I'm not permitting my ship to sit like a duckpin bcause your navy can't locate a lunatic on a sailboat."

"I have orders to stop you from proceeding," said the Iranian. The helicopter moved aft and hovered beside the bridge. Ogilvy could make out the vague shape of the pilot and the man he was talking to.

"I want protection!" he thundered. "Not interference!"

"You'll get your protection when you stop."

"Are you telling me that Iran can't guarantee safe passage in the Persian Gulf?" Ogilvy taunted.

"How do you propose we do that under these circumstances?" the Iranian replied silkily.

"In the same manner that any decent navy protects merchant shipping when it is threatened. Surely, Commander, I don't have to tell you how to do that."

The Iranian waited, then asked reluctantly, "Are you suggesting a convoy?"

"Cover my ship. Give me escorts fore and aft. Sweep the area ahead. That damned rocket of Hardin's has a half-mile range. Create a perimeter and don't let him inside it."

Again there was a pause before the Iranian spoke. "All right, Captain Ogilvy. But I will set the course. LEVIATHAN will follow."

Ogilvy hung up the phone and stalked into the bridge, a smile playing over his face. It was eight o'clock—2000 hours—and the watch was changing. Since they were preparing to berth at Hālūl, formal mess was abandoned tonight. The third officer was just marking the satellite-course readout against the chart.

"Stand easy," said Ogilvy, as the young man stiffened when he saw him. "Better tell your helmsman to keep an eye peeled for wogs. They'll be all over us tonight." He beckoned his steward, who was waiting in the shadows by the chart-room door, and told him to bring his meal out to the port wing. Then he walked back out of the air conditioning and watched the Iranians move to battle stations.

A frigate appeared from the north and took up a position directly ahead of LEVIATHAN. Less than a mile separated the two vessels. Hovercraft stood off LEVIATHAN's bows, to port and starboard. A pair of minesweepers took the beam, and two more Hovercraft covered his stern. Ogilvy smiled again. He was reminded of the war when he was bucketing around on a corvette, shepherding a ragtag lot of rusty freighters and petrol carriers.

The sun slipped stealthily below the horizon as if afraid to compete with the blaze of the gas flares, and Ogilvy's steward appeared with his supper. He laid it out next to the phone console and hurried back with a stool. Ogilvy ordered him to return the stool to the bridge house where it belonged. He ate standing, enjoying the sight of the escort, savoring the food. He was proud of LEVIATHAN and proud of the warships that embraced her. And he was content that he was where he was and not skulking about the oil fields on a sailboat.

Behind him, an icy sliver of moon rose in the dark eastern sky. It hung as distinct as a slice of crystal, seated in blackness, aloof from the lurid glow of the gas flares in the west. Then the heat from LEVIATHAN's funnels shimmied across it. It softened like melting butter and was lost in the ship's oily smoke.

The wing phone rang.

"Yes, Number two."

"The Iranians ordered two degrees starboard."

"Well?"

"What should I do, sir?"

"Tell them to get stuffed."

The steward cleared the dinner tray and brought a trifle.

"Take that away," said Ogilvy. "Bring me a brandy."

He sipped it slowly as the night grew red.

Hardin left the shelter of the abandoned oil rig. He set a course for the sea-lane, the single shipping channel

366

down which LEVIATHAN had to steam to reach the Hālūl sea berth. The wind was out of the northwest—the *shamal* had strengthened all day and appeared to be holding the night as well. He took it on a beam reach, steering by the fireballs and the moving lights of the outbound tankers.

He felt very calm. He had slept well, logging six uninterrupted hours before the sun went down, and he had eaten several cans of tuna fish and asparagus spears, topped off with a glass of wine and a bottle of Perrier.

The Dragon was on the cabin floor, lying in a sling at the foot of the companionway, ready to be hoisted to the cockpit. He would keep the weapon below until the last minute, because it would be a radar target on deck.

The radio was on, tuned to Channel 16. LEVIATHAN's arrival was stirring considerable chatter on the air. Most of the talk was Arabic and Persian, but even in the desert and mountain tongues the ship's Semitic name sounded clearly, an ancient word for sea monster, a giant crocodile once seen in this gulf.

Helicopter engines sounded overhead and their busy lights flickered through the ruddy sky. He heard the high whine of Hovercraft and the lower growl of conventional patrol launches. The search effort seemed to be intensifying the closer he got to the shipping lane.

He looked at his sails. Their white sheen reflected the gas flare's red glow. His fiberglass hull was virtually immune to radar, as was the wooden mast, but ironically he might be seen by the naked eye in these conditions. He furled the mainsail and led the jib halyard back to the cockpit as he had the night before so he could douse the headsail quickly.

He sighted a big can buoy, a marker for the sea-lane. Two or three more miles to the inbound side of the channel and he would turn east to line up his attack.

Suddenly he strained toward the open hatch to hear the radio. He'd been listening with half an ear to an American Aramco helicopter pilot who'd been talking in a western twang to a buddy on Hālūl Island. The pilot was flying east and shortly after he had passed the Sassan oil field, which was about forty miles east of Hardin's position, he spotted LEVIATHAN.

"They got a whole fuckin' navy down there!" he exclaimed. "Goddam! That's a frigate out front. Hovercraft on the flanks—Ooooop! gotta go. I got a Irani bird on my ass and I think he sayin' go 'way. I goin', I goin'."

Hardin was glad he had slept. If he had heard that as he had been yesterday, it would have crippled him. He continued sailing across the sea-lane, pondering what to do. New radio chatter confirmed that LEVIATHAN was virtually surrounded by Navy escort vessels. Their decks would be lined with sailors with low-light glasses and God knew what other gadgetry.

LEVIATHAN was three hours away. The wind was dropping slightly and the air felt heavier. With luck, he might slip between two escort vessels. The Swan's hull was still oily black. He could lower the jib and power close enough to fire before they saw him in the red haze. With luck. He shook his head. He'd come too far to depend on luck.

He had to mislead the escort. Deep in the bilge was the radar reflector he had removed at the Quoins. The rubber dinghy trailed astern. It had been easier to tow than deflate and, knowing that if he needed the boat he would need it fast, he had left it inflated. He wondered if he could step a mast on the rubber boat, attach the radar reflector, and sail it away from him at the moment of attack. Would the new radar blip draw the naval squadron far enough from LEVIATHAN to let him get close enough for a shot?

A tanker loomed to starboard, inbound. He started the engine and hurried across its bows. When he reached the side of the channel he kept going, away from the traffic, into the darkness, steering for an empty-looking patch several miles to the north. It was a broad area bracketed by two sea-rig fireballs. He headed for the dark center where no light from either gas flare penetrated.

A dim, white electric light grew apparent in the

darkness. Thinking it was atop a deserted drilling rig that might offer concealment while he constructed his decoy, he steered toward it.

The light was nearer than he had assumed. The reason for the miscalculation, he saw in its down glow, was that it was much lower than a drilling rig and illuminated instead a bullet-shaped buoy, twenty feet high, that bobbed gently in the low swells.

The water shushed around it each time it rose, and gurgled expectantly when it fell. Hardin circled, puzzled, wondering what it was doing here all by itself. Whatever, the light was too bright. It shone on the Swan's decks, making her visible from the air. He twirled the helm and steered back toward the dark.

The Swan pivoted violently and stopped dead.

Hardin was driven to his knees by the impact.

He scrambled to his feet and hauled in the flapping jib. What the hell had he hit? There'd been no sound of collision, no grinding of fiberglass, but in one instant the boat had been gliding at two and a half knots, and the next she was motionless, as if she had been snared in a soft net.

Something thrashed in the water. He spotted it in the glow of the buoy light, a fleshy-looking cylinder floating on the surface. It was a dozen feet long and at each end it coiled under water. One end submerged immediately ahead of the bow. Hardin stared, trying to fathom what it was. Over a foot in diameter and undulating on the swell, it looked like a giant squid's tentacle.

He shuddered despite the absurdity. The Swan drifted closer to the buoy. Shining his five-cell flashlight on it, he saw Arabic characters, and beneath them western letters. *Stand Clear of Floating Hoses.*

He'd fouled an offshore loading buoy. No wonder it was by itself; the tankers needed room to swing with the tide. He scanned the red horizons with his binoculars. There were no boats or lights heading toward him at the moment, so he got the boat hook and checked the length

369

of the Swan for more hoses. Finding none, he stood in the bow pulpit and leaned out as far as he could.

The hose lay flat on the water. In the flashlight beam it was bright orange. He couldn't reach it with the boat hook. The wind was blowing the Swan past the buoy, increasing the distance between the boat and the hose. Hardin waited, hoping. The hose tightened and the boat stopped. It was stuck on the keel.

He tied a short length of line to a small grappling hook he had stowed with the spare anchors and attached it to the boat hook, which he extended as far as he could and jutted back and forth. The grappling hook swung in a wider and wider arc. He gave it one more thrust and dropped the boat hook's tip into the water. The grappling hook flew over the hose, fell in the water and gripped it underneath. Hardin pulled in the hook, grabbed the line, and heaved.

The hose came closer. Putting his back into it, he slowly pulled the boat and hose together, then tried to lift it out of the water. It wouldn't budge.

He pictured what had happened when the Swan hit the hose. The fin keel had driven deep into a fold of the empty tube. Then, when the boat had pivoted around the centrally placed keel, a loop had formed and tightened. It probably wouldn't have happened if there weren't sharp barnacles on the keel; the plastic hose would have slipped off.

Still, since the keel was neither deep nor straight, a little movement should dislodge the hose. He backed the jib until it filled and, wrapping the sheet around a forward winch, tried to sail her into the wind. She moved forward, then stopped with an elastic lurch. He let her drift back, then tried again. Again she held.

He tried to sail at right angles to the hose, but each time, after he had gotten a few yards, the buoy was still beside him, bobbing up and down mockingly, telling him he hadn't moved. He decided he had to use the engine at the risk of fouling the propeller.

He checked the horizons again, and briefly considered

knocking out the light atop the buoy. But it was protected inside a miniature steel cell like a dangerous prisoner.

He started the engine and tried to reverse away. The back of the fin was perpendicular, which would make reversing free difficult, but it had the advantage of moving the propeller away from the hose instead of toward it.

The hose and the boat remained one. Reluctantly, he eased the throttle forward, his hand poised to disengage. The Swan gathered way. He went back to neutral and let her momentum tug the hose. It stopped him like a rubberband. He tried starting fast, but the short space he could move in prevented him from getting enough way on the Swan to break loose.

He was down to one last possibility. He eased the boat forward to the limit the hose would allow, then slowly increased the power, keeping one hand on the throttle to stop the propeller as soon as she broke free. He held the ignition key with the other hand and watched the tachometer. The engine speed rose higher and higher. A thousand rpm's, fourteen hundred, fifteen hundred. The Swan shuddered with the effort. Sixteen hundred.

She lurched forward.

Hardin yanked the throttle and cut the ignition, but he was too late. Before he had turned the key, he felt the prop bite into the hose and heard a growl which stopped with a loud bang. The engine raced for an instant before the broken ignition stopped it.

The Swan drifted about in a broad circle. Her bow swung away from the buoy, but Hardin slumped in the cockpit, cursing himself bitterly.

He'd snapped the propeller shaft. In one split second of miscalculation he had hurled the Swan back to the nineteenth century. She had only her sails now. Only the wind to propel her and no hope of repair.

If LEVIATHAN came during a dead calm, he was finished. If the wind swung east, he was finished. If they saw his white sails, he was finished. He cursed again. How could they miss them?

The angry words died in his throat. The Swan had stopped drifting. The distance between her and the buoy hadn't changed. The hose had wrapped around the prop. She was still caught.

There was only one way loose.

He couldn't look at the red-black water. His fear was complete, total, as real and paralyzing as steel manacles.

He imagined the anchor chain that held the loading buoy and how slimy and overgrown it must have become. The mooring base and the underwater pipeline would act as a reef and, like a natural reef, every cranny would shelter some fish, or crustacean, or snake. And it would be dark, so dark he couldn't see them, and his flashlight would lure them.

The snake's bite was painless. You might not know it had pierced your skin. Socrates' death notice—numb legs—would be the first you knew. He shivered spasmodically.

If he ditched the Dragon and waited for morning, a patrol boat or a tanker come to load would find him. There would be a lot of trouble, but nothing they could prove. The Arabs or the Iranians might get a bit tough, but with no crime committed against them and, with luck, American extradition for stealing the Dragon, they would let him go. Once he was back on U.S. soil Bill Kline would eat the charges for breakfast. Clean record, military service, upstanding citizen, businessman, doctor, suffering the awful aftermath of his wife's death . . .

It would wash. What other evidence besides the Dragon? . . . Nothing but his log. Hurriedly, he thumbed through it for incriminating entries. Best to chuck the whole damn thing over the side. He threw it, and as it pinwheeled into the water, loose pieces of paper fell from the pages. He hooked up the block and tackle to hoist the Dragon out of the cabin. One of Ajaratu's letters had fallen on the deck. It was the second one, the one he hadn't read. He picked it up.

"Yesterday," she wrote in a bold open hand, "I tried to dissuade you."

> I doubt that I did. I tried again today, but all I had left in me was a love letter. I miss you so. I'm feeling things I never did before and speaking words I never could.
> I love you in ways I'll need a lifetime to tell you.
> I love how you look and touch and feel and smell.
> I love how you rend me and make me whole.
> I love how you hold me and make me fly apart.
> I love the things you are, the things you have been, and the things you will be.
> I love every moment we've had together, every kiss we shared, every caress, every embrace.
> I love the tears I've shed for you.
> I love the laughter and the smiles.
> I love the things you say.
> I love the life you've shown me.
> Please give it back.

She had scrawled tightly at the bottom of the page, "I'm sure this sounds silly to you. Perhaps these are just the feelings I would have felt if we'd had more time. . . . God go with you."

Hardin put the letter back in the chart-table drawer. There wasn't a word in the poem that he couldn't have said to Carolyn.

Her face floated on the red water, the clearest he had seen her in weeks. Tears welled into his eyes. For a moment it seemed as if it had just happened and the emptiness was as horrible as his fear.

Sick and trembling, he looked for a way to protect himself from the snakes. A rubber wet suit would have been good armor against their smallest fangs, but he didn't have diving gear because he hated diving, so he scoured the boat for a substitute. If he was going in, he had no time to waste. The boat was exposed in the glow of the buoy light and LEVIATHAN was steaming closer every minute.

His vinyl-coated heavy-weather gear might stop the snake teeth, but the garments hung loosely. He put on the pants and wrapped the voluminous folds close to his skin with elastic shock cord. Then he donned his sneakers and the jacket and wound the arms with shock cord until they fit snugly. His ankles, hands, and face were bare. He cut strips of material from the spare gear—Ajaratu's—and wrapped his ankles. He tried to cut a mask, but it didn't work and he hadn't the time to try again. He put on work gloves and tightened the jacket hood over his brow and chin. His eyes, nose, and mouth were exposed.

He slipped his three sharpest knives and his cable cutters into the shock cord and tied a line around his waist and fastened it to a cleat in the cockpit. Then he stepped over the lifelines and sat on the gunnel. For a terrible instant, freed of the tasks, he let his mind return to the fear, the things in the water, the snakes.

He tried to calm himself with the theory that animals don't attack unless provoked. But among many species invasion of territory was provocation in the extreme. A grimmer, more satisfying thought came to mind. The venom's paralysis didn't start for several hours; time, perhaps, to sink LEVIATHAN even if he were bitten.

Drawing a deep, sobbing breath, he lowered himself slowly off the hull into the water. It shouldn't have surprised him, but it did. The water was almost as warm as the air. He clung to the gunnel, then dropped off. The heavy clothing pulled him under. He fought the impulse to struggle to the surface, and let himself sink.

The water was pitch-black. He had expected the red sky to glow beneath the swells. He turned on the flashlight. The beam was not up to full power. The batteries had been in the damp too long. He felt the hull and knew it by its curve that he wasn't deep enough, so he stroked up to push down.

Something rubbery brushed his face.

Hardin recoiled. He struck out blindly with the flashlight, and clawed at the knife on his belt. He felt it again and cried out in fear. Water filled his mouth. Thrashing wildly against the hull, he struggled to the surface and emerged coughing and gagging, and shaking with terror. The heavy rubber clothing dragged him under and again his mouth filled. He struggled, sinking, and dropped the flashlight. It jerked up short on the line attached to his wrist.

His lifeline. He grabbed it and pulled himself up to the surface, where he spit water and regained control.

Then he let go the line and pushed under again. The flashlight shone on something that moved. It was sinuous, undulating. His eyes locked on it as he drew closer. The light reflected orange. A piece of the hose. It was drifting from the propeller. He grabbed it and pulled himself under the Swan.

The flashlight beam penetrated about two feet and he found the propeller more by feel than by sight. Passing the light over the blades, the shaft and the rudder skeg, he found where the ripped hose had tangled and where he would have to cut. By then, he was running out of air.

He forced himself to wait while he pulled down his excess line and looped it around the propeller shaft. Then he raced for the surface, filled his lungs, and pulled himself back down to the propeller by the line he had tied.

He turned off the flashlight and let it dangle from his wrist because it gave him the use of that hand and because he feared that the light would attract the snakes. The hose was made of a strong plastic and reinforced with tough, lengthwise fibers that resisted the knife. He drew it tight and sawed until he ran out of air, pulled himself to the surface, took a breath, and went back down into the warm, dark water. The first knife quickly dulled, and when he went up again for air he tossed it into the boat and took out his second knife. Slowly the hose parted, strip by strip, fiber by fiber. He surfaced for air, and when he got back down he turned on the flashlight to check his progress.

Something nudged his arm. He recoiled, thinking snake, then brushed it away, realizing it was a scrap of the hose, and raised his knife to cut some more. It hit him again. Harder. And again. On his chest. Sinuous muscle strained behind the blows. A life. Hardin shone the flashlight against his body.

A snub-nosed head—as big as a fist and mottled with thick scales—smashed into the lens. A sea snake with lidless serpent eyes as black as coal. The scales parted, the mouth hinged open.

Hardin scrambled back and knocked his head against the hull. The snake struck again, thrusting a gaping mouth against Hardin's rubber jacket, forcing him hard against the rudder. A serrated row of teeth, slivery as fishbones, gleamed in the yellow light. It hit repeatedly, with the rhythmic speed of a jackhammer, its venom fangs reaching greedily beyond its needle teeth.

Hardin slashed at it with his knife. The water cushioned his blows, and the snake, fast as light, hit three times for every move he made. Had it penetrated the vinyl foul-weather gear? He didn't know; he kept swinging the knife and trying to dodge the hammering head. It snapped at his neck. Belatedly, Hardin put his glove hand over his unprotected face.

Disembodied by darkness, the gaping mouth shot into the light, hit, disappeared, and hit again. It was only a matter of time or accident before the creature went for his face.

Hardin forced himself to stop struggling. He turned off the flashlight and dropped his knife. Then he covered his face with both hands, pressed the lifeline between his fingers and his cheek so he wouldn't sink, and tried to lie still in the water. Was it alone? Or were additional defenders streaming out of a nearby nest?

He felt the snake batter his legs. Shot after shot. Had it found a place it could penetrate the vinyl? The muscular body writhed against his knees. It curled around his thighs. And hit. Hardin felt himself tightening. It attacked again, higher. He squirmed. It passed between his legs, twitching and shuddering. It struck his groin.

He recoiled violently, unable to control the convulsion.

The snake butted his hip. He hung still again, waiting. It brushed his waist.

His lungs were empty. His head was starting to pound from lack of oxygen and he could hear his heart beating louder and louder. The snake was slowing its attack, hitting less often, tentatively. Was it tiring or probing his defenses? It struck his chest. Then his shoulder. He pressed his hands tightly to his face.

The scaly head nudged his fingers. He squeezed them together, torn between an almost irresistible compulsion to try to grab the thing and rip it to shreds and the sure knowledge that he wasn't fast enough. Again the blunt head shoved between his fingers.

Hardin pressed his palms against his mouth to keep from screaming into the water.

The head withdrew. He waited, his chest aching. Had it gone? It struck his forehead above his fingers on the rubber hood of the foul-weather jacket. It hit hard, several more times, then stopped. Hardin waited for a fresh assault. He could feel his heart pounding behind his eyes. He had reached his limit.

Still holding one hand over his face, he worked his way up the rope, pulling smoothly so as not to threaten the snake with sudden movement. He brushed past the rounded hull, broke the surface, and gasped deep breaths of the reeking air. He held the rope with one hand, covered his face with the other, and waited for the snake.

Had it given up? Had it established its territory? Or had the attack ended because its instincts told it that Hardin must be dead? Or had it, like Hardin, merely retired to the surface for air. Was it waiting below with a full lung, ready to do battle as soon as he returned?

He took a final breath and let himself sink down the rope to the bottom of his boat. Another knife. He pressed the blade to the hose, pulled the material taut, and tried to cut with short, regular strokes, tried to blend with the dark water. It was very quiet. He heard his heart and he felt the vibrations of the blade against the hose. All other motion seemed suspended. He cut and he waited, as if he were watching a paper barrier through which something was going to burst.

The snake was there. Somewhere close. The buoy chain or the submarine pipeline was almost certainly its home. Would it sense his presence as a new invasion, him as a new invader, and attack again? He wedged the long end of the hose under his arm so he could cover his face.

The final strands parted grudgingly, fiber by fiber, thread by thread, opposing the blade to the last. He was running out of air again. Then the knife was through, scraping the metal propeller. He untied his lifeline from the shaft and pulled himself back to the red surface.

In his fear and confusion, he had forgotten to mount a boarding ladder. The Swan's hull, slippery with oil, loomed above him. He gripped the toe rail on the gunnel and tried to gather the strength to climb up. He was drained by the attack and the long periods without air. He tightened his arms and raised his torso until his face was even with the deck. He could go no higher. Water poured from his garments. Locking his elbows, he hung by willpower and waited. When he was lightened, he kicked and thrashed, hooked an arm around a lifeline stanchion, and painfully dragged his body under the lines and into the cockpit.

He lay gasping on the bench, watching the red sky flicker overhead. When he could, he sat up and stripped off the foul-weather gear. The Swan was drifting from the loading buoy. Already the white bullet shape was a hundred yards away and dwindling into the night. He toweled off and put on dry shorts, feeling his way around the dark cabin, afraid that if he turned on the lights he would find the tiny twin puncture marks and know that the snake had killed him.

LEVIATHAN was coming. He had to get back to the sea-lane, loose his decoy, and line up his shot.

Gathering spars, line, oars, a jib, and the floorboards from the Swan's main salon, he pulled the dinghy alongside

378

and wedged the floorboards into the bottom. He lashed one oar across the boat and another fore and aft. For a mast, he stood the boat hook inside the cross formed by the oars, lashed it tightly to them, then guyed it with nylon line from the stern and sides.

He hanked the jib onto a line he had spiraled around the spinnaker pole. Then, angling the pole like a dhow's yard, he lashed the lower end to the dinghy's bow and the middle to the top of the stubby boat-hook mast. He led a sheet from the jib's clew into the dinghy.

The jury-rigged lateen sail started flapping. Standing over it on the Swan's stern, he furled it to the yard and tightened all the guys. Then he fastened a spare oar as a combination rudder and keel.

He sailed back to the shipping lane, attached the block and tackle to the boom, and hoisted up the Dragon. The radio had begun to blare ceaselessly. He moved the block and tackle, then went below and quickly scanned the radio spectrum. The Iranian naval channels were flooded. The VHF traffic could only mean that vast numbers of boats and aircraft were drawing near in concert.

Again, he saw himself at the mercy of luck. At any moment a patrol boat or helicopter might stumble across him. It was ten o'clock, 2200, and he was approximately twenty miles east of Hālūl's sea berth, which meant that LEVIATHAN, due at 2400, was thirty-two miles from Hālūl and twelve or so from him. If he waited, he would meet the monster in forty-five minutes. Three quarters of an hour, during which a searcher might get lucky.

He had to cut the time.

He raised the main and headed east, downwind. The *shamal* was lightening, the humid mists growing thicker and redder in the gleam of the burning flares. He poled out the spinnaker, trimmed it, caught the breeze. The billowing headsail lifted the Swan and set her running. Slicing crimson seas, she flew to meet LEVIATHAN with her little dinghy skidding on her boiling wake.

A Vosper-Thorneycroft Tenacity pulled alongside the

379

commander's Hovercraft, its diesels rumbling easily. Like the Hovercraft, the British-built missile carrier effortlessly maintained LEVIATHAN's sixteen knots. Her twin machine guns were manned by radio-helmeted Iranian sailors.

Miles Donner tried to assess her missile complement. She was roving from flank to flank, but each time she had passed it had been too dark to see. Now a leaping gas flare silhouetted the Tenacity. The missiles were under canvas. Disappointed, he turned his attention back to the Hovercraft's darkened bridge and the officers grouped around the radar screens.

LEVIATHAN was an enormous black presence half a mile behind. The great hull and the towering aft structure moved across the flickering gas flares like a cloud over stars. Two thousand yards to Donner's right another Hovercraft covered the tanker's starboard bows. There were two more Hovercraft astern. The escort began to veer closer to the ship, because ahead the sea-lane narrowed as it passed through an oil field.

Stationed forward of LEVIATHAN, a stately frigate cleaved the Gulf. Donner thought it was interesting that the Iranian commander was here on the Hovercraft off LEVIATHAN's port bow rather than on the frigate. The man moved freely from ship to helicopter, commandeering whatever vehicle suited his purpose, confident his sophisticated communications systems would give him control from any point. Speed, not size, was where the power lay in this modern navy.

Donner had succeeded beyond his hopes. LEVIATHAN was safe; it was all over but the shooting. In addition, he had established a good relationship with the Iranian commander, a competent officer, well placed and obviously on his way up to be given charge of this crack squadron. And, to ice the cake, he had the chance to submit to the Mossad a cracking good report on the Shah's Navy.

An officer cried out. The others clustered closer to the radar screens. Donner shouldered among them. "What is it?" he asked the commander.

"Target a mile ahead."

He shouted in Persian. The Hovercraft roared. Beside it, the Tenacity missile boat cut in its Rolls-Royce gas turbines and the two craft howled side by side at forty-five knots.

The commander finished speaking into a radiophone. He pointed at the officer manning the controls. The Hovercraft shot forward. Sixty-five knots, Donner guessed. A quick glance at the speed indicator told him it was more. They left the Tenacity in their wake and flew past the frigate, which, to judge by its sharply curling bow wake, luminous in the light of a gas flare, had also speeded up. The bridge officers picked up the telephone to speak to their gun crews.

Donner stepped closer to the radar screen. Bright blips marked the ships, dimmer ones the towers of the oil field around the channel.

"Why should we suddenly see him?" he asked the commander. "His boat hasn't shown up on radar before."

"Perhaps it's just a glitch. Perhaps another boat."

"Perhaps not," said Donner. "You've already swept the area. It shouldn't be another boat. And glitches don't usually stay on the screen that long, do they?"

"We'll know in thirty seconds," said the commander.

Donner watched the target light grow stronger. Suddenly he realized what had happened.

"It's his weapon! He's got it on deck. He's preparing to fire."

The Iranian's face tightened. "Of course." He spoke rapid Persian into the telephone.

"I've ordered them to fire as soon as they see him."

Donner was surprised to see distaste in the Iranian's dark face, as if he weren't pleased with the idea of directing such firepower at a single man. The Israeli smiled his understanding. "You had to. You can't take chances if he's ready to fire himself."

The Hovercraft howled into the night, bumping on the swells like a jet liner in rough air. The space between the target light and the center of the radar screen decreased rapidly. Other brighter lights on the scope showed that the Iranians were lining up for a cross fire.

Hardin's boat would be visible in seconds, dead ahead. Donner peered into the wispy burned haze, sighting over the heads of the sailors manning the brace of machine guns on the bow turret. On either side of the bridge were surface-to-surface missiles, their deadly snouts depressed to the lowest angle.

"There he is!" yelled Donner.

Hardin's sloop exploded out of the red mist under full sail. Her booming spinnaker billowed crimson in the light of the flares, tight as a drumhead, glistening with the strain. Her main, an elegant quarter moon, stood tall behind it.

The Iranian commander screamed an order and the Hovercraft, banking into a wide turn, shuddered from the recoil of the big machine guns on the bow. Tracers arced over the water and lighted through the Swan. Fire poured from another Hovercraft. Shell geysers straddled the sailboat. The sails blinked white and red as they were lighted by muzzle flashes and the blaze of exploding shells.

Donner raised his binoculars. He could see Hardin's figure crouching ahead of the helm in the cockpit trying to fire. A missile lanced through the night, holed the spinnaker, and exploded in the water behind the Swan. A shell burst over the cabin. The mast toppled forward, dragging the sails into the water.

They were closer now and Donner could see debris flying from the cabin roof. A line of bullets stitched the hull from bow to stern. The figure in the cockpit was flung to the deck by the impact, and a second later the self-steering vane blew away, gliding for a moment like a disembodied airplane wing. An explosion fragmented the cabin roof and flames flickered in the broken windows.

The Iranian shouted over and over into the telephone

and gradually, as the shattered boat sank deeper and deeper, the gunfire ceased.

For Hardin it was like hearing a murder on the street too far away to stop it, too close not to know. She had carried him over three oceans and her parting gift had been a few more yards of space, a moment or two of time.

He sat in the bottom of the rubber boat, his back braced against the stern, the Dragon half on his shoulder and half in a sling suspended from the mast. Steering back into the sea-lane from a cluster of oil rigs that had hidden him from radar, he let the lateen sail pull the dinghy east. It ran before the wind, self-tending, squatting deeply under the weight of the weapon. Small waves kept threatening to break over the stern.

Hardin peered through the binocular sights, saw nothing, watched over them, squinting to pierce the red gloom. The gunfire had stopped. They'd be circling the spot where she sank, looking for his body.

He sensed a difference on the horizon. A color rather than a shape. It was blacker ahead than it had been. He saw rapidly moving lights off to one side of the shadow. A ship that grew quickly. It was a frigate speeding on a course that would pass close to starboard.

The blackness deepened. Then, in the blaze of a burning sea rig, he saw the white crown of LEVIATHAN's bridge, impossibly high, as high as an office building, and topped by the twin funnels which were LEVIATHAN's and LEVIATHAN's alone. But it was distant, far away. What was closer, much closer, was the black wall that was LEVIATHAN's bow.

The Swan would not sink.

In the cabin the water rose to the chart table, and that flooding extinguished the worst fires.

Her decks were gouged and splintered, her mast gone, trailing beside her, held by her sheets. The radar reflector, clipped to a stay, lay in the water, hidden by the spin-

383

naker. The coach roof, the hatches, and the foredeck had been blown wide open by an exploding shell. She was riddled above the waterline and many of the shots, having been fired from higher platforms, had exited underwater.

She should have broken up, but her stringers and stiffeners held tenaciously to her hand-laid-up hull, and she was still floating, her bow still pointing the last course Hardin had given her.

Donner's quick eyes swept the smoking wreckage, took in the splintered teak, the holes, the fallen rigging. He recalled that he had first seen her driving into a Channel gale, glittering in his spotlights like an expensive toy. Then demasted, drifting into Table Bay. What glittered had been swept away by the sea, and he had seen that the glitter had fooled him. She was a simple and powerful sailing machine. His eyes lingered on the cockpit, fixed on the sailbags scattered around the steering pedestal. One of the seat covers had been blown off and the dinghy locker it had covered was empty.

"It's a trick!" yelled Donner.

The black wall began to fill the sky. Hardin was sitting at wave height and it was higher and wider than he had ever remembered or imagined in his worst nightmares. It didn't seem possible that anything that big could be moving. But it was moving, fast, and looming closer and closer with each second.

He put his eyes to the binocular sight and zeroed the cross hairs in on the center of the black. Then, carefully and slowly, he lowered the muzzle until the cross hairs settled on a line just above the water.

The line flashed like a grin, a malicious smile of waves breaking on the giant's prow. That was his target. The only part of a ship where a hit could sink it. From one shot, LEVIATHAN would not explode, but at sixteen knots, the tanker couldn't stop before the tremendous pressure of its own momentum smashed open its bows after he had blasted a starter hole with the Dragon.

LEVIATHAN was less than half a mile away. A giant black

wall in a blazing red sky. He waited. Closer. A gas flare behind it set a crown of flame between its twin funnels. Hardin sighted the white line on her bow and fired.

The rocket leaped out of the launcher with a loud whoosh. The booster ignited with a startling white light and the Dragon raced across the swells. The smoked glass had protected Hardin's eyes from the booster glare, but it confused him for an instant. Then he found the rocket in the sight and manipulated the guidance switches, steering it left as it veered off center, raising it as it threatened to dive into the water.

The sight splintered, stinging his face with flying glass and metal, and his arm burned like fire. The water boiled around him. Something tugged at the dinghy's side and air began to hiss out of it. He heard gunfire behind him. More bullets plucked at the rubber and the dinghy began to collapse.

The rocket streaked toward LEVIATHAN. Hardin was struggling to control it with the mangled wire guide when a wave curled over the stern and sank the dinghy. The heavy launcher pulled him under and the last he saw of the Dragon was its tail glowing white against the black of LEVIATHAN.

BOOK FOUR

30

Ajaratu pointed her sloop close to the wind. The little boat leaned over at a lively angle and darted across the bay. She gripped the tiller and leaned back, hiking out, her taut body poised exultantly between air and water. The tiller tugged her hands like a friendly animal. Radiant sunlight, hot on her bare shoulders, glittered everywhere on the dancing chop.

She sailed all day, crisscrossing Lagos harbor, shuttling between ocean berths and quiet lagoons. At last she turned back to the marina. She had stayed too late and it was almost dark when she passed the jetty that marked the outer reaches of the sprawling yacht basin.

Her breath caught in her throat. She saw a squarishly built man on the end of the rock pile a hundred yards away. For a long second it could have been him. She strained to see in the facing light, willing a miracle. Then the man turned and walked to a Land Rover. He looked slighter than Hardin had been, and he wore the khaki of a Nigerian soldier.

How often had that happened? How often had she glanced startled at a white man on the street? How often had her mind conspired to deny the news that Miles Donner had brought her six months ago? How often had she prayed her intuition would prove him wrong?

Some level of humanity she hadn't thought the Israeli possessed had compelled him to tell her personally. He claimed he had stayed with the Iranian search teams in hopes of persuading them to give him custody if they found Hardin alive. But all they ever recovered were shreds of the dinghy he had last sailed—mangled strips of rubber spit up by LEVIATHAN's gigantic propellers.

She had been too numb and grief stricken to care if it was true. Hardin filled her mind, and nothing else, including the nature of his death, seemed important. He had left her empty, it was true; she missed him achingly. But she also held a memory of having loved in a full rich way she never had before and thought she never would again.

Miles Donner occasionally detoured through Lagos on his way home from photographic jobs and, now that he was no longer an active agent of the Mossad, he was a welcome guest in her father's house. Ajaratu had long since moved out—much to the delight of her father's mistress—but whenever Donner visited, she returned to play the part of her father's hostess. Donner drank too much one afternoon and they took a walk alone in the garden. She had learned that even retired, he would speak candidly only out of doors.

"Why did you betray him?" she had asked, Hardin's own futile questions echoing in her mind.

"He was no longer an asset," Donner had replied. "We dealt in practicalities."

"But you could have just let him be," she said, sudden anger rising like a choking mass in her throat.

Donner denied it. "As Hardin used to say, 'It doesn't work that way.' Advantage can be found in every situation. By helping try to stop him we were making friends in the Gulf states, just as we found a good friend in your father when we rescued you." He continued, his voice slurring. "Ajaratu . . . if it's any consolation, I tried to save him."

She hated Donner, and yet she tolerated him. She even encouraged his visits, for the simple reason that she was, sometimes, inexplicably and absolutely sure that Hardin was still alive. If he were, Donner would learn of it. But whenever she raised the subject of the hunt in the Persian Gulf, Donner's response was never more than politely noncommittal; he knew nothing. And as the long weeks went by, and then the months, Ajaratu sadly watched time lay waste to her intuition until its wreckage began to look more like hope than truth.

She wondered if Hardin had ever felt about his loss the

way she felt hers. Had he ever blamed his wife for dying as bitterly as she sometimes blamed him? Carolyn at least had been innocent, but he had courted his death. There were nights she railed against his implacable fury, screamed her own anger, pleaded with God to undo what Hardin had done.

But her anger had cooled. She couldn't blame him anymore. Hardin's passion had been beyond his control. Had he denied it, it would have killed his soul as surely as LEVIATHAN had destroyed his body.

She accepted the few links she had to his life—the watch he had given her at Capetown, Donner, and even the cruel repeat of his own experience of loss. But she paid him homage with the little day sailer, practicing the skills he had taught her, taking pleasure in his pleasure.

Now, in the fading light, she approached her dock under sail, the way he would have. A group of people watched her from the dimly lit parking lot. They were young professionals like herself, carrying sailbags and picnic baskets, chatting and laughing around their shiny cars, reluctant to let go the weekend. She pretended she didn't notice their waves, hoping they wouldn't offer to help her dock and intrude on her private, special moment.

Sailing under jib alone, she circled into the wind, taking off way, and wheeled the boat neatly beside the dock. She tied the stern line, then hurried forward to secure the bow. She was reaching toward the dock with a looped line when she heard him.

"Nicely done."

Stunned, she looked up into his eyes. The wind filled the jib, pushing the bow away, and the distance between them began to increase. Ajaratu stared, her heart soaring.

"Toss a line," he grinned.

She threw it automatically. He caught it and she held on to the mast as much to support herself as to brace against his pull while he hauled on the line and drew her to the dock. She wouldn't have been the slightest surprised if his image had suddenly faded to nothing in the dusk.

"If you cleat that line you can let go and kiss me hello."

The thought passed through her disbelieving mind that she had never seen him hold a smile so long.

"Peter."

"I'm alive and well and I'd rather not stand around too long with those people watching us." He said it still smiling, but he added, "Where I crossed the border they weren't handing out visas." His hair was long beneath a broad-brimmed campaign hat. He was bearded and a frayed khaki bush jacket hung loosely from his too-thin shoulders.

"I'll get you a visa," she breathed.

"I had a feeling you might— Now are you going to get off that little boat and kiss me hello?"

"Peter! How did you *get* here?"

He nodded toward a battered Land Rover parked beside the white 2000 she had had shipped from England. "Drove, part of the way. Do I have to get *into* that boat to kiss you hello?"

The shock was more than she could handle so quickly and she said, her own voice coming to ears from a prim distance, "I have to unload my things."

He looked quizzical for a moment, then sat on the dock, his legs dangling over the water, and watched her bag her sails, coil her lines, gather her clothes and Thermos and lunch bag, and pile them on the dock. Ajaratu worked slowly, stealing glances at him, adjusting, wanting him to do nothing but sit there and watch her do things she had done without him so he would know the life she had lived.

She hosed the salt from the decks and by the time she had bailed and sponged the bilge it was dark. The people in the parking lot cast curious looks their way. Finally they drove off, and when they had he relaxed visibly and from that moment on never took his eyes off her.

She looked around for little things to do, did them, then started to climb onto the dock. Suddenly he was reaching for her and taking her hand and pulling her up and into his arms. Their mouths joined, warm and liquid, and she trembled into joyous tears.

392

Her apartment seemed very spartan to her. For the first time she regretted not doing anything with it.

"I've seen steamer-trunk coffee tables," he joked, sounding as nervous as she felt, "but never the suitcase kind."

"I'm moving to Ibadan."

"Back to school?"

"Yes. But it's a secret."

"From whom?"

"My father wants me to marry. I'll tell him after I've begun."

"What about your boat?"

"I'll drive down now and then on weekends," she said, distractedly turning on lights, feeling his eyes as she moved around the room.

"Ajaratu."

She stopped, and returned his gaze. He looked more tired than she had realized at first. He called her name again. His voice, like his eyes, seemed filled with her, even though he lingered tentatively by the door as if unsure what part of their strange life together they could resume.

Holding his gaze, Ajaratu reached for him, loving the awkward way he took off his hat. "Your hair is so long," she marveled. She touched it and her hand drifted to his face. "And your beard. You're as shaggy as a lion."

"Funny you should say lion," he grinned, stroking the beard. His fingernails were still meticulously cared for. "I met one in Ethiopia who offered to trim it for me at the neck."

"Your beard is so gray. . . . I like it."

His lips closed over her finger. His tongue seared her skin. She looked into his eyes, saw confusion, and wrapped her long arms around him.

"I'm so happy you came to me—don't talk!"

She kissed his mouth and pushed against his musculated body. He tried to speak anyway, but she covered his lips with her fingers again. He began to touch her in ways she remembered, molding and stirring her until she was

393

shaking with desire, burning for him. She felt him grow against her. His hands were too slow. She helped him with her clothes, tore at his.

She was astonished by how thin he was, and shocked by his scars. "Aren't you forgetting something?" he murmured, nuzzling her breasts, caressing her bottom; his voice was light with a gentle joke and he seemed unaware she had noticed his maimed skin. "I'm here. Where's my watch?"

Holding him tightly, she backed across the room, led him to her bed, and shyly lifted the pillow. "I wore it on my wrist, at first. I had the band made smaller. I kept the links until Miles . . . told me you had died."

Hardin grinned, clearly enjoying himself. "You know how Miles exaggerates."

Ajaratu wanted to explain. "It was too heavy a watch to wear at the clinic, so I kept it here—I can read the dial easily when I wake up at night."

She closed her eyes as he gently stroked her face. As from a distance, she heard him say, "This is a very narrow bed."

"It was all I needed."

His fingers felt like the sun on her cheeks.

Later, she lay warm on her side, a knee luxuriously up, her head on his chest, listening to his heart beat. Her eyes drifted lazily down his body. His square frame seemed smaller; his muscles were thin and stretched tightly over his bones. An angry red streak furrowed his right forearm and thin white scars striated his sun-blackened legs.

She said, "It's strange to make love and not be on the boat."

"Yes."

"Did you miss the motion?"

"No."

"Neither did I. . . . But what a feeling it was the way she drove! . . . Did it hurt terribly to lose her?"

"She was quite a boat."

"She was . . ." She smiled. "Well I certainly didn't miss sail changes in the middle."

"Umm."

She felt Hardin drift away from her. "Peter?"

"Yes."

"What happened to your legs?"

"Barnacles. I was hanging on to a dhow's rudder." She looked up at his face. He was staring at the ceiling. "They were like round razors."

"And your arm?" Ajaratu asked.

He had described the barnacles unemotionally—a simple point of interest—but now his voice turned bitter. "A bullet . . . It wrecked the sights. I couldn't control the rocket."

Her heart sinking, she listened to his breath quicken and felt his muscles grow tense against her cheek. She caressed him soothingly, but his body grew tighter.

"You haven't given it up. Have you?"

"No."

"Why did you come to me?"

"I need you."

"For that?"

"For everything."

"Including that?"

"Including that."

Ajaratu curled into a tight ball, her head still on his chest. He has to do it, she thought hopelessly. Carolyn still boils in his mind. The passion is still his master, still my rival, and will be until he kills the ghost.

31

It was Saturday and the yacht-basin parking lot was crowded with brightly polished cars. Most of the slips were empty, but Aiaratu Akanke's day sailer was still tied to the dock, partly filled with rainwater.

Miles Donner had already been to her apartment; the doormen hadn't seen her in several days. He'd gone back and broken in for a closer look. Her furniture was there, but her clothes closets and bookshelves were empty.

The people at her clinic had said she had vacation time due and had suddenly taken it. Her father hadn't seen her in several weeks, but that wasn't unusual.

Donner gazed into the rainwater in the bottom of her boat. He was worried, but it was excitement that tingled in his veins. By the time he reached Lago's Murtala Muhammed Airport it was spearing his stomach and racing in his brain. There was no point in trying to make contact with the Mossad in Lagos. He had to go home to try to make them listen.

32

Captain Ogilvy stood between Miles Donner and James Bruce on LEVIATHAN's port wing. The giant ship was steaming down the west coast of Africa, empty, beginning its third voyage since Hardin had attacked in the Persian Gulf seven months before. It was alone on the sea save for an old three-island freighter, plodding the Senegal coast miles to the east, whose tops reflected the setting sun.

Ogilvy was angry. Donner was worried. They had been arguing, oblivious to Bruce's attempts to mediate, since the Israeli and the company staff captain had joined the ship when LEVIATHAN passed Cape Verde. Binoculars hung from each man's neck. Donner used his to scan the water every few minutes.

"Dammit, man!" snapped Ogilvy. "You know bloody well Hardin's dead."

"Then where's his body?" Donner asked quietly.

"Ask LEVIATHAN's propellers."

"But we found pieces of the rubber boat."

"The Iranians made a balls-up of the search," Ogilvy shot back. "Royal Navy could teach the wogs a thing or two about seamanship, eh Bruce?"

Bruce smiled wanly. "Let's call up the helicopter, Cedric. He'll be here in two hours and we'll all feel better with a little firepower. Why don't—"

Ogilvy cut him off. "Or they found him alive and bashed him about so badly they couldn't show the body. The Iranians are torturers, for God's sake. Or didn't you notice when you were buzzing around on their Hovercraft? Maybe they just let him drown. They as much as told me they'd deal with the damned fool before the American State Department could intervene."

"I never heard anything like that," said Bruce.

"They'd hardly send you a memorandum. The point is he's dead."

Donner asked, "How can you be so sure he's not alive and hunting right now?"

"Because he's dead."

"But I've told you that the woman is missing."

"People disappear all the time. Even in civilized places."

"Civilized?" Donner asked incredulously. "She's a physican in the capital city of the most advanced black nation in the world."

"I don't give a damn if she was performing surgery on the king of Zululand. Hardin is dead."

"And will you also ignore the fact that a Nautor Swan was stolen in the Gulf of Guinea near Nigeria?"

"Along with two dozen other expensive yachts. They've more pirates in the Niger delta than they ever had in the China Sea."

"But it's his kind of boat."

"Would you steal a tatty little dinghy if you could have one of them?"

"Do you *want* him to sink you?"

"Absurd coincidences will not sink LEVIATHAN."

"But there are too many coincidences," said Donner. "And not all absurd. *His* kind of boat stolen. *His* body never found. *His* woman missing."

"Political intrigue," retorted Ogilvy.

"She had no politics."

"Then she ran off with a lover."

"She lived alone. She had no lovers."

"A young woman like that alone? Nonsense."

"Ajaratu Akanke loved Hardin in a way you or I could never know. She was as determined to have him as he was to sink this ship."

" 'Was' is precisely the word. He's dead."

"But if he is not, we must allow for the admittedly remote possibility that they're stolen another weapon and—"

"Poppycock!"

"Captain, I'm not the only one who thinks you need protection. Your company does and so does Lloyd's of London, your insurer."

"You're heaping coincidence upon impossibility."

"It's just possible he could have swum to a sea rig," Bruce suggested tentatively. "There were quite a few within a mile."

"Not ruddy likely!"

"But what if he did?" asked Donner. "And later managed to board a dhow. They're everywhere on the Gulf. The monsoon was about to turn. A dhow could have taken him all the way to east Africa."

"*Impossible!*" Ogilvy shouted. His mouth hardened like a beak and his fingers began to drift up and down his leather binoculars strap. "*Hardin's dead.* Didn't you see the serpents in the Gulf?"

"How many serpents would have stayed around while your convoy was riling the water?"

"It would only take one to kill him." He turned angrily on the staff captain. "I'll be damned if LEVIATHAN will carry an armed helicopter for you or the company or even Lloyd's just because one black girl didn't come home on time!"

398

He stared Bruce down.

Donner scanned the horizon with his binoculars.

The sun, a precise red ball low in a cloudless sky, shot a clean red line across the darkening sea into LEVIATHAN's hull. The warm tropical breeze ruffled Ogilvy's thick white hair. He polished the captain's insignia on his left shoulder, glanced back, and inspected the result.

The wing telephone clamored. He picked it up, then handed it to Donner, who had received several radio-telephone calls since he had boarded. The Israeli moved as far aside as the cord would allow and listened, his eyes on the sea.

Ogilvy watched for a moment, then turned to James Bruce. "I can't for the life of me remember," he said casually. "Were you aboard one of the convoy vessels that night?"

"No. I was waiting on Wellhead One."

"Oh yes. Silly of me. . . . Well, you missed something, I must say. I was right here on the port wing, of course, with a weather eye on the wog escort. It was a marvelous sight, Bruce. The sort of thing a man your age has never seen, having missed the war. Utterly majestic. You knew that they laid on a frigate for LEVIATHAN?"

Bruce nodded. He'd heard Ogilvy's story many times.

"And air cover that would have done the RAF proud. You have to hand it to the Iranians. They mustered a very decent force. And in quick time, once I got them sorted out."

"It was quite a night," Bruce agreed.

"You really ought to get off at Monrovia."

"I know, Cedric. It sounds farfetched, but Donner brought pressure—"

"Don't worry," Ogilvy interrupted quietly. "I'm going to sort your Mr. Donner out right now."

Donner cradled the phone, a worried smile playing on his lips. He looked older than when Bruce had met him in the Gulf, and the ease of his manner seemed diminished by a small but telling fraction. "Captain," he said imploringly, "they tell me she is still missing.

Again, I ask you, please consider the remote, but potentially castastrophic, possibility that Hardin is alive and hunting LEVIATHAN."

"Agreed," said James Bruce, mustering his courage. This had gone far enough. He had a responsibility to the company and the ship, as well as the crew. Ogilvy was playing with their lives.

"Cedric, I'm afraid I'm going to have to insist this time. Please have your radio officer call the helicopter."

To his relief, Ogilvy displayed none of the usual signs of impending explosion, and when he replied, it was so calmly that Bruce missed for a second the fact that he was ignoring him and addressing Donner.

"As I understand it, you work for the government of Israel?"

"Yes," said Donner, facing the captain with a wary eye.

"And their intelligence apparatus discovered Hardin's plan last summer."

"Yes."

"And you were asked to bear this information to LEVIATHAN's owners."

"That's essentially correct, sir."

"And to the Saudis and the Iranians?"

"To whomever it concerned."

"Did you know Hardin?"

Donner returned Ogilvy's gaze unblinkingly. "No."

"And what has happened since then?"

"Just as I told you. We assumed that Hardin was dead, until we recently learned that Dr. Akanke had disappeared—"

"No. I mean what have *you* been doing?"

Donner looked uncomfortable. "A number of things have—"

"You've retired," Ogilvy said bluntly.

"Does it show?"

"It shows." Ogilvy smiled. "Not a lot, but at my age I can't help noticing such things. Have you a hobby?"

"I take photographs."

400

Bruce waited patiently. He saw the drift of what Ogilvy was doing. Let him vent his anger, first.

"But wouldn't you rather return to your government work?" Ogilvy persisted.

Donner nodded almost imperceptibly as he said, "It's not a choice open to me."

Ogilvy smiled again. "Well, not until recently."

"What do you mean?" asked Donner.

"You've stirred everyone up about Hardin again. And here you are, back at your job." He chuckled. "And what is that job?" He echoed his own words mockingly. "Your 'government work'? You and your sources and information and radio messages and contacts at Lloyd's—you're some sort of ruddy spy. A *washed-up*, ruddy spy, to be more precise. Don't you see what he's doing, Bruce? He's redundant."

Bruce looked away, embarrassed for both men. Ogilvy's transparent ploy was doomed to failure. Facts were facts and cutting Donner down wasn't going to change the fact that the ship might be in danger. This was a company decision; Bruce would make it.

"He got the sack for some damned reason," Ogilvy crowed. "But as long as he cries wolf—or should I say 'cries Hardin'—he's back in a job. I can't say I blame you, old chap, but I'm not about to jump LEVIATHAN through hoops to keep you employed."

Donner returned his cruel smile, but a vein pulsed in his temple.

Ogilvy chuckled again, a heavy, gloating sound. "Not that I'm not grateful for services rendered, Mr. Donner. It was very helpful to know when Hardin was stalking LEVIATHAN."

James Bruce quickly regained the initiative. "Mr. Donner's troubles are beside the point, Cedric. I am giving you a direct order. The company commands you to carry protection. Radio the helicopter immediately!"

He wondered if he had shouted or whether it only sounded that way in his ears.

Now a pulse was throbbing in Ogilvy's temple. His face reddened. He picked up the wing phone. "Radio room." His eyes sought Bruce's. He thrust the phone at him.

"If you *insist,* Captain Bruce, you had better ring up *two* helicopters . . . and have a pleasant voyage around the Cape, *Captain* Bruce."

He pushed the phone closer to Bruce. Bruce heard the radio officer picking up.

"Now hold on, Cedric."

"Yes!" His voice cracked like a pistol shot.

Bruce eyed the distant bows, his mouth working. Who but God, or Ogilvy, really knew what was going on up there?

"All right, Cedric . . . you win."

Ogilvy hung up the phone. He buffed the braid on his shoulder, looked back at it, then turned expansively to Bruce.

"Hardin came close, I'll grant you that. As God is my witness, that rocket missed me by ten yards."

He led Bruce along the wing, closer to the sea that was frothing far below beside the rushing hull. Donner followed, his face a mask.

"Over there you can still see the fresh paintwork," said Ogilvy. He pointed where the smooth surface of the metal railing was marred by a seam between the old paint and the brighter new. Donner watched his large wrinkled fingers worry the paint seam as he spoke.

"The concussion knocked me to the deck," Ogilvy said, reciting what was, according to his officers, an oft-repeated story. "I fought the blaze with hand-held extinguishers until the bosun arrived with a fire gang. Singed my eyebrows. You can see they're still a trifle short." He paused, exactly as he must have a hundred times, and added with a solemnity they joked about beyond his earshot in the wardroom, "Someone was watching over the good men of LEVIATHAN."

Ten yards, Donner thought, was how close Ogilvy had come to being totally wrong about Hardin. He said, "Fir-

402

ing from a rubber boat. Hardin was resourceful to say the least."

"Bloody lucky is more like it, Donner," Ogilvy snapped back. "Bloody lucky."

"But rather determined, wouldn't you say?"

Ogilvy's hand closed over the railing and covered the paint seam. He stared a long time and Donner wished he hadn't spoken; taunting him wouldn't help matters. The old man's eyes boiled with rage. He had codified his story, ritualized the event, and settled on the facts. Hardin had been a fool. Hardin had been lucky. Hardin was dead.

Donner looked at the weathered hand covering the paint seam as if to hide it. He wondered if Ogilvy repeated his story so often because he had been intimidated by events. Quickly he turned away before the captain could see him smile at an odd thought.

Had Hardin exacted a posthumous revenge? Did Ogilvy tremble in his darkest moments with a fear that Hardin's determined ghost might emerge from the sea one night with a blade in his teeth? Was that why he refused to consider this new information? Donner's smile faded. Or was Ogilvy right? Was he clutching at straws, willing to believe anything to get back in the action?

"Lucky!" Ogilvy spat. "I predicted his every move. It was fool's luck that he penetrated the screen." He fell silent and gazed with opaque eyes at the vast green deck. Donner and Bruce were left to wait upon his mood.

Donner glanced amidships where the spare propeller was stowed on deck. Though it was three days since he had boarded from the Canaries, he was still awed by the size of LEVIATHAN. Along with its brothers that were churning the ship toward Arabia, that was the biggest propeller in the world. What would those blades leave of a man?

He raised his binoculars and scanned the darkening horizon. When his gaze swept a sail, whose presence on the empty ocean had been obscured by the freighter behind it, his hands tightened only momentarily on the glasses. They'd had several false alarms in these warm waters.

"A boat."

Ogilvy muttered an inaudible reply and continued to stare at his decks. The fingers of his right hand slid up his binocular strap. They left the strap to polish the insignia on his left shoulder and the way the captain turned his head to inspect the braid put Donner in mind of a fugitive eyeing pursuit.

James Bruce was already studying the boat in his own glasses. "It's not a Nautor Swan."

"Are you sure?" asked Donner, raising his again and gloomily fiddling the focus wheel.

"Ketch-rigged multihull," Bruce said slowly. "Trimaran."

Donner focused and saw two masts above a broad, flat hull. It was running before the land breeze, westward bound. When he had surmised Hardin's intentions last summer he had read some small-craft voyagers' diaries for a glimpse into the man's character. The trimaran was probably setting out on a warm, pleasant trade-wind crossing to the Antilles. Perhaps through the Panama Canal and into the Pacific. Last summer he couldn't imagine the lure of such simple, lazy isolation. Now, he was not so sure.

"Can you see the crew?" he asked.

"Not yet," said Bruce.

The trimaran was clinging to a course that would take it across LEVIATHAN's path. It was moving quickly, fast enough to clear with plenty of room.

Ogilvy spoke. "I thought you had decided that Hardin stole a Swan."

Donner lowered his binoculars and watched the setting sun lace red light through the tops of the swells.

Like a doctor monitoring a heartbeat, Ogilvy fingered the vibrating handrail. It hummed with an intensity that had been increasing all afternoon. He picked up the wing phone and ordered shaft turns reduced by four revolutions.

Gradually the vibrations eased to a tolerable tremor, but it would be an hour before LEVIATHAN slowed from sixteen to fifteen and a half knots. He continued to hold the railing. The thick seam between the old and new paint began to irritate his palm.

He telephoned the bridge house and his first officer looked out at him on the wing as he answered.

"Yes, sir."

"There's a ridge on the railing, here, Number One. See that the carpenter files it down tomorrow."

"Yes, sir."

"Otherwise it will get thicker and thicker every time we paint."

"Yes, sir."

Satisfied, Ogilvy released the railing and eyed the ship that was his vast domain. She was magnificent, and yet not the titan she had been. The sea had found her wanting. Worse, she bore Hardin's scars.

It had saddened him, at first, but he had come to change his mind. He had been at sea nearly fifty years and he had finally accepted all that had happened as a reminder that survival, and survival alone, was the only victory the sea allowed.

LEVIATHAN had survived. And she was still the greatest ship that ever sailed beneath the sky.

Something intruded on his contentment. He glanced idly at the water. The trimaran had closed to one thousand yards and seemed to be turned directly toward LEVIATHAN's bow.

Again, he spoke into the wing phone.

"Give that damned fool a hoot, Number One."

LEVIATHAN's whistle sounded an imperious blast.

The trimaran turned broadside to the tanker. A figure climbed out of the sailboat's cockpit and leaned over a tripod on the aft deck.

Donner said, "Captain—"

Puzzled, Ogilvy raised his binoculars. "What the devil is that contraption on the stern?"

The trimaran's sails reflected a brilliant white flash.

"Signal lamp?" asked Bruce.

But Ogilvy was racing toward the bridge house as fast as his spindly legs could carry him, his mind screaming that no signal lamp could be so bright.

33

Hardin shook with a fierce joy as the rocket shrieked across the water. He pressed against the tripod, his eyes in the tracking sights, his fingers flickering on the electric switches that controlled the guide wire. The rocket grew smaller in the sights and he heard Ajaratu cry out when its white flame disappeared into LEVIATHAN's bulbous prow.

The black ship swallowed the bolt and forged on.

"Jibe!" he yelled. "Run ahead of him."

Ajaratu, her regal face cast in bold relief by the light of the sinking sun, jibed about and steered ahead of LEVIATHAN on a broad port reach. The trimaran's previous owners had smuggled guns across the Gulf of Guinea to diehard factions in Angola and it was very fast. Her eyes on Hardin, Ajaratu started the oversize auxilary engine. The boat gained speed and hurled spray back to the stern, wetting Hardin's legs.

He hoisted a second rocket from a stack beside the tripod and slid it from the canvas sling he had rigged for the job into the launcher's breech. It was a bigger weapon than the Dragon—Ajaratu had located and bribed a corrupt Nigerian Army officer with sufficient seniority to steal the best—and it was capable of repeat fire as quickly as he could load the high-explosive shells.

LEVIATHAN was catching up, unmarked by the first shot, looming higher. Hardin rejoiced in its nearness. He slid the shell off the sling and pushed the hoisting boom clear of the launcher's fiery recoil. Then he attached the rocket's wire guide, sighted LEVIATHAN in the optical tracker, and forced himself to wait until a long swell lifted the trimaran for a perfect shot.

"Ready?" he shouted, his voice exultant.

Ajaratu pointed the boat downwind so the rocket's backfire would clear the sails. She covered her eyes.

"Ready!"

Hardin swiveled the weapon as the boat turned. LEVIATHAN surged implacably onward, smashing the seas, blotting the horizon. He sighted the bow dead center and fired.

The rocket leaped clear, ignited, the searing flash darkened by the sight's smoked lenses. Manipulating the guide, Hardin drew the second missile twenty feet above the water.

The trimaran plunged into a deep trough and he lost sight of the target. When the boat rose, the last rays of the sun glinted on the guide wire. He dropped the missile to the waterline. A shimmering gold line slashed into the tanker. He felt the wire quiver with LEVIATHAN's pulse.

LEVIATHAN had no collision bulkhead in the sense of a second, powerfully reinforced interior bow, but the foremost cargo spaces were divided into small compartments. Some of these tanks were no more than ten feet wide, which put four vertical cargo-separation steel bulkheads in the foremost fifty feet of the hull.

Hardin's first shot splayed a ten-foot hole in the bow plates and water poured in as LEVIATHAN rammed the sea at sixteen knots. The first separating bulkhead burst immediately, but the second held.

Ogilvy ordered both engines full astern. The giant propellers dug a deep pit in the sea behind the ship as they clawed the water in reverse, but they had no effect on its momentum and LEVIATHAN was still plowing full speed ahead when Hardin's second shot slammed into its bow.

The shell buckled a primary framing member. Bulkheads collapsed. Water and air rushed into the tanks and expelled the inert gases. Huge plates of quarter-inch steel broke the welds that held them together and began to flutter back and forth like eel grass in the tide. The peeling plates scraped each other and scattered sparks.

Ogilvy pushed aside the helmsman and gripped the steering yoke.

The din and clatter of the giant plates rending and crashing went unheard on the bridge a third of a mile away, and he could only wonder what damage the rockets had done. He said nothing when his first officer reported that Hardin had fired a second time. He had seen it. Just as he could see the monster raising a third rocket to his launcher.

LEVIATHAN hadn't slowed a whit. It was overtaking the sailboat, but not so quickly as to stop Hardin from firing again. He put the yoke hard over. She responded grudgingly. He pulled back on it as if to stop the ship with his will. Ahead, the fast trimaran turned with him, darting over the swells, and in a moment Hardin would be ready to fire again.

As the inert gases escaped, air mixed with the residual oil fumes in the violated tanks. The first explosion was small. It too was unheard and unfelt on the bridge. It blasted in the direction of least resistance—inward, because the tanks were empty and the sea reinforced the outside of the hull. The first explosion destroyed several interior bulkheads and the mixing of oxygen and volatile residual oil fumes began again.

Hardin saw a pillar of fire shoot from the bow deck. He heard a sharp bang like a single clap of thunder. A second explosion sent pieces flying into the air about the tanker and the fire vanished like a snuffed candle. The sea rippled toward him and he heard a long deep bellowing rumble spread across the water.

He sighted the ship in the binocular tracker as LE-VIATHAN's decks peeled apart spouting smoke and flame. Flames engulfed its bows. Hardin aimed for the heart of the pyre and triggered his weapon again.

The rocket lanced into the flames. Hardin hoisted a fourth rocket to the breech, loaded, fired. He brought up a fifth. His mind filled with the explosions. The fiery target grew larger and larger. He shot another, and another.

He was out of control and in perfect control. He would fight forever, sailing before the monster, firing again and again until the very weight of his shells would sink it to the bottom of the sea. The closer it came, the faster he loaded. The flames grew hot on his face, and burning metal dropped hissing into the water around him.

He hoisted, loaded, fired, and guided another rocket. It disappeared into the flaming maw and he reached for another. There were no more; the deck was empty. Ajaratu steered out of the path of the burning ship and as the trimaran raced beside it, Hardin leaned on the tripod, his chest heaving, and stared at what he had done.

A great fireball marched aft until only the white bridge tower remained untouched. The bows began to go down, and a canopied lifeboat descended jerkily to the rushing water. Leviathan dragged it like a hooked fish until, cut loose, it fell rapidly astern.

Hardin lifted his face to the holocaust. A tremendous explosion resounded deep inside the tanker and burning shrapnel shrieked by his head. He stared, transfixed. Still charging forward at sixteen knots, Leviathan drove under the waves, its infinite momentum carrying the titan to its grave.

Hardin sailed to the end of Leviathan's wake, looked into the emptiness, and whispered good-bye to Carolyn. The sea had already begun to smooth the steaming maelstrom. When it filled the space where Leviathan had been, he took Ajaratu's hand and they set a course which would let the trade winds bear them to the oceans of the world.

Acknowledgments

Many kind people helped with my research.

I want to thank Stephen Fisher for showing me the craft of sailing.

Captain Guiseppe Catelli, Second Officer Franco Valzania, and the crew of the VLCC Esso *Skandia* were hospitable and informative, as were Esso Marine's Captain Franco Fenucci, and Captain Wlodzimierz Grzesiak, Second Officer Stefan Grosicki, and Radio Officer Czeslan Starczyk and the crew of the M.S. *Roman Pazinski,* and Peter Carling and John Fisher of the Southampton and Isle of Wight Pilots Service. Captain Donald Clark, Norman Toomer, and particularly Donald Ellis were generous hosts at the Esso Refinery in Fawley, England.

Others who shared knowledge were R. J. Moore and Tony Hazell and John Blackwell of Lloyd's Underwriters' Claims Office; Jorma I. Leskinen; Michell C. Gibbons-Neff of Sparkman and Stephens; Greg and Robert Grey; Susan Szita Gore; Daniel David of Sky Books International; John Costello; David James M.P., Ian Brett of the British Information Service; Tom Mahoney; and Kennett L. Rawson.

Many nautical adventurers are dazzling writers, among them Bernard Moitessier, Joshua Slocum, Richard Maury, Errol Bruce, K. Adlard Coles, Sir Francis Chichester, and Hal Roth and, on the subject of ships, Noel Mostert. Marion Kaplan's photographs and writings tell beautifully the story of the vanishing dhows.

And thank you for always being faithful and supportive, Miss Laura Patrick.

James A. Michener

Winner of the Pulitzer Prize in Fiction

The Bridge at Andau	23863-6	$1.95
The Bridges at Toko-Ri	23856-3	$1.95
Caravans	23832-6	$2.25
Centennial	23494-0	$2.95
Chesapeake	24163-7	$3.95
The Drifters	23862-8	$2.75
The Fires of Spring	23860-1	$2.25
Hawaii	23761-3	$2.95
Iberia	23804-0	$2.95
Kent State: What Happened and Why	23869-5	$2.50
A Michener Miscellany	C2526	$1.95
Rascals in Paradise	24022-3	$2.50
Return to Paradise	23831-8	$2.25
Sayonara	23857-1	$1.95
The Source	23859-8	$2.95
Sports in America	23204-2	$2.50
Tales of the South Pacific	23852-0	$2.25

Isaac Bashevis Singer

Winner of the 1978 Nobel Prize for Literature

SHOSHA	23997-7	$2.50
SHORT FRIDAY	24068-1	$2.50
PASSIONS	24067-3	$2.50
A CROWN OF FEATHERS	23465-7	$2.50
ENEMIES: A LOVE STORY	24065-7	$2.50
THE FAMILY MOSKAT	24066-5	$2.95
IN MY FATHER'S COURT	24074-6	$2.50

Buy them at your local bookstores or use this handy coupon for ordering:

FAWCETT BOOKS GROUP
P.O. Box C730, 524 Myrtle Ave., Pratt Station, Brooklyn, N.Y. 11205

Please send me the books I have checked above. Orders for less than 5 books must include 75¢ for the first book and 25¢ for each additional book to cover mailing and handling. I enclose $_____ in check or money order.

Name_____
Address_____
City_____State/Zip_____
Please allow 4 to 5 weeks for delivery.

Sam Durell

"Assignment Series"

Sylvia Thorpe

Romantic tales of adventure, intrigue, and gallantry.

FREE
Fawcett Books Listing

There is Romance, Mystery, Suspense, and Adventure waiting for you inside the Fawcett Books Order Form. And it's yours to browse through and use to get all the books you've been wanting . . . but possibly couldn't find in your bookstore.

This easy-to-use order form is divided into categories and contains over 1500 titles by your favorite authors.

So don't delay—take advantage of this special opportunity to increase your reading pleasure.

Just send us your name and address and 35¢ (to help defray postage and handling costs).